MEDITATIONS IN GREEN

SCRIBNER SIGNATURE EDITIONS

ON EXTENDED WINGS by Diane Ackerman

GROWING UP RICH by Anne Bernays

SOUTH STREET by David Bradley

[illegible] by [illegible]

WHAT I KNOW SO FAR by Gordon Lish

DEAR MR. CAPOTE by Gordon Lish

[illegible] by [illegible]

[illegible] by [illegible]

[illegible] AND OTHER STORIES by [illegible]

[illegible] by [illegible]

[illegible] by [illegible]

[illegible] by [illegible]

BLOOD TIE by Mary Lee Settle

THE LOVE EATERS by Mary Lee Settle

THE KISSING KIN by Mary Lee Settle

[illegible] by Mary Lee Settle

[illegible] by Mary Lee Settle

[illegible] by Mary Lee Settle

[illegible] by Mary Lee Settle

[illegible] by Mary Lee Settle

[illegible] by [illegible]

[illegible] by [illegible]

[illegible] by [illegible]

MEDITATIONS IN GREEN

Stephen Wright

Stephen Wright

SCRIBNER **SIGNATURE** EDITION

Charles Scribner's Sons New York

1988

Charles Scribner's Sons
Macmillan Publishing Company
866 Third Avenue, New York, NY 10022
Collier Macmillan Canada, Inc.

Library of Congress Cataloging-in-Publication Data
Wright, Stephen, 1946–
Meditations in green / Stephen Wright.—1st Scribner signature ed.
p. cm.—(Scribner signature edition.)
ISBN 0-684-18973-9 (pbk.)
1. Vietnamese Conflict, 1961–1975—Fiction. I. Title.
[PS3573.R5433M4 1988]
813'.54—dc19 87-33115
CIP

First Scribner Signature Edition 1988
Originally published in hardcover by Charles Scribner's Sons, 1983

10 9 8 7 6 5 4 3 2 1

Printed in the United States of America

Cover artwork by Paul Bacon

To the graphed, the charted, the data processed
and to all the uncounted

If I knew for a certainty that a man was coming to my house with the conscious design of doing me good, I should run for my life.

—HENRY DAVID THOREAU
Walden

All God's chillun got guns.

—THE MARX BROTHERS
Duck Soup

MEDITATIONS IN GREEN

Meditation in Green: 1

Here I am up in the window, that indistinguishable head you see listing toward the sun and waiting to be watered. Through a pair of strong field glasses you might be able to make out the color of my leaf (milky green), my flower (purple-white), and the poor profile of my stunted growth. In open country with stem and root room I could top four feet. Want a true botanical friend? Guess my species and you can take me home.

The view from this sill is not encouraging: colorless sky, lusterless sun, sooty field of rusted television antennas, the unharvested crop of the city; and below, down a sheer wall, the persistent dead unavoidable concrete.

This is what it means to be torn from your native soil, exiled in a clay pot five stories vertical, a mile and a half horizontal from the nearest uncemented ground. I feel old. I take light through a glass, my rain from a pipe.

Have you talked to a plant today, offered kindnesses to something green? These are crucial gestures. A plant is not free. It does not know the delirium of locomotion, the pyramidical play of consciousness, the agonies of volition. It simply stands in the dirt and grows. Vegetable bliss. But trapped indoors a plant's pleasure becomes dependent upon human hands, clumsy irresponsible hands, hands that pinch and prune, hands that go on vacation, abandon their ferns to northern exposure, cracked beds, stale air, enervations, apathy, loneliness.

Help! My stalk is starting to droop.

Up late and into the street, that was my habit then, the night's residue still sifting softly through my head, I'd wander down to the corner, stand shivering in the sun, waiting for the light to change and my reconnaissance to begin. I was a spook. All my papers were phony. The route was the same every afternoon, a stitching of right angles across the heart of the city where I mingled anonymously with the residents of the day world.

I was under a doctor's care at the time, sixty minutes exercise q.d., an order I probably wouldn't have bothered to honor had not these prescribed walks delivered me into the relief of cacophony and throng. I needed the glow of animate heat, of blood in motion, regular doses of herdlike solidity, curses, jostles, tears, life. I ogled the goodies in the big windows with the other shoppers. I rode express elevators to offices where the receptionists smiled behind bulletproof glass. I burst into violent sidewalk imprecations on the government. Nothing urban was alien to me.

At the end of the day, I'd find myself come to rest atop a public trash can. Same can, same corner, same attitude. I became a fixture of the neighborhood. There were certain faces I learned to recognize, faces I suppose recognized me, but we spoke no words, exchanged no names, in accordance with the rules of metropolitan intimacy. I sat on my can, watching the heads bob up and down the avenue like poppies in a spring meadow until the constant nodding movement turned unreal, the slow agitation of pink marine life swaying in tempo to oceanic tunes. The heart idled, breathing deepened, silver bubbles popped against my ears.

"You're ruining the symmetry," I announced one day to an old derelict tramping unsteadily past. He was walking the street backwards, the rear of his head advancing blindly down the block. His dress was equally distinctive: orange Day-Glo painter's cap, field jacket fastened with safety pins, patched jeans bleached the bluish white of skim milk, purple hightop tennis shoes split at the creases.

He turned and his face was that of a young woman ready to be amused. "*You're* sitting on a fucking garbage can," she said.

"I was tired."

She hopped up beside me. "I like it," she said. "Gargoyles."

I saw her fairly often after that. She'd stop by my post to share a pretzel, a carton of orange juice. "Professional interest," she explained. "I'm a part-time social worker." She said her name was Huette Mirandella. The rest of her history was a series of true-false propositions. Her parents had died in a hotel fire or an auto accident or a plane crash or an artful combination of the three. Orphans at ten and four, she and her younger brother were abandoned to the indifferent care of a senile great aunt. Home was boring. School was boring. Staying out late and running away were interesting and then boring. The five universities she attended were universally boring. She drifted. Minor jobs, petty boyfriends. There was an abortion, a botched suicide, a hospital vacation, "the stupid clichés of an unimaginative life," she said. When I met her she was twenty-two years old, she studied Chinese, played electric guitar, read a science fiction novel every two days, practiced a lethal form of martial arts once a week with a garageful of women, painted vast oil abstracts she called soulographs, and speculated that if there was another Renaissance lurking about the bloody horizon of our future then she was a candidate to be its Leonardo —"the smart clichés of a pop life."

We met on the corner for weeks and then came periods when I wouldn't see her at all. She was home, she was at work, a soulograph required a more steely shade of blue. I continued diligently to push the leg uptown and down, in sun and snow, through needles and cramps. It seemed to change size from day to day in phase with its own moods, its own dreams. On bad days, when it dragged behind me like a sea anchor, the blocks telescoped outward, the pavement all slanted uphill, and I'd entertain notions of traveling in style. Imagine commandeering a tank, one of the big ones, forty-seven tons of M48, cast steel hull, 90 mm gun, 7.62 mm MG coaxially mounted in the turret, and running down the boulevard. Imagine the clanking, the honking horns, the cheers of the liberated masses, the flattening of each tiny car beneath the monstrous tread, the squash of automotive cockroaches. Imagine the snap, the crackle, the pop.

One bad gray afternoon I had just reached home and was rounding the turn on the first landing when, "Bang, bang," a voice echoed harshly up. I leaned over the splintered banister. In the gloom at the bottom of the stairwell a face materialized luminous as a toy skull. I could see shining teeth and that chipped incisor that always seemed to be winking at someone over my right shoulder.

"No fair. I had my fingers crossed."

"You're dead," said Huey. "You're lying out on the front steps with the change falling out of your pockets."

"Yeah? Where were you?"

"Sitting right on the stoop."

"What can I say? Come pick out your prize."

Up in my kitchen she dropped a fat brown package onto the table. Dozens of rubber bands of all colors, red, yellow, blue, green, were wound around it like shipping twine.

"That's a mean looking bundle," I said.

"A prize. For you."

"Wonderful," I said, weighing the package in my hand. "Who wrapped this, a paranoid paper boy?"

"Rafer."

The colors of the rubber bands flipped into bright relief like thin neon tubes switched suddenly on. Rafer was her brother, executive officer of a street gang notorious for reckless drug use and dropping bricks on pedestrians from tenement rooftops. We'd once spent an amicable afternoon together, comparing scars, tattoos, chatting about the effects of various arms and pharmaceuticals.

"Three guesses," she said, rattling open a drawer. "This the only knife you've got?"

I took the bayonet and began to saw. It was like cutting into a golf ball, bits of elastic flying about the room. The wrapping paper was a greasy grocery bag. Inside, pillowed upon a golden excelsior of marijuana, lay a large plastic envelope containing a small glassine envelope containing a few spoonfuls of fine white powder. Embossed in red on the large envelope was a pair of lions rampant pawing at a beachball-sized globe of the earth. Indecipherable Oriental ideograms framed the scene except beneath the cats' feet where appeared the figure 100% and below that in English the identification DOUBLEUOGLOBE BRAND.

"What's that?" asked Huey, peering.

"Ancient history."

"It looks like a bag of dope."

"Yes."

"It looks like junk."

I pulled open the glassine envelope, dipped a finger, and sniffed. A line from powder to nostril formed the advancing edge of a fan that spread in regal succession before inturned eyes a lacquered arrangement of glacial rock, green-toothed pine, unbroken snow, then the shimmer, the shiver, the snaking fissures, melting mountains, gray rain, animate forest, the dark, the warm, the still time of mushroom-padded places.

I was amazed. I hadn't seen those magic lions in years. It wasn't often you encountered an adolescent able to weld a connection into the high-voltage Oriental drug terminals.

I began rolling the unfiltered end of a Kool cigarette between thumb and forefinger. Shreds of brown tobacco sprinkled onto the white enamel table.

"What are you doing now" asked Huey, "sleight of hand?"

I emptied out about an inch of cigarette. I poured in the powder. I tamped it down. I twisted the end shut.

"What are you laughing at?" she asked.

I struck a match, touched it to the cigarette, and inhaled deeply. A dirty yellow dog ran barking into the red muddy road and beneath the tires of a two-and-a-half ton truck.

"You want any of this?" I offered in a strangled voice, leaning forward, the joint poised in midair between us. A thick strand of smoke slipped snakelike from the moist end, raised itself erect into blue air, smiled, and dissolved without a sound. In the corner the refrigerator began to hum.

This is not a settled life. A children's breakfast cereal, Crispy Critters, provokes nausea; there is a women's perfume named Charlie; and the radio sound of "We Gotta Get Out Of This Place" (The Animals, 1965) fills me with a melancholy as petrifying as the metal poured into casts of galloping cavalry, squinting riflemen, proud generals, statues in the park, roosts for pigeons. My left knee throbs before each thunderstorm. The sunsets are no damn good here. There are ghosts on my television set. What are we to do when the darkness comes on and we wait for something to happen, as Huey, who never even knew she shared her name with a ten-thousand-pound assault helicopter, sprawls on the floor with her sketchbook, making pastel pictures of floating cities, sleek spaceships, planets of ice, and I, your genial storyteller, wreathed in a beard of smoke, look into the light and recite strange tales from the war back in the long ago time.

A sweltering classroom in Kentucky. Seated, in long orderly rows, a terrorized company of grimy, red-faced trainees. Stage center, on an elevated podium before their fatigued eyes, a sergeant, a captain, a war.

SERGEANT: (Hands poised on hips. Booming voice.) Okay, gentlemens, listen up! This morning your commanding officer will speak on the subject of Vietnam. I'd advise you all to pay close attention to what he has to say. He's been there, I've been there, we've all been there, and since ninety-nine point nine percent of you candy-asses now sitting in this room will also soon be there bawling and yelling for your mamas you might want to know why. So if your memory ain't too good, take notes. And let me warn you, anyone I catch asleep will wish to Christ he was already safe and snug in a nice bronze box with the colors draped over his face. Understand? (Pause.) Ten-HUT! (The company springs up. CAPTAIN, a collapsible pointer tucked under his right arm, strides smartly to the lectern.) Take your seats! (The company falls down.)

CAPTAIN: (Low authoritative manner.) Too slow, sergeant. Have them do it again.

SERGEANT: Yessir! On your feet! (The company springs up.) Now all I want to hear is the sound of one large butt slapping against the bottom of one chair or we spend the afternoon low-crawling through the gravel parking lot. (Pause.) Taaaaake . . . seats! (The company falls down.) Good.

CAPTAIN: Thank you, sergeant. (He steps to stage left, extending pointer to its full length with a brisk snap.) Gentlemen, a map of Southeast Asia. This stub of land (Tap) hanging like a cock off the belly of China is the Indochinese peninsula. Here we have North Vietnam (Tap), South Vietnam (Tap), and Laos, Cambodia, and Thailand (Tap. Tap. Tap.). The Republic of Vietnam occupies the area roughly equivalent to the foreskin, from the DMZ at the seventeenth parallel down along the coast of the South China Sea to the Mekong River in the delta. Today this tiny nation suffers from a bad case of VD or, if you will, VC. (Smiles wanly.) What we are witnessing, of course, is a flagrant attempt on the part of the communist dictatorship of Hanoi to overthrow, by means of armed aggression, the democratic regime in Saigon. (Clears throat.) Now I know the majority of you could give a good goddamn about the welfare of these people or their problems; they live in a land twelve thousand miles away with habits and customs foreign to our own so you assume that their struggles are not yours. Believe me, this is a rather narrow shortsighted view. Consider the human body. What happens if an infection is allowed to go untreated? The bacteria spread, feeding on healthy tissue, until finally the individual dies. Physicians are bound by a moral oath which forbids them to ignore the presence of disease. They cannot callously turn their backs on illness and suffering and neither can we. A sore on the skin of even a single democracy threatens the health of all. Need I remind you that four presidents—I can't emphasize this strongly enough—four presidents have recognized the danger signs and have seen fit to come to the aid of these afflicted people with massive doses of arms, troops, and economic assistance to ensure their continued independence. (Walks methodically back to lectern.) Certainly, we seek no personal gain; we're just pumping in the penicillin, gentlemen, just pumping in the penicillin. (Long pause.) I'm sure we are all aware that this policy of limited intervention has been challenged by large segments of our own population, but just remember one thing, as far as the United States Army is concerned all debate ceased the moment you raised your right hands and took that one step forward. As men in uniform your duty is not to question policy but to carry it out as ordered. (Grips sides of lectern, leans forward menacingly.) Those *are* the facts regarding our present involvement in Vietnam. Are there any questions? (Short pause.) Very good. We've got a movie here, an excellent one as a matter of fact, produced by the State Department, which will explain the historical origins of this conflict in greater detail. And since this is probably the last time I'll see you together as a group, I'd like to leave you with a few words of advice: keep a tight asshole, leave your pecker in your pants, and change your socks twice a day. (He winks.)

SERGEANT: Ten-HUT! (The company springs up. CAPTAIN departs down center aisle.) Take your seats! (The company falls down.)

Lights dim, film begins, images burn through the screen: bursting bombs, dying French, gleaming conference tables, scowling Dulles, golf-shirted Ike, stolid Diem shaking head, Green Berets from the sky, four stars at Kennedy's ear, charred Buddhists, scurrying troops, Dallas, Dallas, destroyers shuddering, Marines in surf, napalm eggs, dour Johnson: let us reason, come let us reason, plunging jets, columns of smoke, beaming Mao, B-52s, UH-1As, 105s, M-16s, Nuremberg cheers, jack-booted Fuehrer, grinning peasants, rubber-sandaled Ho, Adolf Hitler, Ho Chi Minh, Adolf Hitler, Ho Chi Minh, Adolf Hitler, Ho Chi Minh . . .

Someone flipped a switch and the darkness exploded into geometry. Spheres of light overhead illuminated the angles and planes of an enormous rectangular room. Two rows of bunks faced one another in mirrored perfection and on the last bunk of the left row, a warp in the symmetry, one body, male, inert, semiconscious.

GRIFFIN, JAMES I. 451 55 0366 SP4 P96D2T
USARV TRANS DET APO SF 96384

"Hey, numbnuts, wake up!" yelled a voice slurred with drink. "There's a goddamn war out there."

The lights went rapidly on and off, on and off.

Griffin's eyes blinked once, twice, then closed in defense against the naked one-hundred-watt bulb he could feel even through shut lids bombarding him from above. Planetary-sized spots bloomed on his retina, slid back and forth, black holes in his vision. He hated being awakened like this. It was too sudden, too brutal, it was like being hit on the head from behind. It made him uneasy, subject to disturbing, revelatory thoughts. This is how you will die, said such an interruption, not in the comfortable tranquillity you have always imagined as a natural right, but violently, in shock and confusion, far from home, without preparation or kindness, rudely extinguished by an unexpected light much bigger than your own.

Then a mortar round fell out of the sky into the roof directly over his head.

In the super slow motion of television sports reports Griffin saw the underside slope of the roof shiver into a pattern of stress lines, bow, change color, and had the time to think even this: the barracks is a beer can and we're about to be opened before his eyes and everything in them fizzed up and whooshed out into the warm foreign night. He didn't have time to scream. The smoking rubble of morning yielded one charred finger and a handful of blackened molars

a flap of skin and a torn nail
a left ear, a right hoof
a hambone and the yolk of an eye

He could never decide how to finish. Real death was a phenomenon at once so sober and so silly his imagination tended to go flat attempting comprehension. Like everyone else he was able to picture possibilities. The gathered parts, the body bag, the flagged casket, grief, tears, the world going tritely on, the war too, the sky above an untarnished blue. These were generalities, accurate but lacking the satisfaction of the personal detail. Griffin believed that there existed a proper sequence of final events, which when imagined correctly would give off a click, dim the room, and shut down at last that section of his brain which worked for the other side. Meanwhile, he would learn how to handle these terrible rehearsals that rushed in on him from nowhere. Maybe they were valuable learning experiences. Maybe layers of protective hide were being sewn onto his character. Maybe when the time came he would be brave when bravery was required, calm when there was an excess of panic. He didn't really know. Nor did he know where or when he might encounter real death, but he was sure he didn't ever want to die in a place where in the corner two drunks argued in loud whispers over the juiciest way to fuck a gook pussy.

When you go they put you in a shed there until the computer finishes its shuffle, marked cards, shaved deck, jokers all around. Griffin remained in bed. He chose to pass.

"Got no slots for mattress testers," they said. "We gonna place you in a right tasty location, way up north maybe, where the only lying down is of a permanent nature, heehee."

"Do I get a pillow?" asked Griffin. Hoho.

In the bunk to his right was a randy adolescent ripe with virginal fantasies of wartime sex. He spent hours leafing through pornographic paperbacks reading the good parts aloud. On Griffin's left a twenty-six-year-old baker from Buffalo, New York, who had already received his orders directed a feverish monologue to the ceiling while scratching anxiously at his groin: "I won't go I tell you, no way, I won't go, they'll have to drag me out of here, those people are animals, fucking animals, they *like* to pull triggers, bayonet babies, I've seen the pictures, strings of ears on a wire, Christ! can you imagine that, what kind of person walks around wearing an ear necklace for God's sake, who would have believed it, airborne, me airborne, why me, huh? there must be thousands of guys itching to go airborne, run around like baboons and get blown away, well I'm the winner, I'm the goddamn lucky winner. I don't need this, I got a wife and two kids, I'll shoot myself in the foot first, I'm not gonna get killed for a bunch of crazy glory hounds, that's insane, know what I mean, fucking sick, YOU KNOW WHAT I MEAN?"

Griffin pulled the sheet up over his head. He lay quite still and soon felt himself sinking into an immense bowl of vanilla pudding. It was peaceful and quiet on the bottom, submerged and fetal. From the surface the slow mournful sound of a distant radio filtered down like weary shafts of sun through an unruffled sea:

When the train left the station
It had two lights on behind.
The blue light was my blues
And the red light was my mind.

The song faded to be instantly replaced by the manic voice of a Top Forty disc jockey: "This is AFVN, the American Forces Vietnam Network broadcasting from our Tower of Power in Saigon with studios and transmitters in Nha Trang, Qui Nhon, Pleiku, Tuy Hoa, Da Nang, and Quang Tri."

My God, thought Griffin in astonishment. I really am in Vietnam.

He had been in the country for two weeks.

Meditation in Green: 2

What can go wrong: ants
anthracnose
aphids
Botrytis
caterpillars
chlorosis
cockroaches
compacted soil
crickets
crown and stem rot
cutworms
damping-off disease
earthworms
earwigs
fungus
gnats
improper lighting
improper soil pH
improper temperature
improper watering
insufficient humidity
leaf miners
leaf rollers
leaf spots
mealybugs
mildew
millipedes
mold
nematodes
nutrient deficiencies

root rot
salt accumulation
scale
snails
slugs
sowbugs
spider mites
springtails
symphylan
thrips
white fly
and pollution: animal, vegetable,
and mineral.

And these are merely the threats to common house and garden plants. Consider the problems of backwoods survival.

The white walls dissolved and through my room moved a parade of silent disconnected objects: a bolt, a door handle, a brass eyehole, the black letter U, a steel grill, a pane of glass, a row of wooden struts, disks of yellow light, spinning tires, parts of a truck, of several trucks, a battalion of trucks, a convoy in a fog. A quick skinny dog ran up barking . . .

The country opened abruptly into broad coastal plain. Red sand drifted across the road. Mountains huddled in the mist like blue animals. At the bend the wind took off Sergeant Sherbert's hat. We leaned into the long turn, a rotating curve of rusty barbed wire, stagnant ditch, picnicker's litter, the bursting eye—don't look!—swelling from the socket like a fresh egg, one, two, three scarecrows flung across the whistling wire, melted noses, moldy ears, spilled stuffing, sausage fingers aimed in both directions, lip skin peeled back on purple gums, yellow teeth patrolled by shiny beetles. "The laughing gooks," laughed Sergeant Sherbert, pressing on the accelerator as behind us, inflated with death gas, the bodies floated high above the fleeing jeep down the disintegrating road into Greenlandtown.

It came on like this, scene after colorful scene, rushing in with disorienting abruptness. Memory and desire screaming through my living room at the speed of light, me clinging to the couch. Of course I was in it too, but I was being played by someone else.

The computer opened with a jaunty singsong rendition of "Chopsticks." On the screen clumps of bush began moving from left to right. I gripped the plastic handles of my weapons system. A tiny figure darted out into the sights. I swiveled and squeezed. The tiny figure somersaulted into flying fragments. The computer played "Charge!" Now there were trees and figures in the trees. I zapped three, just, like, that. I jumped the punji pit, forded the parasite stream, skirted the booby trap. In the village tiny figures appeared at the windows. Swivel and squeeze. Burning huts crackled realistically. A head popped out of a tunnel opening, and another, and another. I utilized my laser bomb. Everything blew up. "The Yellow Rose of Texas," sang the computer. A reporter pointed a microphone. How do you feel? he asked. I don't know, I replied. Above us at the top of the screen the number 1,313,000 flashed away in digital delirium.

Panic dwindled into jitters into detached fascination. It was just a show. The longer I watched the less I felt. Events coupled, cavorted, and vanished, emotion hanging in midair before my lemur eyes like a thin shred of homeless ectoplasm. It was cool. It was like drowning in syrup. It was like TV.

Everyone on the helicopter was dead except us. One hung head down out the door, another was draped over the left skid. I was strapped into the pilot's seat. The General was munching on a handful of pistachio nuts. I had never flown a helicopter before. Hard ground zoomed in and out of focus. The General opened his briefcase and dumped a pile of medals into my lap. I touched a button. Rockets leaped out ahead of us, streaming away into bursts of black and white and orange. We landed inside a gray crater. Scattered about were arms and legs and heads and other miscellaneous parts. We hopped around in our pressurized suits. The General drove up in a huge bulldozer. It's okay, he said, scooping cinders, cover 'em up, water daily, and next year you've got a fresh crop good as new.

Gradually I became aware of the heavy paw pressing insistently down on my cheek, sandpaper pads and retracted claws pinning me to the floor. I attempted to think clearly. It was while pondering the possibilities of the situation—a fascinating process that seemed to occupy uncountable hours—that I noticed the dancing lions on the plastic bag inches from my nose, the brown musty rug squashed against my face. The show was over.

I pulled myself up onto the couch and assessed the damage. I could hear trucks rattling down the narrow street, the strange mechanical flap of pigeons' wings at the window. Under the skin the landslide continued to settle, jagged pieces of glass spilling across a xylophone of dry nerves. I had to get away from these ballooning walls.

Outside the air fell in soft glittering flakes over the crystal city. Buildings were lattices of light that shifted pattern as I passed. I couldn't even feel the pavement. The leg went up and down smooth as a piston. Remote-controlled locals with waxed faces too large for their bodies clustered around me. I decided to return to the colony. Arrows pointed the way: Botanical Gardens. I traversed an alien world, I hopped a turnstile. Huddled beneath the poisonous atmosphere were five geodesic domes. I found the sign marked Tropical Rain Forest and went inside. A million leaves erupted into applause. Staghorn fern. Acacia. Betel nut palm. Screw pine. So how you been? Okay, and you? Up and down. Hey, you're glowing. Yeah, so are you. A black asphalt path curved away into waiting green darkness. I went around three times searching for an inviting way in. Finally I just grabbed a railing and leaped over. The ground was warm and spongy. It was like treading on flesh. I moved through curtains of long smooth leathery things to slump against the buttress roots of a strangler fig. The scent of bad teeth drifted up, a cool mist sprinkled down. When I sat still the drug folded in around me like huge silken wings. My spine began transmitting coded messages into the mud, the mud relaying secret signals back. The leaves sighed. I could feel myself slowly emptying, the rushes, the bubbles, the shakes, until I was as blank as a stone Buddha, weather-stained, liana-lassoed, sinking into the jungle depths of some forgotten temple. The void at the heart of fertility. I looked up to see in the spaces between the foliage a skinny white man in hornrim glasses and a maroon turtleneck squinting through a camera in my direction. Study the finished print with a magnifying glass, good buddy, you don't always see what you get. There were dozens of people out there, passing innocently unaware within yards of my position. Over their heads beyond this curious eternally peaking summer stretched a lawn of brown glass, shriveled hedge, skeletal trees. The sky was lowering, the light bleeding away. "Fifteen minutes," called a voice, "fifteen minutes to closing." Lightning flashed across the top of the dome. I crawled out of the cozy forest into bitter wind and the start of a stinging rain. My body was exhausted. It felt as though inner walls had been worked at with a cold chisel. I splashed through the empty streets, water trickling down my neck, wondering if this trough of fatigue was deep enough to connect with that elusive treasure: a good night's sleep. The interludes in my consciousness were uncharitably brief. I'd often wake in the dank hollows of early morning, passing as instantaneously as the revivified monster in a horror film from inert oblivion to raving hysteria. The sheets wrapped so tightly about my legs were made of plastic. Hands, under my arms, were dragging me over rough ground. My heart pounded as though some stranger were trapped inside, lost, suffocating. I would force myself to concentrate on surrounding objects. Gradually the bunker would melt back into a desk, the chair would lower its weapon. When dawn came at last, filling the room with fluid light, I would drift off into an uneasy imitation of sleep, holding between nervous eyelids a child's wish that every vessel, no matter how unsound, might one day ride to the shores of a place where everything was filled with light, even rocks and bones and dreams.

By the time I got home I was The Beast From 50,000 Fathoms, thudding slowly up the stairs, on each step a damp footprint, a clump of seaweed.

In the hallway on the floor below mine Eugene was taking his dog, Chandu, for a walk. Up and down the dim stale corridor. Eugene was dressed in a red bikini, Chandu in a studded leather collar.

"How's it going, lieutenant?" he asked.

"We're getting the medicine through to the Eskimos," I replied.

Eugene smiled, giving me a thumbs up. Chandu lapped noisily at the puddles beneath my dripping clothes.

I climbed the last flight, turned the corner, and stopped. My apartment door was hanging open, the wooden jamb in splinters.

Trips had returned.

"Looking Glass two-zero, this is Looking Glass Control, over."
"Two-zero, what the hell do you want?"
"Yessir. You forgot to fill in the log. What should I put down for this mission?"
"Jesus Christ. Do you ever listen to a damn thing anyone says? I distinctly remember standing right in front of you not five minutes ago and saying I was only going once or twice around the field. This is a check-out flight for Captain (garbled)."
"Excuse me, sir. Captain who?"
"Hold on a damn second, I'm about to take off."
"Looking Glass two-zero, this is Looking Glass Control, over."
(Static.)
"Looking Glass two-zero, this is Looking Glass Control, come in, over."
(Static.)
"Aw, fuck it."

The rain was still falling the night the Old Man went down. The weather had settled into an ugly bloated monotony; forecasts promised no relief. The rain fell in hard straight lines and the shells flew out, the planes moved up and down, the helicopters went round and round. Outside, in the dark, metal and machinery were busy churning plants and animals into garbage. It was the season of the monsoon, the Year of the Monkey.

Inside, three men sat quietly beneath an ultraviolet hum. No one spoke. The skin on their hands and faces seemed rich and dark, deeply textured, the exotic tan of an alien star. The walls, sealed in sheets of plastic against the gray damp months of tropical storm, were glowing like the inside of a picture tube. It was a small room not much larger than a prison cell. There were no chairs. An upended ammunition crate served as a table. Out of the top of an empty Coke can leaned four sticks of smoldering incense, the frail strands of perfumed smoke winding slowly upward among rafters of decayed wood where the rats sometimes crawled and the black light buzzed tonelessly on. The rain banged against the corrugated tin roof like lead pellets.

Crouched on the edge of his bed, Griffin gazed intensely into the pure steady eye of a candle planted in its own tallow at his feet. Beads of hot wax slipped silently to the floor, hardened into tight red clots. He was admiring the cool beauty which rested along the blue-edged curve of its flame. He saw himself, hammer and piton, scaling the slopes of that fire toward the orange air of its wispy peak. He was the hero of heady expeditions bound for the secret temples of ice, the subterranean courts of vanished gods. Pinned flat against a glacial wall by the whip of searing mists, he watched helplessly as his best guide tumbled screaming into icy chasm, arms flailing, body twisting and rolling, the insignificant speck of his white face dying out like a spark. The ropes dangled down empty into darkness. And, leaning curiously creviceward, Griffin's mind detached itself from whatever it is minds cling to and also dropped, a happy plummet, to crash in an explosion of warm color that tickled the groin and lit up the brain.

"What are you looking so goofy for?" asked Simon. "This stuff ain't that good."

"I'm standing on my head," replied Griffin. "I'm turning somersaults."

"Yeah? My head hurts." Impatiently, he shifted his weight on the footlocker where he sat. "My pants are wet."

"I'm bouncing against the ceiling. You look like a tiny person."

Simon began tapping his foot on the floor. He held a hand out in front of his eyes, studied the palm for a long moment, then turned it over and examined the back.

A voice, sharp and clear, whispered his name in Griffin's ear. He turned. There was no one there and he had to laugh. The dog, Thai, a crossbreed of MP German shepherd and Asian mongrel, looked up at him from under the bed through shiny black olive eyes. The dog yawned.

"What time is it?" asked Simon.

Griffin pulled up his sleeve to display a bare wrist. "I don't know. I think someone stole my watch."

"Oh God," said Simon wearily.

The wind rattled the plastic, the rain ran in quick streams off the roof, splashed noisily onto the sand outside. Simon stretched out his arms, let them fall heavily against his thighs. He sighed. He studied his hand again. "Lieutenant Kline put in for a transfer to the infantry," he said.

"Wonderful."

"Says he's bored, says he'd rather run around the woods ducking gook bullets than sit on his hemorrhoids reading *Batman* comic books."

"Kline is not well."

"Major Brand laughed in his face, said the unit was under strength and every swinging dick was needed just in case quote the balloon should go up unquote. So Kline stands there wheezing, says, 'Well sir, then with your permission I guess I'll just go back to my room and jack off.' "

"Funny little Kline."

"I don't know. He wants to play soldier, they should let him. What should we care? We got lieutenants falling out our crack."

The room trembled as an artillery round screeched directly above them to detonate harmlessly in an uninhabited patch of foliage miles away.

"Damn it," Simon muttered. "Damn it, damn it, damn it."

Griffin nodded.

"Seven months and I still jump like that. Jesus Christ, it's either the goddamn shells or the sirens or the prisoners screaming. I don't think I've gotten used to anything. I mean even dogs start salivating after two or three bells, right? Seven months and it's like I just stepped off the goddamn plane."

"Cringing is healthy," declared Griffin, turning away at last from the world of the flame. "I want to be a champion cringer."

"Some night I know, one of those short rounds is gonna drop right in here on top of us, right down our fucking skulls. We'll just be sitting here laughing and blowing weed and zap! A bad fuse, bad casing, I bet there's a hundred things could go wrong. Manufacturer's error. What do these companies care? Government contracts. You could paint string yellow and sell it to the army for gold chain."

"Alex told me a buddy of his in Basic had his sixteen explode on the range. Tore a ugly hole through his cheek."

"You know how it is. They got these gigantic factories with rows and rows of little old ladies in brown sweaters and bifocals screwing rifles together. Cataracts. Arthritis. They spill cookie crumbs inside."

"The unspoken scandal of American industry."

"You know the Lockheed guy was up here tonight examining the wreckage and he comes back and says the plane is a flying death trap and you couldn't pay him to climb into one. The fucking Lockheed guy."

"I guess the trick must be to keep clear of moving parts."

"There it is."

Griffin had personally witnessed the crash, a spectacular failure of moving parts. He had seen them after dinner, just before sunset, strolling casually onto the flight ramp in that characteristic chimpanzeelike slouch of pilots cinched into ejection harnesses, helmets in hand, seat buckles slapping against their thighs, pistols jiggling on their hips, the CO confident, expansive, detailing the company's operations to the other man's attentive ear. Strapped into the cockpit, the bulbous window hatches fastened, propellers fanning up a misty wind, they trundled across the slick black runway, rooster tails of blown water spraying from the wheels. Quickly the plane gathered speed, lifted ponderously as a loaded transport before dropping back, almost unwillingly, landing gear squealing, then lifted again like a flat pebble skipping off a lake as the low rhythmic thrum of the engines drastically changed pitch, unreeling into a frantic shriek of steel under torque and still battling to sustain each desperate inch of altitude banked on a long aching arc down into a foul marsh not five hundred feet off the end of the asphalt and exited behind a mushrooming ball of ignited fuel as Griffin, under a rubber poncho, stood nonchalantly urinating against a revetment wall in the rain.

"I certainly hope the next CO knows how to speak English," said Simon. "The colonel jabbered like an immigrant. I was lucky to catch every other sentence."

"I think all our officers should speak in vague semiintelligible East European accents," replied Griffin.

"We'd probably end up invading Poland."

"Ah, but gently. The good guy's blitzkrieg. Silencers on our rifles, rubber tips on the bayonets, mufflers on the bombs, contraceptives taped to all our dicks. Nice. Calder could decorate the tanks."

"In my last letter home I wrote my mother that if one had to go to a war you were the ideal person to go to a war with. You have an agreeable peasant's sense of the dumb incongruity in things."

"What does that mean?"

"Who knows? My mother liked it. She believes that if you surround yourself with good company you're sure to be protected from harm."

"Isn't there already a deterrent against that: the laser-guided good company cluster bomb unit?"

"I'll tell her in my next letter. I enjoy taking Mom up, dropping her down. She doesn't know anything. She thought Vietnam was an island someplace off the coast of India. She won't look at a newspaper."

"Well, it isn't easy finding out what's going on." Griffin indicated the silent figure in the corner huddled over a day-old copy of *Stars and Stripes* whose pages had remained unturned for more than an hour.

"Vegetable," called Griffin.

After a long pause Vegetable lifted his head. Spokes of golden fire stood erect in the backs of both eyes, as if the corneal grates which normally screened the delicate Self from the raw full rush of the Real were now chemically wrenched open, allowing a peek into that holy furnace where outer meets inner and bursts into wild combustion upon the charged wall of the retina. Griffin was surprised by an appealing intuition: perhaps in the sweep of those beacons playing over fields of newsprint Vegetable truly could divine the arcane pulse that manipulated the world. Such knowledge, of course, would remain private, unspoken, lost to memory, because Vegetable, for all his fine shamanistic air of preternatural wisdom, was ripped totally out of his gourd.

"Huh?" he said at last. A smile slipped off his bright teeth and dripped onto his chin.

"Never mind."

Suddenly the dog came awake, froze facing the door, ears stiffened. Boots began to stumble down the corridor outside. Griffin clutched the bag of marijuana and, bending backward, held it cautiously over the hole in the floor behind his bed. A moment later a soft knock sounded on the door. "Who is it?" he answered.

"Creighton Abrams, asshole."

Griffin relaxed and sat up. He placed the bag against his pillow. "Let him in."

Simon reached over and drew the bolt.

Beaming with the untranquilized delirium of an escaped lunatic, Triplett entered the room accompanied by a pale chubby PFC draped in brandnew but badly wrinkled fatigues several sizes too large. CLAYPOOL read the shining name tag.

"Lookee what I got," he announced, clapping his arm about the rounded shoulders of the open-mouthed boy. "A fucking new guy."

Griffin experienced a dreary film buff's satisfaction. The single character lacking from their B-war had finally arrived: The Kid. His past, his future were as clear, defined, and predictable as the freckles on his smooth face. He had never left home, would write his family once a day, sob himself to sleep each night. He becomes an abused mascot of the company, is kidded relentlessly until the brusque hero (Griffin?), brimming with manly tenderness, takes pity and shelters him from an apparently good-natured but actually quite cruel reality. Friendship cemented, acceptance complete, the next morning The Kid trips a land mine and blows his guts out, anointing his new buddies with a moist spew of panchromatic gore, his large colon, floating in a nearby lotus pond, spelling out good-bye among the fronds. The hero, a tear streaking his muddy cheek, ships The Kid's meager possessions (six comic books, a stringless yo-yo, a smudged photo of Betty Lou) home to a Nebraska farm to be wept over, no doubt, by a pair of simian parents and a bereaved hog. Inflamed by vengeful hate, the hero then goes berserk, slaughtering a division of godless gooks and half the allied general staff before being subdued by a foxhole presentation of the Congressional Medal of Honor at precisely the moment Griffin's dazed mind always congealed to jelly.

"I thought I'd bring him over for the usual orientation," said Trips.

Claypool nodded shyly in acknowledgment.

"Have a seat," offered Griffin, pointing to an empty five-gallon water can. "Sorry we can't do any better, but our furniture's out being reupholstered. The humidity is murder on material."

"Is it always this hot?"

Everyone laughed.

"Enjoy yourself," said Trips. "You don't know what hot is."

"Where you from back in the world?" Simon asked.

"Indiana. New Harmony, Indiana."

"That anywhere near Shit Creek?" asked Trips.

"It's about thirty miles northwest of Evansville, right near the Illinois line."

"What about snow?" Griffin inquired. "You had any snow yet?"

"There was four inches on the ground the day I left."

"Snow," said Simon.

"Where the hell's the weed," Trips demanded. "You ladies can chat about the weather later."

Griffin handed him the bag. He immediately plunked down on the footlocker next to Simon, pulled out a packet of licorice-flavored Zig-Zags, and began rolling a joint as thick as a cheroot. "What's with famous Vegematic there?"

"We figure he got another shipment of blotter acid from his brother," said Griffin. "He's been like that since mail call."

"Thank God for mail call. Packages and goodies from our loved ones."

"Did you hear," said Simon, "that Noll got Sergeant Ramirez to let him use one of the mess hall ovens so he could bake some cookies to send to his folks."

"How cute," Trips said. "He should have mixed some grass into the dough, too."

"He did."

"Oooooooo," Trips crooned. "I love this war. Soooo much. I ain't never going home."

He lit the finished joint and, smiling wickedly through a curl of smoke, brandished it triumphantly under Claypool's nose. "Welcome to Vietnam."

"The Magical Mystery Tour," added Griffin.

Claypool took the jay gingerly between his fingers and puffed delicately as though he were sucking a hot coal.

"You ever smoke before?" asked Griffin.

"Oh yeah . . . sure . . . a couple of times."

"You're in the big leagues now, sonny," Trips said.

Claypool grinned self-consciously and forced himself to inhale. "Gee, that's strong," he gasped, breaking into a fit of spasmodic coughing.

"Again," said Trips.

Gamely, Claypool tried again and succeeded in holding his breath without gagging. "I don't feel anything, maybe it's not working."

"Again," said Trips.

Joints passed from hand to hand and soon the small room was filled with ragged bands of drifting haze, the distinctive scent of disassembly, burning, penetrating, and gosh, Johnny, Indiana is so far away, twelve thousand miles far, day there now, a whole wide ocean away, never saw so much water and sky, guess you either swim or fly.

Claypool looked around as if he were just noticing everything for the first time. "What do you guys do here?" he asked suddenly.

"You're doing it," answered Griffin.

"This and that," said Trips. "Supersecret spy stuff. You cleared for rumor?"

"I've got a secret, if that's what you mean."

"He's got a secret," Simon said.

"Tell you," Trips explained, "we got so many secrets around here they got to run our shit through a shredder. There's nothing we don't know. Why, we even got itty-bitty bugs trained to sniff out Charlie's farts. This is a high-class operation you've dropped into, buddy, dukes of the spooks."

"Does anybody ever have to go out into the field?"

"Ssssshh." Trips raised a cautionary finger to his lips. "Don't give them ideas. What do you think we got all these fancy toy planes and cameras and radar for. We bring the field to us. Only crazies leave the company area. Don't you know what can happen Out There?" He waved his fingers at the walls. "A person could get his head squashed like a grape."

"It did not retain its natural firmness, that is true," said Simon.

"So we just sit right here all comfy and cozy and hope we never run out of dope." He handed another joint to Claypool. "Who was the fool dumb enough to go up with him?"

"Nobody knows," said Simon. "Some new pilot the CO was flight-checking. He only got here this morning."

"Great epitaph for his stone: I only got here this morning."

"The CO had six days left, can you believe that? Six days. His bags were already packed."

"So what do the folks down at Graves Registration always say? If you can't wrap it, bag it."

"I wouldn't be surprised if they discovered he was just plain drunk. He usually started with a couple beers at lunch and by six-thirty he's down to his underwear and singing 'Folsom Prison Blues.' "

"Has anyone mentioned ailerons?" asked Trips. "Tricky parts, break down real easy like iffen they don't get proper maintenance, if you know what I mean."

"Quit it," said Griffin.

"Paranoid humor," said Simon.

"I feel funny." Claypool appeared groggy, his bleared eyes veered unsteadily from side to side.

"More medicine," Trips declared, handing him a joint. "If you don't smoke this instantly to your knuckles and then pop the roach into your mouth you will lose all sensation below your waist for the rest of your life."

There was a pause and the pause grew, lengthened into a space. The room went falling forever through endless voids.

Silence and laughter. Spontaneous giggles.

Stretches of time. Deserts. Hissing sand.

Griffin pointed solemnly to the floor. "Has anyone ever noticed that that knothole there looks exactly like a profile of Richard Nixon?"

Simon bent over to inspect. "My God, he's right. Check the planks, men. Maybe there's one in all the wood."

A shell sailed sedately overhead; and Vegetable, apparently regarding its shrill whistle as his cue, began to recite in a newscaster's drone: "Sergeant Jimmie Parker (above, center), a communications specialist with the 101st Airborne Division, happily counts a portion of the ten thousand dollars in cash he has just received from Reenlistment NCO Staff Sergeant Charles B. Norton (second from left) as a bonus after signing up for an additional six-year hitch. Sergeant Parker plans to buy a new car when he completes his present Vietnam tour."

"Wind him up and hear him speak," said Trips.

The door at the other end of the hootch opened, banged shut. Tense glances were exchanged. Grass and tobacco smoke rose tall-stalked from unmoving hands, a garden of streaming light. Footsteps, heavy and slow. An inner door opened and closed. A light came on. A radio. More steps, shuffling. Bedsprings. Sound of one boot dropping to floor. "The blue bus is calling us," sang the radio, "the blue bus is calling us."

"Alexander," said Griffin. "He had guard duty."

"We're pretty edgy tonight," commented Trips.

"Word is Sergeant Anstin's out on a headhunt."

"Well, fuck him with a hot mortar tube."

"The U.S. Command announced today the loss of three more jets in the latest bombing raids over North Vietnam. This brings the figure of downed aircraft to seventeen for the week. Dead total two hundred seventy-eight Americans, three hundred forty-six Vietnamese, and four thousand five hundred eighty-two NVA and Viet Cong."

"Has anyone ever bothered adding up those numbers," said Simon. "We must have wiped out the entire population of North Vietnam at least twice over by now."

"You can't be too careful," commented Griffin.

"I heard there's a bald E-6 somewhere in an air-conditioned closet deep in MACV with a slide rule and a collection of dried hen bones who turns that stuff out every week."

"My lips are numb."

"It's all a grotesque hoax," declared Trips, "concocted for economic purposes. There is no war, there is no Vietnam. We're sitting inside a secret sound stage somewhere in southern Arizona."

"Yeah," said Simon, "right next to the studio where they faked the moon landing."

Buds of perspiration had blossomed on Claypool's forehead. His left leg bounced up and down nervously on the ball of his foot.

"Members of a Twenty-fifth Division recon unit were surprised yesterday on patrol when they encountered a full-grown tiger less than twenty yards from their bivouac site. PFC Henry Butwinski who first heard the animal's growl and then shot the four-hundred-pound cat says the skin will make a fine rug for the division's orderly room."

"A tiger?"

"Remember when they bombed the elephants in the valley and Wurlitzer flew over later taking pictures and crying all over his viewfinder."

"Not people, elephants."

"People and elephants."

"I think I'm going to have to leave."

"Wonder if anyone ever picked up the ivory."

"Vietnamese ones aren't the kind with ivory."

"All elephants have ivory."

"Well, you can be sure that if there was any ivory someone got it."

"Maybe there were guns inside."

"Guns?"

"Sure, the dinks could have hollowed out the tusks, fit machine guns inside."

"Tear gas canisters in their trunks."

"Those Indian rajahs used to paste jewels on them. To bully the lower castes."

"That's what I'd like to know, where are the jewels. The jewels and the women. What do you think I came over here for? What good is a war without pillage and plunder? Where's our share? The only women around here are these smelly dog-faced hootch maids and they sure as shit don't wear any jewels. Where the fuck are my jewels?"

"Look in your pants."

"There was that elephant in the movies, what's his name, who knew how to fly."

"Dumbo."

"He had to hold a magical cap in his trunk to get off the ground."

"No, no, it was a feather. His friend, the mouse, sat in the cap on his head and whispered instructions in his ear."

"Wow, what if they got a gook mouse to fly an elephant around and snap recon pictures of us."

"They could train hundreds of gook mice to pilot them in, bomb the compound with pachyderm pies. Dusty gray squadrons spread out in V-formation."

"Ears flapping like giant bat wings."

"Evil baby eyes inflamed."

"Trunks thrashing."

"Triangular mouths spilling drool."

"Then they all swoop in at once like this mammoth wrinkled hand pressing down and down, closer and closer. The intimacy is frightening. Dirty yellow toenails. Wispy belly hairs infested with black ticks."

"Dung-clotted tails."

"Hot peanut breath."

"The shock of the weight, the consciousness of collapse, the infinite agony of an unendurable mass."

"Weather for today: continued clear and sunny. Highs in the mid to upper nineties."

The Kid leaped from his seat, knocking over the water can, and darted to the door. "Let me out of here, please," he said. His fingers scrabbled ineffectually at the lock, twitching like galvanized worms. The bolt was already retracted. "How do you." Simon stood and pulled the door open and The Kid tore down the corridor, crashed through the hootch door and out into the rain and the night.

"Bye," called Trips.

"Oh boy," said Simon, reaching out for the wall, "have you people got a surprise when you stand up."

Trips tossed a lighted match through the open doorway, watched its yellow ribbony afterimage hang for an instant in the air. "I wouldn't want to be in junior's path the next time the sirens go off. But he'll be back tomorrow night begging for more. That boy's a head if I ever saw one."

"I've got to go to bed," said Simon, "if I can find my bed, if I can go. Goodnight, gentlemen. See you on campus."

Simon was gone.

"I thought they'd never leave," said Trips. He unbuttoned his left shirt pocket and produced a metallic film canister. "Home brew," he explained, pouring some into a rolling paper. "I'm gonna fix you a nightcap you won't forget."

"I'm getting better and better at forgetting," warned Griffin.

Fifteen minutes later Griffin sensed the first subtle movements of that interior process that shifted the structure of his awareness from a solid to a liquid to a gas. In accordance with the laws of evaporation. On the wall opposite, above Trips's head, a previous occupant of the room had scrawled in crimson Day-Glo the sardonic slogan: KILL A COMMIE FOR CHRIST. Under the soft luminiscence of the black light the words seemed to suspend themselves in space, to ripple ethereally like the swollen palps of an anemone beckoning in a torpid current. Letters revolved, faded, reemerged, sluggishly metamorphosing into a progression of variants on the original:

ZAP A ZIP FOR ZEUS
GARROTE A GOOK FOR GOD
NIFE A NIP FOR NEPTUNE

Amazing how facile the mind, thought a facile portion of Griffin's mind. Something wrong, though, with that last.

Teetering on the rim of complete dissolution, his attention fixed momentarily on that mysterious hieroglyphic which had puzzled him ever since his arrival:

A fraternity letter? An Oriental ideogram? A meaningless military cryptograph? Or only the stylized initials of a long dead or long gone soldier? I.O. Ingmar Olson? No. How many Scandinavians in the American Army? How many Swedes could bear the heat? O.I. Oliver Ingersoll? More likely. Oliver Ingersoll, are you alive, are you well?

Thought winnowed down to a maundering thread. Frontal bone splintered into billowing motes of ivory dust, exposed neural lobes to the cool fall of descending air. Intimate fission flashed with the erratic tempo of summer lightning on a gray horizon. Sheets of electronic rain glided past like heavy theater curtains on oiled tracks. He felt a hand move swiftly inward and seize the flaccid sponge of his mind within the grip of a velvet-gloved fist. Silent static closed over consciousness . . .

. . . and the clouds went slowly through the spectrum of visible light and the sun, just as big and round and red as a penny gumball, plopped between the moist lips of the sea and dissolved . . . into minute grains of sand wedged among the leather cracks of his boot. His focus centered on a large rust-colored cockroach the size of his thumb traversing the uneven wooden floor in a determined diagonal from right to left. He ground his heel down flat against the hard shell, listened for the crunch. There was not a sound. He raised his foot. The undamaged roach scuttled steadily away past the Richard Nixon knothole and disappeared under the bed. Startled, Griffin looked up. The sticks of incense had burned to ash, the candle was guttering in the last quarter inch of its stub. Vegetable and the dog had wandered off; only Trips remained, slouched on the footlocker, head tilted back, eyes shut.

"Trips."

"Hunh," he grunted, without moving.

"Maybe I'm seeing bugs."

"Lucky stiff."
"Maybe I'm seeing bugs and I'm in serious personal trouble."
"Sure."
"Or maybe there are bugs and we're all in trouble."
"Sure, Griffin, sure."
"The quality of my hallucinations is improving. Have you noticed? Do I appear alarmed? Are my eyes red? Am I making any sense?"
"No."
"It's so difficult to concentrate when your head is leaking essential ingredients."
"You're stoned. Go to sleep."
"A word of advice, Earthling, before I zoom away: Beware of the atomic cockroaches."
"Go to sleep."
Halfway to dawn and the guns continued to boom, each successive concussion fluttering the taut membrane that stretched over the dark sky like a vast circus tent, expanding the canvas toward that mystical moment when the balloon would indeed go up. Oliver Ingersoll, where are you? He glanced at Trips, slack-jawed and dumb, his docile face turned up into the black light, and wondered idly if under that warm violet glow he too looked so much like a corpse, and somewhere beyond thought and illusion and war he fell back across the bed and into real dream: of wet stark trees, of arctic wind, and of snow, of falling snow.

Meditation in Green: 3

You stand in a field surrounded by family. Light falls from the proper angles, wind blows from the proper direction, shadows are composed of friendly shapes. Home. Simple nourishment, harmonious rhythms. A fertile tomb where the spirits of ancestors brood over the unbroken seeds of the future. Long green waves swell and ebb across time. The rustle of relatives is a melody. The weather is kind. Nothing will ever change.

Dawn. The first light touches you upon the head, morning's anointment. The dew evaporates, inner chemicals mix and bubble, there is magic brewing. In the pulp, in the frail tissue movement quickens, a push upward, firm, persistent, the imperative of cellular wisdom ancient as the soil which sustains it. The rush expands into leaf after leaf, planes of awareness, alchemist's shops to sweeten the day. A fountain of energy you rise ecstatic into the blue-petaled sky, the pollen-dusted sun.

Centuries pass.

There is a vibration. Rolling in from the west comes thunder louder than the afternoon shower, a foreign key that silences the drone of insects. It advances swiftly, the tremors spread. Boom pause boom pause boom pause boom pause boom boom boom pause boomboomboomboom faster now, the heavy running feet of an animal new to the forest, boomboomboomboomboom-boomboom and a shadow swoops in and the sun swooshes out and a wind and you, you find yourself all at once chewed and torn, thrust head downward in smoking dirt while above in the hot air dangle your shocked roots already begun to blacken and curl at the touch of a light photosynthesis is hopelessly unable to transform.

Framed in the shattered doorway of my apartment Trips lay sprawled across the secondhand couch, combat-booted feet grinding dirt into the faded cushions, a tattered paperback copy of *Ubik* clutched in one grimy fist. He hadn't taken off his coat, a grease-stained field jacket decorated with dozens of division patches surrounded by the colors of every notorious motorcycle club in the country. He looked up from his reading with an annoyed master-of-the-house expression.

"You're melting all over the carpet," he said.

"Hey."

"Okay, I'll buy you a new door."

"You're out."

"Yes, I am out."

"You okay?"

"My friend, I'm a genuine certified okay. Dr. Caligari threw up his hands. Mirabile! A spontaneous individuation. Nothing like it in the entire literature. Gave me a comb, bottle of Thorazine, showed me the gate. They let a bunch of us go every year on the anniversary of Freud's birth."

"How do you feel?"

"About a hundred and two. Got anything special in the house for a weary old soldier?"

"Afraid the cupboard's bare, Pop."

"That's what I feared. Been away a long time." He reached into his pocket and flung onto the table between us a handful of colored capsules and tablets. "Cocktail nuts," he exclaimed, popping several into his mouth. "Courtesy the hospital pharmacy. Try the purple shells, they're great."

I poked through the pile, trying to find something I recognized. The table was a window I had screwed to a set of wooden legs.

"I like this," said Trips, leaning forward. "It's like they're floating in air like tiny planets." He moved his head back and forth over the glass. "I can see myself." He bent closer. "My feet. I can see my feet. That's good, always keep track of your feet, might need 'em to go somewhere."

"How'd you find me?"

"It ain't easy, good buddy, you hop around like a nervous bird."

"Trees keep falling down."

"Yeah, I noticed what a rock this joint is. Who's the wisp in the hall with the mutt?"

"That's Eugene. He's afraid to leave the building."

"I think I'd be afraid not to. What's that skull hanging in the john?"

"Little knickknack I picked up downtown."

"Spooky, Grif, mighty spooky. Don't know what's happened to you since I've been away. What's that?"

I had curled my hands into claws and exposed my teeth. "Our resident three a.m. bogeyman."

"Don't. You're giving me a peak. Peaks and valleys, I've been warned to avoid them."

"Need to get you one of Arden's magic flowers."

"Sheeeeit. That raisin-eyed Green Beret crazie. You still bother with him?"

"Sometimes."

"There's a dude they'd like to see down on Nine West."

"He was talking about you just the other day, wants to make you up a big bouquet."

Trips held up a finger. "Tell him to meditate on this."

"Peaks, watch out."

He glanced around the room. "So where's Rapunzel?"

"I don't know. One day she went down to the corner for a can of orange juice and . . ."

"These squiggles hers?" Oriental ideograms had been painted in black across all four white walls.

"Charms," I explained, "for the demons that abound."

"They look like snakes, nests of snakes. Listen, you want me moving in here for a couple days you're gonna have to tone down the atmosphere. Skulls in the shithouse, gooks on the walls, ghosts in the night, it's worse than the ward. And get some eats. I notice all you've got in the refrigerator is a jar of peanut butter and a bag of leaves."

"Romaine lettuce."

"Yeah? Well, it's wilted. I require minimum daily amounts of the four basic food groups: caffeine, nicotine, sugar, and dope."

"Watch out," I said, clutching the arms of my chair, "I think the rug is starting to move."

Later that night I learned about the hospital—medicated Basic Training—about the daily sessions, chairs drawn in a circle, tall tales around the old campfire: "We had one poor guy raping grandmothers with a bayonet, rolling hand grenades into orphanages, all the time he's screaming and bawling and tossing the chairs, kicking the Ping-Pong table to pieces, chewing padding off the walls, a jazz solo, man, and he finishes up by wetting his pants and collapsing against the Coke machine. He was back on the street in a week."

"Fun."

"Well, you know, we were in competition. I freaked them, though, told everybody I enlisted, I followed orders, I always volunteered, I never complained, I liked it a lot, I *believed*."

"Yeah, that was you all right."

"I was a goddamned maniac."

"Snoring all day at your desk."

"Greasing gooks all night."

"Remember the time Anstin caught you digging up your stash behind the signal shack?"

"That old fucker could really run."

"You must have done a dozen laps around the compound. His face got so purple I thought he'd have a heart attack."

"I was the one who was gonna die."

"Sergeant Mars was shooting that gun into the air. He knew you weren't really an escaped prisoner."

"Into the air, hell, he was firing right at me. That guy *was* from Mars."

"Remember the grass pizza?"

"One of the great home recipes."

"It was like chewing on dirt."

"And you were on guard duty and passed out in your bunk and a rat fell off the rafter into the fan."

"I thought I'd been hit."

"Simon turns on the light and there's your silly face all plastered with blood and rodent fur."

"A laugh riot."

"Yeah, I must have laughed hard twenty times a day."

"You were always laughing."

"You were so goddamned funny."

"So were you."

"We were all funny."

I fell asleep and dreamed of a pair of oversized cartoon hands trying to lace a tiny cartoon boot and then an old gook clutching a bar of blue soap bent over me, face twisted with laughter, and I woke up in the bathtub. I staggered into the other room. The telephone book had been torn apart, ripped and crumpled pages littering the floor and furniture. The door was wide open. Trips was gone.

From the air the compound of the 1069th Intelligence Group was a triumph of military design. Living quarters for both officers and enlisted men consisted of fifty-five identical hootches arranged in five ranks of eight hootches, then three ranks of five. In the open area at the lower right was a concrete basketball court. An L-shaped mess hall defined the bottom corner. The various other necessary structures—motor pool, EM club, chapel, et cetera—were positioned separately off to the side in no particular order. The working offices, long windowless Quonset huts, could be found in the line of hangars, maintenance shops, and supply sheds bordering the airfield. But the unit's basic geometric design possessed a pleasing sense of natural logic and finality that seemed somehow magical to the mind. Approaching from the east you thought of the runway as a pole and the perfectly engineered rectangle of buildings to the right of its top as a flag, a three-dimensional facsimile of a flag. In fair weather when basketball games were a daily occurrence, the tiny players moved back and forth across the court like a handful of loose marbles rolling around a board tilted first one way, then the other. Today the court was deserted, the hoop nets hung sodden and empty, unscored on for weeks. Between the hootches the night rain had mixed sand and clay into yellowish-red stripes that bled like cheap dye.

Outside the compound gate sat a scrawny old man with a face so expressively ancient the lines seemed to have been drawn in ink. Day after day he sat patiently upon his small plastic turquoise mat, a dark wooden bowl centered on the ground before him. Sometimes a soldier on his way to the PX or to town would stop, toss in a wrinkled bill, but such generosities were rare. There was only so much a soldier could care about. Trucks loaded with laughing troops rumbled down the road and often a beer or soda can or even a gob of spit came flying toward the old man who did not move or speak. The thick dust clouds would settle back onto his conical straw hat, his hunched shoulders, and into his empty bowl, tinting everything red. During monsoon season when the daily storms came the old man would cover himself with a rubber U.S. Army poncho and continue to sit, without apparent concern or discomfort, as now the big trucks splashed mud and the bowl filled slowly with rain.

In a plot of spiky grass to the right of the orderly room stood a large painted sign:

1069th MILITARY INTELLIGENCE GROUP

COMMANDING OFFICER — FIRST SERGEANT

LT. COLONEL WILFRED A. DAUER — LEONARD G. BURT

SAFETY FIRST!

KEEP THE GREEN LIGHT BURNING

In the center of the sign was a gaudy portrait of a screaming woman with round crimson mouth, huge yellow eyes, a black nest of snakelike hair: the unit emblem.

The green light was a rusted socket stuffed with sand and bits of broken glass.

Hanging on metal hooks from this large sign was a smaller one that read: 7 DAYS WITHOUT AN ACCIDENT. Even though the sign had been constructed so that the numerals could be changed the same faded 7 had been dangling there as long as anyone could remember. The wind blew and the sign creaked back and forth, creak, creak, in the damp wind.

"See how this pin . . ."

"Was sawed through?"

"Who can tell? These parts is old and decayed. Maintenance ain't what it should be."

"Someone did it."

"Hard to say."

"Someone did it."

Inside a Quonset hut surrounded by high chain-link fence topped with coils of barbed wire behind a red door marked RESTRICTED sat Griffin on a tall stool. His face, strongly lit from below, seemed glazed with silver, moonlike. He held a large magnifying glass in one hand as he studied a frame of the roll of black and white film spread on the light table in front of him. His eyes narrowed. He leaned forward. Something wiggled, slipped into focus, slipped out again. A dead log, not a muzzle brake. He sat up, arching his back to relieve the tightness in his shoulders, the burr in his head. All-night dreams tumbled through him like a wind too quick for memory, leaving behind the sensation of great speed, and, stuck to the morning light, barbs of an indistinct seed, the germ of the headache he would carry to work and the culture of eye strain and tedium in which it would propagate out of control. He reached forward, turned the crank on his right, and the film, unrolling from a reel on the left, moved smoothly across a long rectangle of illuminated glass. The military name for this task was image interpreter. Griffin was required to translate pictures into letters and coordinates that were instantly telexed to such important addressees as III MAF, 1AIRCAV, 25DIV, III MAG, MACV, CINCPAC, and most impressive, JCS. The data went round and round and where it came out he preferred not to hear. A camera fixed in the belly of a Mohawk OV-1A had collected today's images during a morning break in the weather above a sector of suspected hostile activity approximately fifty kilometers southwest of Griffin's stool. His job was to interpret the film, find the enemy in the negatives. He turned the crank. Trees, trees, trees, trees, rocks, rocks, cloud, trees, trees, road, road, stream, stream, ford, trees, road, road. He stopped cranking. With a black grease pencil he carefully circled two blurry shadows beside the white thread of a road. Next to the circles he placed question marks. Road, road, road, road, trees, trees, trees. His eyes felt hard as shells, sore as bruises. Trees, trees, trees, trees. Wherever he put circles on the film there the air force would make holes in the ground.

In the adjacent Quonset hut Captain Thomas Raleigh extended his arm and shook hands with PFC Claypool.

"Welcome to the interrogation section. How's your Vietnamese?"

Claypool grinned. "It was okay, sir, until I heard two laundry girls in Long Binh."

"I know the feeling, son. Don't let it spook you. The field's a long way from the classroom. You've got the basics, but you'll do all your real learning out here." He smiled.

"I was beginning to wonder if I was in the right country."

"Oh, you're in the right country all right. Where else do the people curse each other in six-tone harmony." Captain Raleigh glanced at his watch. "We were thinking of assigning you temporarily to Sergeant Ramirez in the mess hall for a week or two, sort of an undercover job working along side of the native kitchen help who won't know you understand the language. It's something we like to do now and then with new personnel. You get a quick refresher course in Vietnamese and maybe we pick up a bit or two of useful intelligence. I know KP isn't much fun but once we flushed out a whole family of VC this way. Helps to keep everybody on their toes, know what I mean?"

Behind Captain Raleigh's back Claypool could see the cages, all empty except for the nearest one. On the floor, curled into a fetal ball, lay what appeared to be a small woman. Under her body on the concrete was a large wet puddle. Claypool found it difficult to keep his eyes off her. He wondered if she was dead.

"Okay, here's the setup," Captain Raleigh was saying. "We receive prisoners from all army units now operating in I Corps, the 101st, the Aviation Brigade, Special Forces, and so on. It can get pretty hectic depending on the time of year and the size of our staff. Right now we're short about three people but monsoon is usually a slack period, anyway. We try to stay ahead by working quickly. Our facilities are adequate if we can keep the flow running. When we're finished the prisoners are shipped out to the POW compound in Da Nang. Any questions? I would like to emphasize the fact that we are not just interested in speed, we want accuracy, too. This is an important mission we've got here; the information we obtain is read up and down the whole goddamn chain of command from MACV in Saigon to Pacific Headquarters in Honolulu to the Pentagon in Washington. We've got plenty of important eyes peeping over our shoulders, so don't fuck up. Remember, lives depend on our input."

The woman had not moved. She might have been a piece of modern soft sculpture or one of those dummy torsos used to teach emergency resuscitation techniques.

Captain Raleigh looked at his watch again. "I'm afraid I've got a section chief meeting which I must attend so I'm going to have to leave you alone for a couple minutes. Sergeant Mars should be back shortly. He'll brief you on specific duties, help you get settled in. In the meantime look the place over, make yourself at home. We're glad to have you and I'm sure you'll find it interesting and challenging work."

As soon as the captain was gone Claypool sat down at one of the vacant desks and lit a cigarette. Next to the in box was a row of gold-framed family photographs: a pleasant middle-aged woman with short blond hair and glasses, an adolescent boy posed arms folded in front of a gleaming maroon Chevy sedan, a young girl in pajamas clutching a stuffed cat, and a large black setter holding in his mouth a cloth banner declaring We All Miss You Very Much. There was a calendar with all the days of the year up to and including this one neatly X'ed out. Under a Plexiglas desktop were various memos, regulations, schedules, a few humorous birthday cards, a student's crib sheet of typical Vietnamese phrases such as "What is your name?" "How old are you?" "Are you ill?", an anatomical chart with all the body parts labeled in Vietnamese, and two pastel-colored signs. Pathet Lao For Lunch Bunch, said one. VC The Breakfast of Champions, said the other.

Claypool decided that the woman was probably unconscious. Should he do something? For a moment he wondered if perhaps the captain had only stepped into an adjoining room to watch him through a secret peephole in the wall. But if this was a test of some kind, just what was it that was being tested? His compassion or his callousness? Suppose he got up and spoke to the woman. It might interfere with her interrogation. Also, the sergeant might walk in at any moment. He would wait. After ten minutes of uncomfortable suspense he decided to take a look. The woman was on her right side, knees drawn up to her chin, her back toward him. He edged around to the side of the cage. He gasped. Her eyes, large and coal black, were wide open. He bent down, pressing against the wire, looking for the rise and fall of breathing. He thought her eyes moved, blinking like a reptile's. "Hello," he said softly. "Are you all right?" There was no response. He started to repeat the sentence in Vietnamese until he remembered that nationals were not supposed to know he could do that yet. He felt helpless and stupid. The woman stared through him as though he were a ghost. What was so fascinating? He got down on his knees, lowered his head to the floor in the same angle and direction as hers. There was only the adjacent cage and then another cage and another and another, wall after wall of bars and steel mesh receding backward to the blank windowless wall at the end of the building. Claypool got up, brushed his hands on his pants, and went back to the desk to have another cigarette. The ashtray was there and a chair and the light. He wanted to sit under a strong light for a while.

"There's talk the colonel's accident was not as it seems."

"No shit."

"Really, there's rumors of a full-scale investigation. Imported CID, fingerprint experts, trained dogs, the works. We're all suspects."

"Check it out. So are they."

"Watch close, motherfuck." The knife catapulted from Bennie Franklin's fist, went spinning down the narrow corridor and buried itself Plunk! in the door at the far end of the hootch. The blade was still quivering when Franklin yanked it from the wood. "Now, tell me, don't that give a man supreme confidence?"

"Right," said Marvin. "Long as he's standing directly behind you." He shook his head gravely, regretfully. "No, Bennie, I ain't gonna do it."

"Hooooooeeeeee," crooned Franklin, raspy as a witch. He danced around Marvin flashing the knife like a psychotic surgeon.

"Looky here at Mister Uppity, he afraid of taking a scratch, don't want his chrome dented, huh? He don't put a cigarette in his mouth and stand sideways like the good doctor say, this stiletto gonna slip and let the air outta his tire so fast his mama hear him squeal. Now go on before I get extra nasty."

"Get that steel out of my face," said Marvin quietly.

"Maybe I oughta disconnect your hose."

"Try it."

Their eyes locked for an instant. Someone blinked. Franklin backed off. With careful exaggeration he peered over first one shoulder, then the other, and leaned forward to whisper, "You a smart nigger, Marvin." He slid the pad of his thumb along the shiny blade edge, then held it up, displayed the deep horizontal stroke, the blood draining into his palm.

As soon as Lieutenant Tremble took a seat among his men he noticed the crude verse scratched into the table top:

Peace and Grace once ruled this place
An Angel held open the door
Now Peace is dead
The Angel has fled
And Grace is a hustling whore.

The men looked at each other and shrugged. Yes, everyone was well aware of the punishment for defacing government property, everyone certainly wished the unknown offender could be captured and brought to justice, everyone was quite sorry. Specialist Alexander volunteered to sand and repaint the table. Draw your tiles, lieutenant.

Even though Tremble detested playing Scrabble (he always lost) almost as much as he disliked his men (they weren't *serious*) he occasionally allowed himself to be coaxed into a game as a demonstration of plebeian charm, of manly camaraderie, hands across the steely waters of rank. It wasn't always easy. The weight of the entire Research and Analysis Section bore constantly down upon his own prematurely balding head. The nominal chief of the section, Captain T. Hewitt, was no longer competent, having stared long into the crystal ball on his desk—an unfortunate joke, the gift of his predecessor—and seen all responsibilities transformed into distant objects of bathos. He had lost interest in any feats of clairvoyance beyond the summoning of spirits into a shot glass and sardonic predictions about how long the latest ice shipment would last. He was cheerfully spending the remainder of his war in the officers club with Major Brand, the executive officer, the two of them engaged in a joint assault upon the bourbon supply and the weaving of a new age philosophy of life based on the pleasures of college football and imported cars. Papers requiring Captain Hewitt's signature were delivered to a back table in the corner in the dark. Hewitt had not been seen in natural light for months. Like Major Brand he planned on retiring at the end of this tour. He was tired of being a gypsy.

So that left Tremble, a shake and bake looey fresh out of Ohio State ROTC, and already holding down a captain's slot, the makings of a professional career unexpectedly dumped in his lap, and him trying as well as he could not to fumble the pieces. This act had been complicated in recent weeks by The General tossing another ball into the air. The 5th NVA regiment. Where from? Where to? How big? How good? Find it! It was the mission of Research and Analysis to outline shapes, to color in detail. In the back room, protected by steel doors and air conditioning, were banks of vigilant computers, their insomnia tended in shifts around the clock by the men of R&A, working like medieval scribes to copy field reports onto programming sheets, which were punched on keyboards, cut and shuffled by circuits, then retyped with automatic precision on perforated printouts rolling endlessly into cardboard boxes on the floor beneath each machine. Shelves along all four walls were stacked with boxes, dates scrawled in black across the cardboard. Somewhere in those boxes was the enemy. And sooner or later, despite the obstacles thrown around him, Tremble would find it and when he did The General would not forget.

"S," he said, carefully placing a tile on the board, "W, I, Z, Z,

L, E." Tiles were arranged in a vertical column. "Double word, triple letter, what's that—twenty-one, twenty-two?"

Overhead hung framed portraits of the leaders of the National Liberation Front, executives of the Communist Party of the People's Democratic Republic of Vietnam, and generals of the People's Army. Hollow-cheeked men staring resolutely into a Scrabble-less future.

The First Sergeant, sipping coffee behind the morning copy of *Stars and Stripes* acknowledged with a low grunt the madness of the world. Terrorism, et cetera, murder, et cetera, rioting, et cetera, all the usual redundancies. Amateur hysteria. He was glad to be in the company of professionals. There was safety in specialization. Around him his clerks hunched over their machines. The typewriters clattered and rang. Rosters, directives, memoranda, orders. Names and numbers, rat-a-tat-tat.

Trips struck the match with a cavalier flourish and attempted for the second time to start his first pipe of the day. Lungs wheezing like a pair of mildewed bellows, he sucked furiously on the black stem of his seasoned briar. A wisp of pungent smoke came and went. "Well, bite my butt," he mumbled, scowling into the dead bowl. "This goddamn weather." He tamped the springy contents down with a P-38 can opener, which shared the chain around his neck with a metallic swastika and a gold-plated scarab beetle. (His dog tags he had ceremoniously deposited one moonless night inside a Buddhist tomb, one of many overgrown and sand-swept mounds heaped in apparently random fashion back of the perimeter like a distribution of shell craters seen in reverse stereoscopic lenses.) "The rain makes the grass damp and hard to light."

Squatting in a corner, Vegetable dangled a broken watch in front of Thai's snout, trying to hypnotize the indifferent animal. "Sure," he agreed, "and it gives the water buffaloes headaches."

Trips looked at Vegetable. Vegetable looked at Trips. "You simple little shit," said Trips. He took off his cap and began beating Vegetable on the head and shoulders. "Just what are we going to do with you, huh? you simple little stupid stoned shit." They rolled on the floor in convulsive laughter.

At the airfield's passenger terminal the few men waiting for flights out were too tired to do more than smoke cigarettes, exchange stale jokes. No one wanted any conversation. Their restless eyes shifted from the dark surface of the runway to the cloudy sky and back again. No one looked at the pyramid of long narrow boxes also awaiting a ride, the fork lift, and the windowless transport home.

The door was locked, the shutters closed. A small reading lamp projected a cone of light across the desktop mess: a heavy-duty government typewriter; a pile of papers, files, manuals; a pair of bare feet, crossed. Brown smoke drifted through the diagonal light, turning languidly. Slouched in an aluminum lawn chair was the room's occupant, First Lieutenant Zachary Mueller, a corncob pipe stuck between his teeth. The walls were an unmilitary burnt orange. He was dressed in a blue bathrobe. He was writing the unit history.

His literary activity had begun as a search into the structure of a moment. The moment occurred near the end of a routine photo mission when, glimpsing movement at the edge of an empty village, Mueller dropped the Mohawk for a quick peek and a scrawny old woman, all arms and legs, darted out spiderlike from beneath a bush, stopped, planted a pair of splayed feet into the ground and lifted to her bony cheek the long wide heavy barrel of an immense rifle, fixing forever an instant in which horizon rim, banana tree and palm, thatch roof and angular shadow, flowing grass and squinting face, spun about a huge dark oily metal hole. He hung there at the end of a wire, a set of startled blue eyes staring down. Then the plane banked violently away, landscape and cloud resumed linear motion, engines ground unsteadily home where the part of him labeled Lieutenant Mueller made his report, drank his beer, ate his dinner, impersonated bland normality with professional skill as his watch ticked on, sun followed moon, the first wrinkles appeared in the mirror while the moment persisted, refused to change, a note struck and held, through all his succeeding days and nights, a hole that would never close. He read, he jotted down notes, he began keeping track. The Old Man agreed he could start compiling material, in a semiofficial capacity, on a life of the 1069th. Knee-high piles of books and magazines stood about the room like tree stumps. Sheets of loose paper littered the floor. The moment swelled and deepened. Facts, events, objects, and people, himself included scribbling away, descended daily, whirling about the hole, debris down the drain of history.

There was the tale of the first commanding officer, an unrestrained oddball nicknamed Captain Natural who appeared to have undergone a bizarre version of the famous imperialist breakdown celebrated in film and print and who was last seen parachuting bucknaked into the jungle, falling out of the virginal blue like a hysterical nun's wet dream. There was the aged intelligence veteran with impressive credentials dating back to the dirk-and-dark-alley days of the OSS, the very mastermind who had attempted to bribe Hitler's gardener to sprinkle a hefty dose of estrogen on top of Der Fuehrer's cabbage, thereby rendering the symbol of Aryan virility into a bald, moustacheless, wheezing old woman—an agent of flair and imagination whose mind, approaching its twilight years, was unfortunately lit by the sinking sun from strange angles and took to studying esoteric religious tracts printed on recycled grocery bags by one-man publishing houses with names like The Armed Armageddonist and Hot Cross Press. There was the interrogation chief who called his section The Dental Clinic and conducted sessions in information extraction dressed in a barbecue apron depicting a hapless suburban chef behind a backyard grill on which steaks were smoking like a steel mill in Gary over the amusing caption BURNED OR CHARRED? and who, when he wasn't devising such clever innovations as the placement of heated map pins in a decorative pattern on the surface of the eyeball, practiced the Oriental Water Pik, an operation consisting of blocking open the mouth with wooden wedges and flooding the upraised throat, nostrils, and eyes with gallons of unpotable water until the ensuing nausea and suffocation resulted in an uncontrollable expulsion of undigested food, water, mucous, and the precise geographic coordinates of the patient's battalion; an overzealous patriot who was finally escorted, handcuffed and delirious, still chattering about jeep batteries and skin resistance, out to a waiting plane and away. There was the CO found slumped in a latrine stall one gray morning, a large bayonet skewering several important organs in his chest, a roll of damp toilet paper clutched in his right hand. There was the spook who walked the streets of Hanoi in a baggy Bulgarian suit and steel glasses and who died in the bombing the information he radioed out made possible. It was all there in the heap of white leaves collecting on Mueller's floor. The Crevecoeur Hotel murders, the mad boy of Duc Lop, the explosion of Bunker 13, the EM club manager with Mafia connections, the month-long interrogation of the beautiful Xuan Hoa, the gay First Sergeant who staffed the orderly room with his lovers, the black Counter Intelligence deserter who led a squad of VC sappers, the sexual banquets at the CIA estate outside Hue.

Today Mueller was busy working on a complete creation myth. He puffed on his pipe. Smoke billowed upward into the shadows. The light reflected orange suns off the walls. How did it begin? How did it all begin?

He pulled a pad onto his lap and across the top line wrote, "In the beginning was boredom and air-conditioning."

The war might have been a universe away.

His pencil, composing, danced gracefully over the page to the scratch, scratch of its own harmonic accompaniment. Yet in the intervals between phrases, the silences separating thought, he could still feel the hole spiraling through graphite, paper, the pulp of his chest.

"What I find definitively weird is this: a guy, thirty years a pilot, military and commercial experience, last five with the Mohawk exclusively, suddenly dumps his laundry at the end of the runway on a routine takeoff in clean weather that a blindfolded student could pull off without a problem. How come? That's Fort Rucker washout stuff."

"Unless he had a reason."

"For sticking his head in a meat grinder?"

"He didn't know the plane was going to come apart. Hell, they bellyflopped off a diving board. He thought he'd be able to get out okay."

"Emergency ditching lessons for the new man?"

"Flashy stunts for Hollywood. That movie of his needed a finish. He's going home, he wants a grand finale for his war flick. He stations Wendell and camera across the highway, smiles and waves, and takes it down under the nose of the lens. Boom."

"Only he don't get up again."

"There is the movie."

"An amateur job with no sound and scratches all over the negative."

"Our own CO immortalized."

"Long as the freak don't lose the film."

Out on the sloping edge of the runway, squarely centered over a large white numeral 9, a single aircraft stood poised, awaiting final clearance from the tower, an unreliable looking structure of pocked terra-cotta and fissured plaster defaced by the graffiti of three continents, the acne of war, and a perennially pubescent climate. The building had been hurriedly constructed and even more quickly abandoned in the early 'fifties by a disgraced army of fleeing French. (According to Mueller's History, on receiving news of the debacle in progress, the base commandant, Jean-Paul Roipecheur, immediately ordered a bath drawn and, after soaking the filth of Asia from his pores, donned a royal blue dress uniform and sauntered out to greet the advancing enemy. There, in a superb exhibition of Gallic hauteur, he nibbled leisurely from a tin of pâté de foi gras as lead buzzed like vineyard bees about his head and mortar explosions rearranged the topography of his command until the heathen Viet Minh were less than a hundred yards away when he tossed silver fork and uneaten goose liver aside and threw himself dramatically on his sword shouting. *"Et voici comment la France a riposté à tous les despotes!"* Unfortunately, the blade, deflected by a gaudy armorlike row of chest decorations and medals, missed the vital organs and he required five hours to die, during which agony Roipecheur unwittingly divulged every military secret he was privy to. *"Très déclassé,"* muttered the Parisian press.)

Unaware of his proximity to this historical epicenter, the American pilot, Captain Alvin P. Fry, studied his instrument panel with a gruff professional air. The various appliances attached to his head, the huge olive green wraparound helmet, the radio microphone jutting out between his lips, the wide-lensed aviator's sunglasses shielding his eyes, all served to broaden the zone of cool impenetrability that normally surrounded him. His hands, sensitive to the feel of the machine, moved skillfully among the knobs, buttons, and levers of the cramped cockpit. He leaned forward, tapped on a gauge with a gloved finger, the white needle swung loose, settled back into its proper position. When he glanced up at the sky his sunglasses reflected distorted ovals of soft washed light. The man looked good, he didn't at all appear to be suffering from one of the most godawful hangovers of his drinking career. He might have been looking for a place to stick his gum instead of manfully debating whether it was more appropriate for a former Green Beret staff sergeant, ex-Operation Phoenix triggerman, and recently promoted captain to vomit directly on the floor between his legs where that obnoxious jug-eared crew chief who couldn't operate a screwdriver without diagrammed instructions would be sure to discover it caked and rancid on his return or whether to pop the hatch and boldly let fly into the prop wash, risking a faceful of boomeranging breakfast. Neither alternative was particularly acceptable no matter how sick he felt. Actually he would suffocate on his own repressed vomit before playing the fool for anyone. At the age of seventeen he had had tattooed on his right forearm a blue eagle clutching in its talons the banner DEATH BEFORE DISHONOR. An army psychiatrist who examined Fry after members of his Alpha team caught him eating C-rations out of a freshly evacuated VC skull was heard to remark afterward, "This wacko has a real mother of a self-image." So dishonor somehow seemed more of a possibility today in this plane than it ever had on the battlefield. The big Rolls-Royce engines rumbled on in idle, shivering his hams and driving a series of vibrations worse than malarial fever up his spine, and every polluted throb of his heart set off a burst of Claymores behind each eyeball. He wanted to die. For a moment he seriously considered whether prayer might not help, an option he had not taken since boyhood when he had watched a haloed face materialize one dreary summer morning on the creamy wall of his Sunday school classroom, misting gray and ancient against a cloud-shaped water stain, a juvenile's composite of authority: stern and sympathetic, gentlemanly and cherubic, wise and innocent, the features unconsciously gleaned from a sunlit memory of his grandfather and an imposing portrait of enthroned Deity looming above the 26-inch color television set in the parlor of his piously dotty Aunt Victoria, a face which amazed years later when he saw it in *Time* magazine peering owlishly over the canted shoulder of President John Kennedy, the story described the previous week's Bay of Pigs disaster and a caption identified those familiar lineaments as belonging to one Allen Dulles. Prayer, he concluded, would be about as effective as that invasion. There were more efficient methods of dealing with bodily insubordination. There was that moldy agent's dodge: In the presence of ungovernable stress, create a diversionary pain you *can* control. Fry placed his tongue between his back molars and bit down. He thought he would faint. If he could stay cool until airborne there would be too much to do to waste energy on internal discomforts. He had to make it, he had to. He didn't want to be sick, not in his plane, not on his pants, especially not in front of an enlisted man.

The enlisted man in question, Sp/4 Monroe "Spaceman" Wurlitzer, would not have cared or scarcely noticed had the captain begun flopping about the cockpit in the midst of a grand mal seizure. Limp body sprawled in the seat at Fry's right, Wurlitzer was lost in rapt communion with several major hallucinogens. His mind swooped aloft through a pyrotechnic maze of loops and banks aerodynamically impossible for this bulky Grumman to achieve even when airborne. White scarf gaily streaming from his neck, the Red Baron celebrated his latest kill, brazenly taunting the enemy and boosting Junker morale with an aerial victory dance over the pestilential trenches of no-man's-land where far below antlike humans huddled sick and soiled in the wastes of Europe. Ha, ha, you wingless fools, I can fly. A cocky sneer adorned the windburned face of the aviator as he tipped his wings in farewell, good-bye, good-bye all, auf Wiedersehen, zooming off into paradise, machine guns hot for some angels to slay. Boy oh boy, thought Wurlitzer in dazed wonderment, am I high, so high that that oil spurting there on the cowling, those thrown splotches look to be pancakes all bubbly and iridescent, and that real big round one isn't either batter or petroleum but an opening, an opening down like the entrance to a long tunnel burrowing further than conduits, circuitry, and tanks, down, down to dark places, dark and deep. Wurlitzer quickly turned his head away. Something was happening. Things lived down there. A ridiculous notion, but he knew it was true. Shapes were already gathering at the corner of his eye. He wouldn't look. Things like that fed on looks. The harder you looked, the harder they got. He'd just sit like this even if there was a face pressed against the window, tiny fingers drumming on the Plexiglas, nails ticking like avid insects. Suddenly a hand plunged through the windscreen and Wurlitzer screamed, cringing in terror, reaching out instinctively for protection and escape—like a drowning sailor seizing a piece of flotsam, he pounced on the stalks of the throttle.

The plane lurched forward, advancing erratically down the runway in a drunken veer from right to left, left to right, before its apparently searching nose located and finally aligned itself on the broken white center line. The fuselage went fishtailing to a point less than halfway across the length of slick tarmac when suddenly the plane reared up like a stallion and soared almost vertically away, climbing on a pillar of exhaust to topple at the apogee of its spectacular ascension back into the lofty grime of a head of cumulonimbus accompanied by the ground crew's upraised hosannas of "Holy shit!" and "Who is that asshole?"

Late in the morning after all the soldiers who worked days had gone off to their duties and all those who worked nights had settled into their bunks for sleep there could be heard throughout the unit area, if one's ears had not become dulled, the sharp severe sounds of a body being physically abused. And if one's curiosity had not been numbed, the sounds could be traced to a large unpartitioned hootch on the edge of the compound. The room inside was filled with giggling Vietnamese women who smoked odious tobacco, traded gossip, chewed betel, all the while twisting into heavy green ropes the wet fatigues, the empty pants and shirts, of the American army, which they struck methodically again and again upon the concrete floor, beating out the dirt.

On his break Griffin slipped out to the bunker for a quick joint. Homegrown aspirin. Back at the office it was easy to pretend he was up in a Mohawk peering down at the two-dimensional landscape passing below in neat black-and-white-segmented squares. With his hand on the crank he could make the plane go fast, he could make the plane go slow. The only problem was the missions were taking twice as much time as usual. He'd measure the same object on the negative two or three times, read geographical coordinates off the wrong grid square, transpose numbers on the computer sheets, and counting the holes was like counting the dimples on a golf ball—where to begin? where to end? He hardly cared, having been totally absorbed into the fascinating realm of carpet bombing, lost among the oddities of the weave: the not uncommon crater within a crater, Chinese boxes of destruction; the lone untouched tree at the center of a field of matchsticks; the bomb distribution games of connect-the-dots and see a smiling fish, a happy flower; and through it all the long winding road, a living organism of strength and guile, slithering among the damage, easily skirting the small holes, simply passing into, climbing out of, the big ones, interdictions often filled in and repaired before the landing gear of the B-52s thumped down on Okinawa. Trucks and bicycles, troops and supplies, moved in infinite procession through fire and shrapnel. There was no stopping these people, they took to craters like Americans to shopping malls. What wonderful astronauts they would make. At this level there existed a universe in which Vietnam actually was a planet, an entire globe, curious, resourceful, technologically advanced, a confident and impatient world launching missiles in all directions, bombarding the stars, opening frontiers, establishing distant colonies, angry little people with blistered skin and black pajamas roving long ago through the tall grass of Griffin's boyhood and now passing outward, long marching columns, into the city of his future.

On his lunch break Simon picked up an apple and a cup of milk from the mess hall before going back to his room, seating himself at a table stolen long ago from supply, and writing his weekly letter home.

Dear Mom and Dad,

It is after midnight and I don't know how much longer my flashlight can hold out. The shelling has stopped temporarily, and I thought I'd take these few quiet moments to let you know that I am still fine.

We have been living in the bunkers for over a week now, sleeping with our M-16s. But don't worry, no one really expects an actual ground attack. In fact, Louie Sandoz, one of our analyst guys, just told me a couple hours ago that Mr. Charles doesn't have enough troops in the area yet to attempt a full-scale penetration of our defenses. We have been warned, though, to be on the alert for sappers, but so far all has been peaceful except for this constant mortar and rocket barrage. Of course, not even that bothers me anymore. Over here you learn to get used to anything.

I'm sorry but Sgt. Murphy has just ordered me to douse the light so I will have to close. I'll try to write again during the next lull in the action. Hope you are all well. Give my love to Kathy and Junior and a biscuit to King.

Your hot warrior son,
Lewis

P.S. Remember Tommy Brown, the guitar player from Alabama I wrote you about. Well, yesterday he was killed by a stray piece of shrapnel while walking to the latrine. Please send me a chamber pot, pronto. (Joke, joke.)

Simon addressed and licked the envelope, then stretched himself out on a bright red Made in Hong Kong floor mat and started vigorously executing his thirty daily sit-ups. He had noticed lately that his pants were becoming a bit snug around the waist and he absolutely refused to sally forth from the sauna of modern warfare flabbier than when he had entered. What would his parents think?

In an office behind the kitchen Mess Sergeant Howard Ramirez sat rigid as a monument listening to the war in his stomach. Hostilities had begun at lunch an hour ago and since then the rumble seemed to have become less distant, more dramatic. Silently, he measured each twitch and burn. One could never be certain when an attack of indigestion might intensify into a crisis—the commencement of a long-awaited gastric Dien Bien Phu. He knew he shouldn't have touched that meat, greasy army hamburger privates with only eighteen-year-old stomachs usually returned half-eaten, but it had been so long since he had enjoyed any chewable food and he was so sick of milk and cottage cheese and gelatin, meals you could suck through a straw, sick of popping checker-sized pills, sick of licking chalk off his teeth. His tongue had wanted something to taste, his jaw something to bite, and that beef had *looked* so good. Once again his eyes had betrayed his body. Something fluttered briefly inside, a sour belch forced its way out. Reluctantly, Ramirez reached for the bottle of Gelusil. He thought he could actually feel the squirts of acid bombarding his ulcer, deepening a crater he already envisioned as the Grand Canyon of peptic erosion. He saw a tattered army of corpuscles streaming in retreat across a rolling gas-shrouded plain. At any moment he expected to begin hawking up great gobs of bloody phlegm, to fall to the floor in a terminal coma. Died of wounds sustained in an assault by enemy hamburger. He wondered again if he belonged here in a zone where the stomach was only one of an excess of targets, too many of them fatal. Maybe he should have his entire stomach replaced with some sort of synthetic pouch. When his internal front quieted, Ramirez leaned back into the open doorway to observe his kitchen crew. "Noll!" he yelled.

"Yeah?" replied a sulky voice.

"*Yaaay-uh?* Get your ass in here when I'm speaking at you!"

"Yes, Sarge." A lanky PFC ambled into the office.

"You spit on that grill one more time, maybe I shove your cheeks down in the bacon and fry 'em for the troops, huh?"

"Aw, Sarge."

"Didn't I tell you to mop up that grease under the corner oven?"

"Yeah, and I told . . ."

"I don't care who the fuck you told—do it!"

Ramirez gasped like a lanced animal, hunching at the waist, clutching his midsection. He grabbed one of the Gelusil tabs he had left sitting out, swallowed it, then laid the side of his head flat against the desk.

"Sarge, are you okay?"

He was dimly aware of the clatter of men eating in the next room and the taste bud-erecting aroma of percolating coffee. "Oh, my aching gut," he groaned to whoever would listen.

Between haircuts Joe, the Vietnamese barber, paced. He paced from his shop beside the mail room to the mess hall, from the mess hall to his shop, from his shop to the orderly room, from the orderly room to his shop, from his shop to the main gate, from the main gate to his shop. He paced and paced. He couldn't seem to stay still.

Damn, muttered Wendell, trying to hold his hands steady. In the viewfinder the plane wiggled, shrank into a speck, and disappeared. He lowered the Beaulieu movie camera from his eye. "You got anything else to Da Nang in the next hour?" he asked the young Air Force sergeant with the clipboard and the astonished stare.

"Nothing I know about. Of course, there's a lot of stuff goes in and out of here I know nothing about. You might try asking around the 101st helicopter pad."

"Aw shit, I'd probably be too late anyway."

They were standing on the loading ramp in front of the air terminal.

"Was he a friend of yours?" asked the sergeant.

"Hell, no."

The sergeant scratched his chin with the edge of the clipboard. "Well, listen, you want pictures of stiffs I can . . ."

"I needed that one," cried Wendell, pointing up at the empty sky.

For Wendell this had not been one of the war's better days. Sergeant Anstin had forbidden him to leave the signal shop all morning and to make sure his orders were carried out had deliberately sat on a counter doing his paperwork in the same room with him as Wendell sorted colored wires with his hands and various tools of assassination with his mind. He had missed the crash itself, the camera had jammed, so he had been forced to stand there like an idiot with a dead lens while the Old Man took the plunge. Now he had missed the corpse, too.

"Do me a favor," Wendell said to the sergeant. "Hold your clipboard like you're shading your eyes and look up at the sky, and I'll make you into a movie."

The sergeant turned toward the sky and then looked back at Wendell. "What do I shade my eyes for? The sun ain't even out."

Wendell frowned. "You want to be in pictures or you want to be an Air Force chump all your life?"

The sergeant raised his clipboard.

"Hey," he said, crinkling his face at an imaginary sun, "am I gonna be in color?"

Griffin had been drifting peacefully above the same frame of film for more than twenty minutes when a voice from out of the air spoke abruptly into his ear: "Leaf abscission."

"Huh?"

It was Captain Patch, chief of the Imagery Interpretation Section. "Define the terminology."

Whatever "leaf abscission" was, Griffin certainly didn't want to know about it. Abscissa. Coordinates. Mathematical lines.

"Tree geometry, sir?" He couldn't stop staring at Patch's head, he seemed to be seeing it for the first time, seeing *into* it—a vast geodesic dome constructed out of a complex network of brass tubing through which moved streams of dense blue smoke, swift, silent, sure.

"Thought you'd been to college, Griffin. From the Latin meaning to cut, to strip, to denude. Shredded palm, if you know what I mean. Winehaven's scheduled to rotate home in sixty days. I want you to start training to take over his herbicide studies."

"What about my bomb damage assessments?" Small puffs of smoke were coming out the captain's ears.

"We'll pass those on to Specialist Cross." Patch's voice sank into oily confidential. "You know you're the only one I can trust to do this job properly. These studies are top priority. The General has expressed a personal interest. I need someone I can depend on, someone who appreciates the situation." He straightened up. "This duty shouldn't be any problem, you're the brightest boy in the class."

"Yes, sir." Patch had also designated PFC McFarland "the brightest boy" when he appointed him in charge of office supplies.

"This'll look damn fine on your record." He placed a hand on Griffin's shoulder. "I'll see what I can do about some in-country R&R. Have you seen Saigon yet? There's a good chance I can get you there next month. Chief Winkly needs someone to go with, you know how he is about traveling alone. Okay?"

"Yes, sir."

"Fine then, real fine."

"Wonderful," mumbled Griffin, leaning out again over the light.

He had always been interested in plants. The craters shone up at him like watery eyes.

From its position of honor above the bar the painted head of the screaming woman stared into a fog of tobacco smoke, alcohol fumes, and body odor that comprised the constant atmosphere of the 1069th officers' club. The large yellow eyes focused in horror upon an invisible point high above the commissioned heads. Here she was known as Minnie, Sweetheart of the Crafty Eye.

A glass of amber liquid was held dramatically aloft.

"Here's to the colonel, a soldier, a gentleman, maybe not the best pilot in the world, but certainly one ace of a drinker."

"Hear, hear."

"Watch it, Osgood."

"Oh, shut up, Ed, we all know what a flaming asshole he really was."

The stereo twanged out a raucous version of "Ring of Fire." On the corner of the bar stood a table lamp cast in the shape of an Hawaiian hula dancer. A red light bulb stuck in a socket on top of her head lit up a shade depicting a dozen imaginative sexual positions. Slowly the pink plaster hips swiveled from side to side in mechanical voluptuousness.

Even at this hour the club was already more than half full.

"How about a couple more drinks over here. C'mon, Lee, you old lecher, I'll be running on empty in about half a second."

The Vietnamese bartender produced an automatic smile. "No more ice," he said. "Machine broke."

"Whaddya mean there's no more ice? There better be, pardner."

"He said the machine was broken."

"Well get a man in here to fix it, an ice mechanic."

"The beer had best be cold or somebody tells me why."

"Why is the army like a copulating sow?"

"It's a question of technique, Harv, there are those of us who take the time to learn and there are those who, well . . ."

"So I said to the general, 'No, sir, I'm afraid I am unfamiliar with that particular section of FM 380-5' and that's why I'm here now with you guys in this paradise."

"That moron, that bastard, that scumbag."

"I know damned well somebody did it."

"The Twenty-fifth uncovered a big rice cache in the Ashau today. A lotta zip bellies gonna be rumbling out there in the woods."

"Yes, it's my boy's birthday tomorrow."

"Has someone been watering the Scotch or did my tongue die?"

"As far as I can tell, the only way we're ever going to get a leg up on this war is to give every damn gook his own two-bedroom ranch complete with nice shrubbery, a lawn, and a white picket fence."

"What about a garage, they're gonna need a garage, too."

"Okay, they got a garage."

"Built-in."

"Do you know that if this show lasts another three years I can make major before I'm thirty?"

"Say, Jimbo, isn't it about time we organized another joint party with the Ninety-second Evac. I've got something I need a nurse to attend to."

"And at least two cars, preferably Torinos or better."

"Is it true the new CO's father-in-law is an Agency station chief in Chile?"

"No, we're no longer permitted to mention Hill Nine Seventy-six in the briefings anymore. It depresses the general."

"All the major appliances and a color TV."

"Buy me a drink, guys, I just extended for another six months."

"There we were, four thousand feet on a deck of flak."

"That's okay, I always bet on Navy in the Army-Navy game, anyway."

"Did you get a peep at that NVA love letter that came in the other day? 'Though I move in the world's dust, my heart lives in dreams of you.' Pretty steamy, huh?"

"A good job, a private office, a secretary, and a briefcase, everybody gets a monogrammed briefcase."

"The left engine was on fire all the way in to Quang Tri and the TOs bouncing up and down, shouting, 'Jump, jump, you cocksucker, we're gonna die.' "

"So sorry, no more ice, sir."

"No one's ever really ruled out nukes, you know."

"And suburbs, we'll have to build suburbs for all the gooks to live in and gook schools, gook city halls, gook shopping centers with little gook consumer items."

"I love my wife, I really do."

Glasses clinked, matches flared.

". . . and all the time you're fucking her, see, she's got this long silk scarf tied in tiny knots that she's shoving up your ass and damn, if it don't feel surprisingly fine."

"I always wondered about you, Matt."

"Well, at least my asshole opens, Frank."

The officers gathered around the table exchanged knowing smiles. Through a process of bardic repetition and baroque embellishment the tale of Major Brand's R&R had long ago evolved into accepted ritual. Just as much of the comfort of the church depends upon the familiarity of its liturgy, so was Brand's performance enhanced by these good-natured interruptions. Raillery was as much a part of the program as the actual story line. The worst jokes would be tolerated, even welcomed, not simply because Major Brand outranked them and it was their duty to laugh, but because they honestly enjoyed these moments, this communion of belief in some sort of pleasure, no matter how brief or how obtained. Everyone leaned forward for the climax.

"And this little cunt, see, has got a fantastic sense of timing 'cause just when I'm about to shoot my rocks she whips that rag out and My God! my body busted open and shit, piss, farts, and come went flying in every direction all at the same time. And that, gentlemen, is how I got my cock banged in Bangkok."

The round eyes of the unit emblem stared unblinking through laughter and applause. On the bar the plaster hips went up and down.

Behind the secured doors of the communications shack the stutter of teletypes was incessant day and night. The paper spilled out of the machines and rolled on the floor in long yellow tongues. Information. Incoming. Outgoing.

Back in a grove of picturesque palm and other nameless trees and broad-leafed plants, at the end of a neat gravel path lined with cocoanut shells painted white to resemble skulls or cue balls or ostrich eggs, distant in aura and architecture from the uniform mundanity of the rest of the compound, stood a shaggy brown bungalow, quiet, unobtrusive, a CO's quarters perhaps or an enlisted men's day room except for the electrified fence, the gates, the armed guards who answered no questions, turned away all visitors. The list of names of those permitted access was itself the privileged information of a rigorously investigated few. The building was draped in heavy folds of security, its covert projects partitioned into secret fragments. Upon secluded planning tables inside originated operations whose purposes the participants themselves were often unable to decode. For outsiders the only clues to the activity within were in unexpected glimpses of those strange figures arriving and departing day and night by helicopter onto the private pad in back or by field ambulance and canvas-covered jeep, strict military types of every branch and rank, scruffy dudes in nonregulation hair and handlebar moustaches, government civilians with and without gray frame glasses and chained briefcases, pot-bellied corporate tech reps from McDonnell Douglas and ITT; and all the Vietnamese in tailored tiger stripes, facial scars, and dead black eyes. Some you recognized, one or two you were allowed to know. People like Kraft. Or Conrad, "the man from Motorola," who wore Hawaiian shirts, white jeans, canvas deck shoes, and never went anywhere without his Swedish Carl Gustav machine gun. All the flamboyance of the 1069th could be divided between the recon pilots and the "students" of Foreign Studies. The unit, in its boredom, turned toward these two groups for relief, a ride in the sky, an Eyes Only crumb from the bungalow. What was going on behind all that jungle gingerbread? Everyone had an idea. Something to do with shadows, shadows reconnaissance cameras at classified altitudes couldn't photograph, a structure of shadows linking water to road, bush to market, shadows falling, shadows leading in, the shadows everywhere.

Foreign Studies Section, Major Benson Quimby commanding. The Spook House.

Twenty kilometers to the west everything was green and slippery and wet. The sergeant thought he was catching a cold, a stupid Vietnamese cold. He had to squeeze his nostrils to keep from sneezing. There was a stench and a mist that hung like gauze above the paddies. Water dripped from the vegetation above, clung to the vegetation below. When they entered the village the old men, the women, and the children stood quietly watching. Only a skinny brown dog looked them directly in the eyes but he did not bark.

"I don't like it," said the lieutenant.

"Let's torch it," said the sergeant.

Another sergeant named Kraft whispered something in the captain's ear. He had dark skin and dark curly hair and no one had ever seen him before this patrol.

"Round up all the males," ordered the captain.

The males totaled six: two old men with yellowish-white hair and broken teeth and four small boys, one missing his right arm. Kraft and the captain ambled over to this group, inspected them in silence.

Suddenly a shadow detached itself from the rear of a hut and sprinted into the light. A PFC with a flushed face and a green towel draped around his neck took a step forward, raising his rifle. "I'll take him, sir." Kraft brushed the weapon aside and ran off in pursuit. He caught up with the figure at the top of one of the muddy dikes surrounding the rice fields and both men toppled over into the water on the other side. The patrol heard splashes, blows, slaps, grunts, and then screaming in high-pitched Vietnamese answered by shouting in low-pitched Vietnamese and more splashes and silence. They saw Kraft climb out of the paddy, stumble for a moment in the pasty mud, they saw him walk slowly back, his uniform dark with moisture, his reddened nose leaking blood, the clay streaking his face. "Who is that guy?" muttered the PFC with the towel. "Press?" replied someone else. Everybody laughed.

Once a comical newspaper reporter had joined them for what he hoped would be a satisfactory period "waxing gooks." The reporter bragged that already he had dispatched two commies to their Commissar, victims of the Sten gun he flaunted in spite of Geneva Convention suggestions concerning the behavior of journalists. Unfortunately, no gooks exhibited themselves for a waxing so on the way back in the reporter, ferocious with unleashed violence, leaped onto the back of a stray pig that had wandered into the road. Yelling that he was going to kill the beast with his bare hands, he hung there, feet dragging in the dirt, as the squealing animal zigzagged up and down until his grip weakened and he was tossed into a ditch and kicked in the forehead by a departing hoof. No one could stop laughing, all the way in, laughing. That was the famous laughing patrol. The reporter packed Sten gun and duffel bag and rode out on the first chopper.

They laughed, remembering, but this was not the same. Kraft was not a reporter and though he had only been among them for a few hours he did not seem to be a comical person. The look on his mud-caked face was one they recognized. They had sometimes seen it on each other and it had nothing to do with comedy.

In the afternoon a helicopter deposited the new CO at the main air terminal. The colonel's driver picked him up, Val-Pak and briefcase, and drove him back down the spongy red road past the old man and into the unit area. The new CO ordered everyone to get a haircut and then went inside to inspect his new office. His first quotable remark: "What a dump."

And McFarland had crotch rot and Ellis malaria again and Cross worried about his feet and Samuels wet his bed and Trips sat all day in Ops reading *The Mind Parasites* where the flame-proof-suited pilots bearing stained mugs of bad coffee came and went, the metal buckles of their seat harnesses jingling like tiny bells and Sergeant Anstin ran through the hootches at night with a flashlight searching for bags of dope and Lieutenant Hand hadn't spoken to anyone for three days and Noll was out in the hangar trying to tattoo FTA on his arm with a bottle of ink and a hypodermic needle and the bomb craters on the film reminded Chief Warrant Officer Winkly of little pussies and someone cried himself to sleep and everyone hoped that Captain Fry would crash and burn and Hogan claimed he had never had this much fun in civilian life and hoped his home town was blown up so he wouldn't have to go back to it anymore and Feeny counted his money each morning and evening and the woman in Cage 1 wished the Americans would kill her today and Boswell, who was leaving, asked Griffin how many days he had left and when he heard the answer said, "Do trees live that long?" and out on the perimeter girls from the nearby village bared their breasts across the wire, tiptoed in among the Claymores, giggled on the bunker floors, and Wurlitzer dreamed of bald monks in maroon robes descending stone passageways in the far-off temples of Katmandu, and a pack of stray dogs roamed up and down the compound searching for someone to play with.

In the late afternoon the rain began again, gently at first, then with gradually increasing insistence until the tire ruts in front of the orderly room were filled with nickel-colored pools and the earth started to move again. The rain pattered down like particles flaking from some high corrosion overhead.

Griffin turned the crank.

Creak, went the sign in the wind. Creak, creak.

Meditation in Green: 4

2,4-dichlorophenoxyacetic acid
2,4,5-trichlorophenoxyacetic acid
2,4,6-start the engines, pull the sticks
2,4,6,8-everyone evacuate

Days after Trips left I was still finding tiny dust-coated Easter eggs under the furniture and between the floorboards. His exit hadn't bothered me, I was used to abrupt departures. When his burn flamed out he'd be back, depleted, depressed, unwinding some bizarre skein of improbabilities down to the invariable cops and docs—he couldn't warm all his fuses except in relation to uniformed authority—then dropping into an eighteen-hour coma that seemed to be all he required of sleep for a week or more. I was glad to be alone. Those coy Oriental fans inside spreading and folding, spreading and folding. Exteriors were getting remote. I tried going out on patrol. Eugene was in the corridor, strips of electrical tape crisscrossed over his mouth, this week's love slave. He threw me a Nazi salute. Outside the street was impossible. It wasn't overfed shoppers and wired account executives I needed to stare at. In fifteen minutes I was back. I replaced the lock on the door, unplugged the phone, covered the windows with plastic garbage bags. When reconnoitering Yesterday you should begin in a haunted chamber, in a place where there are already holes in the scenery. I was lucky. The first time I saw this room I knew at once I had stumbled upon an opening, one of those ruptures the city is secretly riddled with, a way in under the barbed wire. The decor: Modern Aftereffects. This was the site of an explosion.

In the center of the floor stood a cairn of cascading rubbish monumental in size and odor. Phantom vultures shuffled papery wings, pecked for scraps. From a torn mattress flung across the top of the mound spilled curds of fluffy yellowy stuffing. Beneath this clown's toupee were visible the following: two chair bottoms stamped PROPERTY OF HOLIDAY INN; a bent car antenna; a slide of glossy magazines devoted to the twin subjects of perverse sports and team sex; a scattering of paperbacks (political delusions, paranoid sex); a pair of white oil-stained pants; one cracked combat boot; a jogging shoe without a lace; a powder blue sweatshirt advertising ASPEN SKI MADNESS; four concrete blocks; a transistor radio missing its back; 33 ⅓ record shards; twisted clothes hangers; a coil of climbing rope; a section of rubber hose; a busted television set whose shattered eye framed a large maroon ashtray in which reposed a cluster of shiny prune pits; and everywhere split sacks of garbage leaking empty bean and soup cans, balled-up fast-food bags, crumpled chicken boxes, crushed Styrofoam cups, dry bones, bread crusts, wine bottles, beer cans, chocolate milk cartons. From the base of the pile across the linoleum floor extended a long wide tongue of dark brown fluid that the flies—a busy congregation of them—seemed to find especially tasty. Overhead a mobile made of pipe cleaners twisted into grotesque little men, each man hanging by a different limb, turned slowly in the dusty stillness, frightened astronauts falling.

It was the walls, however, that demanded attention. Every wall from top to bottom had been covered by a jungle of black spray-painted graffiti. The messages were grim. Caught in the center of a demonic merry-go-round your gaze leaped from word to word frantic for security. There was none. The work might have achieved transfiguration as some sort of verbal Guernica of the soul had not every scrawled phrase, without exception, been so worn by age and excessive handling they slipped through the mind with irritating ease. OFF THE PIGS, END THE WAR, UP AGAINST THE WALL MOTHER-FUCKERS, BLACK POWER, STOP THE KILLING, POWER TO THE PEOPLE, FUCK, FUCK, FUCK, FUCK YOU. Slogans, a collision of clichés. But there was nothing counterfeit about the author's agony. Some of the letters were as tall as a man.

"It needs a little work," commented the landlord.

I thought of temples and caves and three a.m. subway stations. You didn't want to linger, in vestments or trenchcoat, unless intent upon disturbing various principalities of unpleasantness above and below. I moved in the next day.

With the patience of an archaeologist I spent hours examining those furious hieroglyphics, trying to imagine the ancient peoples who made them. Tie-dyed hippies who passed around a family-sized bong of mellow yellow, crashed in a tangle of nakedness and beads on a stained flea-infested mattress. Emaciated freaks on methedrine and knives who performed ritualistic murder on neighborhood cats in the kitchen sink. Righteous Panthers in cocked berets and crossed bandoliers who strutted boldly down bad streets. An unemployed vet, black, broke, and bad-papered, who one night in this room unraveled himself like a mummy peeling away its own wrapping and took a gun and headed for the roof. I composed limericks I never showed anyone:

There was a young man from the tracks
Who wanted to know all of life's facts
He found nothing nowhere
So to let out the air
He poked holes in other folks' backs

It was time to slow down the carousel. I covered the walls with two coats of winter white. The room shone. On sunny afternoons it was like living inside a cloud, wandering lonely with angels and harps. At night, during periods of the month when the swollen moon peered anxiously in, the letters became visible again, rose to the surface like bloated corpses. So when Huey began to practice her calligraphy on the walls I did not object. Another layer of paint might help to up the interference level, scramble communications, generate some white noise in the text. Besides, I loved to watch Huey work. Her brush arm, flowing with an orchestra conductor's grace, weaved intricacies of calm as it soon filled acres of arctic space with the bold lines and squiggles of a language I could not understand.

"Okay, now you are safe," she announced, stepping back to study her work. "I've painted protection around you. These are Taoist talismans, ancient charms. You've got one to ward off demons, one to establish order, one to aid a spirit who has died in a strange place to find his way home, one to pacify your mind and protect you from harm." She indicated a poster-sized Chinese crossword puzzle. "These are the one hundred forms of happiness." She pointed to a collection of sausage-shaped ripples radiating from a pond's pebble splash. "And this is a stylized representation of lovers engaged in acrobatic sex." Of course it was drawn over the bed.

But now the walls were turning again and this time I wanted to spiral in so deep I'd either hit a vein of light or slip down stones of darkness into the cold vise waiting on the bottom. How could I fail with roaring lions as my guides?

On the glass table in front of me I carefully arranged my instruments: battered lighter engraved with the cartoon dog Snoopy, half a pack of Kools, plastic bag of DOUBLEUOGLOBE.

I went to work. I picked up a cigarette. I emptied out about an inch of tobacco. I poured in the powder. Et cetera, et cetera. Smoke rings drifted across my face. I jumped through a hole. I was gone.

I traveled.

I knew the euphoria of metal, the atavism of the cell, white nights of burning ice, the derangement of flesh, the deliquescence of dreams, the clarity of death.

I returned.

I stood in the window, mirror propped against the glass, rubbing camouflage stick over face and hands. I rode out under urine yellow skies into a stony desert, scrub grass and dust, crumbling brick buttes and rubble canyons. Trouble on the reservation. I crept up among weeds, peered through binoculars. Indians. Teepees and Cadillacs everywhere. Indians blocked the sidewalks. Indians held open powwows on brownstone steps. Indians had overrun the bus stop. A medicine man outside a movie house was dealing three-card monte. Unemployment lines were dressed in leather and warpaint. Buzzards perched on corroded fire escapes. I entered the tribal council, offered my peace pipe to the chief. He puffed. I puffed. An iron horse screeched in overhead, showering grit and sparks. A fan began to open. The chief seemed puzzled. He picked a piece of tobacco off his lower lip, studied it for a moment, then turned completely black and white, the chilly black and white of a film negative. Red dots bloomed in the cracks between objects, swelled into suns that obliterated space until all I could see was a featureless screen of bloody light. Then the screen went black and I was blind. I tried to speak but I couldn't locate the connections to my mouth. Laughter clattered through me like a bucket down a well. Consciousness was shaken in a bag, dumped into pandemonium, and when all the images disappeared so did I.

I slowly reassembled upon a musty swayback couch, the cushions gone, jagged springs corkscrewing through the thin nap. The couch was set down in the middle of an open lot between abandoned tenements. My head was a vacant honeycomb. The world had a raw after-the-flood look. Even the boarded windows seemed poised to burst into wooden flowers. In front of the couch, fueled by old rugs, rolls of yellow wallpaper, sticks of broken furniture, a huge bonfire sang and danced. Two old men in misshapen hats and torn coats sat together on a warped piano bench roasting sweet potatoes on splintered croquet mallets. I raised myself onto an unsteady elbow. Where am I? I asked, and the words stuck to one another in a wet froglike croak. The old men turned to inspect me with ageless unremitting eyes, the desolate eyes of a turtle. I made what I hoped would be taken for a smile. They said nothing. The fire popped and cracked. When they weren't looking I leaned over, picked up a chunk of brick, hid it under my leg. A cold wind blew through the lot, lifting shreds of faded newsprint, pieces of roof tile. A few stray flakes of snow brushed across my lips. Winter. Was it winter already? I lay on my back, staring up into gray air, watching the crystals shoot out of nothingness, swirl down into my eyes, explode softly against warm skin. The light drained from the sky. The fire leaped brighter and brighter. I wondered how soon the yams would be done.

The trees stood straight up thick as phalluses and cautiously they picked their way among them like blind explorers. The boy in front of Kraft had a plug in his ear and when he turned his head, ducking a branch, Kraft could hear the faint insect sound of transmitted rock and roll. The boy was a smudge. After he died Kraft would use the butt of his sixteen to smash the radio into plastic confetti. Behind him another smudge, out of shape and wheezing, kept stepping on his heels. "Open it up," Kraft had warned. "Don't bunch," he hissed. It had taken the muzzle of his weapon swung into the kid's flushed face to get the message across. Last time he'd come along with this group. Smudges. They didn't care, their next of kin probably wouldn't either.

The only butterfly in all of Southeast Asia fluttered past, settled on a broad-leafed plant ahead of him, quietly fanning its wings, a pair of flat black eyes highlighted by powder blue shadow all around, then lifted gracefully away one moment before Kraft's upraised knee brushed impatiently by. Of course the trail was booby-trapped. It was simply a fact he knew as well as the vital statistics about himself stamped into metal tags hanging about his neck and taped together to eliminate jingle, and the fact that this undergrowth too was somewhere, inevitably, booby-trapped. He began to focus.

Captain Brack, tears of sweat clinging to his cheeks, appeared at Kraft's side. "Five hundred meters," he whispered. "Two to one nobody's home." Another smudge. Kraft ignored him. He continued to focus, projecting his will, bright and clear, through his senses onto the green hostility beyond. In five minutes someone was going to be dead. It wouldn't be him.

They entered a clear space where the brush diminished in size to short, soft leafy plants like ferns and grasses, and the trees, their size and strength wholly exposed, looked like concrete pillars in an underground parking garage. The roof they supported was dense and green. Under this canopy the light was viscid and alive, something given off by the plants, an organic soup of brightness and pollen you parted with your body, eddies swirling away behind. In back he could hear the slob panting like a horse.

The Bush was a professional secret. You didn't talk about it. Words were bars. What was important roamed free. Zoos were for smudges. The Bush had a taste and a touch, a scent and a bite. It moved. It made sounds. It was real. Moving through it, conscious of it, you were conscious of yourself. Irrevocably itself, a presence distinct and unyielding, it offered opportunities for definition. Something smudges would never understand.

There was a click.

A plump white spider dropped through the air, whirling on a thread.

Hidden water gurgled quietly somewhere nearby.

He knew without checking that his pulse was regular, his breathing even. The shock along his nerves would be no more dramatic or intense and of no longer duration than the flash across the gap of a spark plug.

The other men he could see were two-dimensional, clumsy figures cut out of green construction paper, pins stuck through the joints so they could move.

He couldn't tell where his finger ended and the trigger began.

When it finally came, the explosion was like a tree tearing apart in sharp wet yellow splinters. He shoved the boy with the earplug aside, sprinted forward. The firing lasted for well over a minute, a continuous racket and outpouring of metal absorbed without reaction by The Bush. "Herschel!" he heard voices exclaiming, "Herschel, Herschel!" The name was passed quickly back. Up ahead where the screams were coming from he discovered a group of men standing silently in an appalled circle, looking down at another man on the ground, crying now, the shrieks having subsided, lying still at last in the space in the thick blood-stained grass his thrashings had flattened. The man blubbered, staring with horror at his left leg which rested now incongruously beside his head, upsidedown and unattached. "Well, shit," muttered Kraft and kicked the useless leg off into the underbrush. The wounded man's white face looked as though someone had flicked a full fountain pen across it, a spattering of black marks like powder burns or bits of dirt driven by explosive force into the skin. At his other end black blood drained into the ground. Kneeling at his side, Doc quickly tied off the stump, stuck a needle in his arm. Then he cut open the shirt. "Jesus Christ," said someone softly in anger and disbelief. The chest resembled a plowed field. The man looked up at Doc, a child's look, as one hand reached tentatively for his groin, asking in a dry voice, "My balls, are my balls okay?" and Doc nodded, patting his forehead, and the man died. His eyes remained open. "They blew away Herschel, man," someone said and this too was passed down the line of soldiers. Kraft looked at the mess on the ground. The man had a silver whistle on his dog tag chain he liked to blow during fire fights, claimed it scared the gooks. Second KIA in three days, this after two and a half weeks in the field, taking fire on more than half those days. First they had lost the company clown, now the company idiot. Huge holes in the communal bond. The Bush was reaching in. The company's nerves had thinned to wire and judging by the current Kraft could feel now there would almost certainly be a blackout when they hit Ba Thien.

Captain Brack came over to supervise the bagging of the body. They would carry it into the village, chopper it out with the results of whatever happened there. "I'm too old for this," he said to Kraft.

"Save me a talker," Kraft said.

"Well now, I don't believe it's gonna be as bad as all that." He had a twinkle in his eye, a perpetual irritating twinkle. Kraft wondered if he carried whiskey in his canteen.

"All we need is a little war dance around the campfire."

"We supposed to be taking this with a smile?"

Kraft stared off at the trees. "You know as well as I do nobody left in that ville now had anything to do with this."

"Maybe," said Captain Brack.

"I didn't come out here for the exercise."

"Either did I, Mister Kraft. You just take care of yourself and I'm sure we can find a souvenir of some kind for you to take home." He gave Kraft a wink.

"Do what you want. I'm no referee out here."

Ba Thien was easy. Occupied but placid. The average village family. Babies and moms and senile grandparents. Vietnamese males grew normally to age twelve then leaped to age sixty. In the country the middle years did not exist. The soldiers moved through the hootches in a grim fever. A grenade was dropped down a hole. Tear gas and coughing women and children poured out. The people were herded together with rough hands and sharp voices.

"I want everyone in the ditch," ordered Captain Brack, pointing.

Some soldiers stood about nervously clicking their Zippos.

Kraft found a log and sat down. He looked at his watch. When the choppers came in, he would go out. What a patrol. Smudges, all smudges. Let them ask for his help. He'd sit here and wait.

A skinny old man with a blindfold across his eyes, hands tied behind his back, was kicked in the ass, sent sprawling into the dirt.

"Leave him alone," someone shouted.

"Shut up," someone answered.

Two laughing soldiers were pissing into a rice jar. A woman ran up, protesting. Arcs of urine swung simultaneously toward her.

A private sat on the ground, yanked off a boot. A wrinkled wet sock was stuck in several spots to the open blisters on his foot. He glanced at Kraft. "God," he said, "I feel like somebody else has been walking around all day in my legs."

"Shit," mumbled a blond corporal, "these bitches is too ugly to rape."

A tailless dog bounded up yapping at a couple of specialists guarding the detainees. One of the soldiers took a cigarette from his mouth and tossed the lighted butt at the animal. The dog sniffed, pawed, then ate the filter. The soldiers laughed. The other specialist tossed his cigarette. The dog sniffed, turned away.

"Hey," he said, "these *are* gook dogs. They only eat Salems."

One of the women in a group being unceremoniously hustled past smiled bleakly at Kraft. An emaciated woman with a fat baby was screaming.

Some of the hootches were already burning. Lines of fire raced up the thatch walls like released window shades. Thick smoke unwound into the cloudy sky.

A conversation overheard, smudges of sound:

"Like there's gonna be a natural interest when it's over, right?"

"Tours?"

"Air-conditioned buses. Ex-GIs for drivers. They'll be turning people away. This country's got the most beautiful beaches in the world, you know. At least that's what Sarge says."

"Sarge says gook pussies are slanted. Look, up there, a crop-dusting plane."

A chubby lieutenant with a green handkerchief tied around his head approached Kraft. Aunt Jemima, the troops called him.

"Sir?"

"Yes."

"If you'll follow me please."

They walked between rows of fire, the smoke dense and acrid, to an as yet untorched hootch at the edge of the village. Captain Brack was squatting in the shadow of the doorway. He nodded. "Your souvenir," he said, getting to his feet. Kraft followed him inside. He waited for his eyes to adjust. The darkness smelled like a camp outhouse. Gradually images developed: the extension of Brack's arm pointing, a jar, a mat, a table, Sarge in the corner visible only from the waist up like a Buddha statue, in his hands a sheaf of papers that seemed to have captured all the light in this dim space and glowed, yellow.

"A gook personnel office," said Captain Brack. "There's a fucking library down there."

Kraft went over to the hole. It had been neatly dug with square corners. He supposed it connected with a bunker, a tunnel. Sarge handed him the papers. "They had a stove over the damn thing," said Sarge. "Pot of goddamn soup. Warm."

Kraft walked back out into the sunlight. Captain Brack peered over his shoulder. Kraft leafed through the papers.

"These important?" asked Captain Brack.

"Maybe."

"*Maybe?* I'd like to be able to write Herschel's mother he died for something more than a maybe."

"Herschel's dead because he didn't look where he was going."

"You know, once in my military career I'd like to hear one simple fact from you people, just one, mind you, one item of hard unambiguous information."

"Doesn't work that way."

"Two to one the whole village is a nest of VC."

"I doubt it," said Kraft. "Anybody talking?"

"The usual farmer and widow crap."

Sarge came out with another armful of paper.

Kraft was already down on one knee loading his pack. "I think I'm gonna need help with these documents."

"Get Schroeder over here," ordered Captain Brack. Specks of soot were falling through the air, sticking to his sweaty face and arms. "He hasn't done a damn thing all day."

Kraft secured half the documents in his field pack, the rest in Schroeder's. Schroeder was the one with the earplug.

The villagers were still crouching in the ditch, grandfathers tied to one another with strips of torn T-shirt, the women mostly silent, even their crying eerily inaudible. It was like watching the news on television with the sound off. When the muzzles of M-16s occasionally swung toward them, the people looked away. The children's eyes were huge and black as olives, the eyes of waifs in cheap paintings. Kraft focused against this scene. Nothing. No quivering needle. He was certain they could spend all afternoon here, twisting arms, learning nothing. He might be wrong of course, but that didn't happen very often. If it had, he doubted he would be here now. Someone called his name. He turned. Captain Brack pointed to a pair of old men squatting on splayed feet amid a restless green forest of American legs.

"Lieutenant Lang caught these two didiing out the back door."

One man was almost totally bald; the other had a short white goatee. Both had bruises on their cheeks, blood smeared around their mouths and noses. Kraft said something in Vietnamese. The bald one responded.

"Doesn't know nothing," Kraft said. "Doesn't know VC, VC don't know him."

"Sheeee-it," said Lieutenant Lang and spat on the ground.

"What do you think?" asked Captain Brack.

"They're old and scared and sick. That one looks like he has a tumor on his neck."

"If they didn't set that booby trap themselves," declared Lieutenant Lang, "they sure as shit know who did." He tugged hard on the goatee. "This one looks like ole Ho Chi Minh himself." He turned, glaring at Captain Brack. "It's time we did something."

Avoiding his gaze, Captain Brack stared intently into the dark jungle. " 'Bout time for a break," he said. "Then I'll call in the choppers for the detainees, got quite a batch for relocation here, and then I'll call in air to cinder this place, but right now"—he stretched his arms—"I guess I'll go across to those trees there and rest in the shade for a few minutes, the miles get into these bones awfully easily now."

Attended by Sarge and the RTO he walked off toward a stand of banana trees.

Lieutenant Lang turned to a PFC who was missing his front teeth. "Morrelli, take these two out into the field. I think they're gonna require further interrogation."

Lieutenant Lang studied Kraft. "You want in on this?"

"No thanks," said Kraft. "I guess I'm gonna sit down on this here anthill or tomb or pile of dung and I'm gonna eat my lunch."

The lieutenant glared at him and walked away.

Kraft sat down and removed a can of ham and eggs from his pack. Everyone hated ham and eggs, gave ham and eggs away to the Vietnamese kids. Kraft didn't mind. Ham and eggs or beans and franks or the popular peaches. What did it matter? He was opening the can with one of those damned P-38 openers when someone sat down beside him. A skinny milk-faced kid with brown freckles and bright blue eyes and glasses held together with paper clips. And a rifle with the peace symbol scratched on the stock. And a machete in a leather holster under his left armpit. And a ring in his ear.

"Standard issue?" Kraft asked.

The kid shrugged. "Captain don't give a shit. He says I'm a good killer."

Kraft lifted a spoonful of cold eggs to his mouth. He could feel the kid looking him over.

"You're with the CIA, aren't you?" asked the kid suddenly.

Kraft continued chewing, then swallowed carefully. "Now that's the type of question that can have only one answer."

The kid thought for a moment. "Okay," he said. "But like I was thinking when I get out I might want a job."

"Sensible," said Kraft.

"And like I've got all this great experience and I just thought I could be pretty good."

"At what?"

"Like that intelligence stuff, you know, spying and like killing."

Kraft laughed.

"Bet the captain would give me a good reference."

"Tell me."

"Only one way to swing," the kid said, patting the leather scabbard.

Kraft eyed the M-16 leaning against the kid's leg.

"Hell, that they make me carry. Ain't worth a shit. Fucking toy pop-pop-pop. Might as well be punching metal in Detroit. I hate it. Guns suck, like taking a shower with your shoes on or using a rubber for screwing. Now a blade's different, a blade's got soul. Know what I mean?"

Kraft spooned eggs into his mouth.

"Like my daddy'd never go in a restaurant where they had candles on the tables, you know, used to say, 'I got to see what I'm eating.' "

A sidelong glance at Kraft.

"I wanna go on Lurps but I think the captain's saving me for something special."

Out in the field behind them soldiers milled about the prisoners.

The old men sat together on the ground, arms and legs tightly bound with wire. The lieutenant shouted for a few minutes, waving his arms. Kraft turned to see. The soldiers looked as though they were attempting to launch a model plane that wouldn't start. Then another soldier walked over with packages and several men began tying the packages to the prisoners' chests. C-4. Kraft turned around again. He had seen this number before. Sometimes, before detonating the explosive, they would place cash bets on which body would jump the furthest.

"So how much experience this blade of yours got?" Kraft asked.

"Five, six if you count the one I finished with the rifle butt."

"You like your work?"

"I'm the best there is."

"Why not stay in the army?"

"This war ain't gonna last forever."

Kraft chuckled. "But the civilian killing never ends, huh?"

The kid smiled.

Behind them came the shock and echo of a huge explosion. Then another. Gookhoppers.

Meditation in Green: 5

I dream of becoming evil, dangerous, a hazard to insects, small animals, and children. The sawn rung on the evolutionary ladder. Huge purple velvety leaves, bulging seed pods, slender creepers the texture of human lips, prickly hairs, beaklike thorns. A fortress of botanical nastiness.

I'd occupy a park where I could harass dumb campers, urinating dogs. My behavior would be disappointing. I'd throw needles, I'd splash scent, I would be a blot upon the landscape. A visual, tactile, olfactory blot. An indelible vulgarity.

Impossible to uproot I clutch the planet with tentacles of leather twenty-five feet deep. Chemical spray I suck in like rainwater. At the center of a circular plot of earth, black and sterile from the dripping of my poisons, I sit alone, a hardy simple plant of no economic or decorative value, requiring minimal nutrients, swelling annually into obscene fruit, dispensing allergenic pollens, a growth whose single flower, a white corolla of bloody nectar, blossoms just once a month at night in the dark of the moon.

Laughing loudly, Arden spread wide his arms, measurement of a generosity ample enough to shelter any absurdity. "Marvelous!" he cried. "Absolutely marvelous. Transcendental spleen. I should put you in our advertising."

"A misspelled name on a smudged pamphlet."

"There, you're doing it again."

The desk between us held a dozen Chinese vases bursting with assorted flowers above which Arden's face hovered plumply, an October moon.

"I'm wilting, swami."

"I hear you."

"You think it's gone at last, slunk off to die in its own dark corner, you forget about it, and the instant you do, it comes popping out at you like a face leering in a fun house."

"This is interesting. I wonder if the planets are involved. You know I've been seeing things lately, too."

"Yeah?"

"Mum's the word to the pilgrims."

"Your cover is safe with me."

"Flashes, that's all, like white sheets snapping at the corner of your eye except there's no sound, nothing there, just flashes."

"I've had that. It went away."

"What I figured."

"I've got sounds and smells."

"Appears you might need a good transplant."

Arden was in the pacification business. He operated a service for those who suffered from rebellious nerves, insurgent thoughts. Wherever the countryside of the mind was being ravaged there was

Arden to promise peace. He was a relentless peacemaker. Treatment began with a sustained verbal assault upon the infrastructure of the ego, a tactic designed to extinguish any coherent sense of self. Then followed a period of warm baths, solitary contemplation, quiet sobbing. According to the theory, out of the rubble of personality should then arise, like Brahma from the lotus, a newer, more confident "I," wet, mewling, and goggle-eyed. This tiny creature was scolded, coaxed, and trained toward happiness in a series of private exhortatory sessions with Arden or one of his aides. Daily meditations continued the process of reeducation at home. Each sufferer was given a personal flower or flow-image to concentrate upon, these images selected to coincide with desired traits. If an individual was unable to love, then a rose was offered as the image of meditation. For innocence, the daisy; for optimism, the chrysanthemum; for a stronger ego, the narcissus. Each image was presumed to inspire a sympathetic efflorescence of the soul. But don't conclude that the study of smartweed will boost your IQ. Arden's organic calculus was composed of equations more refined than these examples. For instance, how was the unaided psychic gardener to know that an intensive consideration of phlox would reduce the miserly in the spirit or that an equal time pondering bluebells would tend to elevate one's pain threshold. The formula by which Arden arrived at such prescriptions was as complex and arcane as that of medieval alchemy or the Coca-Cola Company. The trunk of his thought grew about a core of pilferings from nineteenth-century language of the flower chapbooks, that quaint hobby of genteel American ladies; the branches were imported graftings, gnarled notions of Oriental religion; and the whole was dusted down with generous handfuls of native positive thinking pesticide. The result was Arden's magnum opus, intellectual fruit of a lifetime, key to harmony, bible of serenity, and guarantor of financial prosperity, an inches-thick loose-leafed compendium of affinities, attributes, idiosyncrasies, character flaws, tics, stutters, and quirks of over ten thousand different species entitled *The Psychology of the Plant*. The book had to be kept in a vault for it was rumored large sums were available to anyone who could provide a privileged peek into its secret contents. There were desperate pilgrims everywhere. The end was at hand. Arden was the messiah of the advent of vegetable consciousness.

He studied me with the gaze of a museum curator. "Well, right away, I don't like your skin. Mealybugs have healthier tone. What kind of evil weed killer you been dousing yourself with?"

"Bag of the old DOUBLEUOGLOBE."

"Jesus Christ, where'd you get that?"

"Huey's brother."

"Where'd he get it?"

"Who knows? It's dropped in the pipe at one end, goes round and round, comes out here. The omniscient communist conspiracy wastes no opportunity to undermine our will. Our minds may no longer be in control."

"I haven't tasted any pixie powder since Vientiane 'seventy. Want to brief me?"

"Standard stuff."

"Sounds and smells."

"But measured, in assimilable cadences. Up, then down. The years in review on a sine curve. You're close, then you're far away. A saraband of shame and folly."

"Remember Nostalgerin?"

"The memory medicine with active ingredients."

"Your buffer against the past."

"Inspired concept."

"Too bad the ingredients would have had to be so illegally active. I'd be sitting on a ransom by now."

"You ain't doing so bad."

"Ah, you can never be sure. The bottom could drop out of this gig in the next hour. Americans have no staying power for this sort of enterprise. They bitch, they moan. They want palaces in every dewdrop or what's the point. Then there's the awareness problem. Problem is they don't really want it, awareness. To be aware is to, well, suffer, can't escape the masters. Instead, they want happiness, little fixes of delight. So I spend all my time pulling weeds. Hard work, especially when they're talking back at you."

"You seem to be displaying the symptoms Nostalgerin was going to alleviate."

"Of course I'm displaying symptoms, who doesn't display them? The great disease of what-if. What if I'd married the neighbor across the street? What if I'd bought Xerox at seventeen and a half? What if Kennedy hadn't been shot? What if the South had won the Civil War? Well, we can go on like this all day and usually do whether we're aware of it or not. That's why I could be sitting in a forty-room estate if we could ever market that product."

"My problem is I don't know whether I'm addicted to the O, the war, or that stupid sweet kid who was once me."

"Your problem is you're just a general all-purpose addict, addicted to addiction, the nearest drug will do. I don't think you're giving my buds a fair chance."

"I think I'm allergic."

"Doing your sessions regularly?"

"Dawn, noon, and dusk."

"In the window?"

"Per your instructions."

"My mistake. I remember your window. Police Street, 1941, Weegee. A philodendron couldn't be happy there. Find a spot without a view. Sit in the bathroom. You might try lounging in the tub. The cool cleanliness of the porcelain, the hypnotic drip drip drip of the faucet. I would imagine it could be extremely restful. Ponder the tile."

"My john's not exactly the Luxembourg Gardens."

"So paste up some postcards. Make an effort. Busting through the accumulated muck of a lifetime is no simple Boy Scout's task. You've got to be ready to split rocks."

"Like the mustard seed?"

Arden smiled. "Like the mustard seed."

"Well, my muck's as tight as a marble floor. I don't know, your worship, but there's something about this process that still eludes me. Somewhere between fleshy pink and chlorophyll green lies a big brown bog of stink and weeds your brochures fail to mention."

"So what? Take time to study the swamp flora. Don't be discouraged. Practice. Sincere practice possesses an extraordinary ability to transform the atmosphere of the heart. That's purity, Grif, and I know that one fine day you'll sniff it, taste it, blow it out of both nostrils. That's when the shoots start to clear the soil. You wait, you watch, I know what you think but trust me, for once trust somebody, you might be astonished." As he spoke, Arden extended his arms in the manner of a priest offering benediction, a self-conscious habit deliberately enhanced by the monk's robe he wore complete with cowl and deep sleeves. The color of the robe, an electric moss green pitched to the very extremity of ripeness and beyond, gave him the appearance of a penitent at a monastery for unredeemed acidheads. Printed in random profusion across the cloth were hundreds of small white circles, mystic signs, emblem of the uroboros, the serpent devouring its tail, image of renewal, immortality, eternity; but also, of course, the chemical symbol for oxygen, final product of photosynthesis. Whenever I sat in this office, staring at that costume, waiting for a monologue to end, I couldn't help but think that all those circles scattered like leper's sores over all that green had the depressed look of craters, mandala of the bomb.

"I'm going to try a couple new images on you. Concentrate, focus your attention. Shape, color, texture, the parameters of beauty. Fill your head. Cultivate your garden."

"It's curious but whenever you say the word *garden,* I always think of that movie *Suddenly Last Summer*. You ever see it, Katharine Hepburn gliding in white out into her hothouse jungle of carnivorous plants and droopy vines and flapping prehistoric birds where Montgomery Clift stands, polite but awed. 'It's so . . . so unexpected,' he stammers. 'Like the dawn of creation,' she replies."

Arden laughed. "You're marvelous, Griffin, a real cocksuck, but marvelous. Why don't you tell me what it is you want from your meditations?"

"Oh, I don't know, some distant kin, a second cousin or a great uncle, to authenticity, I suppose."

There was a pause in which I could hear the mournful chanting of seekers locked in cell-like rooms down the corridor.

"Christ!" Arden shouted, slamming a fist into the desktop. The vases rattled, the flowers jiggled. "And what the fuck is that, huh? 'Authenticity, authenticity.' Marx? Nietzsche? Dale Carnegie? Haven't you been listening? Doesn't anyone listen? Those other voices are dust, murmurings in the dust, so why do all you people persist in following them? Can no one but me see that what is dust is sterile? Always this resistance. Instead of sincere practice everyone gives me hypocritical excuses: 'My analyst claims playing in the shrubbery is dangerously regressive,' 'Doesn't Sartre seem to indicate that vegetation is, *au contraire*, an oppressive presence, a distasteful reminder of the essentially nihilistic and somewhat *de trop* quality of nature's pullulative force.' Well shit, I say, to hell with all that. It's dead, dead, certifiably dead. We have entered the autumn of that overgrown culture and all the dead dry leaves are fluttering down from the great dead trees, piling higher and higher all around until we're choking on the goddamn brittle stuff. Get rid of it! Rake it up, burn it, let the wind carry the ashes away. Let us have done with the season of death and black thoughts and brown funks. Spring approaches. Green is the color of the future. Think green!" And crash! Down came his fist. "Green, green, green." Crash, crash, crash.

The office was clean and spare, a soldier's room. Functional furniture functionally arranged, no decorations. Major Martin Holly was pleased. Apparently his predecessor had also been a simple man. A singular type in a compromised world. Men of spartan vigor were the posts in a fence sagging at the top, buckling in the middle. Erosion was general. The war had gone on too long, a joke without a punch line. Da Nang already resembled a hippie ghetto. In the offices there desktops were concealed beneath dumps of neglected paperwork, personal correspondence, hometown newspapers, cock books, stale food, half-empty soda cans, and Styrofoam cups fuzzy with mold; once-aseptic walls had become infected with a creeping fungus of pinups, film and travel posters, family photographs, and crudely drawn, militantly obscene short-timers' calendars. The living quarters were worse. Officers slouched; privates could no longer accurately recite the chain of command; the salute was an arbitrary flip of the wrist; fistfighting was a nightly occurrence at the EM club; dope was peddled openly in battalion streets; and the pleasant mannered clerk who had typed Holly's orders sat beneath a large color picture of a screaming black man, red bandana tied around his bushy head, huge electric guitar thrust between velvet pipestem pants. Major Holly was glad to be gone. No doubt the 1069th Military Intelligence Group had its problems too, but here he would be in charge, he would correct them. In Da Nang his primary responsibilities had been to sip Pinch and play chess with The General, Holly's uncommon ability at that elegant game of circumscribed movement within a symmetrical space was certainly a factor in winning for him this command opportunity. The General encouraged displays of wit, and those who sparkled found themselves invited to after-hours conversation, special missions, outcountry jaunts. The General's wife and daughter lived in a bungalow overlooking Manila Bay, and each Friday afternoon, if nothing appeared pending in The Territory, The General flew to The Philippines for the weekend accompanied by favorite members of his staff. Major Holly had been a regular guest. He had enjoyed those trips, respite from the pressures of a difficult war, even though it was his unvoiced opinion that such excursions were too frequent and too long and tended to blur the edge necessary for competent tactical thought. The General regarded his weekends as rejuvenations. The family was balm for the soul, he joked, Holly tonic for the mind. "He can speak extemporaneously for more than five minutes without resorting to that nonword 'irregardless,'" The General explained to envious aides. After a few drinks The General particularly liked hearing Holly's seriocomic analyses of the war, his favorite the argument that laid the blame for the origin of intervention upon too enthusiastic a reading of the novels of the late Ian Fleming. The General often requested that Holly repeat this theory to various visitors military, civilian, and congressional even though Holly himself, whether nursing a Planter's Punch in the shade of a date palm on Luzon or watching distant pillars of smoke through binoculars from The General's private helicopter, most often experienced himself not as some romantic adventurer but more like a displaced creature out of Graham Greene.

In the first hour of his new command Major Holly inspected his desk. The bottom drawer, unfortunately, was jammed shut. Then, without bending to look, he carefully ran the fingers of his right hand along the under edge of the desktop, feeling for fossilized deposits of old chewing gum. Happily, there was none. Now he could be assured that sometime in the future when coordinating mission objectives with superiors or reprimanding subordinates his train of thought would not be suddenly derailed by idle fingers stumbling upon a cold clot of sticky gum. No one should chew it. There should be a reg. It ruined teeth and appearance. It turned a soldier into a punk.

Holly himself was blessed with The Look. Blue eyes protected by the thick lenses of gold aviator frames. The hair, short as putting-green grass, too short to reflect any definite color. Firm jaw. Cleft chin. A sea captain's wrinkles. Just one minor flaw, tiny, hardly noticeable. High on the left cheek rested a brown velvety mole his straying hand found unable to resist touching, rubbing, squeezing. Hairs proliferated there despite frequent plucking and the surreptitious application of various depilatories. It was as if one minuscule but prominent spot had deliberately seceded from the austere well-tended country of his face, had gone soft, mushy, fertile. Sometimes he imagined this dot of color added a quaint old-fashioned sexual note to his appearance, but deep in fatigue and depression he often worried about its effect upon his career. In an age when everyone's file was arranged to read as identically as possible, careers could be bent by such trifles as the pitch of a voice, the break in a smile. Appearance. In the military you couldn't ever forget. Burnished surfaces were mandatory.

On the first day of his command Major Holly met with his section leaders, glanced through the late colonel's files, answered affirmatively The General's telephoned request to locate the maddeningly elusive 5th NVA Regiment, and personally changed the air conditioner filter in his office.

Setting. The deployment of objects about a central consciousness. This was crucial. Certain emotional transactions required certain specific settings. Military life sensitized one to the animistic force of things. Grooming, clothes, furniture, wall color, weapons. Minds could be encouraged to coalesce about such stuff. If there was a supernatural it resided in things. The new recruit learned this truth gradually over the course of training as the alien objects of military life transmitted day by day the power contained in their strangeness and thereby became personal extensions of his own enlarged and militarized consciousness. (The General loved this idea too, spoke often of recommending Holly to Basic Training Command.) The settings in the army at their simplest were two: enclosed and exposed. Holly was familiar enough with the latter; he knew what it was like in the bush, he knew about slipping and sliding, that had been two years ago when his mind had been too scattered, dulled, and absorbed to note the contours of its moods. Only a staff officer had the time and personal security to reflect on mental processes, only a bored staff officer could have formulated this theory. So, for the average staff officer then, four objects shared the burden of consciousness: the desk, the bar table, the podium, and the floor. Least pleasant, of course, was an acute awareness of the floor—its solidity, monotony, proximate relationship to you. Holly called this linoleum consciousness, a state that occurred, when it did, in the magnified presence of one's displeased superiors. In the military this state could most often be found within the corridors and offices of the Pentagon where the sight of bird colonels and even generals melting into the linoleum was a too common spectacle. ("Humiliation," remarked The General, "goddamn army runs on it. There's a sex angle too, but you're not supposed to consider that for two more grades yet.") All these buffed floors and polished shoes. Reflective surfaces everywhere. The better to ponder your unworthiness? No, no one wished to be too aware of the floor. The best site for consciousness was behind a well-fortified desk. There the power crackled palpably. How often had Holly sat across from a general at his desk and watched those shoulder stars begin to glitter so much like Christmas tree ornaments you could have sworn there were wires under the coat. One general Holly knew had had all the light bulbs above his head fixed twenty to thirty watts higher than those in the rest of the office. The deviousness of the insecure. Actually, there was no need for such tricks. A commander behind his desk was potent magic without any artificial assistance. Seated in his chair, Holly was plugged in, he experienced radiance.

On the second morning of Major Holly's command, a unit formation was held which all but the minimum essential personnel and their section leaders were required to attend. Uniforms were checked for cleanliness, boots for polish, chins for stubble, hair for unauthorized length. The First Sergeant made notations on a clipboard. Holly spoke of the importance of pride, in self, in mission, in unit. Pride anchored the spirit. Look good, feel good, do good. A soldier without confidence was a defeated soldier. The mission may not be one of actual physical combat, but the lack of immediate perceptible action did not, could not, diminish its importance, its urgency. We of the intelligence branch occupy the apex of the military hierarchy, the eye at the top of the pyramid. Remember the dollar bill. Be prepared. E Pluribus Unum. Our mission. Highest priority. I want. I expect. Don't let me down. I won't you.

Setting. In one corner a gold-fringed Stars and Stripes, in another the colors of the Republic of South Vietnam. Opposite the desk four gray chairs, cushioned; a pair of matching gray filing cabinets; a solid black combination safe squatting on the floor like an overweight toad. On the left a small field table, a set of book shelves packed with all those cream-colored manuals, FMs, TMs, ASDMs, that every orderly room was required to have and no one but the First Sergeant ever consulted. Inserted between FM 22-5 *Drill and Ceremonies* and FM 19-60 *Confinement of Military Prisoners* a wrinkled copy of the February 1968 *Playboy*, centerfold missing. And in the center of the gray-tiled floor an arrangement of rust-colored tiles carved in the elaborate insignia of the intelligence branch. Holly was never sure of the symbolism. The dagger, obviously, represented danger, stealth. The sun was the all-seeing eye shedding light to the four points of the compass. And the rose? The rose was what—seduction, beauty, blood? In official reproductions the center of the flower, a circle studded with clove-like dots probably meant to indicate stamen and pollen, looked to the major exactly like a miniature bug, not the insect friend of pollination, but the electronic microphone, friend of the spook. On the wall behind the major's head a 1:250,000 scale map of Southeast Asia, on the wall opposite a framed photograph of the President of the United States. Overhead the fluorescent light twitched and buzzed, altering the character of the room. New shadows formed. On the wall above and to the right of the safe a dark half moon waxed and waned in nervous rhythm with the rapid light.

In the first week of his command, Major Holly, accompanied by the clipboard-armed First Sergeant, conducted a brisk tour of the unit compound. Dodge City before the Earp brothers. Holly wanted an immediate cleanup, wash and wipe from the motor pool to the flight ramp. He wanted the enlisted men's quarters inspected weekly, they were living like spoiled children. He wanted the hootches painted, hell he wanted everything painted, everything white, clean and white. He wanted neatness, he wanted order. Let's see if we can't at least pretend we're professionals.

War: incredible boredom punctuated by exclamation marks of orgiastic horror. The superior leader understood that his ability to command in periods of stress was a function of his talent in the creative management of boredom. For the rear area commander boredom was the lone, true enemy. Noncombatants had to be reminded constantly of the peril off in the unseen as well as their own positions within an organization of immense and frightful power. Therefore, the superior leader insisted upon the proper bearing, proper decorum, proper preparedness. Traditional remedies. There could not be too little ornament.

In the first month of his command Major Holly announced that daily physical training would be reinstituted immediately and that the partitions dividing the enlisted mens' quarters into private rooms would be torn down, the hootches converted into open stateside barracks. He proposed to allow the fresh air in, gentlemen, see what things look like in the light. We need exercise for our bodies, space for our minds. The mission requires clarity. Let's keep our vision unobstructed, yours, mine, working as a team, emphasis not harassment, you, me, together, forward.

Major Holly opened his briefcase. There was one personal ornamental luxury he did allow himself: a grainy brown photograph of the old ironclad Virginia. The picture commemorated for him the only other voluntary intersection of the Holly family with the military. Cousins and uncles and grandfathers and his own father had been inducted into service of the nation's various wars and police actions but only one great-great-grandfather had, before Holly himself, actually enlisted without duress or regret. The old boy may not have made the wisest decision in choosing the navy but it was a life he *chose* and one he died for when a hot cannonball caroming off the iron hull he had been carelessly leaning against knocked him to the deck a puddle of jelly. That was the legend. Holly liked to have the picture before him. The wharf. The riveted ship. The faded flag. The bearded sailors. The brass buttons of their uniforms. All eaten by the shiny brown sea. It confirmed his obligations. The door opened and the First Sergeant entered, bearing the day's paperwork. Holly glanced through the sheaf of intelligence summaries. The usual brew of facts, falsehoods, and exaggerations a field commander was forced to stir into pertinent sense. There was a coded request from The General advising all intelligence units to devote top priority to pinpointing the exact location of that damned 5th NVA Regiment. There was a message warning all units in the immediate area that the possibility of enemy air/ground attack for the period 13–14 November was 75–80 percent rising to 90 percent the early morning of the fourteenth. Holly checked his watch, then tore the dispatch into pieces he tossed into a burn bag. Today was 19 November. He decided that tonight he would order a surprise shakedown of the 1069th. Drugs, weapons, miscellaneous contraband, let's shake it all out, get on with the job at hand.

In the second month of his command Major Holly, humming and glowing, returned from the nightly O club festivities, unlocked his door, and found square in the center of his clean floor . . . a rolled-up sock? . . . a bottle of mouthwash? . . . a human turd? He flipped on the overhead. An authentic fragmentation grenade tightly packed with powder, pellets, and anonymous threat.

Setting. The walls were bright with fresh paint, the wastepaper baskets reeked of disinfectant. Major Holly sat at his desk, studying the latest order of battle analyses. Looking up, he thought he saw an unpleasantly large bug scurry along the baseboard and disappear behind the safe. He got up to check. The safe would not budge. From where he now stood the buzzing light reflected differently and he could see quite clearly mop streaks on the floor and about halfway between his desk and the door a dirty sticky splotch the shape of one of those vague South American countries. He shouted through the open doorway for the First Sergeant. He wanted a cleanup detail in here right after dinner to scrub, wax, polish, and buff. This floor was a scandal.

Meditation in Green: 6

Bounded by a nutshell then, secure in the vise of the earth, a unity whole, free, and organic, a voyager beyond time. And outside, a hull thickness away? Cold, wet loneliness, the agony of growth, total struggle in total night. And up above, a gap of infinite inches? The blindness of light, storm, drought, frost, and the monstrous food pyramid.

Happiness is a pristine seed coat.

Huey had no telephone and she wouldn't tell me where she lived—she came and went as she pleased. When I wanted to talk I called her at work down at the Social Services office.

"Hi."

"No, not exactly."

"Sounds like the Happy Face sticker on your phone has come unglued."

"The forest deepens and darkens."

"You're not goofing on that wall poster again?"

"Thoughtfully provided by the state in lieu of a window. Every thirty minutes another client shuffles off into the woods and out again, looking for bread crumbs."

"Have you had a break yet today?"

"We don't get breaks here, we sob quietly between interviews."

"How's the soulograph business?"

"You know how it is when you suddenly remember something you didn't even want to know and memory locks into a pattern you never saw and can't quite understand as long as you stay you?"

"Is it something like being a lost dwarf?"

"I'm painting that."

"Wonderful."

"Yes. It's one of those surfaces that won't stay fixed to the canvas. It hovers."

"Hovers?"

"When it's ready you can see."

"You're working hard."

"Yes."

"So that's where you've been."

"What do you mean, that's where I've been. Where have *you* been?"

"Same old stand. Puttering about, mumbling, peering between the curtains."

"I was there."

"Really? I must've been out."

"You were out all right, laid out under the table, staring up through the glass. Me staring at you staring up. Get the picture?"

"I think that's what I was trying to do."

"Is there any left?"

"You can't eat just one."

"Please don't ask me to bring you more. I don't think I can."

"Not even a hint."

"Rafer was in here yesterday, breaking pencils with his knuckles, reciting the rosary on a chain, thoroughly terrorizing the front desk."

"I'll bet he didn't have any trouble getting his food stamps."

"He doesn't look well."

"Nobody looks well down there. All that tile and fluorescent light. The waiting room's like one big toilet."

"I think you're starting to look the same way."

"No, no, you haven't been around. I've turned over a new leaf. Arden's straightened out my program. I'm all vigor and glow and capillary action. Come see."

"Do you hear that noise?"

"No."

"Mrs. Armstrong is screaming at Dolores in the next cubicle. This is what I listen to every month."

"Maybe Rafer could start regular deliveries of DOUBLEUOGLOBE. Get all the corners in that office rounded off."

"I don't know. Some of the clients are so rounded off they're barely whole numbers anymore."

"Guess who's back?"

"Who?"

"Trips."

"Oh no, they let him out again?"

"He's cured."

"Yes, like a Virginia ham. Is he raving about that ridiculous sergeant person?"

"Anstin? Not yet."

"He will."

"No, not this time."

"Yes, he will. You encourage him."

"We're friends."

"Together the two of you are an entirely separate creature."

"Well, you'll be pleased to hear he's gone again. He only stayed a couple of days."

"Good. Where'd he go?"

"How should I know? I don't know where everybody goes."

"You're starting to sound funny."

"I'm standing up here behind my dirty window, looking down, and you know what I see? I see little colored rectangles shuttling around a concrete board. Too many pieces, too many rules, not enough turns."

"How long have you been alone?"

"I think I see a wino in a gas mask trying to shinny up a street lamp."

"I'll be over."

"Now I hear a noise."

"Yes, sounds like Mrs. Armstrong is finally having her breakdown. I better go. Listen, I will be over."

"Soon?"

"Soon."

Out in the waiting room the clients paused, frozen in place, dark brittle bodies gleaming in the light, antennae threshing the air—time to bolt for shadows or can clinging resume?—the hard-won purchase on furniture and walls slowly giving way to a long backward slide, legs locked, down a sleek molded curve and then off the bright plastic chair into pure space, free fall, no chute.

It might have been a wall, a green garden wall opening to display rare scarlet blossoms within—the uniforms parted and for an instant Claypool was presented with a glimpse of brilliant gum and lip tissue. A pornographic sight. Then Captain Raleigh screamed, the green wall shook with violence, grunt, snap, and everyone stepped back into a moment of silence.

Sergeant Mars pushed his glasses back up on his sweaty nose. "I think you broke his arm, sir." He wiped his fingers on his pants.

There were eight of them gathered inside the cramped interrogation shed: three Americans, two prisoners, and the three representatives of the National Police. Lieutenant Phan was seated in the captain's chair with a copy of *Playboy* spread across his lap. His two subordinates squatted in a corner playing some sort of dice game with a handful of weathered bones. Neither man had expressed the slightest interest in the scuffle that had just taken place. Perhaps there were large stakes involved.

One prisoner now lay on his back in the dirt, arms extended, white-rimmed eyes examining the tin roof with intense abstraction. The dark bony chest rose, then fell. There was an audible sigh and the prisoner began to moan. It was a peculiar sound, formed with an economy of breath and movement Claypool later came to characterize as distinctly Oriental. Each exhalation, from beginning to end, was accompanied by a constant high-pitched noise, which was then answered by a sudden gasp of inhalation. It was the most disturbing sound Claypool had ever heard a human body make. A buzz saw was more melodic.

The other prisoner, hands and arms bound behind his back with commo wire, leaned sideways against a wall, his eyes closed.

Claypool sat in a corner on top of an empty ten-gallon drum rescued from the trash piled behind the photo lab. Large block letters on the side read DEVELOPING FLUID.

The falling bones clattered on a floor of smooth bare earth.

Captain Raleigh stood in the open doorway rubbing his right hand, then studying the skin in the sunlight. "The hell with his arm," he muttered. "I think my goddamn finger is busted."

Lieutenant Phan looked up from his magazine. When he grinned he revealed teeth identical in color to his staff's dice. "You number one John Wayne cowboy Western man," he said.

"Yeah, well it still hurts like hell, pardner." Raleigh held up his hand. The index and middle fingers were bruised and slightly swollen. Then he noticed the expression on Claypool's face. "Fucking gook," he said. "You see what he did?"

"Yes, sir," replied Claypool. He didn't know what he had seen.

Raleigh turned away. "Fucking gook."

Lieutenant Phan chattered in Vietnamese to his men. They looked at the Americans and laughed.

"You should go down to the Ninety-second, have 'em check out your hand," suggested Sergeant Mars. "You can get all kinds of ugly shit from a human bite."

"That poor gook don't know yet all the shit he can get from me."

The prisoner had stopped moaning. Now he too closed his eyes.

"Look at this," said Raleigh. "They're waiting for Buddha to come take them away."

"Buddha not fairy godmother," said Phan.

The air inside was warm and stale, heavy with the scent of fear and unwashed flesh, a scent Claypool was attempting to ignore.

Hands on hips, Raleigh stood over the prostrate prisoner. "There's nothing wrong with him," he declared. "These gooks are made out of bamboo." Suddenly he slapped his palms together. The prisoners' eyes flickered. Even the gamblers looked up. "Sergeant Mars," he proclaimed. "Once again if you please."

"Roger," replied Sergeant Mars.

Squatting over the prisoner, Mars placed his hand under the man's chin, slowly squeezed the skin of his cheeks together, then shook the head briskly several times. He lifted the head off the ground.

"Tên māy lā gī?" Mars shouted. (What is your name?)

He twisted the face into rubber shapes.

"Tên māy lā gī!"

He let the head fall back. With his hands free he began slapping the prisoner again and again. Sweat flew from his face. On impact his hands made sharp popping sounds. Claypool wanted to scream.

"Tên māy lā gī?"

The prisoner's upper lip was split but it appeared to move, it made a noise.

"Phuong," repeated Mars.

"Good," said Captain Raleigh.

The South Vietnamese police spoke to one another and they all laughed again.

"Māy ō dâu?" (Where do you live?)

The parts of the prisoner's mouth no longer worked in coordination but functioned in separate movements. Brown fluid dribbled onto the chin. He looked like a feeding grasshopper.

"Binh Doa," said Sergeant Mars.

Captain Raleigh consulted one of the maps tacked to the wall. "His tag said Tuy Long. That's more than twenty clicks from Binh Doa."

Lieutenant Phan said something to his men. This time they did not laugh.

"Tuy Long," said Sergeant Mars. "Tai sao māy dā dến dó?" (Why did you go there?)

The prisoner looked into each of the faces hovering around him. He might have been memorizing details.

"Tôi dā dến dó thăm chi tôī," he murmured.

"To visit his sister," said Sergeant Mars.

Captain Raleigh grunted. "And what's she, a VC nurse?"

"Your football more exciting than this, yes?" inquired Lieutenant Phan.

Sergeant Mars bent closer. "VC," he whispered.

The prisoner shook his head. "No VC, no VC, no VC. Tôi lā nông dâu."

"He says he's a farmer," translated Mars.

Raleigh peered at the prisoner over the tops of his glasses. For a moment he reminded Claypool of his grandfather. "Well, son," he said, "I was a farmer once myself and the one thing I never forgot was the smell of horse manure." The hard polished toe of his boot slammed into the prisoner's groin. The prisoner screamed just once, then rocked from side to side, the mouth working, tears sliding back into his black hair. "Get this fucker up on the table. Let's call his sister up and see if he ain't lying."

In the center of the shed was a large wooden table sturdy as a butcher's block. Field pack straps and web belts had been cut, altered, and nailed to the top. The rough surface was covered with stains, the nailheads with rust. Sergeant Mars and Lieutenant Phan lifted the prisoner onto the table, fastened the belts and straps tightly about the thin arms and legs.

"Pay attention now, Claypool," ordered Captain Raleigh. "You're about to see something you never saw. Know what I mean?"

Sergeant Mars was unraveling a pair of wires which were attached to a mechanical contraption that resembled a bicycle exerciser. Each wire ended in an alligator clip. Weren't they going to lock the door? Claypool knew what was next. This was the one they told the stories about, seasoned instructors dispensing trade secrets and coffee between classes at Fort Holabird. It was during these breaks that the students received their most important lessons. The classrooms were reserved for official reality, the corridors for what really happened. Claypool had been disturbed. He hadn't wanted to hear such stories, to have confirmed as true what was printed in leftist magazines, shouted by hysterical war protesters. It was like learning your family dentist overcharged for extractions or drilled into healthy teeth. It meant there were cliffs where he had always assumed there were fences. It meant he might be required to participate personally in events he had imagined as the aberrant behavior of Marines or Green Berets or airborne paratroopers, angry soldiers out in the boondocks with the heat and the pain. Intelligence personnel, stationed in cozy rear area quarters, conducted interrogations across office desks or seated at the hospital bedsides of wounded prisoners. Preinduction fantasies. Now an actual field phone interrogation was about to take place not six feet from where he sat. He didn't know what to think. He just hoped he wasn't going to be asked to turn the crank.

"Doesn't hurt as bad as it looks," explained Captain Raleigh. "Think of the lives we're saving."

The National Police were joking among themselves again. From the few words and phrases Claypool was able to decipher they seemed to be discussing the relative designs and performances of various American cars. The bottom of Claypool's stomach felt as if it were floating in a pond of cold green water. Lieutenant Phan sat down at the contraption, hands resting across the handles of the crank. Sergeant Mars clipped the wires to the prisoner's right ear. Shouldn't the American turn the crank and the Vietnamese be the one to apply the electrodes? Claypool was distressed by the procedure. He wanted to turn away. The prisoner was breathing quite rapidly now.

"You VC?" asked Sergeant Mars in an expressionless voice.

"No," answered the prisoner. "No VC." He shook his head. It was obviously painful for him to speak.

Lieutenant Phan turned the crank. It made a harsh grinding noise like a pencil sharpener. The prisoner made an "ai" sound and tried to lift his body off the table. Lieutenant Phan smiled at Claypool. Those bony teeth.

"VC?" repeated Sergeant Mars.

The prisoner shook his head.

Lieutenant Phan turned the crank.

The prisoner was still a farmer from Binh Doa on a visit to his sister in Tuy Long. Her name was Mai.

"Try his balls," said Captain Raleigh.

Sergeant Mars ripped the prisoner's black shorts in half. Leaning forward between the prisoner's legs, he clipped the wires to the scrotum.

Lieutenant Phan turned the crank.

Claypool had never heard such a cry, not even in the movies. It pierced the skin, continued unbroken between cranks. Once the prisoner seemed to admit that yes, he was VC, a sapper lieutenant, but then he seemed to deny it. Then he talked on and on, a babbling brook of disconnected Vietnamese running out of a ruptured dike.

"I don't know what he's saying," said Sergeant Mars in disgust.

"He praying hard," Lieutenant Phan explained, "but Buddha not answering his phone."

Claypool was experiencing difficulty understanding anybody. It was lunchtime and across the compound normal people sat before trays heaped with hot food, a gentle cooking aroma settling over their shoulders like a spell, and in clean well-lighted offices air-conditioned clerks were typing on clean white paper, and down in the motor pool boyish mechanics with greasy fingers were lying on their backs screwing bolts into silent engines, and up in the sky leather-gloved pilots weaved and dipped over land green as a garden hose, and on the other side of the planet, wrapped in a familiar darkness, his mother and father slept peacefully together in a warm locked house.

The prisoner began to weep.

"Shut up," screamed Sergeant Mars.

He yanked a wire from the prisoner's groin and whipped it across his cheek. Tears dribbled down into the prisoner's ears. Mars and Raleigh exchanged looks.

"He disappoints me, this prisoner," said the captain.

"Hog-tie to jeep," suggested Lieutenant Phan. "Drive to PX. Number one penalty play."

"I tell you, Phan buddy," said Captain Raleigh, "when I leave here I'm gonna put you on a leash and take you with me."

Lieutenant Phan nodded. "Fine for me. I go States double-time."

"Don't look at me!" shouted Sergeant Mars. "Fucking gook was looking at me."

"Oh yes, Sergeant, happy to cut off your head, number one trophy for mamasan."

Sergeant Mars raised a threatening fist and Lieutenant Phan, in a mockery of fright, backed away into the corner, stumbled on a neglected bone, and fell on his butt. Even Claypool smiled. The session seemed to be nearing its end.

"All right, gentlemen," announced Captain Raleigh. "I'm afraid we've got a bad connection here. Time for a conference call."

Winking at Claypool, Lieutenant Phan spoke rapidly to his men. One of the policemen stood up and pulled a sheet of muddy canvas off a second field phone, which had been hidden behind a pair of upright fifty-gallon drums. Claypool couldn't imagine what the drums were used for. The phone unit was dragged to the table and the Vietnamese policeman took his place at the crank. The second set of electrodes was attached to the prisoner's lips by Captain Raleigh. "Okay," he said, "on my command—four, three, two, one, now!"

There was the noise of several pencils being sharpened simultaneously. The prisoner's body tightened against the straps. Claypool couldn't watch. His own bones were being ground into points. He thought he had seen a thin wisp of blue smoke rising from the prisoner's groin. The policeman cranked away as if anxious to drop a couple pounds by day's end. A hundred miles later he stopped. The silence afterward reminded Claypool of those uneasy moments following a test of civil defense sirens. The prisoner's screams must have been shattering. In the air there was a curious odor of spoiled cottage cheese.

Captain Raleigh seized handfuls of the prisoner's wet hair, lifted the head off the table. "VC?" he shouted. "VC? VC? VC?" Spittle sprayed the prisoner's pale face. For a moment the prisoner studied him, as if pausing to compose the proper reply, then the dull black eyes rolled back into the head and the body went limp.

"Is he dead?" asked Sergeant Mars.

Captain Raleigh felt for a pulse. "Hell no," he answered. "These gooks are made of bamboo."

"He must be NVA," said Sergeant Mars, "or he would have confessed by now."

"Well," Captain Raleigh said, "let's let the fucker dream about what's gonna happen when he wakes up. You know what a good rest can do for a man."

"Maybe the demons will fly out his ears," said Lieutenant Phan.

Captain Raleigh turned to Claypool. "Learn anything, specialist?"

"Yes, sir."

"He learned not to mess with Ma Bell," commented Sergeant Mars.

"I think Charlie freak him out," said Lieutenant Phan.

Claypool was relieved he hadn't been expected to translate the prisoner's responses. He hadn't even understood those simple phrases. His ignorance frightened him. If you couldn't translate they handed you a gun and pointed to the bush. Try interrogating a little return fire.

"Let's break for chow," said Captain Raleigh. "Lieutenant Phan and his thugs can have a go at the other one after lunch."

"Very good," said Lieutenant Phan, rubbing his hands together. "You Americans number ten in art of persuasion. Always so impatient."

"Like it or leave it, Phan."

"I think I wait and see."

The mess hall was a haven of activity and light. Human bodies, human noises. Claypool could hear the clean sound of the surf in that company of voices. Standing in line he watched with affection as Sergeant Ramirez insulted his cooks. A week earlier, sweat stinging his eyes, Claypool had stood before a back sink arms plunged to ruddy elbows in a pool of pans and greasy water. That seemed like a holiday now. His stint as kitchen spy had been largely undistinguished, yielding only two items of hard intelligence on the Vietnamese help: 1) female nationals enjoyed joking about the size of PFC Noll's nose; 2) neither sex would touch American hot dogs believing them actually to be boiled dog penises. Claypool carried his loaded tray to an empty table. There was no one in the room he knew. He sat down and examined his lunch: instant potatoes, creamed chicken, watery Jell-O, khaki-colored beans that appeared to have been carved from a bar of soap, and a square of chocolate cake coated with green frosting. The old gag: Why do you think they call it mess? The food resembled an unfinished painting, an action abstract in which the oils had not yet set; even as he watched shapes and colors began to change character, to flow, to blend. Chunks of chicken dissolved in the too yellow gravy sliding globules of fat down a mound of collapsing potato into the red Jell-O sea floating a flotilla of soggy beans. Everything moved toward the stability of mush. Claypool tried his fork. The food dripped between the tines. Everything was moving and then so was his stomach and he too up and out the door moving toward the latrine. This was going to be unpleasant. He hadn't eaten all day. Dry heaves could really hurt.

Meditation in Green: 7

an apple
a pomegranate
a squirting cucumber
a gypsy's wolfbane
a pickled cactus under a pregnant moon
the trimmed hedge of a diabolical maze
the fungus in the basement
the rose between Groucho Marx's teeth
the money tree in the backyard
a sprig of mint in the senator's drink
a weary sunflower
a merry maypole
the carved pineapples on a fourposter bed
the dandelion on teacher's desk
the orchid on a corporate breast in an air-conditioned
  box high above the Super Bowl
a morning glory on Bikini Island
the cherry tree George Washington chopped down
the cork in the bottle
the olive branch in a taloned claw
the mushroom Alice ate
the ivy spelling obscenities upon institution walls
the moss between the cracks
the yeast in the body politic
the wreath on a tomb
a pod from outer space
a hyacinth
a forget-me-not
an evergreen

In the cafeteria we were required to occupy the table nearest the door, standard operating procedure when dining out with Everett Triplett. The exit had to be close and unobstructed in case of an emergency. Trips had always been a sensitive. Atmospheric fluctuations most people chose to ignore could send him bolting for the street. And any room whose proportion of packed bodies per square foot approached that of a stockyard he simply refused to enter. He had a great fear of animal madness.

"You still owe me for the door," I said.

"I don't want to talk about that."

"So what have you been doing?"

"Hunting Nazis."

His eyes were so bright all you could see in them were reflections.

"Yeah? How many did you find?"

"You'd be surprised."

He unscrewed the cap from a saltshaker and dumped the contents onto the table. Wetting his finger, he pressed it into the salt, then with elaborate deliberation licked it neatly clean.

"That's bad for the blood pressure," I said.

"Maybe it'll kill me, huh?"

It was lunch hour. The place was full of open mouths, talking, chewing. The room breathed an aroma the color of the walls, weak gravy brown, a fragrance that seemed to accompany every meal through all changes in menu. Cafeteria spoor. Salisbury steak monster. At the adjoining table a middle-aged couple (floral print dress, tan leisure suit) were pretending they did not see the unpleasantness they saw, a difficult pose requiring intense whispers, a furtive eyeball dance, distant looks of concentrated abstraction. Trips had not cut his hair since his discharge. It hung unsanitarily to his waist. He looked like a mobile willow.

"If that toothless fart peeks over here once more," Trips declared in a loud voice, "I'll tie his glasses in a pretzel he can eat."

A murmuring surrounded us like drums. Leisure Suit studied his macaroni as though it were a treasure map. Lips pursed, Floral Dress contemplated a vanishing point above the chandelier.

"Ain't it disgusting," complained Trips. "The decline in manners everywhere. Corruption of the social contract. Death of civility. These are disappointing times we inhabit, my boy. As a member of the species, I am fucking outraged."

"Here," I said, nudging a ketchup-doused plate toward him, "have one of these dehydrated French fries."

Again he dipped a finger into the salt, licked it clean with one swift audible suck.

"Someday," he said, "I'm going to turn around, walk right out of this city, keep going until I come to a big empty place with a big hollow sky over it and I'm going to dig a hole and sit in it and rest, just listen to the blood beating in my ears for a long, long time. No horns, no voices, no fucking creeps. Think maybe I'll walk to Australia."

He stared dreamily out the window at the usual street turmoil. "I saw the Sarge today," he said.

"Uh huh."

A large box of limp greenery served as the cafeteria's window dressing. Dust had coated the plants with a fuzzy gray fur. A dead fly, resembling a shrivelled berry, dangled from one of the stems. I reached over to touch a leaf. Plastic.

"He was walking a dog."

"Uh huh."

"I've never seen him with a dog before. It's like he knows."

"Uh huh."

I had been wondering when the Sarge sightings would resume. UFOs, macrobiotics, former army sergeants, one learned to tolerate the eccentric interests of friends. Since Sergeant Anstin's rumored retirement more than half a decade ago, Trips had claimed to have spotted either him or a cleverly disguised double in almost every quarter of the city. The Sarge was a traveling man. He was North, he was South, he was all around. He rode in cars, cabs, buses, and trains. He ate lunch in the East, dinner in the West. He was a doctor, a traffic cop, a guy unloading fruit off a truck. He washed his clothes in an all-night laundromat, he sat in the back of a Mercedes, he chased a dragon kite through the park. Once he jumped from a fifth-story window, rode screaming to a hospital where he died. Once he held up a federal bank and appeared that night on the evening news. In the summer on Mondays, Wednesdays, and Fridays he sold flowers in the street to pale people rushing home. But always, every day, he ran around the corner of the signal shack and saw the freshly opened hole, the uncovered can, the vegetable matter. He ran around, he saw the matter. He ran, he saw. The Sarge was here, there, everywhere. He was nowhere.

"Let me get you a salad," I offered, pushing back my chair. "That salt's going to need some sociable company."

"His name is on the mailbox."

I sat down.

"His name, Anstin, is on the mailbox. I followed him home."

"Are you positive?"

"You know I could spot that name in agate type from across a room. There's no mistake. This is the one."

"It couldn't be a different . . ."

He looked at me as if I'd just proposed we reenlist.

"Hey," I said. "It's not like I haven't heard this tale before."

"You want pictures, I can get them."

"I believe you. Give me a minute to adjust. Sergeant Millard Anstin, the terror of I Corps, alive and well and you found him. Incredible. After all these years."

"They call it bad time."

"Okay, so now what? Rape the little woman, slip acid in the daughter's malt, choke Daddy black and blue with a gold lamp cord?"

"The dog. I'd like to begin with the dog."

"For Christ's sake, it's been almost seven years. Nobody stays mad that long."

"I'm not mad, I'm cool, I'm Frosty the Snowman. No heat, no sweat. Cool me. Cool Trips. I can't get a job, my family doesn't speak to me, the VA wouldn't give me a Band-Aid if I slit my wrists in their lobby. That's okay, I'm cool. I learned this in the army."

"He was just an ignorant E-7 alcoholic."

"And Thai was one beautiful animal."

"So what are we supposed to do? Wait around, look for your name in the papers?"

"You'll never see it. I've had an eternity to construct cunning plans of Gothic splendor. Will the execution flawlessly match the design? Believe it."

"He doesn't matter anymore."

"Don't forget, the link between us is old and private, the chances of any connection being established practically non-existent. No, this will be a modern event without apparent motive, cause, or origin. Should the authorities ever happen to meet our friend at all—and it's not likely—they will know him only as Millard R. Anstin, U.S. Army retired, victim of random urban crime."

"You're joking with me, right?"

"I'll tell you a joke." His forefinger glistened with salt crystals. "You're gonna help me kill the bastard."

Deliberately now, behind a static of unbroken rain, light began to phase steadily in, a plasm of dead silver dilating on the darkness. Gradations of gray laminated the sky, assumed structure, a subtle pressure, a fluorescence tepid and shadowless, pervasive as blight. Soon the vibrancy of these green latitudes lay stunned beneath a screen of modulated obscurity. Generators purred in contentment; cathodes glowed merrily. There may still be thunder in Rangoon and Mandalay, but here the dawn came up on the hushed click of a rotated dial.

"Gooooooooooooooooooood MORRRN-ing, Viet-NAAAM!"

This happy whoop, reveille horn for combat's latest hybrid, pierced the deep winter of Griffin's sleep like the howl of a rutting wolf. Shuffling through immaculate, endlessly extended spaces, the Bearded Explorer feels first the air emptying around him, prickling the skin, alerting the hair, and then a pause and before he can even hear the crack as crisp and final as a twig snapping at thirty below, everything is moving all at once very fast. Dry tundra collapses into a schema of bladed clefts; multiple avalanches leap from mountain shelves, range beyond range; caps of ice unlock, settle out on less polar currents. The crust buckles under him, folds itself into sculptured waves, a massive white sea undulating rapidly away, rushing to the safety of a vast silent beach no map has ever located. Equilibrium dislodged, B. E. is flung prone, spread-eagled across the top of the world, devoid of shelter, handhold or rock, a simple X of flesh revolving like a dizzy ornament fixed to the hub of a great wheel until the axis begins to tilt, the blizzard to speak. A brass band swung lustily into the virulent opening bars of "The Colonel Bogey March" and Griffin, semiconscious, rolled onto his side in apparent pain. He clamped the pillow over his exposed ear as though applying a compress to the puckered mouth of a sucking chest wound. Instantly the volume was amplified, melody banged all around, the martial strain ricocheting through his makeshift bandage, note impacting on note, tinseled sharps and flats bouncing like loose ball bearings against his resonating eardrum, and the music parted and obstinate Alec Guinness led a whistling regiment of Ruddy Tommies down an avenue of chords and across the doomed Kwai bridge. Griffin's body obligingly contracted with tension. I am a British officer, colonel, a devoted subject of His Majesty and I simply do not break. Eastern eye-slants narrow to Western gunslits. A smile passes across betel-stained lips like wind over grass. I find your bravado amusing, English . . . Dee-dum dee-dum-dee dum dum da. Griffin whipped the pillow away, sat bolt upright, and slammed his fist into the wall.

"Goddamn!" he cried. "Goddamn."

"Whatsa matter, troop?" It was Trips calling across a gap of sand and crumbling bunker from his room in the adjacent hootch. "Roach in your shorts?"

"Turn that damn thing off!"

" 'Up lad: sunlit pallets never thrive.' "

"Wonderful."

" 'Clay lies still but blood's a rover.' "

"What is that, goddamn Kipling? Goddamn Housman?"

" 'Breath's a ware that will not keep.' "

"Goddamn Mother Goose."

On a shelf behind Griffin's head between a pile of unread science fiction paperbacks and a stack of tape cassettes stood an open bag of rolled joints. The radio played on, a chart-busting love song about dunes, moons, and orgasms. Seated in the center of his bunk, Griffin set about doing some serious smoking. Trips never slept. He napped; up all night on dope and verbal inspiration, he spent much of his duty day sprawled across a desk in Flight Operations where Sergeant Perkle had given up badgering him about production. Sergeants still bothered Griffin, he was expected to rest, he was expected to work, in the proper sequences, at the proper times. "Isn't there someone who'd appreciate hearing from you today?" asked the radio. "Take a moment and write that letter home." A pleasant confusion settled over him and his head became music and light, music and sleep.

When Griffin awoke, hours later, the rain had stopped, the air smelled of lunch, the radio was silent. Outside he could hear Vegetable talking to Thai. "You're a good ole puss, ain't ya, hon, give Daddy a kiss, c'mon puss dog, please c'mere." Between the wooden slats of his wall the visible sky resembled the color of cement. A sandbag atop Trips's hootch had burst open overnight, spilling its contents like wet brown flour across the corrugated tin. No leaves yet on the TV antennas. For reasons unknown every roof had one even though there wasn't a single set in the entire compound and the nearest broadcasting station was out of reach in Da Nang. Griffin liked to suppose the army, in a typically misguided outburst of lunatic generosity, had erected them as props, morale aids. Hamburgers, incoming, and TV. All the comforts of home.

Griffin got out of bed and still in his green underwear staggered down the short corridor to the back porch where he slumped into a sagging deck chair. He rubbed his eyes, pulling the skin of his cheeks downward so the bottom lids turned out, red and pulpy as a movie monster's. There wasn't anyone around to frighten. The hootches stared back with the shabby dispossessed look of a Depression-era Hooverville. Griffin stuck his hand inside his shorts, jiggled his balls like a pair of dice. Already there was something wrong. The roundness of the day had an imperfection, a bruise. It wasn't the dream, that now familiar uneasiness, this was something new. Then he remembered. Today was the start of his botany lessons. He wished he could stay home, have his mother write a note.

The door at the other end of the hootch creaked open.

"I'm back here," Griffin called.

Someone came down the corridor. It was Simon.

"What's for lunch?" Griffin asked.

"Baked canteen covers, sautéed malaria pills, and that disgusting chocolate cake you like with the purple frosting."

"Yum, yum."

"Look at me," said Simon, spreading his arms dramatically.

"I'm looking."

"The paint, damnit. I've got fucking paint all over my fatigues."

"And now you can't go to the prom."

"Jesus, you people who work nights. I'm there every day right in the middle of it."

"Sounds like the action's getting a bit heavy at the front."

"Now he doesn't want to see any spots on our fatigues. That was the word he used, spots. So the other day Hagen comes in from the motor pool with grease stains on his back pocket and the

CO goes crazy and rips the whole damn thing off. So today he says he wants the whole orderly room painted."

"I thought Uncle Sam did that a couple months ago."

"He did, but the CO doesn't like the color and he says there's a hole in his wall he wants covered. Says it stares at him."

"He's seeing that stuff already?"

"And we've got to do it ourselves because Uncle Sam's still out there working on the stage for Bob Hope."

"I hope all those singers and dancers have insurance."

"So we're supposed to paint whenever we get a chance, in between typing out memos on haircuts and shoeshines and rinsing out the coffee urn."

"Intense cross fire."

"The Board's got to come down, too."

"No."

"Anarchistic ornament. Top made a notation on his clipboard."

"When was this?"

"Who knows. You were probably asleep. He and Top toured the hootches together. He came through here like Queen Victoria visiting a leper colony."

"But The Big Board's a work of folk art."

"Subversive junk."

"So the colonel said. The late colonel."

"Hey . . ." Simon leaned backward into the corridor, checked both entrances. "Don't even joke."

"Well, I'm pissed. Think of all the man-hours spent leafing through newspapers and magazines, the calluses on my scissors hand. Look at the one I found yesterday, up there near the top."

Simon stepped back to see.

The back wall of the hootch, protected by the screened porch, was covered with a monstrous collage of news clippings, paperback book covers, army manual pages, C-ration boxes, record albums, letters, photographs, and food labels from cans and boxes sent from home. There was no one in charge of The Board, no one to arbitrate questions of form, harmony, and taste. Any member of the 1069th with an item he considered suitable was free to paste it up himself using the jar of glue that could usually be found kicking about the porch floor. The cutting and pasting had been in progress for years now and though rain and humidity had managed to bleach out most of the earlier contributions or caused them to peel off limp and faded as dead skin, fresh clippings went up often enough so that the board continued to renew itself like some exotic snake. Griffin had proposed that when the war ended The Board be preserved under a coat of liquid plastic and left to the patient scrutiny of the North Vietnamese. What would they make of these inscrutable Occidentals? There would be much to ponder: presidents and penises, officers and orifices, history as an illustrated stroke book, from the ancient mamasan in conical hat and black latex to last year's Playmate of the Year from whose glossy pink ass a stick of five-hundred-pound bombs dropped onto a football field mined with pizzas where one team marked AFL rushed another team marked NLF for possession of the oversized head of Mickey Mouse decapitated by the blades of a Cobra helicopter streaming rockets into the U.S. Capitol dome that was a beanie on the head of Ho Chi Minh. In the upper right where pigs grazed on the White House lawn under a rain of pubic bushes cut into the shape of hydrogen bombs and Jesus with golden halo and folded hands lay on his side in a pile of charred Asian dead from which rose the Statue of Liberty who was taking it stoically in the rear from Pham Van Dong's dong, Griffin had pasted his latest addition atop the handle of freedom's torch. The photograph, clipped from the front page of Captain Patch's *Chicago Tribune*, showed the President shaking hands with a Marine corporal about whose neck he had just placed the Congressional Medal of Honor. The President was smiling. The boyish corporal was smiling. The parents were smiling. The mother clutched a handkerchief. But the senator who represented the soldier's home state had been caught by the camera in mid-yawn or mid-laugh with eyes rolled comically upward and mouth stopped in a huge black O.

Simon laughed. "It looks like the Vice President just stuck a thumb up his ass."

"We need a picture of the CO, stick his head in here somewhere. That's probably why he got so upset, he couldn't find himself with the rest of the gang."

"You know Major Quimby isn't talking to him. They communicate through typed memos Ellis carries back and forth. He's the only one with a security clearance the both of them trust."

"Interesting. Now where would our CO be the happiest?"

"I think they know each other from the Missile Crisis or the Berlin Wall, one of those great intelligence convocations."

"Let's put him here on the moon between Frankenstein and Nixon."

"Knock yourself out. I've got to go write a letter to my parents."

"Or maybe up there sucking on Miss April's skull tits."

"Have a nice day."

By the time Griffin finally got dressed and over to the mess hall Sergeant Ramirez was bolting the door. "Goddamn sorry about that," he said, smiling through the screen.

"Aw sarge, c'mon, let me in."

"Ain't no restaurant goddamnit. You know the hours. No special catering to night people goddamnit."

"How about a piece of cake? Is there any cake left? A teeny piece of cake?"

"You like my cake?"

"Purple frosting?"

"No, all gone, only got green, plain green, goddamnit. Wait here."

A moment later a slab of chocolate cake smeared with bright green icing was passed through the door as cautiously as atomic secrets.

"Next time be here sooner, understand? No more favors, goddamnit."

Munching on the cake, Griffin strolled over to the mail room, a trail of brown crumbs marking his path. There he found one lonely letter forwarded from home. A national oil company offered him the use of a credit card. As a busy college student he probably often found himself with an empty tank and an empty wallet. He tossed the application in a Dumpster outside.

He walked down the red dirt road, still soft from yesterday's rain, past the orderly room where Simon, headphones clamped to his ears, struggled daily against bureaucratic clamor and the nervous chatter of his own typewriter, 7 DAYS WITHOUT AN ACCIDENT, through the gate, pausing to deposit a wrinkled bill into a wooden bowl, the fist darting out, the money gone without a trace somewhere beneath that mud-splattered poncho. The old man. Sometimes he didn't seem quite real.

Out on the highway Griffin hitched a ride with four privates, a maintenance crew from the 511 FAC, who were on their way over to the Happy Smiles Massage Parlor, a small concrete block building painted flamingo pink and conveniently located across from the PX. Griffin had made the obligatory visit early in his tour. Directed to a musty cubicle behind a torn shower curtain, he had found a girl younger than his sister whose childlike features were more emphasized than obscured by a hideous coating of adult makeup. Griffin had never been back. The privates were arguing about whose turn it was to have Number Three, apparently a girl of incredibly nimble fingers. Finally they decided to let her choose. Then they congratulated themselves on the easy availability of certified and inspected Grade A prime instead of village leftovers who all carried the Black Syph for which there was no known cure except an indefinite confinement in a military hospital on Okinawa until a treatment could be found and who were all VC sympathizers anyway with razor blades concealed up their snatches to mutilate imperialist pricks. Griffin left them in front of the Happy Smiles arguing about whose turn it was to stand guard over the jeep. They decided to solve this disagreement with a round of one potato, two potato.

The PX was the largest building on the base, bigger than the air terminal, bigger than the hangars, a fat ripe apple still unsplit by VC rockets. Four garage-sized doors opened into a metal cavern dense with cardboard stalagmites, shipping pallets of soap, toothpaste, and deodorant towering upward into the gloom, through which fell a fine steady snow of red dust and yellow watery light. Soldiers of every rank crowded the narrow aisles, touching with dirty fingers the stacks of electric shavers, Japanese cameras, Olympic swimming trunks, the plastic packaging of hair driers no one but an officer's mistress would ever use or want, not even having to buy, the touch alone sufficient, a moment's respite from the strife outside in the intimate contact of hand to synthetic as if these various goods and appliances were the last relics of a distant age of faith whose remaining magic, dim and uncertain, lingered about the few surviving objects of its worship. Then a newly-arrived crate would be unpacked at the electronics counter and Griffin would be dodging a mob of shoppers in the backlot annex of a chain of super discount stores where the clearance sale signs never came down and there was always just one remaining Sony AM-FM stereo receiver with two frog-voiced teenagers ready to kill for it.

At the magazine stand Griffin leafed through a month-old newsweekly. Comic book America. He picked up a package of chocolate bars, taste of Pennsylvania, and moved toward the exit. Vietnamese women in long black hair, Hollywood makeup, and pastel smocks stood in rows punching cash registers with professional abandon. Between the checkout counters and the doors was positioned a final claim on homesick attention: a ruddy man with a gray crewcut, orange polo shirt, and the melancholy look of a retired master sergeant seated at a rickety table spread with slick pamphlets, glossy cardboard displays of General Motors' latest models, and a paper coffee cup stuffed with soggy cigarette butts. Order now, your personalized car will be delivered upon your arrival home. Griffin wanted to know what happened to the cars whose intended owners got blown away. Was there an underground garage of gleaming Chevys hidden away somewhere? The salesman was looking the other way. He leaned back in his chair and yawned.

Outside, the jeep was still parked in front of the Happy Smiles. Unattended. Griffin wandered among the vehicles beside the PX, searching for 1069 markings. The damp air smelled like the late morning wind that rolls through the empty stalls of a metropolitan produce market. The sky resembled a gray field dressing. A helicopter the shape and color of a rotten banana passed from west to east, swinging a howitzer on a steel cable.

"Homes!"

Griffin turned.

"Yeah, you. My man." A black hand beckoned impatiently.

Peering around the corner of the PX was a tall angular PFC wearing a 101st patch. His boots and fatigue pants were plastered with red mud up to the knees. A puckered pink scar adorned his left cheek. The bushy globe of his Afro was bisected by a leather headband decorated with skull carvings. He shifted nervously from foot to foot, arms and legs rising and falling in the sudden irregular movements of a marionette whose important strings were being worked by different hands.

"Let me see now," he said softly.

Griffin's field of vision filled with a pair of wet black eyes, the whites yellow and shot with broken vessels. The lids snapped once like shutters collecting images. The eyes zoomed back, resolved into a face again.

"Sheeee-it, you ain't even high."

Griffin smiled.

"No, you ain't." The PFC stopped, cocked his head as if listening to faraway sounds. He chuckled quietly to himself. "Out of uniform, my man. What's your First Sergeant's name, boy?"

A short-timer's stick, a length of black wood ending in a carved fist, appeared in one hand. He displayed the open palm of the other, closed it, then tapped the back of the hand with the stick, wooden fist to flesh fist. The hand turned over, opened to reveal a thimble-sized plastic vial of white powder. "Cocaine," he whispered, "in-country R&R, a head honeymoon." The eyes were clicking like aerial cameras.

Griffin looked and looked. He had never seen cocaine before.

"Smoke it, snort it, stuff it up your ass. You owe it to yourself."

But there wasn't any cocaine in Asia. Was there? Didn't those trees grow in Colombia?

"Buck a vial. How many you want?"

"I don't think so," said Griffin, still staring, still wondering. "Looks a little too potent for me."

"Hey, your choice." The PFC bowed. "No sweat." He held up the first two fingers of his right hand in a V. "Here, a complimentary sample." He offered the vial.

"No, really," said Griffin.

"Hey, I understand." He crossed his fingers, kissed them, crossed his chest. "Don't worry, don't worry 'bout nothing." He made shooing motions with his hands. "Catch you later, huh?" His high unsettling laughter followed Griffin down the hill and onto the road. When Griffin turned around to look, the PFC, all teeth and hair now, flashed him another V sign.

A jeep pulled up beside Griffin.

"Need a lift, soldier?"

It was Ellis, the CO's driver. Griffin climbed in.

"Who's your friend?"

"I don't know. I don't know what he is."

"Hundred and first?"

"Yeah."

"I don't go near any of them. They're all demented."

"No worse than the rest of us. So what are you doing over here anyway, hiding out?"

"Oh, I just dropped Hollyhock off at the terminal. The General's holding another one of his seances in Da Nang. Figured I'd take the opportunity to get some air. Driving this character around is like sitting in a john with your mother. Told me on the way over I should rent out the insides of my ears for truck gardens."

"Witty fellow, isn't he?"

"Look, I gotta get out of here. I don't know how much more of this I can stand. I haven't been feeling well either. I think I've got scurvy or beriberi, some kind of tropical disease. Gonna see the doc this afternoon, beg for a confinement to quarters, anything for a rest, or I'm going out of here wrapped in wet sheets."

The jeep slid down the mushy road, past the motionless old man, through the gate, under the eye of a tracking camera, the orderly room, 7 DAYS WITHOUT AN ACCIDENT, the barber shop, the basketball court, around the mess hall, the smoldering gray dunes of the dump, wisps of smoke rising like torn tissue paper from the decay where an old man stooped over a stick poked impatiently at the garbage, and down into the motor pool.

"Was that Wendell on the roof of the photo lab?" Ellis asked.

"I didn't see a thing. Let me out here."

Griffin climbed the hill behind the chapel and peeked around the corner. In a moment Wendell would probably be running down into the motor pool with a bottle of dye wanting to pose him as a corpse under the wheels of a deuce and a half. He sneaked around the officers mess where he could hear someone favorably comparing combat casualties to traffic accident victims. Joe the barber stood there, his ear to the wall. When he saw Griffin he grinned, bobbed his head up and down like a mechanical toy. Vegetable was stomping through the puddles on the basketball court, showering Thai and himself with water. Short Time Suzi sat on the steps of Trips's hootch, polishing boots, her bag of pharmaceutical wares between her knobby feet. Sergeant Mars, a towel around his waist, stepped to his door and spat into the sand. Someone was singing off-key "Ruby, Don't Take Your Love To Town." A Mohawk roared in overhead, buzzing the compound. Franklin's knife went thud into a wall. Outside the Spook House Conrad lifted his Gustav, pretended to spray a laughing trio of Green Berets. Sergeant Anstin put his hand on Griffin's shoulder. "You don't mess with that dope, do you, son?" His eyes were turquoise marbles, splintered glass that had been hit with a hammer hard enough to crack but not destroy. "No, Sarge, of course I don't." "That's right, I know, I know you're one of the good boys." Lieutenant Phan rushed out of the interrogation section, looked at the backs of his hands, rushed back in. In the latrine the toilets were overflowing again and "George," the Vietnamese attendant, was hosing down the floor. A used rubber lay in the bottom of the urinal like a dead fish. Along Officers Row there wasn't a sound. The doors and windows were all tightly closed. Sagebrush ghost town. Griffin climbed creaking steps, cautiously pushed open the door to Mueller's room. The lieutenant, stripped to his shorts, was stretched out on the white sheets of his bunk leisurely absorbing ultraviolet rays from the sunlamp nailed to the wall above him. One eye squinted open.

"Don't explain," said Griffin. "You heard me coming and knew I needed a good laugh."

Mueller sat up, flicked off the lamp. "No way I can go home without a tan. I'd be laughed off the beach."

"At least that lamp keeps your room dry. I feel like I've been sleeping in a mushroom cellar."

"I always suspected you had a secret stash. Those astonished eyes. The surgeon's studied composure."

"I had one of those snow dreams again."

"Don't worry about it. You get to escape for a few hours. Exotic adventures, novel climes. What are you complaining about? I lie down and see SAM missiles and the ground rushing at me like a big lime pie. Awake I suffer from daymares. Now where the hell is it?" His arm rooted around under the bed, came up with a book he waggled in Griffin's face. "You ever read this?"

Griffin shook his head.

"Curl your hair. Listen, fact: January nineteen nineteen, Paris, Nguyen Ai Quoc, a twenty-nine-year-old ex-mess boy, former pastry cook for Escoffier, and Parisian photo retoucher, believing that Wilson's Fourteen Points were not in fact a practical joke on a naïve world, attempts to see the great man with a list of eight points for his own small country. Naturally he is shown instead to the door. Who was that man?"

"The Lone Ranger?" guessed Griffin.

"Ho Chi Minh, yes, wandering the corridors of Versailles in a bowler hat and a rented tux, for God's sake. Between all those mirrors. An infinity of yellow interlopers. Did you know that, you with your rich American education for God's sake?"

"No, I guess not."

"Or in nineteen forty-three and four his guerrilla operations for the OSS?"

"No."

"Or in forty-six offering Ben-Gurion Hanoi as the site of an Israeli government-in-exile?"

"No."

"Or his final petition to the government of Washington and Jefferson for help against European tyranny?"

"No, but look, what does it . . ."

"Or the A-bomb business, Dulles offering the French the use of a couple nukes, just the tiny ones you understand, enough fireworks to frighten the Viet Minh to the peace table, having noted, of course, a couple years earlier, the encouraging effect these weapons have on the little colored people of the world, did you know about that, does anybody know about that?"

"No."

"I'm still tracking this line down, just sent another list of books to my mother yesterday, thank God she lives in Berkeley."

"Why?"

"What do you mean why? You sound like a whiny freshman. So we can know what's going on why. So we're not political zombies why. So we can begin seizing the controls why. You seen my latest addendum to the unit history? Here, have a copy."

"But why torture yourself? I mean, we're already here. Ferreting out obscure facts ain't gonna help us now because this whole grand pageant of idiocy simply condenses down to you and me trying to make it through another day. You've got to be the only fool on this entire damn peninsula who beats himself over the head with these political horror stories. Me, I can barely get through a comic book."

"Well, I have a separate speech on that topic, 'Apathy or Paranoia: How to Know the Difference,' but I just remembered I'm not even supposed to be talking to you, I'm supposed to be informing you that if you have any questions or problems regarding the military and your role in it you may visit me in my office during posted duty hours or arrange for an appointment."

"Another turn of the screw."

"Another poor individual with Swiss cheese for a historical consciousness. I think someone should take him aside for a quick briefing on the particulars of the colonel's short unhappy reign."

"There's movement in that direction and speaking of which I see by my waterproof shock-resistant, macho-man wrist watch that I'm gonna be late for my next class, Botany 101."

"Here, take this," urged Mueller, pulling a thick book out of one of the several huge piles strewn about the floor. "Check out pages ninety-two to a hundred and ten when you get a chance. As a favor to me."

"*The Bamboo Maiden*?"

"Memoirs of a former French infantry officer. He spent two years in a mental hospital in Dijon."

"Wonderful."

An hour later Griffin stood on a metal flight ramp in the shadow of a wing, staring up at the plumbing attached to the underside of a twin-engined C-123.

"We've got the boom there with fourteen nozzles on each wing plus the eight on the tail," explained the pilot, gesturing with a dead cigar butt. He wore a zippered gray flight suit and a .38 revolver in a shoulder holster beneath his left armpit. When he stepped in front of him, Griffin smelled whiskey and Old Spice. "The tank holds a thousand gallons and at air speed we're laying down about three gallons per acre. Average coverage three hundred acres, elapsed mission time five minutes. Of course, in an emergency we can dump the whole thousand gallons in thirty seconds."

Griffin studied the scattering of holes across the plane's belly, the crazy-quilt pattern of dark and light squares, the result of replacement and repair, and the fine coating of some oil-like substance so complete it appeared the plane had been totally immersed in a bath of preservative and then set down here before them to dry, dripping excess from every point and edge. The liquid smelled like kerosene. Carefully painted along the nose were the words WE EAT FORESTS. Under the cockpit window on the pilot's side were drawn several rows of small green trees with bright red **X**s centered through each one.

"How safe is this stuff?" Griffin asked.

Without a word or hesitation the pilot squatted down, dipped his finger into one of the puddles growing on the ramp beneath the wing nozzles, and stuck it into his mouth. Incredulous, Griffin swung around to look behind him. About twenty-five feet away Weird Wendell, camera for a face, held up an arm, thumb and forefinger forming an O.

"Is he intelligence too?" asked the pilot.

"The very embodiment," Griffin replied. Both he and Payne had removed the rank insignia from their lapels before driving over to the Six-oh-third Air Force squadron, the 4-H Club as the crews preferred to call themselves. The pilot had no way of knowing he wasn't addressing equals.

"Wanted me to go that route once. Turned it down flat. Dead-end work. You know they did one of those psychological studies a couple years back analyzing all the military jobs and know what they found? You guys and the cooks are just about tied for the highest percentage of alcoholics in any job category. No feedback. Too much frustration. You put out and you put out and get nothing back. Like fucking a dead whore. Let me take you boys up and I'll show you results, a couple roads we cleaned last month and a manioc field up in the mountains VC were using for food. Ever see a load going down? A fucking blizzard. Beautiful sight. Come on out in the morning. Be glad to have you."

Griffin looked at the holes again. "No, thanks, afraid my colleague and I will be locked up all day in one of those marathon strategy sessions."

"Too bad. Tomorrow we're going after mangrove."

"Maybe another time."

"It's different out there, you know. Can't really taste the full flavor without air time. Helicopters don't fly any lower than we do, puts an interesting perspective on things, it's a glorious sight out there, I tell you, absolutely glorious."

"I know," Griffin said. "I see the film."

His field trip completed, Griffin spent the remainder of his duty day in classroom work under the tutelage of Specialist Fifth Class Ronald Winehaven, master of applied science. Lessons in the detection and measurement of organic death. The physics of infrared, the chemistry of poisons.

"The first time I heard of Agent Orange," Griffin confessed, "I saw a piece of fruit wrapped in a trenchcoat."

"Try an ester cocktail," explained Winehaven, "a jigger of 2, 4-D to a jigger of 2,4,5-T."

"Yum," said Griffin.

"It's usually diluted with diesel fuel to get a better spray effect. Stuff sticks to the leaves, absorbs right through even waxy skin. And here's the fun part: it mimics plant hormones so once inside it starts to heat up the plant's economy, everything commences to grow and grow until the plant grows itself to death. Sort of a botanical inflation."

"Or vegetable cancer."

"The morbidity period varies according to species. Some shrivel up in a week or so, others linger on for months. We've found that good visibility often requires two applications."

"You like this work?"

"Haven't cracked a rifle since my last qualifying round at Fort Dix."

Griffin learned about need: that peeling away sections of the enemy's green umbrella exposed his activity to the light of return fire, that crop denial disrupted his activity, that without food or a place to hide he could not win.

"At least that's the story," Winehaven concluded. "I guess it's better than carpet bombing."

Appraising the carpet had been Griffin's specialty until now. "Yes," he said. "I suppose."

"Of course it's not as if bushes were innocent. Ever been out on the perimeter?"

"No, not yet, thank God."

"Well, you ought to go out there sometime, sit on top of a bunker, stare at the tree line for a while. You have to concentrate because if you blink or look away for even a moment you might miss it, they aren't dumb despite what you may think, they're clever enough to take only an inch or two at a time. The movement is slow but inexorable, irresistible, maybe finally unstoppable. A serious matter."

"What movement, what are you talking about?"

"The trees of course, the fucking shrubs. And one day we'll look up and there they'll be, branches reaching in, jamming our M-60s, curling around our waists."

"Like Birnam Wood, huh?"

"Actually, I was thinking more of triffids."

That night, lying in the dark of his room, head throbbing like the ancient engine of a tramp steamer laboring upriver, Griffin reviewed his work since his arrival for duty in RVN. First the bomb damage assessments, now these defoliation studies. He'd seen the land develop acne, now he'd watch it lose its hair. Sooner or later, he realized, it only a question of time, they'd have him on his hands and knees, polishing the skull, measuring the brain pan with a pair of steel calipers.

Dear Mom and Pop,

Everything fine here. Nothing much to report since my last letter. The war drags on, the food grows worse. We have a sadistic mess sergeant who serves us a stew about every other day that no one has yet had the courage to ask what the lumps are. You might want to send me some canned meat and fruit and some cheese if you get a chance.

Glad to hear Dad is now Republican county chairman. See what you can do to help support us over here. We need all the encouragement we can get.

Please do not worry. I am as safe as anyone can be in this country. I'll bet the Ambassador has taken more fire. In the last rocket attack the hootch next to mine was wiped out by a direct hit and all the pieces of shrapnel could do was cut open a few of the sandbags around the bunker I was in. So don't worry. I'm healthy, as happy as you could be in this environment and I'll see you all in 264.

Love,
Lew

The surface of the mirror was dotted with flecks of shaving cream. Leaning forward, bringing into view the stubbled underside of his jaw, Major Holly drew the razor rasping across his skin. "Outstanding!" The razor plopped into a sink of milky water. A hand reached for the damp washcloth. Third nick this morning.

"You okay, Major Marty?" called a voice from the other room.

"Yes, yes, damnit."

He inspected the wound. Minor but noticeable. He was certainly going to look like hell at today's Numbers Conference. If The General asked he'd say Anh had scratched him, accumulate points early in the game. The General encouraged hints of sexual activity among his subordinates. When Holly was on the staff he used to make up tales for The General's pleasure. Iron cocks, hot pussies. The General slept like a baby. Days later Holly would hear details he had invented stuck like cloves to The General's overdone accounts of his own fictitious exploits.

Holly swished the razor around in the water, leaned into the image of his face. He couldn't look any worse than Captain Fry this morning. Break your nose and sometimes both eyes would blacken. Those carrier deck landings. He'd have banned them the first week had not Lieutenant Peary, the earnest morale officer, assured him such antics were absolutely necessary to the flight crews' emotional well-being—"Take away belly landings, sir, and you might as well ground the planes." And there were The General's last words as Holly departed for this command: "Remember, my boy, there's the army and the army and then there's aviation." Pilots did seem to operate out of an excess of spirits even combat missions couldn't fully dissipate. So each evening, regular as the 2100 artillery barrage, they'd line up, once a proper altitude of intoxication had been achieved, to take turns leaping, chest thrust defiantly forward, arms spread defenseless as wings, from the top of the bar onto the unit emblem, that screaming woman's head painted in garish color on the hard tile floor of the O club. Shouting, crashing, sliding into tables and chairs. Shirts sopping with spilled beer. Cigarette butts mashed to their chests. An insane business. Obviously too late for him to apply brakes. O club injuries honored with an aluminum heart: a pop-top pinned to the pocket. Captain Marovicci of the white silk scarf and gleaming silver bars—he refused to wear the standard combat subdued black—still strutted about, right arm encased to the shoulder in plaster, the result of a "miscalculation" that occurred before Holly's arrival. "Forgot to drop my landing gear, sir." Compound fracture. For which he had put himself in for a genuine Purple Heart. The orders had already been cut.

"Like meel-lows," said Anh. She stood in the doorway, hands buried to the elbows in the boots she held up for inspection. Round leather paws. Holly nodded.

"The General give you more leaves now," she said, gesturing toward his lapels.

"Yes," Holly replied, amused by the pun she wouldn't understand. "I may have to apply for another branch."

"I can see my face. Can you see yours?" She thrust a boot under his lathered chin.

"Like chrome fenders," he said. "Like mirrors. How about the pants?"

"This time you cut youself on crease for sure," she replied, obviously pleased at using the expression correctly before the major.

Holly laughed. "What would I ever do without you?"

"Have someone else," she answered. "I put boots by bed."

He turned back to the mirror, saw himself still smiling. He'd like to take her with him, show her off to The General. Classified or not, what could she understand? He often had difficulty himself. A Numbers Conference, ostensibly a meeting to coordinate hard data on enemy activity in I Corps, was in fact a complicated game in which all participants attempted to guess the numbers already written on a piece of paper concealed in The General's pocket. The first person to guess correctly and prove his own figures matched The General's won the game and The General's grace until the following month when the competition started all over again. This ritual had been amusing when Holly sat behind The General. The view from the other side of those stars was not so funny. The General gave away nothing, silent and expressionless throughout each presentation, sucking patiently on his pipe, the closed air of the briefing room gradually filling with the vapors of his special aristocratic blend of Egyptian tobacco—a reek of smoldering mummy wrappings. He'd wait, noncommittal to the very end, when, leaning back in his seat, the leather squeaking like chalk on a blackboard, he'd speak with magisterial finality into the expectant silence: "Bullshit." The sound echoed in a tomb. Captain Danzinger, paling to his boots, looked at Holly. Holly shrugged. The tip of Danzinger's pointer began to tremble. The last slide, frozen in the projector, burned a graph into the wall. Holly shifted position in his seat. "Well, sir," he said at last, "perhaps if you'll give me a moment to clarify the . . ." "What's this five thousand odd figure here?" gesturing toward the screen with tooth-scarred pipe stem. "We don't have anything like that." The General turned to his left. A hand clutching a sheet of paper appeared from behind his chair. "What figure is that, sir?" asked Holly. "I'm afraid I . . ." "Right there, of course, in the last damn column," the pipe stem quivering. "Aren't you people familiar with your own damn numbers for Christ's sake?" "Yes, sir, but allow me to . . ." "What is that, anyway, number of rounds expended per gook?" A titter traveled through the darkness across the back rows. Holly knew there was no way out now. "No, sir, I believe that's the total of service personnel." The General snorted, a cloud of smoke exploding around his head. "How many g.d. gooks do they need to change a frigging bicycle tire?" He turned again to his left. "What's our figure?" "Three hundred and eight," answered a disembodied voice. The General nodded, eyes resting on Holly like weights. "Bit more realistic, eh, Marty?" Holly went through the motions, he defended his numbers, his men, unsure of both, but playing the game to its proper conclusion. The General was enjoying himself immensely. "I used to think this young man had a future in the United States Army." On cue the staff chuckled. "I like to think I still do," Holly replied. The General nodded without comment. Then The General went on to speak of the virtues of systems analysis, the sanctity of the data base, the effective utilization of common sense, he talked about the program, getting with it; he elaborated on progress, the correct tallying of figures, the latest consensus upon which everyone should clamber aboard or be left at the dock with the gooks. The General's rebukes occupied only the median ground of subtlety. Holly remained polite, attentive, his deodorant melting under his fury. Today, he was afraid, there'd be more of the same. His latest numbers were even less "realistic." He had gotten to know his men since the last conference, unreliable soldiers, superb technicians; no reason to doubt the results of their work and despite their cavalier attitude and slovenly habits he had yet to behold a single one of them in the pitiable condition achieved last night by Major Brand, the executive officer, who dumped a Black Russian on his head, crawled under a table, and made sounds like a pig. When Holly ordered him to his feet, he demanded a refill, and, before the glass touched his lips, collapsed to the floor, almost cracking his skull against the bar. Hewitt and Patch carried the inert body out to a jeep where it sat, the skin pale and cold as cemetery marble, the facial expression so oddly fixed it resembled a Halloween mask, eyes wide, unblinking, unseeing, the trunk of the body propped in the front seat like a tailor's dummy all the way to the 92nd Evac where the stomach was pumped. Not the first time either, Lieutenant Tremble thoughtfully informed Holly. A colorful lot.

The flecks of lather on the mirror gave his face a diseased look as if he were suffering from some rare, particularly ugly species of boil. Holly ran his fingers across his cheeks. Smooth as The General's contoured chair.

"Anh," he called.

"Yes, Major Marty," she answered, appearing with the suddenness of a genie.

"My pad."

She returned in a moment with a black leather notebook and a pen. Across the top of the first blank sheet Holly scribbled the word ROCKS. Another idea about improving the general appearance of the unit area. Make a border for the walks. Keep it neat. He put the pad down and splashed green aftershave into his palms, slapped them across his face. A satisfying sting. Friends in CID had dusted down the grenade without finding a single print. Big surprise. This was an intelligence unit after all. He would have been disappointed had the culprit left any clues. Let them play their games. He wasn't going to bother ordering a headstone yet. Holly scribbled in his pad again. SAND. All the ramps, both aircraft and motor pool, should be swept daily. Better appearance. Cleaner machinery. He checked his face again. With a pair of tweezers he easily removed a short black hair that had apparently erupted overnight in that blemish on his cheek.

"Major Marty, look." Anh stood in the doorway, holding up his large freshly washed and ironed shirt. For a moment in the mirror he had mistaken her for his daughter, home from school, dressed in one of his old fatigue shirts.

"Yes," he said. "The General will be most impressed."

"Not enough starch?" she asked with concern. She was still learning how to handle the cans of spray starch Holly's wife sent from California.

"Just right," said Holly, hanging the shirt on a nail behind the door. "Stiff as a board, the way we soldiers like 'em."

"You like this stiff, too, huh?" She yanked the towel from around his waist. In her other hand she held a spray can. "Here I make this hard." She pressed on the nozzle. "Why you . . ." Holly exclaimed and naked chased her squealing into the other room. Behind him the round shaving mirror slid off the top of the sink and slipped soundlessly into the white foamy water, disappearing without a trace.

Christmas came and went. In the mess hall the enlisted men were served a traditional dinner of creamed chicken on toast, instant potatoes, soggy green beans, and chocolate cake with fire engine red frosting. (Where's our goddamn turkey, demanded the men. You eat what you got, replied Sergeant Ramirez.) Upon leaving a party at the 92nd Evac a red-cheeked Santa Claus fell out of a helicopter and broke his wrist. In Research and Analysis lights were strung between the map pins representing confirmed sightings of the 5th NVA Regiment, a pin in every province of I Corps. Out on the perimeter each bunker was permitted to shoot off one festive flare, make its own star of Bethlehem. In the morning nobody got what they wanted and only four people showed up at 0530 in complete combat gear for the truck ride over to the Bob Hope Show eight hours later. The Vietnamese carpenters had done their job well. The stage was broad and firm and did not collapse. Good work, Uncle Sam.

Meditation in Green: 8

These transparent elevators are sucked rapidly upward into blue and red light. Machinery gurgles like old plumbing.

"Do not fear The Conversion," murmur the speakers. "Be proud you have been chosen."

We are packed naked together for movement to the outer levels. Apprehension surfaces in our solemnity as nervous laughter, the stupidity everyone takes as a joke.

When the elevator stops we crowd into a narrow corridor. A yellow line painted on the floor indicates with arrows the proper direction.

"The Conversion is a privilege, The Conversion is an honor, The Conversion is a duty."

We are herded into a large chamber. The light is more intense. The air is rich. The chamber is filled from floor to ceiling with stacks of gigantic green coins. Too late for protests and exits. Silently we move toward the doors opening into the coins.

"Let go, people, simply let go now, there is no pain, let go of your O."

Just before the doors close it is possible to glimpse the conveyor belt moving away, bearing upon its sliding back coffin-shaped tins of sweet food descending one after another into the darkness.

"Do not fear The Conversion. It's as easy as getting your picture taken."

Up ahead flashes, pounding, the whirr of machinery.

I was in the john, hunched on the seat, clutching several pages torn from *National Geographic.* Hawaiians in native dress (Sears muumuus, polymerized leis) looked up at me with Kodachrome smiles. I was supposed to be concentrating on the orchids in their hair. The flower of testicles and death. Is that why high school kids wore them to proms? The mind is a magpie, say the masters.

Trips was in the other room, making obscene calls on my phone. The moment I shut the bathroom door he was on the line. I could hear him out there, dialing, whispering.

Sun. Sand. Pineapple. Little grass shack. Orchids dangling from every ear like splayed skin, pretty nut brown heads beginning to rupture. I tried another picture. A gleaming aluminum trailer. Ohio plates. Foot-high picket fence. Behind the fence and around the trailer a dense cordon of stiff gladioli. Spears of red, of yellow. Flaming stalks. Nature itself spontaneously combusting. In a minute the whole trailer will go up like a storage tank in a refinery fire.

"Hey," called Trips, "turned into a dandelion yet?"

"The trick is not to turn into," I said, opening the door, "but to discover you already are, a dandelion."

"What do I know," he said, moving past me, unzipping his fly, "I slept through zoology."

"Botany."

"I told you I slept through it."

On the glass table were the scattered remains of a couple issues of *Time,* a pair of scissors, a jar of white paste, and an open tablet of children's construction paper. Various sized and colored letters had been cut from advertisements and pasted onto a red sheet to spell BUCKLE UP FOR SAFETY. The photograph underneath showed a type usually described as "a prominent East Coast mobster" seated behind the wheel of a recent model Lincoln Continental. Head pitched back, mouth yawning blackly. In the center of the forehead a modest round hole. This was the fourth, or was it the fifth? such message Trips had composed to Sergeant Anstin. Simple murder, it had been decided, was too quick, too clean for that worm. His varied crimes, his very presence in life, demanded that he twist on a hook. Uncertainty, dread, and impotence—particularly able demons of the NCO mind—set cavorting among the slick hills and dales of an alcohol-softened brain. There should be pain, a lot of pain. I was being encouraged to assist in this campaign, lick envelopes, breathe into the phone. I didn't say yes, I didn't say no. I was distracted. Big green trucks plowed through my walls every night, chewing up my pansies.

Trips came out of the bathroom, rubbing his hands. "You ever watch a toilet flush? I mean really watch, positioned directly over the bowl. There's this still pond, then there's this roaring vortex spiraling away. Know why the water whirls around like that? Cause the planet is spinning like mad and you're not even aware of it till you flush your commode. Makes me dizzy to contemplate. Below the equator all the toilets spin the other way."

"Thank you, Mr. Science."

"Point number two. The tarnished mirror above the sink. It's not me looking back. I don't know who you got stuck inside but it ain't me."

"Well, sounds like you had quite an adventure in there."

"I try to be fully conscious of my surroundings at all times, Grif. A word to the wise."

"Were you on the phone before?"

"You asked me not to do that."

"Then who were you talking to?"

"Anstin."

"You just said you didn't use the phone."

"Don't need no wire to talk to him. When de obeah man make de magic he like to croon over de charms."

"I saw your latest here. Pungent."

"It's like an ad campaign. Escalation of effect. All day the itch is working under the skin; at night he sits up in bed listening for the sound of breaking glass."

"Our Sergeant Anstin? He may be sitting up trembling in bed but it's not because of your letters."

"He wonders about bringing in the police. Will they be suitably concerned or merely polite?"

"If it even is him."

"Don't start on me again, Grif. You're just pissed because you've finally come to realize that Hardon or whatever the hell he calls himself now is a fucking fraud."

"But I always knew that."

"Then why this horticulture crap?"

"I want to get back to my roots. What's more American than good honest fraud? Your consciousness can't be that full of the gritty day-to-day without an appreciation of the delights of deceit. It's a fun head, knowing and pretending not to know or not knowing and pretending to know or not knowing and not pretending. Wheels within wheels, forging cash value. It can get pretty elaborate but once you work your way in, shake off those qualms, there's all these cozy layers between you and the outer chill. Delusion is a national pastime."

"I don't know, Grif, do I know you anymore? You're out in the boonies. This creepy apartment, your weird friends, hunkering down in the toilet all day. The boonies. Know what I think? I think that war's got you bent out of shape. You're all twisted up." He began to chuckle quietly. "The war turned you around. You ain't the same since you shipped out. Yeah, you're all fucked up."

"I'm in a world of hurt."

"And it could be worse. You could be all fucked up *and* getting cut-and-paste threats in your daily mail."

On the wall above Trips's right shoulder was a faint dark spot (one of those surfacing scrawls?) I realized I had been staring at for some time when it erupted into blossom, unfolding moist petals of unbelievable color, a liquid-quick stem plunging to the floorboard, extending curly tendrils and acid green leaves, vines whipping right and left, flowers exploding, seed pelting the room, fecundity gone mad. No, I thought, not this, not now. In seconds the entire wall was covered over, a riot of vegetation that seemed to heave and pulse.

"Here's another one I did this morning," Trips continued, thrusting into my confusion a sheet of yellow paper on which had been pasted a grainy night photograph of a dented semi, a crumpled Ford, state troopers reaching in through a smashed window, wet pavement, the head of a dog, possibly German shepherd, no carcass in sight, caption: MAN'S BEST FRIEND GOES ON A TRIP.

"Don't give it to me," I snapped. "You know I don't touch any of that stuff without gloves on."

The floor was bobbing gently up and down like a dock in the wake of a departed speedboat. I dropped onto the couch.

"He paces, gripping his pill bottle. He sits in the window, waiting for the screeching car, the shoulder at the door. The night is no longer his friend."

"He calls for flares," I muttered, "but the line is dead."

My heart was thrashing like a rabbit in a gunny sack. Attend to specifics, fasten on detail. Sergeant Anstin, yes, Sergeant Anstin, the vodka vampire. Slinking through the compound, flashlight at the ready, sniffing for narcotics, listening for the telltale creak of bedsprings.

Do not look at the wall, don't look.

"That's the spirit," Trips declared. "Start with a little sarcastic abuse and work your way on up. I knew you'd get with the program sooner or later."

"Eugene told me you took a kick at Chandu."

Dogs. In the hallway. On the street. Roaming foreign lands. The need for submissive companionship. Shit everywhere.

If I do not choose to see foliage, the foliage cannot be seen. Think winter.

"Chandu? Who's Chandu?"

"The dog. His dog's name is Chandu."

Thai. He liked to chase cockroaches. He liked to swallow cigarette butts. He liked to sleep on top of the bunker, howl at the stars when the sirens began.

Take a peek. Is it still there, writhing at the periphery?

"Chandu? What kind of name is that for a dog?"

"He says you were on your way downstairs and deliberately came down the corridor to kick Chandu. You were wearing steel-toed jump boots."

He liked to get stoned. Crawl inside the big plastic bag we'd, huffing and puffing, inflate with brown smoke. Circle the room on rubbery legs, collapse on his belly like a rundown toy.

The imagery has become self-generating. The mind's gone organic. There's no control.

"Why would I do that? I love dogs."

"That's what I said."

Where were they now, those hounds of yesteryear? Fur and flesh sucked down the hopper for processing into the vegetable level, the vegetable level then compressed into the mineral level, the whole cycle pointed toward the perfection of stone, the bottom level. A passage noted in a careless configuration of forgotten bone, a last graffito scribbled into the surface of the planet, Kilroy was here, our mark.

What will I do when I look down and see the frondage sprouting at my feet? Twining about my arms?

"What did he say?"

"He made me feel the bruise."

The place where I slept, the space where I worked. Who lives there now? Do the buildings remain or have they been razed to make way for the Nguyen Giap Golf Course and Country Club or, more likely, a wire-enclosed Reeducation Center. Bulldozers to uncover the canine skull, the rib cage—now prize exhibits in lectures on the natural depravity of imperialist Americans.

This meditation business is not working, it is not working at all.

"Hey, this Eugene character better watch his mailbox."

No, I can see them still, those huddled ramshackle structures. They didn't even bother to dismantle them, torch the planks with souvenir Zippos. The ultimate insult: they ignored them, left all that Western redundance and engineered craziness to time and rain and wind. It is not the water that flows but the bridge, say the masters. The runway buried in sand. Duty rosters bleached white on the bulletin board outside the orderly room. 7 DAYS WITHOUT AN ACCIDENT. The basketball court sunken and cracked. It is night. It is always night. Cold moonlight gleaming across tin rooftops, row on row. Silence, the total haunted silence only possible in a place once devastated by noise. Rusted screen curls away at the windows. Mosquitoes pass whining in and out, the ceaseless blood quest. A rotting T-shirt on a nail. Empty bunk frames, overturned lockers. A nodding table fan plugged directly into the void. In the corner a dimpled helmet, home to the cockroach. Between the floorboards poke the tender tips of new life, shoots of marijuana, naturally. There is growth everywhere. Plants have taken the compound. Elephant grass in the motor pool. Plantain in the mess hall. Lotus in the latrine. Shapes are losing outline, character. Wooden frames turning spongy. The attrition of squares and rectangles. The loss of geometry. Form is emptiness, emptiness is form.

Mind is a magpie.

Forward brothers
Forward sisters
Marching the long road to Victory
The suffering of our beautiful
land calls out to us
Hasten to the battlefield
Our will is strong
Our foes tremble
Let the truth of our struggle
sweep all obstacles away
Let the blood of Vietnam flow
through one heart
Let our people unite in the cause of
peace and

tựdo or tựtử?

Claypool scraped at the mud specks with a bent paper clip. A hole opened in the rice paper. He sighed. If there were special tools for this sort of work Claypool hadn't been told where to find them. Now the last word was lost and he would have to guess. He leafed through his English-Vietnamese dictionary. Well, this shouldn't be difficult. Certainly the people were not being asked to unite in peace and suicide. So it was "tựdo" then. The line ended in "freedom."

When he began his study of the language at the army school in Monterey it seemed that too many of the words not only sounded alike but looked the same on paper, as if the Vietnamese would be quite content with just one word that, depending on subtle variations in spelling and pronounciation, could represent all the known objects of the world. A beginner's impression. Unfortunately, he did not think his understanding had improved substantially since then. Two hours to translate a simple DRV marching song. Struggling on with a weakening will.

"Drop your cock!"

Claypool flinched. He hadn't heard Sergeant Mars come through the door.

"Saddle up, kid." Beer breath. Rough hand on his shoulder, squeezing. "The one-seventy-sixth needs an interpreter ASAP and you're our volunteer."

"But I'm . . . this document . . ."

"No sweat. They've got the best kill ratio in I corps. Never lost a lady yet, ha ha. What an opportunity. See the country. Brush up on your dink. Wish I could go."

"I don't have . . . I'm not . . ."

"Helicopter leaves in forty minutes. Have your gear and your ass out on the ramp in thirty."

The office had a double bank of fluorescent lights, two air conditioners, buffed linoleum, a green refrigerator stacked with cold soda, a clay ashtray molded into the shape of a duck on Captain Raleigh's desk. This wasn't supposed to be happening. Claypool had reenlisted, exchanged a year of his life for the security of a noncombat job. He wasn't supposed to carry a gun, to hump, to get shot, the army had promised. There was a guaranteed contract on file in St. Louis. He couldn't go. He didn't know what gear one packed to the field.

In the shower room, fully dressed, Claypool twisted all the squeaky handles back and forth. Finally, from one rusty nozzle a thin trickle. He held up his canteen. Someone passed the door whistling "The Colonel Bogey March." Passed and reappeared. It was Griffin.

"What's the matter?"

"There isn't any more water . . . and, uh . . . this canteen, I guess I need it."

"What's the matter with you?"

"I don't know."

"Are you ODing in here or what?"

"They're sending me out."

"Out? Out where?"

"The field . . . the boonies, I guess."

"Wonderful."

"The one-seventy-sixth. Are they really the . . ."

"Wonderful."

"How can they do this? I can't shoot. In Basic the drill sergeants cheated on my scorecard to pass me through. I flunked the PT test twice."

"Look, listen to me. There hasn't been any noise out there for a couple months. That area's been so worked over there's nothing left but stumps and stones."

"Then what do they need an interpreter for?"

"Well . . ."

"Who's the beneficiary on your GI insurance?" Trips stood behind them, dark eyes shining, fingers tugging at the string of beads around his neck.

"Leave him alone," said Griffin.

"Hey, I'm only trying to be of service. If the kid here's really going out, there's certain information he needs to know, certain attunements to the reality."

"I've already 'attuned' him."

"I heard. Now he's all set for Boy Scout camp. Or a nature hike. Or a botanical expedition. What's he gonna do when the botany starts blowing up?"

"No one's going to dump some green MI type out into the middle of VC land."

"Hang loose, kid. Watch your step, don't touch anything."

"Don't worry," said Griffin through a smile that made Claypool feel terribly lonely.

"Take as many magazines as you can carry," said Trips.

Had Claypool known a good place to hide he might have been absent from the battered jeep bouncing over the airfield to the helicopter skimming above a landscape of green on green to a slash of brown crammed with bunkers and tents and a bucktoothed major; a captain whose cousin sold stationery in New Harmony, Indiana, Claypool's home town; a distracted first sergeant; a snoring buck sergeant; and a nervous PFC whose name tag read SMITH and who said, "I guess I'm supposed to take care of you."

"Thanks," Claypool replied.

"Do as I say and you'll be around to thank me later."

"He's the best shot in the company," offered someone with a crooked nose and pimpled cheeks. Claypool glanced at the name tag. JONES.

"In the division," said someone who looked Italian. JOHNSON.

"If it moves, The Mouth can kill it." A soprano in a boys choir. BROWN.

Half-circled around him, stale as wild dogs, an expensive camera dangling from each sunburnt neck, they peered at Claypool with such intense good humor he felt compelled to check his fly.

"Mouth?" he asked.

A pink bubble appeared between Smith's lips, swelled slowly to cover his head. When the gum burst it collapsed over his face like a wrinkled mask. Smith peeled it off, popped the wad back in. "I don't know." He shrugged. "I can't stop."

"He ate five steaks at the last company party," said Jones, "and sucked the marrow right out of the bones."

"Once I saw him swallow seventeen eggs," said Johnson. "Intact."

"On R&R he bit off a whore's nipple," Brown said, "and spit it out the window."

"You don't want to get too close when he's hungry," advised Jones.

Mouth clicked a button on his Minolta, recorded an image of Claypool: forlorn surprise.

"You got a lens?" Jones asked.

"No, I never wanted to . . ."

"I'm putting together a slide show for the Rotary back home."

"I had an Instamatic once years ago."

"Let me hunt you up one. There's that Canon of Taylor's but I think Top already sent it out with his effects. Frank's in Taipei with his Miranda. Lewis, Peterson . . . Let's see, I think Matthews is still in the dispensary with the trots. He probably won't be using his tomorrow."

"Tomorrow?"

Mouth's camera clicked several more times. "We were supposed to go today, but they can't find it. Captain Miller says to be ready at dawn."

"What can't they find?"

"I don't know, some gook village supposed to have a VC headquarters buried under it or something. Listen, you know how to shoot?"

"I was a marksman in Basic."

"I don't mean that, I'm taking care of that, I mean you know how to shoot." He aimed his camera at Claypool's head. Click-click-click.

"You look through here and press here?"

"Last MI we had he couldn't shoot worth a damn either. You better stick real close to me."

That night Claypool couldn't sleep. As he was getting ready for bed Johnson strolled in stripped to the waist and offered Claypool his back, the knobby ridge of scar tissue traversing his shoulders, go ahead, touch it if you want. His bunk smelled of feet and mildew. The man in the tent with him kept mumbling Is that you? I know it's you. Is that you? The light from intermittent artillery fire burst across the canvas roof like popping flashbulbs. When Mouth came for him he was staring quietly down the length of his body having become convinced several hours earlier that a poisonous centipede was attempting to crawl up his leg. He got up and walked out into one of those startling Asian dawns that go from dim to bright in a matter of minutes. Claypool examined the distant black tree line. It looked as if it never slept.

Breakfast was soft eggs and stiff bacon, neither of which Claypool touched. He was forcing down a cup of bitter coffee for the caffeine when Brown took his picture.

"All my photographs are perfect," explained Brown, taking the seat opposite, "cause my hands don't shake. Used to be I'd blur everything. The guys would even have to light my cigarettes. That was before the bags. Mind if I take another? You've got the changingest face I've ever seen."

Claypool tried to assume that fresh serene look most often found in nearly every high school graduation photo except his own, soldiers of life confident the fray ahead can do them no harm.

Click.

"There I was, standing on the tarmac, all scrubbed up, my khakis pressed, watching the freedom birds going in and out. I must have been high, I think I shared a couple joints with this goofy Marine in the latrine, anyway I know I was feeling good, I was on my way to Hong Kong, I was on R&R and for a week there wasn't gonna be any war when this little bitty truck that had been unloading crates off the planes tooled by and this box fell off and broke and all these shiny plastic bags slid all over themselves across the concrete and I had never seen them before so when this Marine told me what they were I just knew that one of 'em was mine, my personal bag. It just had to be. I mean, that was a moment. Hey, could you take my picture. It's this button here on top. Let me . . . okay, great."

"Sorry, I'm afraid I might have jiggled the camera."

"That's cool. This pic can be part of my mortar attack collection. All my earlier stuff looks like we're taking heavy fire."

"How bad is it?"

"The faces are fuzzy but you can still recognize the people."

"I meant the enemy, how bad is the action?"

"You ever kill somebody?"

"No."

"Don't mean nothing. You'll understand, after you've seen your bag."

Mouth finished gobbling down the food on Claypool's tray.

"Should have eaten breakfast," he said. "Now you're gonna feel like hell all day."

The leather case was there waiting on Claypool's bunk along with the rest of his gear, the field pack, the web belt, the helmet, the prescription sunglasses he had worn at home whenever he went downtown. Jones sat on the opposite bunk, licking out the inside of a pear can.

"Matthews said you put a scratch on it he'll slit your throat with a roll of Kodachrome. God, he makes me laugh. He's the funniest guy in the company."

Claypool snapped open the case. Inside was a glittery Nikon F studded with enough knobs and dials and buttons to outfit a Phantom cockpit.

"I can't take this."

"Suit yourself. Like, there's no reg or nothing but you'd be the only one without and that could make things kind of spooky, know what I mean?"

"I've never been out before."

"Shit, no one holds it against you. Everybody's got to get laid the first time."

Claypool tried hard to smile. He had never been laid either.

The sun was a ripe blister overhanging the tree line when the company walked single file through the wire. Claypool's heart running like a mouse on a wheel. Against the perimeter gate lounged a soldier without insignia or name tag, his uniform stiff and white with dried sweat. Silently, he watched them pass, one by one. A set of flat lizard eyes pinned Claypool's own distant blues. "Do it," the soldier said. Claypool looked away, pretended not to have heard. A piece of barbed wire caught at his sleeve and, yanking it away, he tore his shirt. Behind him someone laughed. Ahead stalks of tall grass drooped across a narrow trail winding off into the trees where half a dozen bamboo and thatch huts posed as a new life hamlet. The sharp grass cut at his face and hands. The sun went behind a cloud. Claypool wiped his forehead with a green handkerchief. He was in it now. Beyond the perimeters. In the village a woman nursing a baby went inside at their approach. The children stopped playing. The dogs refused to bark. Everywhere the clinging odor of charred wood and rotting fish. The patrol moved on through the trees and out into another field where two farmers, conical hats, brown faces, splay feet, turned their backs to work the hard ground with their hoes.

"Look, here they come again, so many."

"They move like apes, funny white apes."

"Don't make such a face. They will think you are a VC."

"No, I think they will take my picture."

"They are strong and healthy."

"They smell like apes."

"Look at all their big guns."

"Look at their big feet."

No one in the passing column understood a word of this dialogue, least of all Claypool. At the sound of the language he reached down to feel for the portable dictionary in his thigh pocket and tripped on a root. "Watch it," Mouth hissed. Off in the distance stretched paddies thick with shoots of green rice. A buffalo ambled through the water, a small boy clutching a stick perched on its dark back. Turquoise sky, silky clouds. A travel poster. An Occidental romance.

The patrol entered the jungle. At first Claypool was grateful for the shade. Five minutes later his uniform was heavy with sweat. He had difficulty breathing. It was like being locked in a sick room with a vaporizer jammed on high. A cloud of tiny bugs swarmed about his face, flew in and out his mouth. He spit out some, swallowed the rest. Fat drops of sweat slid across the lenses of his glasses, transforming the forest into a swirling blob of shimmery green. His pack grew heavier. The straps cut into his shoulders. His back ached. His feet hurt. He was afraid to check his watch for fear the four hours his body had ticked off were only thirty minutes by the clock. He couldn't see, he couldn't breathe. He thought he would pass out. Then everyone sat down. Claypool lay on his back staring up into the deep green canopy. He felt like one of those miniature porcelain divers fallen unnoticed in the silt of a neglected aquarium. A bird flashing blue and gold through the trees startled him for a moment. He had thought it was a VC flag. He closed his eyes. The ground was so soft, a nice warm sponge. Someone punched his shoulder.

"Get up," Mouth said.

Claypool rolled into a sitting position. Mouth was unbuttoning his shirt, Jones was pulling up his pant legs.

"What's going on?"

"Leech check," said Mouth.

"What?" said Claypool. "Where?" He yanked his own pants out of his boots. "No one told me about this." He ran both hands up and down his sticky white legs.

"Looks like one on the back of your neck," Mouth said.

"Aaaaaaaaa!" Claypool screamed, leaping to his feet. His hand touched something slimy.

"Don't do that," cautioned Jones. "You'll tear the skin."

"Get it off, get it off."

"Hold still," said Mouth. Inserted in the elastic band around his helmet was a small plastic bottle. He squeezed some liquid onto Claypool's neck.

"Is it off?"

"Yeah," said Jones, pointing to the shiny black worm writhing in the mud.

Mouth stepped on it. Blood squirted from under his boot.

"Yuck," said Claypool, rubbing his neck.

"Fucking MI," muttered Mouth.

In ten minutes they were up again, staggering through vines and humidity. Claypool started seeing creatures darting across the corners of his vision but he kept quiet. Behind his smeared glasses everything looked sinister and alive. A florist's nightmare. He concentrated on the round scuffed toes of his boots stumbling on over the undergrowth. Rhythm. If he could establish a comfortable rhythm. Then everyone sat down again. He could hear whispers, rustling movement up ahead. His finger folded around the trigger of his rifle. Heart pounding like a parade drum. "Move out." Following the words SQUEAKY CLEAN bobbing on Jones's helmet through creepers and thorns, his breath an asthmatic wheeze, stumbling surprised into a clearing arranged as a movie village.

Grass huts, coconut palm, banana trees, a stone well, a cooking pit, a dirt path running in and out spiked with booby traps. No one home. A ghost town. The open space made Claypool more nervous than the jungle. A scrawny chicken, its tail caked with filth, rushed out to greet them. Jones lowered his rifle. "No," said Sergeant Wilson. Squads of men moved quickly from hootch to hootch, probing the walls with bayonets, banging rifle butts on the earthen floors. Several of the roofs had collapsed and inside weeds grew in the bright light flooding through the holes. Food jars were overturned. A rusted Coca-Cola can rolled out onto the ground.

"I don't know," said Captain Miller to Claypool. "This was where you were supposed to strut your stuff." He unfolded a map. "And us sucking hind tit on body count. Williams, give me the damn horn." The man with the radio strapped to his back handed the captain the phone.

Captain Miller consulted the map, spoke into the phone, consulted the map again, then tossed the phone at Williams. "We're in the wrong goddamn village," he said.

Lieutenant Davis looked toward the well where some men were filling their canteens with green water. Then he turned to study the surrounding bush. "I've got a feather in my nose," he said.

"I know," replied Captain Miller, staring at the sagging hootches. "Colonel White's fingerprints are all over this operation."

Claypool edged casually away. In the event of ambush, he remembered, these people were primary targets. He found a patch of shade under a huge tree that smelled of furniture polish. What were the symptoms of heat stroke? Would the skin on his belly appear flushed or fish white? He longed for a chunk of ice. To suck on like candy. To rub against his steaming face. He couldn't understand how the others were able to go on.

"You dropped this," said Mouth, holding out a wad of damp green cloth.

"Thanks." Claypool shoved the handkerchief into his back pocket.

"Lucky I found it. They could've used that rag to sic the dogs on you."

"Who?"

Mouth walked away. "Fucking MI."

The CO was still in a huddle with his subordinates. After hours of tramping the bush his helmet still sat perfectly centered upon his head. It must have been glued there after having first been adjusted with a carpenter's level. The man even sweated like an officer, neat half moons under his arms, a large cross imprinted on his back. Claypool heard a Colonel White's name mentioned several times. Then Brown came up to report the results of the search: no weapons, no food, no tunnels. It was time to go. As the group broke up the chicken reappeared, walked over to Captain Miller and stood solemnly at his side in a hen's parody of attention.

"Looks like you got a friend," declared Sergeant Wilson.

"He knows leadership qualities when he sees them."

Lieutenant Davis dropped to one knee, staring at the bird's head. "This chicken is blind," he said.

Several men crowded around for a look. The left eye was indeed fogged over, a tiny gray marble.

"That's okay, sir," said Sergeant Wilson. "One eye is still good."

"A rare tribute," replied the captain, "from a one-eyed gook chicken."

Brown was on his knees, stroking the bird's yellow back. "Let's take him with us."

"No pets on patrol," said the captain. "Never know, he might be working for the other side."

But when the company started to move out the chicken followed.

"Sergeant," said Captain Miller.

Flapping his arms, Sergeant Wilson chased the bird back into the village, answering squawk with squawk. He turned to go. The bird followed. He threw a rock. The bird looked at him, then stepped closer. Sergeant Wilson lunged forward, seized the bird and with one deft twist broke its neck and tossed the carcass into the dust like a wet towel.

Claypool studiously wiped his glasses with a corner of his shirt. Wiped and wiped. He couldn't see a thing without them.

The patrol crossed a field of long dry grass and reentered the forest. Noon to twilight. The change was that abrupt. Like passing out or entering a cave. There should have been bats hanging down and flitting about. Vampire bats. Rotten jungle odor pitched camp high up in the nostrils. Lumps of dog shit turning white in a damp basement. Water dripped from every leaf tip though it hadn't rained in weeks. The mud was slippery with moss or algae. In the broken light falling through the tiers of vegetation massed above their heads everyone's face looked green. Claypool was exhausted. The undergrowth tugged at his feet. He was experiencing difficulty staying erect. When they stopped for breaks his body seemed to keep moving. Except for the chop of machetes and the occasional stumble or curse there was no sound. None. The forest generated silence. No clicking insects, screeching parrots, chattering monkeys. And the plants, the plants were all wrong. No movie had ever been made in here. Claypool recognized nothing. Had a dinosaur's head poked down between the branches he would have laughed. For a moment he lost sight of Jones, then panicked that he might be left behind, blind, dumb, dead. When he caught sight of Jones again he wanted to stick a boot up his ass. No one lived in here. No one had ever lived in here. No one had ever passed through here. Even communists must require something more than this . . . this organic inferno. Claypool ran out of water. "Fucking MI." He licked the sweat from his upper lip, which only made him thirstier. He wished he had a machete to hack with too, just for a couple minutes, he wanted to let go with his rifle, hurt those gray trunks, blast them into soft stumps, shred some leaves, tear out a hole so he could breathe. His face and arms were cut, scraped, and bitten. "Christ!" cursed Jones. "I can't fucking stand it." He pulled a long knife from a leather sheath strapped to his calf, the bright blade beaded with moisture. He reached down between his legs and sawed out the crotch of his pants. Cock and balls dangled freely, runny sores exposed to the air. "We should only be wearing paint anyway." Claypool tossed his dictionary into the bush. It had been chafing against his thigh for some time. Let the mushrooms learn Vietnamese. He began to itch. But when he scratched he made ugly red furrows down his arms, soft dirty skin rolling up under his nails. Heat steamed from the soil. The sun was green. Claypool was being baked. They were all lost. There was no way out. Endless circles. Gnawing on bark. Shooting each other over the last stagnant drop of the last canteen. Flesh finally eaten by the plants. Snakes slithering in and out of their skulls. He didn't want to die. He wasn't supposed to be here. He was punched from behind. Sprawled on his nose into the tanglewood. Flash. Boom. What happened? "I can't see," someone was crying, "I can't fucking SEE!" Claypool shut his eyes and squeezed his asshole as tightly as he could. Here it was. The Big Scene. Yells. Screams. Exploding metal. Guns were barking, stuttering, coughing except that no human or animal had ever made sounds like these. Something sharp hit him in the side. He reached down to feel for the blood. "Your weapon," Mouth shouted, shoving the rifle into his ribs. What was he supposed to do with it? There was nothing to see, nothing to shoot at. Bullets zipped overhead. There was a second explosion. The ground shook. He didn't know whether those were mines or grenades or artillery shells or mortar rounds or bombs. "One six two six one niner," Captain Miller shouted, ". . . six one niner!" A confetti of wood chips and leaf fragments cascaded onto Claypool's back. He didn't know what he was supposed to do. He curled up as round and small as he could get and he screamed, let it all come loose, guts in a flutter, wind howling through his chest. When he opened his eyes, Brown was lying across from him taking his picture. Brown lowered the camera, held up a hand with thumb and forefinger forming an O, and his jaw disappeared, yanked away by a hidden wire. Brown fell over, hands clutching his throat. He couldn't talk or scream. He gurgled. He gurgled on and on until Claypool wished he would die. Why wasn't someone helping Brown? Where was Mouth, his protection? He looked behind him. Jones was lying there on his side, back to Claypool, shirt stretched tightly across his shoulders where blood beaded through the green stitching like rain on a window screen. Like a sweat stain, just like a sweat stain. His helmet lay uselessly on the ground beside him, SQUEAKY CLEAN upside down. Claypool wished he had asked him what those words meant. Shrieks fell from the sky. The air brightened. The earth trembled. Claypool could see the trees rocking back and forth. Holes were being opened in the jungle. He held onto his knees and cried. Then

Mouth was there again, pounding on him. He tried to hit back. Someone started screaming off in the bush in front of them. Mouth leaped up, crashed into the jungle. For the first time Claypool was able to distinguish the sound of M-16s cracking all around him. Sergeant Wilson scurried in on hands and knees. "Where's Mouth?" he shouted. Face smeared with mud the color and texture of human shit. Blood dribbling out of one ear. Claypool pointed into the forest. "Jesus Christ." Brown was bubbling quietly. "Help that man. Jesus Christ." Claypool obediently crawled over to Brown. He couldn't look above the chest. What was he to do? He felt for Brown's pulse but already the arm was cold, a freezing subzero cold that attached itself to Claypool's skin, he jerked his hand away but it was too late, the cold was on his fingers, it was in them deep as bone, moving up his own arm, his wrist, his elbow, past the shoulder down into his chest. Claypool started to shake. He shivered, he had the chills, even his sweat turning icy as he sat there between Brown's jaw and Jones's back waiting for winter. The rifle fire stopped. Silence. A hive of pain. Lieutenant Davis ran back in a crouch to ask, "Where's the sarge?" Claypool pointed and the lieutenant gave him an odd look. "Kill me," someone screamed, "don't leave me like this, please." Someone else was crying loudly in shudders rapid as Claypool's own, which he now thought were probably the incipient symptoms of malarial fever. Suddenly the bushes erupted into noise and motion. Claypool didn't move, he simply sat there alone in a tangle of weeds that had been his home forever and waited for whatever it was to emerge and do whatever it had to do to him. It was Sergeant Wilson dragging Mouth out of the jungle. Mouth no longer had any legs. How convenient, thought Claypool, legs were so heavy, no one should be required to carry anybody with legs.

Then Claypool was standing with the rest of the company in a ruined corn field surrounded by dead stalks. His eyes were blinking. The sunlight was dazzling. Everyone seemed to be waiting for something. Johnson was drinking from his canteen when his face froze, his mouth opened, and blood came pouring down his chin, soaking into his shirt. He laughed at Claypool. "Kool-Aid," he said and took another swallow. Claypool couldn't stop blinking.

Then, instead of precipitation, the sky brought helicopters and after everyone's jaws and backs and legs had been loaded on, Lieutenant Davis helped Claypool aboard saying, "Guess we really didn't need you after all," as the helicopter sprang upward from the revolving ground piled high with green mountains Claypool stared at for some time before realizing that the snow on their peaks was only clouds. Then the door gunner leaned over and, shouting above the engine noise, offered Claypool a hundred bucks for the camera around his neck. His girl had been begging him for months, she wanted to see some photographs of what it was really like.

In any other war Wendell Payne would have been instantly recognizable as the goldbrick with the thick money belt (easy loans to close friends at special interest), the one with the cap on backward catcher-style and the pile of chips and bills spreading beneath the hand holding the flush and the suspiciously uncanny luck. In this war he was making a movie.

"Okay, listen up!" Wendell shouted through a battery-powered loudspeaker. "I want all the Americans over here on this side of the bunker," pointing the broken half of a meter stick he handled like a riding crop, "and all you VC out there in the field."

He cracked the stick against the rim of the loudspeaker.

"VCs, be generous with the camouflage paint. I don't want to see any white skin."

He slapped the stick against his thigh.

"Are we ready? Hell for leather now. I want controlled insane hysteria."

Crack.

"Go ahead, people, laugh your heads off, you want to laugh, I'll shoot laughing, if all you want to give me today is a field of laughing painted people I'll take that, I'll use it, must be something I can do with it."

Slap.

"Let's go, let's go, another hour and all the good light is gone."

Crack.

Today Wendell was staging a minor ground attack upon the unit compound. Lying on his stomach on the floor of the guard tower, his assistant Vegetable holding his legs, he wanted to shoot from directly overhead as his VC stormed the bunker below. He envisioned the clash of bodies as a ripple, a repulse, a sweep, and a release, a collision of line, a resolution of tension. He wanted grace and beauty of movement, he wanted to see a spring flower open and quietly close. He wanted choreography, a dance of death.

"Action!" he screamed, hanging out into space over his viewfinder.

Motion and light poured through the lens, the black chamber, the speeding film, and stopped against the backs of his eyes. "Chinese fire drill," he muttered, already mentally editing today's incoherency into harmonious design. He'd probably be up all night.

This movie was the latest and certainly most obsessive in a series of projects that had, to the displeasure of several superiors, diverted Payne's energies so thoroughly he could rarely be found on the set of the real war. In fact, the war and Wendell's duties pertaining to it seemed to be at best props, at worst temporary hindrances to his continuous unfolding delight in the toylike mechanisms of his own mind. Wendell often gave the impression of having wandered onto the wrong bus somewhere, and, finding himself uniformed in Southeast Asia, had hardly paused to express annoyance before carrying on with his life much as he would have in another time, another place. To Captain DeLong, his section chief, Wendell was just one of the loose wheels occasionally thrown off by the Green Machine as it lumbered through the soggy unmapped waste of this unfortunate war.

His first project, begun only days after his arrival, had been the creation of the famous all-star rodent circus, a warren of cages constructed from pilfered wire and ammunition crates and stocked with dozens of unsavory-looking black rats he trained to fight for sport and gambling or to run through mazes equipped with no-no panels of flattened C-ration cans connected to jeep batteries. The show was forced to strike its tent one night when a starlite scope in the perimeter tower detected movement in the wire and bunkers were alerted, machine guns manned. The flares sputtering overhead turned the VC shadow into a frozen Wendell, crouched in surprise, a trap in each hand. On the wall of his room now hung a black-bordered photograph of him emptying a sack of poisoned little bodies into a Dempsey Dumpster.

His second project was made possible by "borrowing" electronic parts from the signal shop where he ostensibly worked. Cages, rat ring, and maze were soon replaced by colored wire, tubes, transistors, circuit boards, instrument panels all soldered together until the crammed room resembled a cockpit to the moon. At night people gathered on the floor while Wendell plugged in some plugs, switched on some switches, and tubes glowed, lights blinked, as a series of unearthly sounds escaped from huge stereo speakers placed at intervals about the walls—mercury dripping from a faucet, galactic winds, ball bearings rolling across the floor of a vacuum—a sort of sonic doodling. Fans were entranced for hours, Wendell's Thing, they called it. This was also the period when Wendell himself began to be known everywhere as weird.

Then he got his camera, lost interest in his Thing, and suddenly wherever Colonel Dauer went there was Wendell hunched behind a lens. *The War In Vietnam*, he called it, *Leadership In Action.* How he had managed to convince the CO, a notably saturnine man, of the pleasures of cinéma vérité was a mystery no one understood. There had always been rumors of a book, a little black book in which were recorded certain violations flagrant and minor of military regs concerning blackmarket activity, illegal equipment use, doctored files, et cetera, et cetera, complete with dates, times, names of witnesses, but there was an apocryphal black book in every unit and as far as anyone could determine only one genuine Wendell in all MACV. When questioned about his Svengali-like power over immediate superiors, Wendell's reply was, "I took a lot of crystal in LA back in 'sixty-seven." No one knew what that meant. The unit's response to these Delphic utterances, to Wendell himself, was a curious confusion of wonder and discomfort similar to the emotion once inspired by the village idiot. Kraft believed he was a genius. "He's not a serious person," said Simon. The problem was that Wendell's edges remained perpetually, maddeningly out of focus: brilliant or dull? sincere or deluded? talent or fraud? Another edge: as a sound engineer prior to his induction Wendell Payne had helped mix the *Are You Experienced?* album, an achievement regarded by most of the enlisted men as being equal to successfully managing a presidential campaign. He certainly seemed to possess the electronics knowledge and he had amazing tales of Hendrix, lost, rapt, fingers dancing on wires into paradise—but who could know, who could be sure?

Meanwhile, Wendell was having an exhilarating time. As the colonel's official photographer he occupied a cozy position warmed by the artificial light of bureaucratic power. Temporarily freed from the tedium of routine duty he lived like the colonel himself, traveling about I Corps in guarded comfort, dining in country-club splendor, making influential friends among the field grades, a heady style spiced by that journalistic sense of being on the inside, in the know, privy to information mortals didn't have, and then too, to have all this high life strangely negated by the very act, filming, which had given access to it, so that at the same moment Wendell was luxuriating in his luck he could also take delight in the fact that he was and always would be a hopeless outsider.

In a month he was bored. The colonel, his face, his mannerisms, the way he sipped his wine, had begun to depress. Wendell's camera began to stray. Quite often the colonel, midway through a pulse-quickening address to the troops, would look up expecting to see the familiar eye of the lens staring blankly back and instead, with dismay, discover it inspecting some rotting telephone pole, meaningless puddles in the road, the undistinguished profile of some private's face. "Backgrounding," Wendell explained. "Objective correlatives, you know." The colonel didn't know but his young man seemed so capable, so assuring. By the time the Old

Man died his unexpected end barely affected the course of what was now The Movie. His story had become only one strand in a coil that would embrace the complete complexity of the American experience in Southeast Asia. Wendell photographed indiscriminately, confident that form, like invisible writing exposed to a flame, would reveal itself beneath the heat of his talent. For a couple days he even followed Thai around on his hands and knees for a short section entitled *The War In Vietnam: A Dog's Point Of View*.

Company clown was a role that had already taken shape between himself and the rest of the unit before Wendell, gauging its possibilities, simply stepped forward into it, adding flesh to shadow, thereby multiplying his intensity in accordance with that peculiar arithmetic of human behavior, which often yields the largest sums to the smallest fractions of personality. As a caricature he was granted a personal freedom "normal people" were not. No one else in the unit was permitted to spend so much public time on private matters doing exactly as he pleased. The price for such exemption, however, was a frequent lapse of sympathy and a loosing of laughter. Several of his peers, Griffin and Trips included, suspected that his eccentricity was only a mask, a white boy's military version of the antebellum black's Uncle Tom. They had a phrase for it: "You know Wendell," chuckling good-naturedly over his latest antics. Payne himself used the phrase, had invented it in fact, to deal specifically with the impossible demands of his immediate superior in the signal shop, Sergeant Anstin. "Okay, I give up, just where have you been for the last day and a half?" Smile. Shrug. "You know Wendell."

Up on the guard tower Wendell pleaded through the loudspeaker for one last take. "C'mon team, before it's too dark." Out in the field his "actors," booing and jeering, began to disperse. "Thank you," shouted Wendell. "Thank you for your patience and wholehearted cooperation." A hand disappearing around a hootch corner showed him a single greasy finger.

He sent Vegetable to drop off today's film with Speed Graphic, his man in the photo lab, and then, portable loudspeaker in one hand, empty Beaulieu camera in the other, Wendell trudged through the sand to the silence of his room. There he stretched out on his bunk, a beaded can of cold pop pressed to his forehead. A vague flylike thought buzzed through his preoccupations. Had Sergeant Anstin told him to do something today, some specific what? Check the wiring in the mess hall? Sort through the parts box in the radar trailer? Test the VHF circuits on one-seven? Hadn't he done those jobs? The thought flew away. Military trivia. Impedimenta, up to our asshole in impedimenta. The army nagged without interruption like someone you borrowed money from once and paid back long ago but neither had had enough sense to retain a proper receipt. Nagged until artistic breakthroughs collapsed into fuck-ups, the most carefully planned scene fell apart in hopeless tatters, streaks of boredom staining the celluloid like plastic fingers scratching at a closed window. And it got inside all the moving parts like the sand in his camera always working to stop the advance, to freeze the action. Boredom. From the thigh pocket of his fatigues he extracted a well-worn paperback copy of Ayn Rand's *Atlas Shrugged*, front and back covers both gone, the book itself only two-thirds its original size. When Wendell read he tore off each page as he finished, dropping it wherever he happened to be. The densest concentrations, modest piles on the floor beside his chair, his bunk, were swept up daily by the hootch maid, but page after page had been found throughout the unit, I Corps, all of South Vietnam: in the latrine, the mess hall, the EM club, the chapel, the hangar, the detention cells, the supply room, in the bunkers, on the floors of cockpits, in air terminals up and down the coast, on helicopters, C-130s, Cobras, Beavers, Birddogs, the whole zoo of military aircraft, page one hundred and eighty-seven was even rolled up and smoked one desperate night. Once a couple loose pages got sucked up into the right engine of one-nine and Sergeant Anstin had to be restrained, his swollen face contorted into obscenity and a threatened legal reprimand which never did materialize framed in the viewfinder backing steadily away. Taken slowly, a few pages a day, the book, thick as a flak vest still, could last weeks, months, perhaps the whole tour, a further antidote against the boredom real as the enemy out there in the weeds. His bed began to shudder as the local artillery commenced its regular early evening barrage. The book jiggled between his hands but he read on, wholly absorbed in the text, thinking, yes, reason is happiness, selfishness is virtue, A is A.

At night Griffin burned classified trash. An unusually popular detail. He never lacked help, even at two in the morning. Every night, a stapled bag of secrets tucked under each arm, he'd lead a modest procession out behind the intelligence hut to the Restricted Area incinerator, a converted fifty-gallon drum with a hole cut in its side and mounted on waist-high metal legs. There a half dozen or so security-cleared "assistants" crowded around the drum, watching Griffin unroll reels of aerial film into the flames. The acetate bubbled and sizzled. Oily smoke moved in clouds over the sleeping company, sprinkling rooftops with black snow, the acrid scent also masking the classified odor of burning dope. The pleasures of combustion. Once Griffin burned so much trash he lost his balance on the wooden sidewalk, fell off a board laughing into the sand, too giddy to stand up; once he tossed in a handful of money to see what that felt like; once he saw trees shrieking in the fire. Sometimes they'd take turns spitting against the drum, the saliva hissing like snakes as it went to steam. Personal habits were going up in smoke too, rules Griffin had formulated to ease him through his tour. For instance, he wasn't supposed to incinerate until his desk work was done; but one exceptionally tedious night it had suddenly seemed perfectly reasonable, the height of clarity, to go outside rather than to stay in plotting targets and reading out infrared missions. Afterward, his self seemed to sit easier inside his body, his body to fit more comfortably inside the uniform as though certain restraints had been lifted, certain straps loosened. Sometimes now he even forgot there was a uniform, although those rare occasions still managed to frighten him; he preferred a more orderly madness, a middle class ecstasy you could stroll in and out of at your leisure; deep sofas, pile carpeting, the lounge chair in front of the TV while the wallpaper crawled with unpatented colors, the mirrors screamed, demons danced in circles past the windows. Tonight there was no hysteria. He simply felt good. Cross had brought a ring of sausage and a box of Ritz crackers. Wurlitzer was retelling the famous story of Captain Ferris and the SAM missile. Vegetable had a canteen full of cockroaches he had trapped in his room and was dropping them, one by one, into the singing incinerator. His friends. The Thai sticks tasted of burnt roses. The stars strobed in unison across the heavens. Mere breathing was a sensual event. The flames crackled. He felt himself blacken around the edges, begin to melt. For one whole hour he was in love with Vietnam. Until all the secrets turned to ash.

Now if he was careful he could carry this head through the remainder of his work shift and then on out into dreamland. Guaranteed unconsciousness. Better than Doc's sleeping pills. He mustn't rush, though, or get upset, must guard against molestations. Carefully he made his way back to the office. He spoke to no one. At his desk he hunched over the map boards, a parody of concentration, Do Not Disturb, I've got a soufflé cooling in here. It was slow work now, requiring twice the time it would have taken without an incinerator visit. The dots on the maps kept shifting around like checker pieces. Careful, careful. Maintain. If tomorrow the recon pilots missed their targets by a grid square or two, well, close enough for government work. Let the damn planes go where they would. He'd dipsy-doodle on back to his room. Where the brownies were.

He fell into bed, seeing himself falling in multiple selves, a fan of after-images, slices from the reality sausage slipping in succession into the original body now prone on the mattress. Swoon. Unspeakable bliss. If he weren't so tired he'd attempt a replay.

Griffin liked to fall when he was stoned. He liked to fall like a stone.

He was in New England, red houses, white rocks, cold drafts sliding over the homemade quilt atop the maple fourposter when the hootch door opened, rubber shower thongs slapped down the narrow hallway, the door banged shut. Mamasan. His ancient hootch maid. The other women had all been given Western names like Suzi or Nan or Molly, but she was old and balding and half deaf and stubbornly herself. She remained Mamasan. Griffin's nose flooded with menthol. When she was sick she wore around her neck a packet of herbs strong enough to stun a polar bear. Griffin buried his face in the pillow. Her arrival meant it must be eight or eight-thirty and he wasn't asleep yet. The increase in temperature was already unpleasantly apparent. If he could doze off now he might be able to sneak in a couple hours sleep before the climbing sun transformed his room into a sauna. He turned to the wall and closed his eyes. A jolly snowman in scarf and top hat bent over, shot him a round icy moon. The door to his room quietly opened and, lying still, breathing regularly, he heard: the sighing of Mamasan, her constant sigh, the weary exhalation of Asia, a sound she must practice nights; the cracking of her brittle knees, calcium fragile as dry chicken bones; sigh; the rustle of material, shirts and pants, a zipper lightly scraping across the floor, laundry being gathered; sigh; the door opening, the door closing, quietly, quietly; the sandpapery shuffle of her bare feet moving on into Simon's room; sigh; the creaking of bedsprings. The creaking of. The door quietly. What the hell was she doing? Then he knew. Griffin rolled over and leaned out of his bunk, hands braced against the floor. For once a petty military regulation proved useful. The army fire code decreed that partitions between rooms descend no farther than two feet from the floor. Through this space Griffin had a clear view of Mamasan perched on Simon's bunk, his own pants across her lap, a wad of MPC in one hand, his elephant leather wallet in the other. He was sober in an instant. Several straps snapped loose. He screamed. "What you do?" Mamasan leaped off the bed as though struck. Bills fluttered through the air. "What you do? What you do?" Griffin couldn't stop screaming. Mamasan stooped over, scrambling for the money as quickly as she could. She neither replied to Griffin nor looked in his direction. Her body was shaking so severely she resembled a child's windup toy. Griffin didn't care. He was bouncing up and down on his hands, a maniac's push-ups. His face was flushed. His eyes bulged. "What you do? What you do? Get in here! Get in here right now!" He sat back up in bed and waited. He was trembling too. He wanted to frighten her so badly she would never sigh in his presence again. He wanted to overwhelm her with intimidation. He wanted her to believe she would suffer obscene technological torment for this transgression. He wanted her to think she would lose her job. Tossed off the gravy train. No more castoff combat boots. No more complimentary drinks at the NCO club. The door creaked open and she approached his bed, thrusting pants and money stiffly out before her. She began to jabber in Vietnamese. "What you do?" Griffin shouted. Her body shook with pathetic vigor. She hastily stuffed the ball of money in a pocket and laid the pants back on Griffin's shelf. Then, holding up her hands, fingers wide, she waved them around, displaying palms and backs like a stage magician. "What you do?" Griffin knew she was the only hootch maid who understood no English beyond "Hey you" and "Okay" but he was upset, he wanted an explanation. Her Vietnamese turned shrill, quavered toward tears. She lifted her blouse, showed her body naked of money, shriveled breasts, cracked nipples, shiny yellow scars across her wrinkled waist. She started to pull down her pants. Griffin impatiently waved a hand. "No," he said, "I don't need to see your dried up cunt." He wasn't screaming any longer. He was muted with shame. Look at this woman. What was he doing? He pulled the pants into bed with him and counted the money. Two hundred and forty dollars. Twelve twenties. Had there been more? Were there a couple bills shoved up her snatch? He didn't care. His anger had flared and died. "Get out," he said, "go on, you get out of here." She was chattering still, pointing now at Griffin's locker, now to the pants, shaking a horny finger in his face. Then he realized what she was doing: she was scolding him, scolding him like a mother, the tone of her voice, her gestures, saying to him, you stupid soldier, take care of your belongings, lock your valuables away like one who has respect for himself and his property, I don't enjoy such humiliation, I do not steal happily, I am so frightened, you ignorant boy. "Yes, yes," said Griffin, "now go, go on." She backed through the door, bowing as deeply as her aged body would allow, unable to conceal completely the anger in her eyes. Griffin turned away. He couldn't stand looking at her anymore. Clever, these Orientals. The whole sorry episode was now his fault. Corruption of innocent East by boorish cash-besotted West. He could hear her sighing and muttering as she swept the hallway, the oldest, most trusted Vietnamese employed in the compound. The shock equal to learning your own mother was a petty thief. And you were to blame for her disgrace. He wanted to dash out into the hallway now, beat her black and blue with his fists, crack a couple ribs with his boot. The urgency, the strength of this impulse. What was happening to him? Totally unbuckled by noon? This wasn't the real Griffin. The real Griffin bought pencils from blind men, listened politely to old women's troubles. Where was he? What was wrong with her? Why would she jeopardize her job? She should be grateful she was working, grateful she even had an opportunity to be exposed to criminal temptation, grateful to the army of the United States whose gargantuan needs provided her with a salaried position to fill, a position she required, of course, because the armed presence of that army had also deprived her of a husband and a son and converted the family farm into a field of poisoned mud puddles.

Go and apologize.

She wouldn't understand.

Give her the whole two forty.

And reward her for stealing?

If Griffin were a white rat in a behavioral lab he would have learned all about electricity by now. He got up, put his pants in the locker, turned on the fan, and adjusted it to aim directly at his head. The wind was warm. He tossed restlessly from side to side. Quite a low point performance today. Dropping back into the pack in the competition for the Hands Across The Water Award. At last, after several changes, he discovered a posture that enabled him to achieve a state of semiconsciousness that, while not exactly genuine sleep, would do for the moment, was close enough for government work.

He opened his eyes, aware at once he had been watched. Who? What? She was squatting patiently on the floor, arms resting easily across her knees, waiting for the bus that would carry her off to a stop only slightly less boring than this one. All Vietnamese squatted like this. No bus ever arrived. How many disagreeable sleeping habits of his had she noticed? The drool on the pillow, the unconscious hand in his shorts? He recognized her immediately, of course, Missy Lee, the interpreters' hootch maid. Come to case the joint for the next attempt. The locker was still secure, the key still chained around his neck.

"Yes?" inquired Griffin.

Her face closed in a frown. "You no want Missy Lee?"

"No, thank you," he replied. "My room's already been cleaned out once this morning."

She stood up. "We make fuck," she said. Her eyes the glossy black of charred cardboard.

Griffin laughed. It wouldn't have been the first time a girl had been sent into somebody's bed for a joke. There was the memorable night Trips paid Suzi, EM club bar girl and resident whore, three dollars to take off her clothes and crawl into the bunk of Private Edwin Norris, supply room incompetent and resident virgin. Poor Norris had bolted upright, clutching his sheets. "Woman," he'd shrieked, "have you no shame?" The laughter still echoed. Missy Lee, though, never joked; she performed her housekeeping duties with the sour efficient disposition of a head nurse. Her age, like that of so many Orientals, was difficult for foreigners to guess; she might have been twelve, she might have been thirty. Still, she had about her the look of a daughter, of someone whose family ties were sufficiently complex that the idea of sex with her seemed ringed with ancient taboo. Everyone in the company wanted to get inside her pants as soon as possible.

On hot mornings, unable to sleep, Griffin often sat on the hootch steps and watched her hanging laundry across a string of commo wire. She'd have to strain to reach, lifting onto bare toes, arms outstretched, slender body leaning gracefully forward as if poised for flight, the gusts of wind tightening her loose clothing around the curves of her buttocks, the lines of her thighs, the long black hair shining down her back. He'd watch until she was just a pair of legs behind a curtain of wet fatigues.

Now she sat beside him on the bed.

"What are you doing?"

"You make fuck with me." One hand scratching his back, the other fumbling across his thigh. His excitement readily apparent. She smiled. Her teeth dazzling as snow. "We make fuck now, okay?"

What was it she wanted? Money? food? stereo tapes? She need only ask. Or was she VC, an avenging seductress intent on information and reprisal? What would be the price of this visit? Her hand burrowed into his crotch. He opened his legs.

"Sure," he replied.

There was also the less paranoid possibility she simply liked him.

Then Missy Lee stood and with as much ceremony as if she were preparing to step into a bath she stripped off her blouse, pulled down her pants, and climbed into bed.

Griffin tried to kiss her but she refused, shaking her head no. Without a word she settled herself under him, seized his penis and began guiding him in. Griffin came all over her thigh. "I'm sorry," he stammered, wiping her with his bed sheet. She giggled. "I go now, okay?" "No," he said quickly, "please don't, not yet." He liked Missy Lee. He wanted her to like him and despite his ineptitude, the uniform he wore, the color of his skin, he knew she would if presented with a full view of the real Griffin. At least one Oriental woman today was going to experience his capacity for tenderness and understanding. He leaned forward and kissed her lightly on the shoulders. Her skin was so soft, softer than his lips. He kissed her back. Brown satin. He eased her down and began moving his mouth across her chest. Breasts the shape of bananas. A taste of salt. He sucked them clean. Beneath her passivity he detected the wary eye of a modest tension questioning each movement. Okay. He didn't know her too well either. That was what these kisses were for. But below her navel she stopped him with her hands. "We make fuck," she said firmly. "Fine," he answered. There would be no hesitations, no clumsy pauses. Carefully he climbed on top, he seemed so heavy, she so small, so alive. Once he was in he didn't ever want to leave. For a moment he just lay there, allowed himself to be buoyed by the comforting tide of her breathing. It was like coming home to a place you had forgotten you left. You were ready for a lingering visit. He moved slowly at first, edging into the current, prolonging the savor. How to be here every day. Missy Lee could meet him each morning, hands cool from wringing out the laundry. He'd get a bigger bolt for the door, more boards for the window. Naked, they'd sit in the dim light, discover with their bodies where trust began. He'd wind her hair about his penis, he'd teach her how to kiss. He'd tell no one, Their Eyes Only, a secret the war couldn't classify or burn. Later perhaps—who could know?—two seats back to The World. Suddenly all the scenery changed. Walls, banks of rubble, stands of damp forest were looming through him. What the fuck? Space telescoped away like the dropping of an elevator. Things were larger, slid further apart. She was here and now she was gone. He was lost in uncharted immensity. Frightened, compass gyrating, he went humping away. Down a tunnel toward a hope, openings, that burst of light. On and on until the glow drained off like poison. There was no exit. Her legs tightened around him and he experienced a moment of pure panic, sharp as a needle sliding under skin. Joined by the heat, friction-fused, they'd rock and roll forever, shake themselves down to bone and fear, yellow skeletons grinding mechanically in the dust. He looked down into Missy Lee's face. All expression had settled out. Her eyes locked, blind to him heaving above her, slick with sweat, ass pumping frantically. He was on a rock ledge, peering down into black pits deep as starless space, a cold shifting of voids and vertigoes, the one recognizable shape the reflection of his own head drifting over the surface like the shadow of a monstrous bird. His foot touched metal, the end of the bed frame. His penis scraped sand. He thrust again, once, twice, long threatening licks, a promise of future action, a denial of defeat, and, preparing to disengage, turned his head and saw the crack in the door and the dark curious eye peeking back at him.

"Hey!" He was up in an instant, hopping into his underwear. "Who is that?" He flung Missy Lee her clothes, hit the door in one step, forearm slamming the planks backward to miss by an inch the huddled form of Mamasan out in the hallway cringing like a wet dog. "What you do?!" Griffin shrieked. This was the absolute worst day of the war. Tonight, on his guard shift, the perimeter would be breached at last, the base overrun.

"Get in here," he ordered.

Mamasan shuffled obediently into the room. Without a pause the two women began exchanging bursts of angry Vietnamese. Missy Lee started to cry. Mamasan reached over and squeezed a pinch of skin above Missy Lee's elbow.

"What the hell's going on?" demanded Griffin.

"Mamasan say you no like Missy Lee," she said, letting the tears fall freely.

"Of course I like you. What is this?"

"Mamasan say Missy Lee make bad fuck."

He wanted to hold her, to tell her what had happened, but he couldn't trust himself yet. He felt as though he had been in an accident. "No, hey, that's not true."

Mamasan silently studied the unmade bed.

"What the hell does she care about the quality of your fucks anyway?"

"She say she lose her job."

"What?"

"She say you tell people Mamasan bad person."

"Good God." Now he understood.

"She say you tell honcho man she lose her job."

Worse than learning your mother was a thief. She was a pimp, too.

"I won't tell anyone," said Griffin. "I promise."

The girl spoke to Mamasan who listened without comment. She bowed once to Griffin and left the room.

"Mamasan no steal," said Missy Lee. "Mamasan good worker."

"Yes," replied Griffin. "She good worker." He sat on the bed. He was tired. If he could find a cool bunker . . .

"I go now," said Missy Lee.

"Fine. You go."

"You good man."

"I don't think so."

She assumed an expression of mock surprise. "Yes," she said emphatically. "You good man. You make family very happy."

"What family?"

Should he offer her a twenty? Would she be pleased or insulted? His mind was too weary to explore consequences. Let her ask.

"Mamasan's family."

American military uniforms should be woven with money, fives, tens, twenties, stitched into combat durable shirts and pants, all most civilians saw anyway: a fool wrapped in cash.

"Wait a minute. *Whose* family?"

The girl looked puzzled. "Mamasan's family," she said.

Griffin pointed at her, then toward the door. "Is Mamasan *your* Mamasan?"

"Oh yes," she answered, smiling, nodding eagerly. "She number one Mamasan."

"Number one." Of course. What else was a daughter to think?

How much innocence went to make up this person he imagined was himself, how much remained to be shredded?

"Yes, she work very hard."

"Go on, Missy Lee, you go back to your work, too."

She nodded and slipped out the door.

Griffin sat on the edge of his bed, watching his bare feet roll back and forth over the grains of sand on the floor. As a kid he often perched on a warm dock, dangling his legs above the cool water of a forest lake. Where the fish leaped like silver birds and agile water bugs skimmed the bright surface. A million years ago. There had been terrible heat in those summers too but relief was always at your feet, spreading out blue to a pine horizon. He cried when he had to go home. Today, those fish, their brains pickled in pollution, flopped in the sun until they died. He reached for a corner of the sheet to wipe his dripping forehead and touched something clammy. He had to get out of here. He stood up, pulled on his clothes. For three days Weird Wendell had been filming in the dispensary, with the enthusiastic cooperation of Flight Surgeon Beams, the crucial medical scene in which wounded dozens in various degrees of distress were miraculously repaired by a heroical surgical team dressed in greasy coveralls and gorilla masks. Griffin could be a casualty.

He opened the hootch door on a collection of smirks. His friends. Gathered outside like a gang of teenage virgins.

"Who would have guessed," exclaimed Trips, "that you'd be the first to pop Missy Lee. How was she?"

Griffin carefully descended the wooden steps. How long had they been out here, moist lips, cocked ears? He understood now about long-range reconnaissance patrols: deep in the bush were fatigue, terror, the possibility of death, but also clearings of privacy. He looked around. They were waiting. He smiled. "Best I ever had," he replied, already moving through the laughter, the pats on the back, not even bothering to turn or pause but walking away as he said, "And you know, she never once asked me to take her to America."

Cheers. Laughter. Whoops of delight.

You shits. You fucking shits.

Dear Ma and Pa,

I'm learning how to play the harmonica. My first tune—"Row, Row, Row Your Boat." Last night a few of the guys gathered in my room to share some conversation and that tin of chocolate chip cookies (Thanks Mom) when Sam, you remember Sam? He's the boy from Arkansas who stands guard duty in his bare feet despite the danger of snake bite. Anyway, he pulled out this mouth harp (another word for harmonica) and started playing a rendition of "Shortening Bread" that was absolutely amazing. I never realized what a rich sound you could get out of these things. He's the one who's teaching me.

Sometimes I think it's moments like last night that redeem the other times of this awful war.

I try to keep busy but seems like these days never want to end. Sometimes the boredom is so terrible it's enough to make one wish for a little excitement, not too much though, I know how something like that would worry the both of you so.

I guess that's all for now. It must be beautiful back home now. At night when I close my eyes I see snow on our roof. Ah well, next season I'll be there. Take care of yourselves and please don't worry about me. See you in 203.

Love,
Lew

P.S. The other night one of our sergeants went crazy from tension and started running around screaming and shooting at people with his pistol until the OD hit him over the head with an entrenching tool. Lucky there was no one seriously hurt.

Meditation in Green: 9

In the morning dew condenses on the spiky flowerlike knots of metal arranged in regular intervals along the wire fence surrounding them. The mountains appear huge and blue in the far distance.

She doesn't feel well today. She misses home, not home as it is now, but home as it was then, in the time of the Stone Buffalo. Bieng-the-Golden-Eye was still chief then and even though Ndoong-the-Son took his own life near the Water-of-the-Elephant's-Trunk and everyone was sad for so long the Spirits had not run away yet and the land talked back and The Jar was always full. If all the soldiers would only . . .

She heard stirring in the hootch behind her. She recognized the voices of Mae-Jieng and Dur-the-Widow already arguing over the metal spoon. She sighed, her breath momentarily visible in the cool air. Their quarrels made her tired. If the guards heard them they would rush in and beat up some people even before the counting and the eating of the morning rice. She was afraid of the Vietnamese and she hated them very much. They laughed and called the Montagnards "monkeys." Then they took out their sticks and beat somebody. They beat somebody every day unless the American Whites came and stopped them. The American Whites were a mystery, sometimes friendly and nice, sometimes angry and terrifying. It was their machines that had dropped the Medicine Cloud into the Forest of the Singing Tigers the summer of the Sky Sickness when the corn died and the water tasted bad, so much illness, Troo-Wan and her children died.

She can no longer hear the voices inside so the argument must have ended. Maybe today there will be no beating. She has heard that trucks are coming to take them to another camp. She hopes there will be a doctor there. Her belly has begun to ache. She is afraid of the pain and wishes her husband Bbaang had not gone away with the Green Hats. Maybe he will be in the new camp. Her belly aches. She is afraid of this baby. She feels something move inside her and she touches herself. Her fingers come away wet. She has begun to bleed.

"You sounded like *The Return of the Mummy* coming up the stairs," I said. "I was ready to pile furniture behind the door."

"You look utterly devolved," said Huey. She had on a Tibetan goatskin cap pulled down over her ears, a black leather jacket, purple pants, and tall boots. She stood in the doorway, studying me for a moment. "Okay, where is he?"

"I haven't seen him in days. Honest. Three days." I held up fingers. "Count 'em."

She stepped warily into the room. "I can feel his presence. It hangs about like greasy smoke. It clings."

"Yes, well, there have been a couple 'incidents' since last we spoke."

"Let me sit down."

"Trips found Sergeant Anstin and is at present feverishly engaged in plotting against the man's sanity and life. I, on the other hand, have begun hallucinating freely, even during daylight hours."

"What a pair."

"The Aquarian Abbott and Costello."

"I thought you had turned over a new leaf."

"Apparently it had bugs on the bottom."

She smiled. Dimples and the chipped tooth. I loved that tooth.

"At least your eyes, I see, are relatively clear."

"Walden ponds of limpidity."

"What's this head business?"

"My botanical life has become a shade unruly. Things grow whether I want them to or not. I try to pretend not to notice. They keep growing. Now I'm trying to pretend to be used to them. Motley faces gloating off the walls, broad green fingers reaching out. I don't know what's gone wrong. I have a session with Arden next week."

"I knew this would happen sooner or later, stuff growing right out of you, you've always been so full of shit."

"Everyone is so sympathetic."

"People in your condition should not be indulged."

"What condition is that?"

"Vegetopsychosis. Donahue did an hour on it last month."

"Did you know your eyes have got these soft maroon crescents under them?"

"A new look I'm experimenting with. Haute Fatigue. The fashion for today's up-to-the-minute woman."

"Like you've had an injection under each lid."

"A bitch of a week. I've an 'incident' to report, too. You know the world goes on out there . . ."

"Coherent as a stroke victim."

". . . yes, and hemorrhaging is everywhere. This is a story from work. Did you catch me on TV Monday?"

"Trips and I were at a Marshall Thompson film festival. You were on television?"

"Channel 4 Action News."

"Someone planted a bomb at the welfare office."

"No, not yet."

"Your supervisor leaped from her window."

"Don't we wish."

"Is this a tale of woe and desperation? You know how much I like those."

"You'll be in ecstasy over Altoona Brown."

"Altoona?"

"She has a brother Scranton."

"And a sister Towanda."

"How did you know?"

"It's one of my favorite states."

"Mrs. Brown is a remarkable woman. She's got eight kids seven months to nineteen years. She's got arthritis, bad teeth, and a dream she will meet a man at the laundromat who's got a bed and money she can share. She hasn't got a job or a live-in husband.

Anyway, last Monday Charles, the father of at least half the children—she can't be more specific as to number—showed up at the door, knocked her down, stole every cent in the house, which was every cent she had, and left threatening to return at the end of the week for more. She didn't know what to do. That night Charles broke in, locked her in the bedroom with him, and apparently initiated a resumption of conjugal activity. In the morning she called me to ask for money. I told her if she came down to the office, filled out some forms, we could probably give her some food stamps and pay her utility bills. But no cash. Charles got on the phone. He said no one was leaving the apartment until he got some money, the woman and the kids were getting free money and he, who hadn't had a job in six years and couldn't get one because of a poor work record which wasn't his fault at all but was due to his liver that had had jaundice when he was a poor little baby, he wanted his share too. He also said that I was a white cunt bitch. My supervisor called the police. An hour later the police called me. Mrs. Brown wished to speak with her case worker in person. I went down there and stood in front of a door while Mrs. Brown asked me to look after her children. She was certain they'd get good care from me because I wasn't one of the ones who spoke with disrespect or spied on her home. Charles yelled that I was a white cunt bitch. He told the police he wanted lots of money and for him and the woman to be flown to Algiers where Eldridge Cleaver went before God messed up his mind. There were negotiations. The police said he could have his money and plane ticket right after the hostages were released. Charles shouted out that he was going to tie up Mrs. Brown, hang her from the ceiling, and give her a spin. Whichever kid her head happened to be pointing at when she stopped, that's the first kid to go out the window. Charles was having a real good time. By midafternoon, realizing he was going nowhere, he said everyone could leave if he could just be allowed one decent meal with his wife before going off to prison. He wanted a thick porterhouse medium rare, a baked potato with sour cream, a green salad, and one bottle of Chivas Regal with ice."

"Chivas Regal?"

"International financiers sip it in magazine ads Charles had seen. The police said they'd be glad to serve him as soon as the children came out. Almost immediately there was a sound of sharp blows and Mrs. Brown began screaming. The police took down the door. Charles was standing in the middle of the room with a belt in his hand. Mrs. Brown was seated on the couch with the children gathered around her. 'I guess I'm caught,' Charles said. Everyone was smiling, even the babies. It was a big joke. All the way down the stairs and out to the wagon Charles kept asking if they'd settle for a hamburger, just one burger and a Coke, that's all he wanted before being shut away."

"Did he get it?"

"He got an official knee in the crotch."

"A great menace weighs over the city."

"So you've told me."

"There's gross vegetation coming up through the pavement, the lobsters are crawling out of their tanks at Captain Jack's Loins and Claws."

"I'll be careful."

"You're known now, you're a heroine of the evening news."

"I was on for fifteen seconds."

"Every slimy creep and cheesehead with a portable TV is gonna be after you. The Dolly Doughnut of Social Services. The phone's never gonna stop."

"I don't have a phone."

"I'll have to shadow you all over town, skulk around corners, a wrinkled trenchcoat and a rolled-up newspaper."

"Oh no you won't."

"In my pocket the hand's friend, a packed Luger."

"You see, this is what happens when that maniac hangs around. Guns, paranoia, delirium. He's gonna pop out of a closet any minute, isn't he?"

"I think he's out touring local wrecking companies. He mentioned something about the beauty of smashed windows, twisted steel. The aesthetics of junk. Salvage yards as museums."

"And where does he sleep, in a Dumpster behind a Chinese restaurant?"

"He's here, on and off."

"Why, I would like to know, is he even at large?"

"He's not as bad as you think."

"This is the guy who masturbated on the television. Right on the warm screen."

"Maybe he liked the show."

"Maybe he hated it. God, you people."

"Someone's got to be there to talk, to listen at least."

"He's a terrorist. Like Charles. He shouldn't be out on the streets."

"Who should?"

Later that night we fell into bed and learned that painted patterns on the wall were not always dependable magic. The bedclothes severed her legs. Shadows tore scoops of flesh from her side. The moonlight burned her face. Outside in the street the sirens wailed all night long.

After my return from foreign fields there were periods when things (lampshades, door knobs, bathroom mirrors) began to move with unusual velocity. The trees wriggled more than the wind required, the walls performed a visible suspiration, faces defied resolution. I stood on a long metal bridge, back braced against a concrete post, and watched the traffic until my eyes hurt and my jaw ached from the action of the chewing gum.

I borrowed Arden's car, an emerald Datsun with a comfortable defeated look despite the painted chrysanthemums growing out of the chrome strips on its doors. I never went out before dusk. The day couldn't really begin until the light had died and all the edges were gone. Then the city became a terrarium. Electrical life scurried out into the open, the exotics of artificial illumination. I cruised around for a couple hours admiring the flora, then drifted up a ramp and out onto the petrified coils of the interstates. Destination was unimportant. What mattered was rapid movement between points, traversing vast distances, intersecting possibilities. Here the only distractions were the road, the night, the wind, and those large luminous green mileage and exit signs that come up into the headlamps as if lifted by the night's pit crews.

The right foot presses into the accelerator.

The radio, glowing like a plastic saint on the dashboard, pumps out the beat and chatter of urban monsters gliding along out there beyond the highway. I hear the voices, the names, the sweet regret as one radio station fades into a penumbra of static from which another inevitably emerges. The night country howls past, the cities race across the windscreen like planets. Even the cells seem to understand they are engaged in extraordinary movement. Here is a chance to rhyme, to equal at last the incredible speed of things.

The foot rides the accelerator down to the floor.

The tires, working the road outside, pick up a rhythm from the radio, drum a rhythm onto the pavement, roll a rhythm through the body, lock a rhythm into the wheels of the head, and bam! blood explodes in the piston chambers, axles rotate along the spine, gears mesh, transmission achieved. Interstate consciousness. I could drive like this forever, swift and loose, senses drowned in a shriek, headlights boring holes in the void, because somewhere out here there must be a way home.

The minute the phone rang Major Holly knew who it was. The General had taken to calling every Tuesday morning at 1000. Today he wanted to harass him about Hamlet Evaluation figures.

"There's no consistency here, Marty, we need some g.d. consistency."

"Well, I'm afraid I don't see it that way, sir."

"Didn't think you would. What about that Fifth NVA? Any new leads?"

"The most recent is a D reliability interview with a dispossessed grandfather. I believe I sent you a copy."

"Yes, I've seen that. Well keep it cooking, Marty. The cost-benefit equation on this operation is already shot to shit."

At lunch Major Holly was informed by the mail officer that Private Franklin had received two crates of revolutionary literature from Oakland, California. Home of the Black Panthers.

In the afternoon Captain Fry demanded that one of the crew chiefs be reduced a grade for giving him the finger as he taxied out on a highly important mission.

Major Quimby sent over a message saying he couldn't possibly spare any of his men for unit guard duty, washing trucks, or any other quote yardwork unquote.

The First Sergeant reported that two of the cooks seemed to have gone AWOL.

The General called again.

The swivel on Holly's chair broke.

"This place looks worse than a ghetto," the CO informed the First Sergeant. "How's that painting coming along?"

"About half. We're waiting on another shipment of white."

"Let's get the torn sandbags on all the bunkers replaced. Looks like hell."

"Yes, sir."

"And First Sergeant."

"Sir?"

"That sign out front. Didn't I tell you to get it fixed?"

"I don't believe so, sir."

"Well, have it taken care of. 7 DAYS WITHOUT AN ACCIDENT. Must be in the double or triple digits since what?—the colonel's crash."

"Yes, sir."

"Well, count it up and get an accurate number up there. And change it daily! Let's get some pride in this outfit."

"Yes, sir."

"Let's go for the record, First Sergeant, let's kick ass in the accident department."

"Yes, sir."

One night, returning from a latrine so filthy from use and lack of water—stools stuffed to the rims with wadded paper, globs of crap—he had had to breathe through his mouth, Griffin saw them in silhouette against the dark sky perched like monkeys along the peak of the roof, three men, their backs to him.

"See no evil, huh?"

One of them turned, looking down. "Come on up," Trips invited.

Beside each hootch was a "bunker"—a section of corrugated sewer pipe buried in sandbags, the top reinforced with a piece of portable steel plating, the open ends protected by sandbag walls. Under the weight of his boots the weathered bags tore, crumbled apart. Sand slid hissing in the dark. From the top of the bunker Griffin stepped easily across onto the slanting tin roof, clambered up to the peak, and found himself a seat on one of the sodden bags that helped hold the roof on in tropical storms.

Off in the distance beyond the clustered lights of the base the smooth rock surface of night was split by—he paused to count—five magnesium flares, hung like lamps at various altitudes, each dangling on a parachute between a twisting coil of gray smoke and a cascade of sparks, artificial suns drifting down into extinction, their replacements bursting brightly into illumination further above, the whole show like a student's model of genesis and apocalypse, planets spawning and dying in unbroken succession, a parody of eternity. From below a long red line of tracer fire arced back and forth like a sluggish windshield wiper. A second red line appeared, the two swung slowly toward each other, intersected with no perceptible effect, swung slowly away.

"Wire probe?" asked Griffin.

Trips shook his head. "Too far out. Looks like Deadman's Curve again."

"Yeah," said Griffin. He knew about Deadman's Curve. The unit had lost one jeep, a deuce and a half loaded with Mohawk parts and two drivers on that blind secluded section on the road to Da Nang. That was where he had seen the three bodies flung like highway litter into the concertina-choked ditch. VC, explained Sergeant Sherbert, ambushed in their ambush. Griffin ambushed by the spectacle of his first dead. And tomorrow looked like there'd be more trash in the ditches out there where three or four red lines joined occasionally now by spurts of green weaved about like colored hoses. Two flares burst simultaneously at similar heights, moved through the smoky sky like a great pair of dragon's eyes. From where they sat the four on the roof could hear no sound except the low lawnmowerlike growl of the generators powering the installation through the night. The distant fire fight proceeded in eerie silence. It was like watching the electronic display of a fancy pinball machine on which all the bells and buzzers had been disconnected.

"God," Griffin exclaimed, "it's beautiful."

Noll turned to look him full in the face, his features breaking languidly apart into a facsimile of a grin. Griffin could see the silver flare light reflected in his shiny eyes and teeth.

"Regular Fourth of July," mumbled Trips, smoke streaming from his nostrils. He passed the weed along the roof top.

"Who's the third who sits beside you?" Griffin asked.

"Who the hell does it look like?"

"Claypool?" said Griffin, leaning forward. "Is that you?"

There was no response. The figure sat motionless as a gargoyle, his knees drawn up under his chin.

"Why doesn't he answer?"

"I'm not his goddamn mother."

There were bursts of white in series along the ground, bright rapid explosions like a string of bulbs popping one after the other.

"Those ain't machine guns," Trips said.

Noll started bouncing up and down on his hands. "Juice 'em," he shouted, "give 'em the fucking juice."

"Hey. Noll," warned Griffin, "watch it. You're gonna fall off the damn roof."

"Oh, this isn't Noll," said Trips. "This is . . ."

"Mutant Man!" cried Noll. He jumped to his feet, staggered for a moment waving his arms at the lights like a drunken conductor before falling back down again. Griffin and Trips each seized a leg, eased him into a sitting position.

"Tell Griffin about that atomic bomb you got too close to."

"It knocked me down," Noll boasted. "Knocked me down like getting a picture taken with a giant flashbulb. Pop. Bang. Sit on your butt. Every year Dad in his lawn chair laughing."

"What is he talking about?"

Just below the roof in the wall of the nearest hootch in the next row was a space in the shape of a right triangle glowing blue. Griffin remembered the day Wurlitzer had cut out the wood, nailed on the hinge. Even Death Row inmates get a window to look out of, he had said. Griffin could see right into his room. Beneath the blue light Wurlitzer was stretched out on his bunk, masturbating.

"The famous A-bomb of Lantern Park—you haven't heard? Biggest bang of the biggest fireworks extravaganza in all western New Jersey."

"Of course then I was just a kid."

"And now you're Mutant Man."

"The A-bomb and the army, man."

Trips turned toward Griffin. "Every day they made Mutant Man low-crawl for an hour around a gravel parking lot. Under the drill sergeants' cars."

"The worst was the dunes, man, the fucking dunes. What a shithole. It was so hot the lizards tried to crawl into our canteens. God, they'd run us up and down those fucking dunes until everybody was falling down and passing out and puking all over their rifles. It was bad if you went down because the sand would burn your hands. There were guys with blisters on their palms big as balloons. Once we were spread out over the dunes panting and gagging, everyone's face turning sick white when Sergeant Boley, one gung-ho asshole, going for Drill Sergeant of the Year Award and everything, starts going crazy punching and kicking, screaming fucks and shits at everybody in his platoon. He stomped on one guy so hard it busted a kidney or something and they gave him a medical discharge."

"Lucky fucker," said Trips.

"If you're too psychotic for the infantry," said Griffin, "they make you a drill sergeant." The flares were still blossoming and fading. Tracer fire streamed out like neon tubes. There was no sign of an early finale. Griffin began to wonder if this was one of those shows in which the audience would be required to participate.

"Fucking Basic," Trips said. "We had a guy, dumb sorry-ass bastard didn't have a muscle in his body or a brain in his head, father supposed to be a colonel or toy general or something, big expectations for his boy, and one afternoon just after we'd come in from the range he sits down in the latrine and blows his head off, from the eyebrows up—nothing. So the drill sergeant has the guy's best friend wipe up the mess. We were having a big inspection next morning and he wanted to be sure the shithouse was real clean."

"Fucking pigs," muttered Mutant Man.

"Guy in my platoon tried to brain our drill sergeant with an entrenching tool," said Griffin.

"Yeah?"

"Drill sergeant threw him down the stairs."

"We could write a book."

"A fucking exposé."

"Famous Drill Sergeants We'd Like To Off."

"Volumes one and two."

"I bet Claypool's got some good stories," said Griffin. "Claypool, tell us about your adventures in Basic Training."

There was no answer.

"Claypool." Griffin stared at Trips. "What the hell's wrong with him?"

"I ain't his mother."

A flare, igniting prematurely, soared upward like a roman candle, trailing a shower of white sparks. "Ooooooo," moaned Mutant Man, rocking back, "dig that rush."

"I wish Claypool would say something," said Griffin. "Why the hell doesn't he say anything?"

"Leave him alone," said Trips. "Just because someone ain't shooting off ninety words a second . . ."

A half dozen flares filled the sky with burning light. For the first time the distant landscape was visible, chrome bumps and curves, inky pools of shifting shadow. "What the hell *is* going on out there?" asked Griffin. A ripple of bright crimson appeared, moving from left to right like a stage curtain. The curtain passed back and forth several times red as molten steel being poured from a huge bucket in the sky. "Gunship," said Trips. Mutant Man bounced up and down on his hands. "Yeah," he whispered, "yeah, yeah, yeah," in fierce cadence.

"God," Griffin said, "it's so beautiful."

"Better than acid," Trips said.

The curtain fluttered about like a scarf on a dancer's neck. Still there was no sound but the persistent drone of the generators and someone's radio cycling in and out, the music too faint to be recognized rising and falling in volume, the murmur of a remote argument.

"Hey!" a voice called out. "You people up there." The beam of a flashlight swung up at them, flicked across Griffin's eyes. "What's going on?" It was Sergeant Anstin. Trips cupped his hand behind his back. "Nothing, Sarge," he said. "Nothing at all. Just out enjoying the war on this pleasant evening."

"Who's up there with you?" The flashlight played among their faces. "Who's that back there in the dark?"

"Claypool, Sarge," answered Trips. "And that's Griffin and that's Noll."

"I hope, gentlemen, I'm not smelling something."

"You're not, Sarge."

"Noll."

"Yes, Sergeant."

"Am I smelling something?"

"No, Sergeant."

"I'm not smelling something, am I, Specialist Griffin?"

"No, Sergeant, you are not."

"That's good. That's fine. Certain odors bother my nose, know what I mean?"

"Yes, Sergeant."

"My eyes aren't always the best, but sometimes they get a little sensitive, too. Certain sights make them twitch, know what I mean? For instance, why, right at this moment, am I seeing four of this unit's finest stuck up on a roof like targets in a damn shooting gallery? Could someone explain that to me?"

"It's the view, Sarge," said Trips.

"The view."

"Quite a show out there tonight."

"Quite a show we'd have in here if a lucky round sailed in and knocked four pretty heads off. Luck like that would make me most unhappy. Do you know why, Specialist Griffin?"

"No, Sergeant."

"Because I'd have to walk in to Captain Patch with my hat in my hands and tell him one of his boys lost his head out here tonight when I wasn't looking. And then Captain Patch wouldn't be very happy either, would he?"

"No, Sergeant, I guess not."

"And it would make me even more unhappy. Do you know why?"

"No."

"Because I'll have to spend all tomorrow, tomorrow my day off, typing the paperwork on four young corpses. On my day off. Have you ever seen me type, Specialist?"

"No."

"A quadraplegic could do better. And on my day off. You don't want to see your poor sergeant suffer like that, now do you?"

"No, Sarge."

"I didn't really think you would. I'll be back in an hour. Anyone still sitting on the roof gets written up. *Comprende?*" The flashlight danced across their faces.

"Yes, Sergeant," replied Griffin.

"Thank you, gentlemen. Have a pleasant evening." The flashlight wavered across the sand, disappeared behind a corner.

"Fucking pig," muttered Trips.

"Fucking . . ." Mutant Man's voice trailed off, unable to locate a sufficiently damning noun.

The curtain sparkled like red cellophane.

"Running around like that," said Griffin. "He's supposed to be on duty for Christ's sake."

"What'd you expect," Trips asked. "Keen eyes? A steady hand?"

"Somebody ought to . . ." said Mutant Man.

"Nice time we'd have tonight," said Griffin, staring off at the fireworks, "if something did happen and him to lead us."

The curtain fell like blood from a wound in the skin of the night.

"I bet he used to be a drill sergeant," Griffin added.

"Look," said Trips and the curtain snapped out as if a cord had been pulled. As they watched, the last flare slid down and out leaving only the darkness to consider and the afterimages hanging like movie ghosts or the moldy shroudlike webs various species of insects and disease leave behind to mark their passing among dying trees. Except that even these ghosts possessed more form, solidity, and permanence than the rapidly vanishing real objects and beings of Griffin's prewar existence. And each time he witnessed another raw incident like tonight's (the bodies by the road, the ragged line of blindfolded wounded prisoners shuffling from truck to cell) his past took on more and more of the insubstantial characteristics of fantasy. The war was real; he was not. It was like memory, and therefore his most profound sense of self was a tub of tepid water into which chunks of rock (the war) fell almost daily now in wide splashes, spilling his past and his life onto a cold black-and-white linoleum floor. Griffin couldn't help but wonder what the displacement would be equal to finally.

"That's all folks," announced Mutant Man.

Griffin looked over into Wurlitzer's room. The triangle was gone, the blue light extinguished.

"There's a couple cans of that Scandinavian smoked salmon still left in my room," Trips said.

"We ain't there yet," said Griffin.

"No," said Mutant Man.

"No?"

"No. I'm not moving, not for that lifer. That juicehead. Let him write me up. I ain't doing nothing."

"Mutant Man takes a stand," declared Trips. "Okay, here's what I paid my money to see."

"I'm going to bed," said Griffin.

"No one's going anywhere."

"I'm tired."

"You heard The Man. A line's got to be drawn."

"Yes, and every line you ever drew they stepped across with an Article Fifteen. Excuse me, my dreams of snow are waiting."

"Look at Claypool. He's staying."

"Claypool obviously would sit out here through a mortar attack."

"Wait, take Mutant Man's hand and Mutant Man'll take mine and me Claypool. Now everyone close their eyes and squeeze. Think about the other guy's hands, think 'em into your own until they feel like your own, until they are your own, like your hand is squeezing your hand. Now quiet, quiet . . . do you feel that?"

"Yes," said Mutant Man.

"What?" said Griffin.

"We used to do this on patrol sometimes," Trips explained. "Afterwards, when I reached for my rifle, sparks would jump. If Sergeant Anstin was to come by now he'd take one look and keep on going."

"Isn't this what the Dallas Cowboys do before a big game?" Griffin asked.

"I saw a bullet pass through a man's chest once without touching him."

"I guess things get a little spooky out there."

"Things are spooky everywhere, good buddy."

"Wheeeeeeee!" exclaimed Mutant Man.

"Okay," said Griffin.

"Don't worry. You heard him, he hates paperwork. You ain't gonna lose your precious status as captain's pet."

"Don't forget my trip to Saigon."

"Or your ficky boom-boom."

So they all four sat there waiting. There was nothing to look at now but the scattered lights of the base stretching off like a suburban housing tract toward the mountains of the night.

"What do you suppose was here before we came?" Griffin mused.

"Rice," said Trips. "Rice and buffalo shit, same thing that'll be here when we go."

The airfield was at their backs. Occasionally a C-130 rumbled in with the sound of huge vague objects breaking apart and the dark air would fill with the dead scent of expended fuel. After a while Griffin seemed to hang suspended there, the roof rocking gently above it all like the top seat of a Ferris wheel that had stalled. They talked, letting the silence grow naturally in the pauses between those stories anyone who ever wore a uniform anywhere could exhale easily as breath until finally they were simply sitting together in silence, comfortable, content, unalone in each other's presence.

"Probably he passed out by now," said Trips.

"I can see him," said Griffin, "snoring across Top's desk."

The sound came in two directions at once, out of the sky falling, up through his insides like something slippery and hard he couldn't stop, the answer to the soundless repetition what is that? what is that? already begun in his body's downward roll over the bruising corrugated roof into sand still moist from the late afternoon shower. The explosion was like the sudden collapse of an immense tin can. Crump. Plunged in sand, his fingers felt the trembling of the ground. Darkness fell in pieces around him. Crump. The sky was punched bright with flares. He heard screaming. INCOMING! screamed the screams. INCOMING! The siren on top of the mess hall began its mechanical shriek. Griffin scrambled into the bunker on his hands and knees. "Move over!" he shouted. "Let me in here!" "Sorry," someone muttered. Inside it was too dark to recognize anyone. There was a faint odor of stale urine. Crump. Arms around his legs, head against his knees, back pressed against the steel ribs of the pipe, Griffin smiled. An image had just come to him of someone—it looked like Alexander—bursting naked through a door, helmet clutched firmly over his penis. First the sound like a knife slicing the darkness in half. Then crump. Metal buzzed past outside.

"Oh my God." It sounded like Simon.

"Simon?" Griffin asked, surprised that his voice worked so well. "Is that you?"

"Yes . . . unfortunately."

"Nice alarm clock, huh?"

Crump.

"Shit." Other voices started up.

"What?"

"What do you mean what? I'm scared."

"Think happy thoughts."

"Anybody got a flak vest? . . . a rifle?"

Crump. Griffin heard an echo, an iron twang.

"What do they want with us, anyway? We're peaceful, I am, anyway."

"My mother told me I'd regret coming over here. She said I'd get my ass in a crack like this and praying wouldn't help because any God that permitted this war wasn't gonna be much interested in the fate of my skinny little prick."

"Your mother always talk so dirty?"

"She's a pinko leftist. I almost lost my clearance because of her."

Crump. Crump, crump. Griffin couldn't tell if they were closer or further away. A direct hit would resolve this huddle of sandbags and bodies into bits of glass and bone buttons.

"Okay, who's been pissing in the bunker?"

"It wasn't Calloway. He does it in bed."

"Griffin?" Trips' voice.

"Yeah."

"Griffin?"

"I said yeah."

"Oh."

"Claypool?" called Griffin.

"Don't touch me," said another voice, pitched with tension. "Don't."

"We didn't leave him outside, did we?"
"He's here," Trips said. "He's fine."
Crump. Like a giant sitting down hard on his butt.
"Oh God."
"What's wrong now?"
"I can't find my wedding ring. I was just playing with it and it dropped and I can't find it."
"Jesus Christ."
"When are they gonna stop?"
"She was just getting her legs around me good and tight, too. Goddamn, it makes me mad. I haven't had a decent wet dream since I got to this fucking war."
"Samuels, you are a wet dream."
Someone flipped on a Zippo and all their white faces, suddenly illuminated and turned as one into the circle of light, resembled those in newspaper photographs of a carful of coal miners descending a shaft.
"Jesus Christ, shitbird, put that fucking thing out. You ain't got any more sense than a goddamn gook."
"Sorry. I only wanted to see what time it is."
"Time? Time to kiss your ass goodbye."
In the flickering light Griffin saw Claypool, pale, eyes closed, and beside him Trips looking as serious as he had ever seen him but where had Mutant Man gone? Either he was in another bunker or he had turned into a sandbag.
"Does this happen often? How long do we have to stay in here? When will it be over?"
"Yes," someone answered.
"I think I might pass out."
"Shut up, you're all right."
"I don't think so."
"Yes you are goddamnit shut up!"
The siren rose and fell in metallic hysteria. It reminded Griffin of civil defense drills when he was a kid, all six grades of the elementary school packed face first against brown tile walls in a dark gleaming corridor in case the communists ever attack us, dear. Well, Mrs. Lundquist, now they are.

Crump, crump, crump. Griffin could hear only the muffled explosions, not the incoming sound.

"Sounds like the One Hundred First is taking a beating."

"Airborne's turn to dance."

Crump. Crump.

"Chopped eagle meat.'"

"Hey, everybody knows airborne don't bleed."

"Yeah, they suck."

Griffin concentrated, hardly daring to breathe, his ears focused outside on the sappers flowing like shadows among the hootches. Under cover of air attack they slipped silently in, detonating bunkers into tombs. He never thought he could want an object like a rifle so badly. No one, though, was armed. Major Holly had ordered all weapons locked in the supply room. Griffin was afraid, but he was surprised to learn he could still be all right; his mind seemed to be operating logically in refrigerated sequences carefully numbered. He'd get the keys, he'd open the arms room, he'd pass out the weapons, he'd form a defensive perimeter, he'd secure his position. Logic. The method of heroes. Question: When the satchel charge came in on him would there be time enough to toss it back? Answer: probably not.

"Oh, ow, shit."

"I'm sick of your crap. Shut it."

"My leg. I've got a cramp. Oh, it hurts. I've got to stand up. Let me out of here."

"There's shit storm out there."

"Hey, watch it, you . . ."

"You stupid fucker."

"Let him go. Who cares?"

"Who was that?"

"I don't know."

"Fucking creep."

Crump.

"I hope he dies, spitting blood." Trips.

A flashlight shone into one end of the bunker. "Is there a Paul Michaels in there?"

"Who?"

The flashlight pointed to a clipboard. "Paul Michaels. Spec Four Paul Michaels. He's supposed to be on Reaction Force tonight."

"You mean Paul?"

"That's what I said."

"You said Paul Michaels."

"Correct."

"But it's Michael Paul. Paul is his last name."

"Michael is his first," said another voice.

"Okay, Michael Paul. Is he in here?"

"No."

"Where is he?"

"How should we know?"

The flashlight disappeared. A helicopter flew in low overhead clap-clap–clap.

"Yay, here comes the cavalry."

"I wonder if our hootch is still standing."

"If it ain't we're gonna be fighting the rest of this war in our underwear."

"What's going on? I've never been in a bunker this long before."

"Did someone just poke a flashlight in here?"

"Sergeant Anstin."

"Thank God. I thought I was having a hallucination."

"Hold one. What's that?"

Everyone quieted, listening.

"What?"

"It's stopped."

"Is it over?"

"My mother was wrong about prayer."

"Now they wait a couple hours and zap us in our sheets."

"Who's going to bed?"

"Right, I'm sleeping in here tonight."

"Got a stick to beat off the rats?"

When at last the siren sounded all clear they crawled out of the bunker and stood about for a moment in small uncertain groups, astonished that the surrounding buildings appeared as intact as they had left them.

"So where's the damage?"

"I told you I was having a hallucination."

A figure hurried breathless out of the shadows. "One of the TO hootches is gone," said Simon. "A direct hit."

"Anybody in it?" Griffin asked.

"They're looking," and hurried away.

"Sergeant Anstin?" Trips had come up behind him.

"Are you kidding?" said Griffin. "He'll leave here without even needing a Band-Aid." Claypool stood in back of Trips, staring dumbly up at the stars. "So Claypool," Griffin said, "how'd you like your first mortar attack?"

Claypool was blinking as if the sun were out.

"I said, how'd you like it?"

"He told me," Trips said, "he was personally disappointed."

"Maybe I'd like to hear his voice. I've forgotten what it sounds like."

"Tell him, Claypool, tell him how you liked it."

Claypool's head moved with ponderous care as though a delicate system of gears and weights were necessary to lower his gaze ninety degrees, then revolve the lens machinery until the visual field contained only two, specimens perhaps of an alien life form. The mouth opened. "Fine," he said.

"Fine?" repeated Griffin.

"Everything's fine with the Claypool, isn't it, kid?"

"Fine?"

"Try it yourself sometime," said Trips. He laid a possessive arm across Claypool's shoulder and led him away, the suspicious attendant guiding one of the infirm back to his room.

Griffin followed the flashlights, the sound of voices. A crowd had gathered, standing subdued about an absence that minutes ago had been the TO hootch, home for the enlisted men who during reconnaissance flights operated the radar and infrared equipment, and was now a heap of splintered sticks and a hole in the ground, a space, a gap in the fence. One section of the roof had been driven into the wall of the neighboring signal shack where it protruded like a solar panel on a space station.

Simon came over, still breathing heavily. "Spatz was in bed," he said grimly. "They just finished taking away what was left."

Spatz was one of those "old guys" Griffin knew only by sight. His year almost completed, he had been due to go home next month so there hadn't been much point in getting to know him well. Now Griffin was glad he hadn't.

"Guy flies two hundred missions without a scratch," said Simon, "bites it on the ground in his own bed. What irony."

"I guess it doesn't really matter what it is," replied Griffin.

A blinding light flashed through the crowd. Several men dropped to the ground.

"You shithead,'" someone shouted.

It was Weird Wendell, filming again. The camera lights illuminated the remains of the hootch with the same stark dimension-obliterating intensity that had destroyed it.

"Don't anybody move," he commanded. "I need bodies for scale."

"You'll have one by God," someone threatened.

"Who let him out?" asked another.

"Payne in the ass."

"Yes," said Wendell, "yes, yes. Could you guys over there," he called, pointing, "try to look a little more horrified. Somebody died in here after all."

Under Wendell's eccentric direction the thick light flowed like a blob of mercury over the scene, coating rubble and spectators in a momentary brilliance, unable apparently to choose or find an object suitable for focusing.

Someone ran by, shouting, "They got an officer, too," and at once the crowd moved swiftly away toward Officer's Row.

"Wait a minute," called Wendell. "Hey, wait a minute, I'm not finished here yet."

"Shoot for the moon," somebody yelled, dropping his shorts as he bounded off.

"Do you think it could be Captain Fry?" asked Simon.

They turned a corner.

"No such luck," replied Griffin.

A jeep and a field ambulance were parked beside Captain Patch's hootch. Half the structure had collapsed. There were pieces of wood and metal strewn up and down the dirt road from the officers club to the main gate. Griffin reached down, picked up a chunk small and heavy as a meteorite. It was still warm. Wearing only his green underwear, Captain Patch came staggering backward out the open doorway, gripping one end of a long loaded bag. At the other end came Lieutenant Hand, grunting. They worked their way carefully down the wooden steps, the crowd silently clearing an aisle to the rear of the ambulance. The bag was lifted inside, the metal doors clanged shut. Captain Patch, barefoot, still in his underwear, continued on down the road without a word or glance to anyone, down toward the darkened O club. Lieutenant Hand settled back against the hood of the jeep, pulled a green handkerchief from his back pocket, and blew his nose.

"Who was it?" Griffin asked.

He looked at Griffin for a moment, then looked away. "Lieutenant Kline," he said, looking back at Griffin angrily, then staring off across the road. "There's a door on the roof of the photo lab," he said, his voice casual, even, so that at first Griffin thought he was merely remarking upon some sort of architectural oddity, rarely noticed, hardly worth the comment until Griffin himself looked and saw the door undamaged and intact lying on a slant across the tin roof where the blast had put it down.

Kline was one of the operations officers, one of Private Trips's nominal superiors, an obsessive gin rummy player, a man with a high nervous laugh like the psycho killer in a bad movie. His men called him Peaches. He hadn't yet begun to shave.

The engine coughed, the ambulance drove away.

Lieutenant Hand looked down into his handkerchief.

The mortars were still for the remainder of the night. Griffin lay on his bunk, fully clothed, watching the darkness until the spaces between the wall planks turned pewter, and then, even before the CQ came through shrilling the morning whistle, he went out into the cool gray dawn, a white mist lifting over the field of weeds behind the unit's guard tower, to look at the rubble in natural light. The changes were only subtle ones. The sand appeared ashen, the shattered lengths of jutting wood metallic. The wreckage was totally anonymous. Not a boot nor a locker nor a bed frame. Griffin stood there, patiently, expectant. At first it was like inspecting a construction site. Then it was like pausing before the Sphinx and he knew that if and when this hootch was ever rebuilt there would always be a hole here—fatal rounds tearing thought like rocks through tissue paper. He felt a weakening, collapsing sensation as if all his nerves had retreated into their burrows and suddenly he was exhausted, tired enough finally to sleep. On the way back to room and bed he stopped in the latrine, watched his piss arc steaming out of him into the corroded trough. He looked at himself in the stained mirror, saw eyes looking back through eyes, and vision was just a pair of hard black dots like nothing, like targets. The feel of the sink, cold as stone beneath his hands, brought him back. He turned on the faucet. Nothing happened. There was no water, he had forgotten. He glanced again at the mirror. His face was thinning out. He was beginning to look like an Indian. When he left the latrine he remembered to exit by the other door, walk around back by the empty water bladder lying flat and black in the musty sand like a dead slug, under the guard tower with Cross leaning out calling hey, what time is it? Can I come down yet? Hey, hey, and up between the cooks and the mechanics then a right turn back to the weathered door that opened into the closet-sized space that was his room and the unmade bed he had littered with sand lying on it all night in his boots. It was the long way around but today, this morning at least, he preferred a different route home.

||||||||||||||||||||||||||||||||||||||||||||||||||||||||||||||||||||||||||||||||

Wurlitzer had been thinking about it for some time now. If you extended your tour, volunteered to spend another six months in Nam, you got a thirty-day leave to any place in the Free World and the army provided or paid for the transportation—They had to!—and your thirty days didn't even start until the moment you set foot on your destination. There was this sergeant in the 131st who pored over maps for months and finally found this little bitty island off the coast of Africa, see, and the only way to get there was into Nairobi where you had to change planes, fly to this minuscule dirt strip deep in the heart of darkness, transfer to elephant caravan across mountains and bush country until you got to this virtually uninhabited trading post that ran a leaky motorboat out to the island maybe every two weeks. Took a month and a half to get to this hole. Month and a half back. That's three months just traveling and it's all good time! Some guys went to Sweden for thirty days of blond pussy, some never came back. But for the truly discriminating traveler there was only one spot for relief from the miseries of global handball: the diamond clarity and saffron mystery of Katmandu.

A procession of blue-skinned monks in orange robes filed down stairs of stone, a yak's butter lamp in each hand, the tinkle tinkle of tiny bells echoing through a vast and cold emptiness.

And there was dynamite dope virtually lying in heaps all over the place.

Daydreaming again, Wurlitzer hopped into a jeep for a quick trip to the PX to buy a bag of M&Ms. Outside the gate he felt a bump and discovered he had run over the old man. The beggar was dead on arrival at the 92nd Evac. His bowl was cracked in half.

"What can I say?" said Wurlitzer.

Accident, said the MPs. Stupid gook, sitting like that beside a major thoroughfare, don't he got any brains at all?

Meditation in Green: 10

Plastic

no need soil
no need water
no need light
no need air

got no roots
got no seed
got no insects
got no disease

Styrofoam earth
alcohol rain
chip my paint
staple my brain

weather don't matter
seasons stay away
bloom forever
a perfect green day

Plastic

"Not the London Fog in the hat, the whitewall head behind him."

"Behind what?"

"At the light now, the one beside the purple dress."

"Gimme the binoculars."

We were up on the roof of an apartment building, leaning across the warm tiles. I focused down the length of the block, elbows propped among the pigeon droppings.

"That's him," Trips whispered fiercely. "That's The Man."

"I can't believe the dog."

"Penance."

"A Yorkie?"

"He's got a shitload of karma to mine."

"But this guy has a moustache."

"Part of the disguise, new life civilian identity."

"I don't know."

"Look at that walk, that cob-up-your-ass strut I'd recognize anywhere."

"I don't know."

A nondescript man in a gray high school janitor's windbreaker turned up a set of clean concrete stairs, braced the door open for the animal with a canvas-shoed foot, then man and dog disappeared into the pink brick building.

"His ass has gotten bigger."

"I don't know."

"Imagine what we could have done with a pair of scopes. Bam, bam, both kneecaps simultaneously."

"I'm afraid my hands aren't too steady. My meditation hasn't been going well."

"You could use a sandbag."

"It's not him, Trips."

"Of course it is. The name on the box. The dumpy wife in lavender tights. The teenage daughter I watched the other night undressing for bed. Yum, yum."

"Coincidence."

"Try this." From his jacket pocket he extracted a hand grenade, one shiny chrome-plated hand grenade. The top flipped open and out popped an orange flame.

"What about it?" I asked. The lighter wouldn't work for me.

"Look on the bottom."

Engraved in Gothic letters were the initials **M. A.**

"Ma," I said. "So what?"

"M. A.," said Trips. "Millard Anstin."

"Sure. Where'd you get it?" I was certain he'd had the lighter engraved himself.

"Through the bathroom window. Tore the place apart. Looked like a DEA raid by the time I was finished. I even took a piss in his fish tank."

"But, listen, it's not even him."

"The next time there will be two rifles, one in each corner, we'll triangulate the bastard. Maybe I'll rent a helicopter for a stylish getaway."

"Will you listen to me for a minute?"

"Don't pull out on me now, Grif."

"Slow down. Think. Look this guy over again. Look hard."

"I'd counted on you, buddy."

"Then pay attention to what I'm saying."

"Friends."

"There when you need 'em."

"A circle of hands around a casket."

Two hours into the all-night frolic of drinking, arm wrestling, and war-gaming that was Captain T. Hewitt's farewell party, Major Holly suddenly realized he could not remember what his wife looked like. He could picture her face easily enough but that specific arrangement of specific detail distinguishing her exact face from all others remained vague, indecisive, as if viewed through a sheet of frosted glass. No doubt she worried about him, about his health, his safety, his intimate proximity to girls like Anh. Excusing himself, he left the O club for his quarters. He would write a chatty letter to reassure her.

Outside the night was warm and peaceful. Up in the black sky the red lights atop the signal antennae winked languidly on and off like the warning lights on a pier. At the end of the dirt road running past Officer's Row he could see the gate guard lounging against a telephone pole, probably asleep. He'd let the OD handle that. He walked to his hootch down a sidewalk (the only one in the compound) almost completely buried in sand. Note: tell First Sergeant to have it swept daily. As he fumbled through his pockets —Where the hell were those keys?—there was a whirring in the air above his head and something went thwack against the planks of his door. He turned around. The guard had not moved, the shadows were still, there wasn't a sound. He found the knife under the steps where it had fallen, and, cradling it in a handkerchief, he carried it inside to his desk. The blade was huge and extremely sharp gleaming there under his table lamp as he dialed Captain Rossiter's number. He hoped there were fingerprints all over it, big as moons.

Then the rains ended and the dry season began. The sun, its brass nozzle aimed directly downward, burned away the overcast, baked the sky to a glossy enamel blue. The ground, its glue of moisture evaporated, came quickly apart, concrete solidity crumbling to slippery sand. Somewhere a furnace grate had swung open and all the cellar doors and windows were locked tight. The office air conditioners stopped working, the showers ran dry, there was a shortage of ice for drinks. The buildings were kindling for the carbonization to come. It looked like a long summer.

On duty all night, Griffin would waken less than an hour after he had fallen asleep from dreams of suffocation and premature burial to sweat-slick face, arid throat, head stuffed with straw, and the big floor fan in the corner of his room spewing jet exhaust across his tired, hot vibrating body. Struggling to his feet, he'd pull on his damp uniform and stagger bleary-eyed about the compound —movement seemed somehow preferable to wilting in place— until the sun gave out and hell cooled sufficiently to permit sleep in the few dark hours before work. But as the days built up like a pile of coals and the temperature settled into a fixed variation at the upper limits of human habitability this schedule of steady work, inescapable heat, and intermittent sleep started to have an effect. Beneath the moist rapidly browning skin his nerves were disintegrating into particles as fine and as irritating as the sand whose progress he noted dully from his hootch steps. All objects, outdoors and in, seemed to be breaking down into this basic granular stuff. Every available surface displayed its own thin coating of sand. It was everywhere. There was sand in the orderly room, sand in the food, sand in the telephones, briefcases, classified files; it collected in crankcases, engine housings, rifle chambers, and handcuffs; there was sand under the beds, in the sheets, between the pages of unopened books, piling up in the dark corners of closed lockers, hiding inside the CO's safe. It jammed tape recorders and typewriters, clogged shower drains, and scratched reconnaissance film. It got under clothes where it chafed against sticky skin; it got inside boots, rubbing sores into sweaty feet; it got in the ears, under eyelids, between the teeth. The sun made the sand sprout from the ground and there was no escape from either this mineral crop or that ball of molten lead dripping out of the sky.

Marijuana, happily, elevated tolerance levels and seemed to produce a beneficial air-conditioning effect on the body—whether psychological or organic he couldn't decide—but still, sometimes when he was quite stoned, the light itself would shatter into particles, glittery grains of falling sand. The world sparkled like a freshly split rock. And him without the vaguest comprehension of geology.

Seated on the hootch steps, he leaned over, scooped up a handful of warm white clean sand, and let it trickle slowly onto the hard round black toe of his boot. The separate grains bounced off the leather like tiny rubber balls. Down in the hollow behind the EM club, washing laundry with the other maids, Missy Lee was carefully ignoring his stare.

Occasionally there were brief sandstorms when the wind would quicken, the light darken, and everyone scurried inside. Sand blew against tin roofs with the sound of snow brushing a windowpane. Inside, tongues of sand crept under closed doors, drily licking the smooth wooden floors.

Griffin scratched his head, sand rolling up under his fingernails, mineral dandruff.

He'd lie, eyes closed, in the shade of a bunker, and hear it hissing out there in the sun. He saw ribbed dunes, sculpted shadows, glaciers of sand sliding down valleys into secluded hamlets. Deep inside his powdered nerves set up a constant itch where he couldn't reach to scratch. He figured he probably was going mad. He rolled over, glanced at his watch. It had stopped.

"Let me take you away from all this."

Griffin looked up and saw himself, a pair of distorted heads in the convex silver lenses of Lieutenant Mueller's sunglasses. "You look like an insect," he said, adjusting the wet washcloth across his forehead.

"I feel like an overdone vegetable. Listen, you want some relief?"

"Of course, but I don't think Sergeant Ramirez will allow me to sleep in the refrigerator."

"Jellyroll's got the shits again. You want a ride?"

"What are the targets?"

"Bac Nham, the Monkey's Tit, 1033, 906, Chu Dan, that squiggly little stream looks like a line of worm crap, the usual."

"That's nice. Watch out for the AA on 906."

"It's cool."

"Cool?"

"You'll need a jacket."

"Cool?"

Cinched into a flight harness, Griffin felt like an astronaut except for the .38 revolver strapped in a holster around his waist. No commies on the moon—yet.

"You know," Mueller had joked, handing him the weapon, "in case of an 'incident.' "

Inside the Mohawk cockpit, Griffiin sat helpless as a baby in a high chair as Mueller leaned over, attaching the numerous buckled straps to all the proper metal loops. He reached between Griffin's legs and clicked a red switch. "Your seat is now armed," he announced, smiling pleasantly. Griffin began to wonder just how disagreeable the weather actually was. "Look in the rearview mirror," Mueller directed. "See that basketball hoop above your head? To eject just reach up and yank, hard. You'll know when it's time because you'll look over and I won't be here anywhere."

"Having a good time?"

"Put on your helmet. From now on if you want to talk press this button here." Mueller strapped on his helmet, adjusted the mike so that its stubby gray rectangle grazed his lips. "How do you read me?" he said in a fuzzy metallic voice.

"Reading you five by," answered Griffin. This might be fun.

"Let's crank up this bird and get out of here." With the hatches locked both of them had begun to perspire heavily.

Mueller started the engines. The cockpit shuddered, then settled into a steady not uncomfortable vibration. Staring out his window, Griffin was cheered by the words ROLLS-ROYCE in shiny chrome insignia fixed to the engine housing, but once the plane heaved itself forward and began to move, a stiff old-fashioned buggy trundling over the metal flight ramp, wings bouncing awkwardly up and down, he wondered who had constructed the fuselage—American Flyer? At the end of the runway the Mohawk turned and came to a halt. Griffin looked down a diminishing length of rubber-streaked pavement. A dirty white passenger prop rumbled in over them, tires squealing and smoking down that pavement. As the plane taxied toward the terminal Griffin saw the lettering AIR VIETNAM and, pressed against each oval window an anxious Oriental face. Tourists in for the season? The static in both ears synthesized into the words "Looking Glass zero eight something something" and the engines began to scream. Griffin clutched the map boards in his lap. The plane was bouncing again as though some delinquents were outside rocking the tail, the black strip of runway moved toward him, rolling up on a reel beneath the nose; the hangars, the supply sheds, the offices on either side of them were moving too, scenery attached to the same reel as the runway blurring now, and the plane, moments before a frail toy, took on sensations of hardness, strength, and stability. Griffin glanced out his window and realized they were up. The Mohawk dipped, circled once over the airfield, giving Griffin his first aerial view of the base. Arranged in such precise straight lines and right angles, the 1069th resembled a concentration camp or a movie lot, the Quonset huts housing sound studios. The plane climbed, pushing through foggy wisps of cloud, and headed west, out toward Indian Country. Air streamed in across Griffin's face, strong and cool. Griffin, his focus consistently limited to the blemishes recorded on film, hadn't ever experienced the simple beauty of the land. There was a lushness of organic color he had never seen before. Fifty-seven varieties of green and off in the distance a row of emerald mountains supporting a balcony of blazing clouds. A natural greenhouse. Toss a seed from this altitude and it would sprout before it touched dirt. The plane flew over rice paddies, a patchwork quilt divided by dikes and flooded now so that the ground seemed like an immense latticed mirror over whose unchanging surface moved a small bright airplane chased by a somewhat larger and darker shadow. Griffin imagined a stick of bombs shattering the polished glass. How many years bad luck? Far off in the distance, hanging in the sky like a string of lights, were the sunstruck windscreens of hovering helicopters. Then, as though it were suspended on a wire between Griffin and the ground, a single engined Cessna floated by at a ninety-degree angle to the Mohawk.

"Forward Air Controller," explained Mueller. "Wanna hang around and watch?"

"Show me the war," replied Griffin. He wondered if the Cessna might not be one of the very Bird Dogs serviced by that gang of horny privates who had given him a lift to the PX one long ago day.

Higher up in the sky, between Griffin and the sun, a flight of F-4s came streaking in, bodies camouflaged in splotches of brown and green paint, wings and tails cut to resemble shark fins. Griffin's ears filled with cool professional voices so near their owners might have been jammed into this cockpit with him.

"Good morning, Spud, how are you?"

"Looking good, Bluebird, what size eggs you got to lay for me today?"

"Five hundred pounders, four rocket tubes, some twenty mike mike, all that good shit."

"Make me happy."

"There's heavy fire coming from the tree line. The village has got a damn stone wall around it. I count about a dozen structures, same-same bunkers, spider holes, looks like a tunnel system all through it, I think they're probably stuck in there pretty tight."

"Need some loosening, huh?"

"The province chief says the whole place is lousy with VC so knock yourselves out. Didn't bother with the phosphorus. Figure you can line it up on the road and work your way in along that axis."

"Affirm."

One by one the F-4s peeled off and came swooping down in over the tree line. Griffin could see shock waves along the ground as clear as the rings in a pond of water when a rock is tossed in. Columns of smoke lifted into the blue sky.

"Oh boy!" shouted someone in Griffin's ear. "Oh fucking boy!"

The separate columns of smoke joined together in one solid wall rising high and thick from the combustion below. Palm trees swayed in the fire, turned black and shrank. The burning hootches became visible, collapsing in slow motion into the flames. There was no sign of life anywhere on the ground.

"Shit hot, Bluebird, that's a one-oh-oh. Six structures, at least twenty KBAs. Thank you very much."

"Thank you, Spud. Glad to be of service."

"Hold one, Bluebird. There's a definite unfriendly scooting out the back door. Can someone handle that?"

"Roger."

Griffin could see a speck moving along a brown road.

One of the jets knifed swiftly downward, swept in over the road. Its black nose twinkled. A dust cloud rose up. The speck stopped moving.

"Right on. Thank you, Bluebird, it's been a pleasure working with you."

"Any time, Spud."

The F-4s soared into the haze.

"Wonderful," said Griffin.

"See all the fun you office boys miss out on," said Mueller.

Their plane climbed a spur of jagged mountains and entered a valley of the moon, barren earth pounded into dust and pocked with craters more numerous than skin pores, a bowl of holes, depressions in an ashtray.

"What the hell was down there?" asked Griffin.

"Nguyen's Pizza and Hamburgers, Commie Community Drive-In Theater, who knows? I think what we're looking at here is actually a site of random mineral exploration. Chop up the ground with explosives, see what rises to the surface. Damn country's loaded with tungsten, you know. For filaments, light bulbs. Bombing this place is really keeping our homes back in the world clean and well-lit."

"Never heard that theory before."

"New shipment of books from my mother."

The Mohawk passed over a huge rectangle of dry brown larger than any Griffin had ever seen on the film, or perhaps on film the size of defoliated areas simply appeared smaller than life. Beneath the rectangle, in the corner typically reserved for the artist's signature were the large letters USA, also in brown. Soil sterilants, thought Griffin. Our mark.

The plane stepped over a second mountain range and then swung down over the jungle.

"Enough sightseeing," Mueller announced. "Here we go, target number one."

Fumbling with the maps, Griffin finally located the target box, a grease-penciled area centered on a route interdiction in the middle of the valley floor. The plane dropped abruptly toward a threadlike road, Griffin's stomach bouncing around off the walls of his insides like an overinflated basketball; the ground, a bowl of undulating pea soup, prepared to dump its contents on top of his head.

"Now," signaled Mueller.

Griffin's white finger found the appropriate button and pushed. Somewhere under his feet a camera clicked off frames.

"Okay," said Mueller.

Griffin released the button. The plane climbed rapidly cloudward, captured and securely preserved in its belly possible tracks of the invisible enemy.

"Well?" asked Mueller.

"I thought you guys worked for a living."

The green half of the picture before him slipped off the screen and, pinned to his seat, Griffin gaped at a deep expanse of unblemished blue. His body's position on the seat shifted and, lifting his head backward, he was presented with an equally breathtaking view of solid green. Then, as someone began dribbling his stomach down a tilting court, the green started to revolve like the painted surface of a child's top, accelerated and blurred into a long green tunnel narrowing to one immobile dot of black toward which

Griffin plummeted in a state of fear so intense it was exhilarating and, as memory preceded the physical body down the drain, he realized that beneath his spinning consciousness there was an identical dot toward which the other moved as if into a mirror, and the ground did a somersault over the sky and there was the green and there was the blue each in its proper location and, nestling on his lap, inside the plastic map bag, were the warm soggy remains of Griffin's breakfast. Mueller hadn't turned on the intercom but Griffin could see he was laughing, the fillings in his teeth.

"Thank you," said Griffin, wiping his mouth on the corner of a 1:50,000 chart of Thua Thien province.

"Sorry," said Mueller. "I don't know what came over me."

"Never trust a pilot."

"But you're cool aren't you, tell me how cool you are."

"Right. These drops on my forehead are nothing but snowflakes."

Except for terse comments relating to mission business they hardly spoke to one another for the remainder of the flight. Mechanically the camera collected images: roads and trails, river crossings, streams, an abandoned hamlet, rocks, trees, and a remarkable field of craters arranged in such neat nearly symmetrical rows as to resemble a bizarre species of farm crops. Banking away from the last target, a suspected truck park hidden under an impenetrable canopy of vegetation, Griffin was gazing indifferently out the window when he noticed to his surprise a long wide brown sear winding sinuously into the northern horizon through an immensity of dense jungle, a gigantic earthen snake warming itself beneath the tropical sun.

"What the hell is that?" he asked.

"Nine two two," said Mueller, swinging the Mohawk around for an extended look.

Griffin recognized the number immediately, the route designation of a well-traveled section of the notorious Ho Chi Minh Trail. He was astonished at the difference between the insignificant tracing on a map and the broad avenue of actuality.

"It looks like an eight-lane freeway," he exclaimed.

"Industrious little folks, ain't they?"

Griffin turned to inspect once more this marvel of engineering and in the next instant the marvel was completely upside down as though the slide had been improperly inserted in the projector.

"Whoops," said Mueller.

Griffin looked up at the platter of land, the mossy tombstone teetering madly over his head. This time he was determined not to get sick. Someone clinging to those bushes up there was signaling him with a hand mirror. Then there were glints of light like sparks from flint against stone. Behind him he heard the sound of a metal door being slammed shut, again and again. Who was getting out? He checked to see that Mueller was still beside him and saw black smoke streaming off the wing, the blades of one engine were no longer rotating. The ground descended with the speed of a palm slapping a bug; the jungle began separating out into individual trees, blotches of light and shade into distinct swells and depressions. When he finally realized that this was not another of Mueller's jokes and that he actually was going to die the slide changed and Griffin beheld a pleasant composition of creamy cloud and baby blue.

"Bit of a problem back there," said Mueller, still engaged in a wrestling match with the controls.

"What happened?" asked Griffin. His fingers were curled about the bottom of his seat.

"I'm afraid some camera-shy natives just tried to shoot us down."

"Is that fuel spraying all over out there?"

"Don't worry, I think we're moving faster than the tank's leaking. Boy, for a minute there it was like being back at Fort Rucker again. Surprise! You've only got one engine, now what?"

Suddenly everything got brighter, as if his hands, his knees, the instrument panel, the cockpit, the nose of the plane, the brilliant sky had all turned to crystal. His seat began sinking hydraulically downward. He grabbed for the handhold just under the windscreen. Vertigo descended over his head like a spinning dunce's cap, his face went hot, then cold, the skin studded with greasy beads of sweat.

"Hey," said Mueller, "are you okay?"

"I'll never complain about the heat again."

"This was not a routine mission."

Griffin gave him a blank look.

"Usually there's a couple SAM missiles to dodge, too."

"Wonderful."

Mueller contacted Looking Glass Control, informed ops of their situation. "We'll roll out the fire trucks," answered a bored voice Griffin thought might be Trips's.

"Think I'll put us in for a couple DFCs," said Mueller. "How'd you like to star at the next awards ceremony?"

"The feel of firm ground under my feet will be adequate reward."

His eyes kept darting toward the gas gauge. He felt violated, bruised. Like a peach that had been bounced against concrete. It wasn't until he glimpsed the glittering sea shading off into the sky that he was able to begin to relax.

The landing was an exercise in delicacy. The plane seemed to float in softly as a ball of fluff. The wheels squeaked, the frame shuddered once, then coasted smoothly down the striped tarmac.

"Beautiful," said Griffin. "That's one I owe you."

Mueller brushed the compliment away with a gloved hand. "Maybe someday you could doctor a mission report for me."

A modest crowd had assembled on the ramp to watch them taxi up. The Mohawk rolled to a stop amid a circle of beaming faces. Griffin popped the hatch and was instantly enveloped in a bath of wondrous heat and friendly humidity. Then he saw Weird Wendell below him, aiming that obnoxious lens at his face and he smiled, he smiled and he waved cheerfully, so absorbed in impersonating Charles Lindbergh or Errol Flynn he failed to notice until he began climbing from the plane that the hand with which he had been greeting the happy ground crew still held firmly clenched in its tight fingers a colorful bag of fresh vomit triumphantly displayed as though it were a prize, an award just presented by the president of a grateful nation.

There were journalists in the hotel too, most of them experienced enough to recognize someone like Kraft. They were tolerable company for brief periods despite their sophomoric idea of relaxed conversation.

"Hey, Kraft, how many kills you got by now? Fifteen? Twenty-six? Forty-two?"

"Lost count, I guess."

"But what's it like, to kill somebody personally. For the reader back home. Intimate details, please."

"What's it like? Well, I guess I'd have to say it's like taking a shit. You know, some are good and satisfying, some okay, some just plain messy, but one way or another, it's always nice to get the crap out."

Then they'd all laugh and pass around the dope.

Kraft, of course, had forgotten nothing—he was well aware of the precise number—but whenever he thought of the dead he always pictured American corpses and heaps of boots at impossible angles still attached to limp doll-like legs, the edges of the Corfam soles worn smooth and round on their journey through the war, tread clogged with dry mud, black leather uppers scratched and creased, boots safe now from future wear, boots ready for the dump. Enemy dead were jagged lines and shaded bars on plastic graphs and colored slides. Yes, that was how it was except for those solitary dark-of-the-moon scenes upstairs in his room when it was conclusively proven that even here in the ersatz luxury of the Hotel Golden Gate, joking with journalists and flicking lizards off the walls, there could still be found telltale traces of messy shit.

Hanging behind the desk in Major Quimby's Spook House office, next to a mounted letter of congratulations from General Edward Lansdale, was a framed motto: A Guerrilla Swims Among the People As A Fish Swims In Water. From the sayings of Chairman Mao. Beside this was one of those bleached-out watercolors torn from a children's Bible and depicting a golden haloed blue-eyed Christ knee deep in water, surrounded by an adoring mob of robed believers, the first two fingers of one hand erect, raised in benediction, the other casually yanking in a net of leaping silver fish. His superior's famous sense of humor. He thought often of that picture now. In from the field, his lone-wolf status temporarily modified, Kraft operated his own net out of this hotel. Vietnamese agents and informers came and went bearing news, sometimes reliable, of arms and rice and communists. Kraft listened and wrote reports, which were added to the eternal round robin of reports that circulated from hand to hand until the outlines of a consensus formed in the murk. A wish became a guess, a guess an estimate, an estimate the reality. Kraft sat in the middle making lists. Names were added to lists, action was initiated, names were deleted from lists. Sometimes a name on his payroll list appeared on one of these other lists and then Kraft himself often participated actively to assure a proper and complete deletion.

His counterpart on this present job was a short skinny Vietnamese with a face as unexpressive and grimly humorous as Buster Keaton's and a name—Le Thong—more appropriate for a pair of stylish French sandals. Kraft neither liked nor trusted Le Thong and was expecting his ludicrous name to appear momentarily on a list. But at least Le Thong wasn't a smudge; he was neat, he avoided mess like a cat, and for these characteristics Kraft respected him and occasionally accompanied him on those various outdoor jobs Le Thong enjoyed so much more than sitting in a hot office "waiting for Mister Charlie to knock on door."

Doan was a cab driver. Hardly a section of the city he did not pass through daily. Friends and acquaintances everywhere. Good man, eyes and ears always open. Unfortunately, too often also his mouth. Le Thong, sitting in back, waited until the cab had come to a stop at an intersection before shooting Doan through the seat. Passersby thought he had passed out from too much dope.

Dong was a merchant. A prosperous businessman dealing in consumer items from toothpaste to Scotch and shelter halves, goods stolen from rich American PXs and provided to him at special rates. He was a good mingler, flypaper for buzzes of useful gossip. At night, though, after locking the steel bars across his store front, he'd hop on a Honda for a ride into the country and meetings in the moonlit bush with gun-toting men in black pajamas. Le Thong placed a bomb in his gas tank. One bystander killed, six severely injured. VC, whispered the street, VC everywhere.

Thich was an assistant to the mayor. Friend and confidant of American officials, military and civilian. Le Thong slit his throat. Five days later, bloated belly up, Thich joined the morning sampans moving downriver to the open sea.

Pham worked for AID, Kim was a bar girl, Nguyen a province chief . . .

Of the making of lists there was no end.

At night Kraft returned to his room in the Hotel Golden Gate, a concrete-and-tile cubicle designed for easy maintenance and quick cleaning. Dirt, urine, vomit, blood, unwanted guests could all be hosed down and flushed out the circular metallic drain embedded in the center of the floor. Kraft would lie on his bed, an inadequately disguised military hospital model, studying for significance the wonderful patterns assumed by the lizards on the institutional green walls of this enlarged shower stall of a room. Sometimes a clear shape or letter would almost form but the moment he looked away the positions would shift, a cruel poltergeist would alter the ornament. On the ceiling light and shadow, reflections from the street, slid back and forth, one over the other like blobs of oil and water attempting desperately to mix until the curfew when the game became more subtle, the movement measured, then finally the inevitable but agonizing triumph of white over black and Kraft would assume he was rested, that sometime during the night he had slept, and he would get up, brush his teeth with bottled water and go down the creaking elevator to breakfast.

The hotel dining room was long and wide with pillars and

arches opening into a stone courtyard complete with fountain and fish pond and then beyond what had been in the building's French epoch an immense, carefully tended garden of tropical color. The owner at the time, an amateur botanist, had taken full advantage of the fertile climate to create a natural beauty that back home in Normandy would have been possible only beneath glass insulation. The Vietnamese owners of the American epoch had no interest in horticulture and today the garden was overgrown, the pond a refuge of poisonous snakes, and the fountain, still visible from tables set with linen and silver, a trickle of brown fluid sliding down the stained beak and algae-furred breast of a stone bird into a bowl of stagnant scum. And of all the places in all of Vietnam that he had ever been this dining room was Kraft's favorite. Except for the quiet, excellently trained staff there were no stray Vietnamese permitted in the restaurant. Pushers and cab drivers were kept strictly to the street. Women were allowed to sit in the lobby but not to enter the dining room unaccompanied, a vestige of colonial decorum the management attempted to preserve. His table, the same one reserved for him each day by the windows, was a good spot for drifting. Such quiet, such simple peace. Sometimes the cultured voice of a waiter inquiring politely if the gentleman might not be more comfortable upstairs in his room told him he had dozed off again. Or sometimes, nursing a cup of green tea and staring out the open windows, he'd try to rearrange that meaningless jumble of trees and weeds and stones into the garden that once had been and his nose would be teased by the tickle of a scent, a plume of perfume briefly fanning the air, and, glancing about, he'd find the room empty. Perhaps it was an aroma insufficiently appreciated back in the days when the tables were moved aside for dances and all-night parties. Paper lanterns among the orchids, champagne in the fountain. The old botanist had a daughter who required diversion. The hotel then, La Fleur des Champs, was the gathering place for the local European society; military officers, administration officials, missionaries, jewel exporters, rubber plantation managers, the whole white-suit crowd Kraft had forever missed. A waiter approached with a silver tray bearing a modest white card, on it the emblem of the snake-haired woman. Kraft finished his tea—adieu, mademoiselle, save me a dance—and strolled out to the lobby where Le Thong waited. Another crisis, another deletion.

Once Le Thong had come for him here reeking of fish and garbage and Kraft had immediately sent him upstairs to shower. But that was when he had been angry; he didn't seem to be so angry anymore. Once there had been a captured cadre official with only two visible teeth and a look full of laughter that seemed especially grotesque when you knew he was lying with such flaunting delight and after strangling him with a wire and cutting out his eyes Kraft had placed in the sockets a pair of small round mirrors. But he wasn't angry anymore. He wasn't even angry when the name Le Thong turned up at last on a list at Corps headquarters. One day after lunch Kraft simply shot him in the head and had the body dumped into one of the ARVN latrines, a dead jeep battery tied to his waist. More reports, more explanations.

He sat in the dining room, stared into the garden. Sludge oozed from the fountain. A snake darted into the weeds. He was assigned to the field again. A fortified village. Hardcore VC. NVA regulars. Probable HQ, weapons and/or food cache, double agents, hidden lists. When the American infantry received fire the CO called in artillery. After the pounding stopped, the fire withered, the smoke drifted away, a cluster of frightened nationals were found huddled between the stacks of charcoal that had been their homes and families. Kraft stood beside the CO who was radioing an action report back to battalion. He was tired of looking at so much waste. This country was a goddamn garbage dump. A scrawny sickly child, female, walked toward him, her deep black eyes focused determinedly on his. Her left arm was cut in several places and bleeding, the side of her face was burned, some of the hair singed. She must have been nine or ten years old. She needed medical attention. Seeing him beside the honcho with the bars, she must have thought he was a medic. Kraft smiled. "Holy shit!" someone shouted. "She's got a grenade!" Bodies flopped to the ground all around Kraft as men took cover. He could see the grenade now big as a melon in such a tiny fist. He couldn't tell if the pin was in or out. The girl kept coming steadily toward him. "Stop!" Kraft shouted. "Dung lai!" He raised his rifle. The girl kept on. "Dung lai! Now stop! Stop right now, stop where you are!" The CO, speechless, held the crackling handset of the radio frozen in space away from his ear. "Stop, just stop, goddamnit!" he yelled. He waved the M-16 at her. "I'll do it, I'm really gonna do it!" Her hand began to move. His rifle was set on automatic. She wasn't more than fifteen yards away now. What he could never forget were those chips of bone flying up off her face like the shower of particles from a Fourth of July sparkler and her small head just coming apart in all directions like a paper sack blown up with air and then popped.

He sat at the table sliding a silver butter knife across the white linen and looking out at the garden. The stone bird seemed to be getting fuzzier about the edges. It was losing its shape. One day he'd probably come in from the field, seat himself down for lunch, and glance out, to be confronted by an eroded length of sculpture resembling a baseball bat. Ah, but what the hell did you expect? This weather ate away at cloth and leather, at wood and stone. There was rot under everything. He raised the butter knife into the light. His fingers had left smudges all over the mirrored surface. Messy shit.

Dear M & P,

Few changes since my last note. Between the mortars and the wire probes our defenses have been kept pretty busy lately. We had three casualties on our section of the perimeter last week. However, so far we've counted forty-nine enemy bodies. That's a kill ratio of almost one in seventeen which is even better than the

ROKs, the most efficient fighters over here. And they're Korean. Just goes to show you all gooks aren't weak and cowardly. Two days ago a couple sappers did manage to sneak through the perimeter sometime before dawn, but some of our eagle-eyed boys manning the guardposts around our unit took them down with some fancy machine gun work before they were able to inflict any serious damage. Each gook had two huge bombs tied to his body. Lucky none went off when they were killed. What a spectacle that would have been and only a few yards from my hootch.

Still just routine duties for me. In between pulling guard duty and dodging incoming it's type, type, type. So you see there's nothing to worry about. See you in 147.

Love,

L

P.S. Last night one of our guys hung himself from a rafter in his room. Guess he couldn't take it anymore. Glad I didn't see it. Gook bodies are okay but seeing one of your own is kind of weird.

On the advice of his morale officer, Lieutenant Peary, Major Holly issued orders for the organization of an official awards ceremony. Each section, regardless of how recently it had done so, was directed to submit the name of at least one deserving individual for appropriate decoration. Cheered by the generous distribution of reward, the men would turn to their work with new vigor, cease quarreling among themselves, lay down their dope pipes, and quit throwing stones at the O club roof.

Lieutenant Tremble received word of this plan with no special joy. As far as he was concerned, no one presently assigned to Research and Analysis had demonstrated the least achievement worthy of the most insignificant award. What to do? He needed a name. The solution was so obvious he didn't see it until the day before the deadline. Alexander. He'd nominate Alexander for a medal. Alexander, who openly mocked his orders, encouraged disrespect, laughed at the mission. Alexander, who had initiated those damn Scrabble games. What was the word for this stratagem? Yes, he'd "co-opt" the troublemaker with the mittened claws of approval. Examined from this end of the telescope, Alexander was practically a model soldier, he did whatever was asked of him with care and efficiency, he worked overtime whenever required, he was smarter than anyone else in the section, he knew more about the total operation than anyone else. And once, during a mortar attack, hadn't he run back into the office, dodging shrapnel, to make sure the safes were locked and been cut on the cheek by a cinder of hot metal? And hadn't he fixed one of the computers himself when it had broken down during a critical week and the technician couldn't come up because of the monsoon and wasn't he always polite to The General and wasn't his printing on the briefing slides so very neat? This guy should be recommended for the Bronze Star. What exquisite revenge.

As the date of the ceremony approached, the awards desk, normally a busy place anyway, quickly disappeared under a snowdrift of applications. At night, during lulls in devastation measurement, Griffin would go next door and help Grumbacher sort through the claims. Because Grumbacher had completed a couple courses of collegiate creative writing (one effort even published in the University of Minnesota literary magazine), he had been promptly appointed to the job of awards and decorations clerk though few of his own compositions, he later admitted without false modesty, could equal the naïve narrative flow, the melodramatic suspense, the unconscious wit of those fabulous mission reports the officers themselves had written as testimony to their deeds of heroism meriting special recognition. The best of the recent batch was Captain Fry's breathless tale of a flight for which he had proposed himself for a Distinguished Flying Cross. "Dusk was approaching," it began, "when Captain Marovicci and I climbed into the cockpits of our sturdy aircraft and took off for that fortified area of Southeast Asia known as The Valley of Death." Grumbacher dropped the form behind a filing cabinet. "Oops," he exclaimed, "I believe I've misplaced Captain Fry's paperwork."

At last the great day arrived. The hangar swept and mopped, the tools cleaned and hung in their proper locations, the missing bulbs replaced in the fixtures overhead, the unit, also scrubbed and polished, arranged in perfect formation opposite the double rank of nervous awardees. "Where's the punch bowl?" whispered Trips. Despite Major Holly's clear forceful voice his words—bravery, dedication, honor, inspiration—kept phasing in and out of Griffin's attention like an editorial on a car radio. His mind was hopelessly wandering, he was thinking about something else, sex actually, the specific brown legs of Holly's hootch maid Anh who had taken lately to romping about the compound dressed in a pair of scarlet silk shorts. The speech ended, Anh disappeared around a corner, and Holly stepped smartly to the first man in the first rank, the First Sergeant right behind bearing the sacramental box of ribboned medallions the major began to pin, one by one, to these deserving chests. The smiles and handshakes were proceeding smoothly until Holly, Bronze Star between thumb and forefinger, leaned toward the starched fatigue shirt of SP/5 Colin Alexander who had begun almost imperceptibly to shake his head. His mouth, trembling, formed a word. "No." The major's hand, metal star dangling, paused in midair. Major Holly smiled. "What's that, specialist?"

"I don't want it," said Alexander, "the medal, I mean."

Puzzled, Holly turned to his First Sergeant who was glaring with full NCO intensity into Alexander's face. "But this is yours," the major replied, "you've earned this honor."

Alexander shook his head. "No," he said, "I did what was required, that's all. I haven't earned anything more than my pay. If that," he added, staring straight ahead, focused on the grease gun on the far wall.

"But whether you accept this from me now or not," said Major Holly, "the award is part of your official record like it or not."

The grease gun was hard and bright.

"Yes, sir. I would prefer that it be removed from my record also."

The major moved closer, blocking the line of sight to the gun. "I don't know what sort of game you're playing here, specialist, but I wonder if you have stopped to consider all those other individuals past and present who have received this decoration with gratitude and dignity and I wonder if you don't think your behavior today is an insult to them and their accomplishments."

"No, sir." There was a fascinating mole on Holly's face.

Holly cocked his head to one side. "No sir what?"

"No, sir, I didn't stop to think that."

"I won't banter any further with you, specialist. If you don't want your award we'll simply send it home to your parents." Holly dropped the star back into the First Sergeant's box. "Your mother might have a different feeling about the country's recognition of her son's achievements."

"I'm sure she does," said Alexander.

"At ease, soldier," Holly snapped.

Holly stepped to the next chest, a muscle in his cheek conspicuously twitching. Close behind, the First Sergeant now assumed the vacated space in front of Alexander and allowed the cold stones of his eyes to press heavily upon the young specialist's insubordinate head. He did not blink. No First Sergeant ever blinked. Alexander focused on the distance. That grease gun seemed to have moved to the left since he last studied it.

Major Holly held up an Air Medal before a man who had taken control of a Mohawk flight after the pilot, the Executive Officer of the 1069th, passed out during a routine radar mission. "You're not about to disappoint your mother, are you?" he asked.

"No, sir," replied the man, Adam's apple bobbing.

"Glad to hear it," said Holly.

The rest of the heroes received their awards without complaint and after Major Holly had completed his presentations, he saluted the recipients, about-faced, and stalked from the hangar.

Tubs of iced beer were carted in, steaks tossed on hot grills, and the party began. The first beer cans were still being popped when Lieutenant Tremble backed Alexander against a dismantled fuselage, hissing like a maniac that Alexander was through, finished as an R&A specialist and if he was very lucky he'd spend the rest of the war scraping burned meat loaf out of greasy pans in the mess hall instead of toting a sixteen through the Ashau where he belonged and where he Lieutenant Tremble would pull every lever within reach to see that he went. Several officers applauded. Wurlitzer dropped his pants and showed Tremble a moon he could jump over. Sergeant Ramirez produced a pan of chocolate cake, the American flag in green and purple icing on top. "We all ought to get Purple Hearts for eating this crud," said Captain Marovicci. Sergeant Mars split a pineapple open with his machete. Simon strummed on a cracked guitar, singing, "Oh Lonesome Me." A group of pilots gathered in a corner reminiscing about Captain Lemington who crashed five planes during flight training. The black contingent abruptly appeared in the open doorway, surveyed the scene with consummate cool, and marched off with an entire tub of beer. Conrad, the "Motorola man," showed up for the first time in six weeks and everyone took turns guessing where he had been, Phnom Penh, Vientiane, the streets of Hanoi? Lieutenant Phan demonstrated his quick draw. Trips sneaked about, dropping tiny pills into people's drinks. Griffin was bored. More beer cans popped. The sun went down. Noll was engaged in an intense explication of the genetic theories of Alfred Rosenberg for a cluster of fascinated NCOs. Balanced on a wing, Wendell filmed Chief Winkly, stripped to the waist, attempting to rotate a pair of tassels pasted to his pendulous breasts. Lieutenant Mueller sat on the floor, gnawing on a steak bone and reading a book. Sergeants Anstin and Sherbert, taking a break in their drinking contest, stepped outside for a moment to see who could piss the furthest. Leaning forward for extra distance, Sherbert tripped and fell into a drainage ditch. Unable to get back up he lay there in the dirt helpless as an overturned turtle to the raucous amusement of a group of enlisted men who had been huddled in the dark passing a pipe stuffed with Thai flowers. Captain Patch, recipient that very afternoon of the final communication from his now ex-wife and her attorney, was propped against a garbage can too drunk to move. "Sergeant Sherbert," he bellowed, annoyed by this laughter from the lower grades, "I order you to remove yourself from that ditch ASAP." Sherbert tried again, arms and legs waving about uselessly. "Sorry, sir," he replied from his supine position, "I'm afraid I've been the victim of a slight miscalculation." "Sherbert!" There was no reply. "Sherbert!" Captain Patch ordered Griffin and Cross to carry their sergeant back to his room so Griffin wasn't present to hear Captain Raleigh comparing the Vietnamese people unfavorably to the retarded unfortunates his wife, a physical therapist volunteer, worked with daily back in the world or Sergeant Cott's tales about the early, less economically restricted days of the war when a friend of his left this land of green with about a quarter of a million in green stuffed into his ditty bag or see Captain Fry brandishing a yardstick and demanding that everyone present their penises for immediate measurement or the memorable look on Captain Raleigh's face going down under Alexander's quick return when he decided to teach this damn hippie a few lessons about patriotism and respect or the XO stepping between with words of caution to both men sufficient to break the mood and within an hour send the revelers staggering off in twos and threes into the warm night until only Vegetable was left sitting all alone in the cockpit of an incredibly expensive piece of aerial machinery, crooning a tune recognizable only to himself, while one greasy hand tilted a can of stale beer foaming over dials and gauges into wires and gears gurgle gurgle gurgle giving the hot thirsty plane a nice long drink.

Lieutenant Phan sat outside in the shade of the interrogation hut, straddling a gray office chair, his hairless arms dangling over the back, in the casual style he had learned at the movies: American

Cowboy. The smoke from the Salem cigarette in his right hand flowed upward along brown bony fingers like machine-made fog. When he took a drag, his head tilted to one side, an eye squinted. From where he sat he could see far across the runway and beyond the perimeter to distant water buffalo roaming over a flooded paddy. Claypool slouched in the sand at his feet, chipping away with his thumbnail at the black paint on the eyelets of his boots.

"Every day I see you coming and going," Lieutenant Phan said, "doing good work and everything is very fine but there is no smile, no talk. Such a serious face. Isn't this so?"

The thumb flicked away paint.

"I worry about you, Claypool." Lieutenant Phan's mouth opened to emit at precise intervals a series of progressively smaller smoke rings that fit inside each other like a set of Chinese boxes. In the air, circles wheeled, scattering. Lieutenant Phan looked up at the clouds and smiled. "You make me wish for a son of my own."

Chip, chip.

"See how you never talk, my American friend, but if I were to say, PFC Claypool, on the double, get me that report from yesterday, you would say, Yes, sir, Lieutenant Phan, I shall return immediately. Isn't that so, PFC Claypool?"

"I suppose." Claypool hunched over his boot like an ancient cobbler.

"There, you see, you can talk and isn't that much more friendly. You know, sometimes I think you do not make enough of an effort winning my heart and mind." His laugh was long and high, the screech of a prehistoric bird. "A day of many jokes." He smiled at Claypool. He was always smiling at Claypool. "This morning when you wouldn't even say hello I thought of our friends inside and I say, yes, I know many ways to help PFC Claypool talk." He screeched, he clapped his hands together in delight. "How did you like that one, good buddy?"

Claypool's thumbnail had turned black with trapped paint.

"Maybe when war is over I go to your Hollywood and tell jokes." Lieutenant Phan licked his thumb and forefinger and squeezed them hissing about the tip of his cigarette. Then carefully shredding the butt and filter, he tossed the pieces into the air. He reached in his shirt pocket for another.

"I think you are troubled, my young friend, and I think you are troubled because of a confusion. I think that you do not understand. Sometimes, I admit, I myself do not understand and this is my own country so I see how confusing it must be to someone like yourself." He stared up at the billowing clouds. "Which of the states did you say you come from?"

Claypool looked up at him for the first time. "Indiana," he said.

"Ah, yes, I forget, Indiana where the Indians live and the cowboys. You are a real cowboy, huh?"

"No," said Claypool. "There aren't any Indians."

"No? Then why is such a place called Indiana?"

"I don't know."

"Ah there, you see, sometimes you do not know about your country, either. How amusing. I think we are all funny people, don't you agree?"

"Yes," said Claypool.

"Sometimes I start to laugh and I cannot stop myself. Very bad manners but sometimes I cannot help it. Have you ever felt such a way?"

Chip, chip.

Smoke rings slipped skyward. "So," said Lieutenant Phan, "I will try to make you understand. Then you will not be troubled anymore."

Claypool started work on the other boot.

"My country is old, you understand, very very old. Many many wars. Many enemies, many deaths. Death all the time, a terrible business. So many ghosts sometimes you not always sure you are talking to a real person. Sometimes it does not matter. The ghosts talk back and they are very wise. Sometimes they are stupid. The killing goes on a long, long time. Chinese kill many ancestors of mine. Japanese kill great grandparents. French kill grandfather. VC kill aunts and uncles. Two sisters are prostitutes. Older brother leave for Paris many years ago. Younger brother drive cab in

Saigon. VC cousins try to kill me all the time." He smiled, puffed on his Salem. "Now, do you understand?"

"No . . . I . . . What?"

Lieutenant Phan was watching the clouds drift across the sky. "Live fire number ten," he said.

Claypool nodded gravely.

"VC very, very bad but VC understand." He slammed a fist into an open palm. "Captain Raleigh, Sergeant Mars, they understand also. Very good men. So now, do you?"

"I don't know."

"My family is very, very poor. Have nothing for long, long time. Now Lieutenant Phan has stereo—" he shot out his arm "—fine watch, and Playboy book. Maybe someday I go to Indiana. Look for Indians." His laugh broke into a hacking cough. "America number one, okay Stars and Stripes." He held out the green-and-white pack of Salems. "You want a cigarette, young Claypool?"

Claypool shook his head.

"No? You don't smoke. But this is a very bad mistake. Look here. You see how one time I blow smoke out mouth, next time out nose? You see? Do you know why? I will tell you. Everywhere all around there are angry ghosts too, who have no homes and they will try to come into your body, build hootches in the holes in your head. I no bullshit you American GI." He screeched merrily. "This very bad trouble, so you should, my friend, smoke, smoke all the time your wonderful American cigarettes or number ten trouble will get you." Lieutenant Phan stared down at Claypool, smoke pouring like steam from nostrils and lips.

"I think you're insane," said Claypool.

This was Claypool's last conversation with another human being. In the following week he was occasionally seen in the company of Trips, silent, expressionless, unresponsive. He took to his bed. Once, hearing a noise in his room, Griffin peered in to find him huddled under a yellowing sheet, eyes huge and bright. "You okay?" Griffin asked. The eyes shone like fog lamps.

Then Claypool abruptly disappeared. Two days went by before he was even missed. One afternoon, Sergeant Mars, requiring a pair of arms to wax and buff the office floor asked about The Kid. The General was coming, all hands were needed to apply cosmetics. Claypool couldn't be found, his room had been left unlocked and empty. No one knew where he had gone. Sergeant Mars put Mulhavey to work on the floor and in the confusion Claypool was forgotten again. Charts and slides were being hastily prepared, walls painted, speaking parts memorized. Captain Raleigh had spent a week writing and rehearsing to bored officers the briefing he was to present. Records were updated, reports harmonized, whole filing cabinets of disagreeable information locked and whisked out of sight. The cages were hosed down, the wire and bars polished. Certain unkempt prisoners were transferred to a hut behind the Spook House. One of Lieutenant Phan's men, outfitted in black pajamas, was placed in a cell and handcuffed to the wall, befitting his status as an uncooperative and unruly NVA intelligence officer. (The General would be so impressed by his chat with "Major Quang" that the next day a mountain in western I Corps would be flattened by B-52s on the assumption it contained the top secret headquarters of communist intelligence for all South Vietnam.) Who could concern themselves with Claypool? The General was coming, The General was coming.

Claypool couldn't have told anyone where he was either. He seemed to have awakened from a nightmare and found himself trapped in completely unrecognizable surroundings. Alone and frightened, he sat in the dark, looking out into the light. He took off his shirt to study the letters stenciled above the right pocket: CLAYPOOL. Whose clothes were these? They couldn't be his anymore. He had abandoned that name and the life clinging to it like dead meat, he had thrown it away and gone on as easily as one removes a pebble from a shoe. Now, if he was anything at all, he was simply a spy, squatting in the dark to peer between slats through a screen, watching. He watched and wrote in dirt upon the wall notes for his superiors of what he saw. Through wire mesh that sparkled like a theater screen he could see outside bands of the green people walking to and fro with buckets of liquid. When they applied this liquid buildings would vanish. Of course he knew the liquid was white paint but it wasn't. He couldn't be fooled again. The paint was a chemical like typewriter correcting fluid and soon all the mistakes would be erased. As they worked, the crews of green people drank the liquid from smaller cans. He knew this was beer but of course it wasn't. Like the walls and the hootches these people would disappear too, as surely and completely as mistyped letters in an interrogation report. Day after day, as he watched, the crews of green people continued their work and the light got brighter and brighter. It wouldn't be long until the screen was as clean and white as a page upon which nothing had ever been written. In the sky green machines flew back and forth carrying drums of the liquid everywhere. When they came to do his wall would he disappear too? He thought so. He knew he was a mistake.

One morning, after The General had come and gone, the unit had settled back into routine, a tall sunburned man, dirty from weeks in the field, dull from too many nights without sleep, came in through the front gate. All he could see before him was a cold shower and a clean bed so he failed to notice Major Holly exiting the orderly room and walking past in the opposite direction. "Forget something, soldier?" called a voice. The man turned. Major Holly stood in the middle of the company street, hands on his hips, his mouth twisted in an expression of childish disgust. The man shrugged his shoulders and walked away. Holly returned to the orderly room to find out just who this insubordinate troop could be. The First Sergeant, who had witnessed the little drama from his window, was delighted to inform him. The man's name was Kraft, one of Quimby's personal favorites.

Kraft unlocked the door to his room, dumped his gear in a corner, and was seated on the edge of his bed, unlacing his boots, when he heard the rustle behind his locker. Quietly he picked up his weapon. The last rat he discovered in his room escaped with half a tail. This one he'd beat to death with his rifle butt. He crept to the locker, raised his arm. That was how Claypool was finally found.

"Who are you?" Kraft demanded.

The figure huddled deeper into the dark.

"How the hell did you get in here?"

He hauled Claypool from his hiding place. There was a pile of shit on the floor. He shook him roughly. "Who are you, smudge?" Claypool's mouth opened and closed, his eyes rolled backward, his body went limp in Kraft's hands. He hadn't eaten in over a week.

Sergeant Mars wasn't surprised. He had begun his military career as a Fort Polk drill sergeant cultivating amoeba and jellyfish into sharks. He had recognized Claypool's species immediately and knew that sooner or later much work would be required. Now he could begin. First, he hustled Claypool off to the showers, watched to be sure he got clean; then he escorted him back to his room, made sure he dressed in fresh fatigues; then he marched him to the mess hall, made sure he ate; then he took him to the office to type interrogation reports for the rest of the day. At 1700 he escorted him back to the mess hall, watched him eat dinner; then accompanied him back to his room, watched him get into bed and before he left, leaned over Claypool's ear and whispered that if he Claypool were not up and ready to work by 0800 the next morning he would be treated to further on-the-job training, which might include experiencing certain interrogation techniques from the novel point of view of the "interrogatee." Understand, cunt? Claypool's head rubbed against the pillow. Yes.

That night was Griffin's turn to pull guard duty in the tower. He sat, armed and alert, on an ammunition crate behind a low wall of sandbags high above the sleeping company. The tower always reminded him of the cab of a monstrous semitrailer truck. Bolted to the platform were a pair of huge arc lamps that searched the humid darkness for the center line and dangerous hitchhikers. Clouds of strange insects swarmed through the cones of light, the constant buzz loud and monotonous. It was always a struggle not to fall asleep at the wheel. Even the amphetaminelike thought that in the event of an "incident" the tower guard made the best target lost its effectiveness over the hours. The mind tended to wander. By two in the morning Griffin was Angst Angstrom, pilot, mystic, and lover, hovering at the controls of his star cruiser as it rocketed on to the rim of the universe and beyond. The insects were stars streaming past, the sizzling noise every few seconds as another careless bug cremated itself against the hot lamps was a laser explosion, the shattering of a world. Angst's mission was to penetrate the edge, cross over into a realm where space was light, the stars were black, and death an eruption of color. Holes had appeared in the membrane of energy separating the two universes. Evil forces were seeping in. Angst had been sent to plug the dike. A risky business, but Angstrom wasn't worried, in a tight situation he could transform himself simultaneously into both a wave and a corpuscle, slip undetected through enemy strongholds. Stars rushed at him. Angstrom checked his instruments. This was it. Insects crackled against the light shields, wisps of blue smoke sputtered up. He leaned forward. Ahead of him infinity began breaking down into doors. The field phone clattered.

"Hello," said a voice.

"Hello," said Griffin.

"Hello," said Sergeant Mars, tonight's CQ speaking from a desk in the orderly room.

"He's here," the voice announced.

"Who?" asked Sergeant Mars. "Who's here? Who the hell is *this*?"

"Hello?" said the voice.

"Noll," said Sergeant Mars, "is that you?"

"Holy shit. His body was all white and glowy like."

"Whose body? Noll, what are you on tonight?"

"It's real, man. I could feel the wind when he flew over my head."

"Say again."

"I turned the corner and next thing he's leaping out the back of a deuce and a half right at me. He's here, I tell you, he's really here."

"Who, Noll? Who's here?"

"I don't know, Sarge, I think it's God."

From his elevated position between the latrine and the EM club Griffin had an unobstructed view into the motor pool. Phone in hand, he turned, curious for a glimpse of the Almighty down there among all those neat rows of jeeps and trucks and, as he did, was startled to see a naked man leap the sandbags behind the garage and come bounding up the hill back of the chapel. Griffin lost sight of him somewhere in the shadows between the cooks' and mechanics' hootches. That flash of skin was hardly a surprise; any day now he had been expecting one of them—Vegetable? Wurlitzer? Trips?—to unwrap, to go natural; you could feel the adhesive coming loose in the humidity, the edges beginning to curl, then you knew your own bare body hurtling through the night, limbs in flame, running from, running toward, the exhilarating fear of how easy it would be simply to keep on, past the regs, across the laws, over the code, boundaries bursting like ribbon, on into a jungle of hair and teeth, raking the darkness with extended claws.

At dawn the following morning a man dressed in plaid shirt, tan pants, gray Hush Puppies, and clutching a black leather briefcase was apprehended by Air Force security attempting to board a C-130 to Cam Ranh Bay. He carried no wallet, no identification card. "It is time to go," he announced. "I am under orders." Captain Marovicci, who happened to be at the terminal awaiting delivery of a package of contraband from a government connection in Thailand, recognized the prisoner and offered to take him off Air Force hands. Back at the 1069th orderly room the man was questioned. He smiled, contemplated his feet. The briefcase was opened. Inside was a miscellaneous jumble of wires, transistors, and tubes obviously stolen from the signal shack and, curiously, one used paint brush. "What is this?" demanded Major Holly. The man held a reel of recording tape to each ear. "Listen," he said, staring into space, "stereo." Major Holly and Captain Marovicci looked at one another. The man was driven over to the 92nd Evac. The diagnosis was back by the end of the day: acute alcoholic poisoning. The officers were relieved. The enlisted men laughed. Claypool had never once even swallowed a single sip of beer. The last the 1069th heard of him he had been bundled aboard a planeload of brain and spinal injuries for transport to a military hospital on Okinawa where, as Trips liked to joke, he could spend the remainder of the war, sitting in a closet and drooling in his shoe.

Meditation in Green: 11

I want to grow big as a house, strong as the wind.
I want roots that are deep and complex and secure.
I want birds in my hair, squirrels on my arms, children
climbing over my skin.
I want to cool, to comfort, to inspire.
I want to expand the day with oxygen.
I want to cast shade on lovers.
I want to catch lightning bolts in my fists.
I want to pose nude against a flaming sun.
I want to die in a shower of color and return from
the dead with annual regularity.
I want to live a long long time.
And when at last my body withers I want the bones
converted into pencils and baseball bats.
If Daphne's pleas were answered, why not mine?

I found Arden in his office closet, stacking shelves with plastic flower pots. In his green cowled robe and high-top sneakers he resembled an eccentric elf with glandular problems. Perhaps it was the location. The Green Bean occupied the entire second floor above a magic and costume shop. On the way up you passed plastic vomit and rubbery body parts, lifelike masks of flesh-eating ghouls and modern presidents.

"One free to the first hundred people signing up for our introductory course," he explained. "You'll see them, big letters everywhere, newspapers, wall posters, mimeographed handouts: FREE POT. Thought of it myself, Grif, what do you think?"

"Don't call me Grif."

"Oh? What do I call you?"

"G."

"G?"

"Just the initial. I'm down to the initial."

"You're not sleeping well, I can see that."

"Everything's fuzzy. Everything looks like there's mold growing on it."

"What about the bathroom, what happened there?"

"I went tile blind."

"Do me a favor, Grif—excuse me, G.—don't tell anyone you're a student of mine. Years of painstaking analysis and perfected technique roll off your back like water. Thank God you never appeared in any of the advertising."

"What can I say?"

"Let's hear the gory details."

"Insomnia. Migraine. Vertigo. General phantasmagoria."

"I've had visions. I told you about those, didn't I. They went away."

"Teeming walls. Fornicating furniture. Cockatoos in the curtains. I crawl into bed with a machete and a canteen."

"You familiar with the term 'China syndrome'?"

"What, I'm having a meltdown?"

"I think you concentrate extraordinarily well."

"My karma's radioactive for the next ninety-nine years?"

"However, I also think that all your considerable attentive abilities are beamed at present onto too flimsy a screen. Temperature mounts, collisions abound, and soon you've got yourself a critical breeder."

"I don't think I can handle the lead suit."

"I like this resistance, you know that. What's a rose without thorns? Listen, I'm sorry about the shouting when you were here last. Sometimes the robes get unduly heavy. It ain't easy being serene day and night. The paradox of tense tranquillity. I believe there are references in the ancient masters. It's something I'm still working on myself. But to return to your problem, have you ever considered gardening?"

"Isn't that what we've been doing these many months?"

"Let's speak nonfiguratively for a moment. Blistered palms, damp knees, gummy soil under the nails gardening."

"No, I have to admit I've never engaged in nonfigurative gardening."

"Yes, I think we need to go 3-D with this."

"Wonderful. I love those little cardboard glasses."

"I remain serene. You see me, a fountainhead of equanimity. The pure abstraction is, of course, the meditative object of choice among true devotees, but someone with your psychic reserves requires more than mental images and two-dimensional photographs for their energy to effloresce properly. You need the concrete. The objectification of interiority. So we turn the glove inside out before reinserting the hand. Do you understand?"

"No."

"Sowing, tending, watering, whatever one does to produce a healthy plant. Target on the actual green thing. Prune, mulch, hover."

"Should I wear an apron and sing to them, too?"

"Cooperation, please, a little patience and cooperation. Give it a chance. Choose a plant you can relate to, something you feel good about. Here, to begin." He handed me a plastic pot. "Free."

"This doesn't mean I have to sit through the course again?"

"Be nice, G. Say it with flowers."

The CID was sympathetic but they simply had no legal grounds for holding Private Franklin. There were no witnesses, no evidence, no telltale stains, no fingerprints of any kind on a knife no one could prove was his. "Favorable odds do not a case make," said Captain Rossiter who was thoroughly sick of Franklin's antics but tired of running a hotel for misfits and delinquents. Their detention facility was already crowded with certain convictions and the notorious LBJ had exceeded its official capacity years ago. There simply was no more room to house a man who was a perpetual suspect.

So that was how Private Franklin came to occupy a special chair in the orderly room of the 1069th where he could be found from morning formation to evening chow under the custodial eye of the First Sergeant. And if Major Holly expected Franklin to break down and confess, thought Simon who worked at a desk across from the detainee, everyone within range of Franklin's mouth was in for a long siege. No quiet on this front.

"Hey, Top! How long I got to sit here?"

"All day."

"How long for all day?"

"Till the CO says otherwise."

"Shee-it. This the use the army makes of a man's talents? I got multiple talents. What kind of contribution can I make here?"

"You can shut up and let the rest of us get on with the business of winning this war."

"Winning? *Winning?* You people are even crazier than me. I ain't never figured you folks out yet."

"So sit and watch, learn something."

"Can I smoke?"

"No."

"Can I read? Give me that paper there."

"No."

"Well, what the fuck am I supposed to do?"

"Think about being a good soldier."

"How can I think in here with all this chatter? And my chair's too hard. Hey, Top, give me one of them like yours with a cushion on it."

The clerks looked at one another. The First Sergeant fired a sharpened pencil at Franklin's head. Simon put on his headphones and typed to the music. A betting pool formed with the pot going to the one who came nearest to correctly guessing the date upon which the First Sergeant reverted and dealt with his tormentor on a more primal level. The afternoons were usually less tense since Franklin dozed in his chair. Major Holly came out of his office to glare. Franklin snored away in the corner. As word spread, officers and NCOs from other units dropped by to check out the sassy black in the orderly room and Franklin, who was already a celebrity among members of his own unit and the nearby military police companies, was soon famous throughout I Corps as the voice and symbol of the exotically secret 1069th Military Intelligence Group. Inspired by the attention, Franklin's personality quick-shifted into a variety of gears.

"I'm a hairy eyeball," he proclaimed, swaying in his chair. "I see galloping moons, I see green fire, I see little bitty yellow men running through the woods, I see you, I see me, I see bad shit, whoooeeee."

The mania in his laughter evidence enough for most onlookers to convict him of all charges.

"I'm hungry," Franklin declared. "How about a slice of watermelon?"

At the O club conversation became speculative. Was the graffiti in the latrine turning ominous? The list of missing weapons in the supply growing longer? The drums in the night beating louder? What *was* going on down in the Voodoo Hootch? The rituals conducted within that closed building were as mysterious to whites as the clandestine activities of the Spook House across the compound were to those with insufficient clearances. As far as anyone knew only one honky had ever been permitted beyond the door decorated with painted drawings of fierce masklike faces and Weird Wendell's standard reply to the curious was that the occupants partied each night by opening veins in one another's forearms, toasting the demons with brass canisters of blood, and dancing about a flickering Sterno can clad in their jockstraps. This segment of his film was entitled *The War In Vietnam: Going Native Or Getting Down?* The party was nonstop at the Voodoo Hootch, laughter, shouts, dope scent around the clock; someone was always up and tending the flame. One night a lonely Griffin searching for company was attracted by the noise and stood outside in the dark listening to Franklin, founding father, chief interpreter of the white man's military ways, and major drug dealer, engaged in a fabulous harangue to an audience of recent black arrivals: "You ever see a *black* man punching buttons over in the fancy computer room? See a *black* man climbing down out of a pilot's seat? A *black* man with thick glasses showing slides to The General in that air-conditioned whorehouse they got underground? Tell me, any of you ever see a single one of those miraculous sights? No? You say no? And why ain't you seen that and why ain't you ever going to see that no matter what garbage comes spilling out The Man's mouth? I'll tell you why, because Marse Sam he don't want no coons up in the big house on the hill, don't want no filthy black fingers on all them shiny new buttons, don't want no real spooks mixing with the white spooks. Here it is, brothers, this here's a white spook's war. Only way we get into it 'sides Sambos and cannon fodder is to put on white sheets. Put on white sheets and go off scaring and chasing these yellow folks same way The Man's been doing to us for two hundred years. Time has come to stop this jive, time to say no, brothers, time to break the chains, time to go free, time to make up a mess of trouble for this nasty white boogie man, time to end this war, time to bring down this devil army, bring it down, that's right, bring it down, you heard me, bring it *down*!" A burst of shouts, handclaps, a stamping of feet on the wooden floor sudden as rifle fire, then the screech of a guitar as the music came on and under cover of the cry, "Scuse me while I kiss the sky," Griffin crept back to his room. No place for him at this party even though Franklin had once in a fit of wicked generosity said to both Trips and Griffin, "Hey, I like you guys so much that come the revolution I'm gonna personally shoot the two of you myself so your suffering won't be dragged out." Whether or not Franklin's daily detention was a factor in hastening the arrival of that day couldn't be determined but racial tension had certainly become more dangerous. Hagen, the motor pool mechanic, who enjoyed getting drunk and prowling for a fight, was found behind the garbage dump bleeding and unconscious after a night in which he had declared he was going out on one of his periodic "coon hunts." Doctors at the 92nd Evac tactfully ascribed his injuries to "a fall from a jeep." A couple weeks later a scuffle erupted in the mess hall in front of the milk machine. An overturned table, some spilled food, a couple of tossed chairs. The blacks took to marching to and from the mess hall and the EM club in a silent swaggering group armed with pieces of scrap lumber they called "freedom sticks." The XO worried about a race riot, Major Holly advised calm or at the least a convincing facsimile.

More weeks passed, without violence or further incident. Then one morning Major Holly, consciousness swarming with the homilies and admonishments he had planned to release at the day's formation, stepped out the orderly room door and was confronted by a double row of black soldiers blocking his path. "Excuse me, gentlemen," he said in an even voice. No one moved. The blacks stared at the major, he stared at them. The moment expanded with inflammables. Then, as though a telepathic signal had been passed, all the blacks turned around and took their places in the regular morning formation. Nothing more was spoken, nothing more needed to be spoken. "Spooky," muttered the XO, "real spooky."

Franklin, of course, knew nothing about nothing. "Ise right chere on de bench, massa, doan see nuffin wat dat trash do outdoor." Major Holly was silent. The First Sergeant snorted all day as though something was caught up his nose. The XO slept with a revolver under his pillow.

Weeks passed without incident. "They made their point," said Major Holly, "it's over." "No," said the XO, "something's brewing, something big." The CO smiled.

One morning Franklin reported for his chair warming session wearing on a chain around his neck what appeared to Simon to be a small dried apricot.

"Okay," said the First Sergeant. "What's that?"

"Lucky charm."

"Some sort of African mumbo jumbo?" asked the First Sergeant, coming from behind his desk for a closer examination. "May I?" He reached out a hand.

"Be my guest," said Franklin, leaning confidently back into his chair.

The First Sergeant felt the apricot with his fingers.

"Y'all can line up here," said Franklin, "behave nice now so everybody can get a turn."

"Where the hell did you get this?" exclaimed the First Sergeant, voice rising in volume on each word.

"Guess I found it."

"Now listen here, son, you best come clean with me or I'm gonna break you into so many pieces we'll have to have a police call to put you back together."

Simon checked the calendar on his desk. One of his dates in the pool came up this week.

"It's my part," said Franklin. "I got to do my part in this war, too."

The First Sergeant stormed into the CO's office. The clerks looked at one another. Franklin picked his fingernails with the point of a pencil. The First Sergeant and the CO came out of the office. The CO picked up the offending apricot, then dropped it instantly.

"Where did you get this?" asked Holly.

"I thought you'd be real proud of me."

"Answer the major," said the First Sergeant.

"I snuck over the wire last night, crawled out into that gook village and got me a VC. How's that for initiative?"

"Take it off," said the CO, holding out a hand.

"Jesus, you fucking white folks." He tore the chain from around his neck. "If you want it that bad. Should pay me something, too."

Holly, the confiscated apricot in his fist, returned to the inner sanctum of his office. The clerks looked at one another. Simon put on his headphones. Franklin sat in his chair, cracking his knuckles. Finally, the First Sergeant emerged from the CO's office, settled himself at his desk, and began leafing through a pile of paper work. Long minutes passed. Then the First Sergeant looked over at Franklin, studied him for a moment and said, "If I had an entire company composed of individuals such as yourself, private, I think I would seriously consider my chances with the gooks."

Franklin adjusted his face into a crafty smirk.

If there hadn't been such a stigma attached to welfare assistance Chief Warrant Officer Ernest Winkly might never have joined the army. Intimidated by the idea of college, insulted by the actuality of work, dismissed by his family, he was, in his late adolescence, a young man in need of a plan. An older cousin, on leave from the magic kingdom of Basic Training, brought Winkly Technicolored tales of drinking, swearing, and screwing. "You get paid for this, too?" Downtown, over Cokes and cigarettes, the local recruiter confirmed the details. He offered Winkly a pen. Later, lying awake listening to the sighs and sobs of his fellow trainees, Winkly would smile up at the bulging bunk springs above him thinking, that was a good one, cuz, you really got me this time. A regular prankster himself, he could appreciate the cruelly skillful execution of a "good one." He soon realized, though, that beyond the immediate nooselike horizon of hysterical drill sergeants, pulled muscles, and Brasso there was a special civilized world of quiet duty and loud nights. Instead of revenge, Winkly plotted to apply, at the earliest opportunity, for warrant officers school, a rank high enough to earn salutes, low enough to escape the imprisonment of command. The career had turned out rather well, better than his marriage, fifteen leisurely years of guaranteed paychecks, hot meals, and discount booze linked to a dim succession of identical gray steel desks scattered throughout the Free World where he sat, eye on the clock, shuffling cards and retailing shelf-worn anecdotes. The cards were notorious, his private collection a frequent bar topic from Heidelberg to Fort Hood. The center of each playing card bore an invariably grainy photograph (fifty-two different poses per deck) of a naked woman either having sex or about to have sex or thinking about sex with either herself, another woman, or one of an assortment of lonely farm and zoo animals. To Winkly these blurred off-tone reproductions were artistic wonders deserving repeated consideration and comment; certainly they occupied his time, those seductive games of solitaire spread pink and glossy across his bare desktop, hour after hour, day after day.

"Ho ho, the seven of clubs. Griffin!"

In the back room Griffin's petitioning eyes rolled ceilingward. "Yes, chief." He was alone in his counting house, counting defunct nipa palm, acre after blighted acre of leafless trunks like dandelion stems gone yellow to white and dispersed by the wind. Except that these breezes sowed no seeds.

"Get in here! You ever see what a pig's dick looks like?"

"No, chief."

"About time you did. Get in here."

The card, erect in a stubby fist, greeted Griffin rounding the corner to Winkly's loud, "You see that?" pointing a dirty fingernail. "It curls up into a corkscrew like the tail."

"How do you know it isn't?"

"Isn't what? Curled?"

"Isn't the tail. It looks like a real pig's tail to me."

"So tell me the last time you saw a pig's tail."

"Her face is green."

"Of course it's green. What color do you think your face would be sucking on a pig's dick?"

"I like the eight of hearts. The snake must have been drugged."

Winkly shuffled rapidly, raised a second card in smirking anticipation.

"Good God," Griffin exclaimed. "Don't tell me *that* turns you on."

"Griffin, my boy, I don't have a choice. If you could pull back the top of my head and peep inside all you'd see would be little pussies."

"With that crowd up there how can you possibly concentrate on your game?"

"I can't, that's why I want to talk to you. There's been a change in mission plans."

"Again?"

"Now hold on before you get your balls in an uproar. This guy with the Americal called who he and I go back a long way, Dix in 'fifty-nine, and he's gonna be in Saigon then, too, so I'm flying down on the twenty-third before he flies back to the field and you fly down and meet me on the twenty-sixth only two days later than we planned. Not disappointed are you?"

"Of course not."

"I figured your pecker would keep and all the girls'll still be there, walking stiff-legged with cock burn maybe, but still there. Got your bag packed yet?"

Griffin cupped a hand over his groin. "Roger, it's packed."

"That's affirm," whooped Winkly, slapping Griffin on the butt. "We're gonna have a great time, you and I, a real grunt time." His voice dropped to a dramatic whisper. "You're not gonna bring any of that stuff you people smoke, are you? I'd hate to see what the captain would do to the both of us if you got caught."

"What stuff is that, chief?"

"Roger," Winkly replied, "over and out."

Griffin returned to his palms, temples throbbing like the sides of a bell.

For the next sixteen days Griffin was unable to pass Winkly's desk without undergoing similar interrogations that left him feeling like an erotic immigrant. He began to arrive late for work, hoping the chief was already gone. Instead, he'd be greeted by "Hey stud, watcha doing, getting in some practice sessions before the trip?" Drawn through time his carefully composed smile turned brittle, had begun to crack when Winkly, sunglassed and cologned, departed at last for the open legs of Saigon. Griffin went limp with relief. He seemed to have just been expelled from the musty interior of a dirty joke that had no punch line. For two days even the office was not unpleasant. He toyed with phoning the chief, sorry, sudden onset, bones ache, skin burns, asshole leaks, maintenance required, can't be helped, things happen, another time, huh? But seven days without Winkly were also seven days with bleeding trees, sore eyes, stiff muscles, the dead stink of warm film, the same faces, the same complaints, the same ugly hootches, the same stand, the same sky, the same sameness. The entire area occupied by the 1069th Military Intelligence Unit was no larger than one fair-sized city block. Griffin hadn't set foot outside this area except to visit the PX, a dull warehouse well within the protective confines of the base, and to accompany Sergeant Sherbert on that disturbing jeep trip to Da Nang, the memory already clouded with a sort of perverse cheer which said, now I have seen that, now I can put that behind me. He needed to get out again. The signs were everywhere. He had started to enjoy abusive arguments, he couldn't sufficiently concentrate to read a comic book, he yawned a lot. Childhood claustrophobia had returned. When he slept, the walls moved so after he got up everything was smaller. This must be what a convict feels, he imagined, with his cell, his daily work space, the shuffle to chow and back again, the slow turns around a sandy yard, and outside, beyond the wire and guard towers, the hostile population that kept you locked in. Saigon would be a temporary parole, in the custody of a difficult probation officer to be sure, but at least an outing, a change, a chance to breathe. Trips's favorite joke wasn't so funny anymore. Sensory evidence provided no clues to contradict his theory that they had not in fact left the United States at all but were simply prisoners in a bizarre behavioral study somewhere in Utah. Except for a few KPs, a couple latrine attendants, and a handful of maids, everyone around was quite American, speaking American, eating American, driving American, reading American, rocking American, the sky itself crisscrossed dense as grandma's knitting with American aircraft and American telephone poles and American wire. The difference of Saigon might allow him to believe he had been somewhere.

"You'll be sorry," Trips warned.

"The chief said he'd loan me one of his rubbers," replied Griffin.

So on the scheduled day Major Holly's driver, Ellis, drove Griffin to the air terminal. He was fizzing with news.

"The CO's sending me home," he said.

"Yeah?"

"Seems like I've got this here weird skin disease now, they don't know what it is, see." He lifted his hands into the air. The jeep veered toward the ditch. "I've got to wear these here gloves. The steering wheel hurts my fingers."

"Yeah, is this contagious?"

"They don't know that either, but I'm sure hoping. Don't see why it shouldn't be, and let me tell you, if it is you'll have to pay to touch me. I think I can make enough to buy a new car when I get home."

"Well, good luck, Ellis."

"Thanks, I scratch it every chance I get."

Inside the terminal, a huge metal shed stuck next to a runway of portable steel plating, Griffin was informed he had been bumped by a lieutenant colonel on emergency leave. "I don't know," said the Air Force sergeant behind the counter. "I think one of his warehouses in New Jersey just burned down. Afraid there's nothing till six tomorrow morning."

"Fine," said Griffin. "Wake me."

He spent the night curled up on the concrete floor, his AWOL bag for a pillow, dreaming of his mother washing windows, a stone mansion of a hundred windows, gray and brown streaks across the glass, the water in the bucket turning ink black and even when all the windows had been washed no one could see in or out.

At five-thirty the Air Force sergeant tapped him on the top of the head. "Our turbo prop service to Da Nang is now loading at gate three."

On the plane Griffin was the only passenger below the rank of E-7. He knew he was out of place, he should have been on the ground, slogging with his peers through the grass and the mud. He sat beside a pale grim major in dress uniform whose briefcase looked inappropriate without being handcuffed to his wrist. There were a pair of captains who resembled twins, a lieutenant wearing love beads, and various other bars and stripes he barely glanced at. No one spoke to anyone else. Two minutes after take-off Griffin was sound asleep again.

The thump of the landing gear locking down jolted him awake. Da Nang. Marines, whores, bands of five-year-old beggars. Parked on the ground amid all the armed clutter of Phantom fighters and Cobra helicopters was a massively incongruous jumbo jet blue-lettered PAN AM. In a matter of hours this airliner would screech down into Tokyo, Taipei, Hong Kong, Bangkok, or some other mythical R&R spa too distant to imagine. In the open doorway an awkwardly poised stewardess tried to keep the wind from lifting her skirt.

Inside the passenger terminal, in addition to the usual airport confusion, a group of Australians in bush hats and tailored camouflage fatigues, their plastic chairs drawn into a cozy circle, were singing in accented English and to harmonica accompaniment a bawdy version of "Home On The Range." Griffin headed straight for the counter. The Air Force sergeant here said there was nothing for him until possibly 1000. Griffin stretched himself out across several uncomfortable chairs and closed his eyes. The terminal sounded like the noise inside a sea shell. At 1000 the Air Force sergeant told him to come back at 1300. At 1300 he said to try again in an hour or two. Griffin wandered outside to watch the jets take off, plumes of fire and soot spurting from their tails. In a rusty trash barrel he found half a magazine. After Hours With Your Senator—A Lively Guide To D.C. Sex Clubs. Enhance Your Pleasure With Our Amazing Erection Extender. Debbie's Favorite Foods are Shredded Coconut And Bananas. At 1500 there were still no vacant seats headed south, but around back there might be an army helicopter with some room leaving for Chu Lai in about twenty minutes. The overhead blades had just begun to turn when Griffin found the Huey parked behind a row of F-4 revetments. Holding onto his cap, he ran up in a crouch. "Chu Lai?" he screamed. The door gunner nodded. Griffin clambered aboard. The helicopter seemed to tighten for a moment as if screwing itself into the ground, then it leaped into the air like a grasshopper.

There was only one other passenger, a Spec Four with black rimmed glasses and pimples on his chin who looked almost twelve. He and Griffin nodded, mouthed "Hi" to one another. The engine noise made any conversation other than an exchange of shouts impossible. Griffin held his cap in his hands. The sharp humid wind roaring in through the open doorway stung his eyes and turned even the short strands of hair the army permitted him into tiny whips across his forehead. The chief, of course, had been chauffeured nonstop to Tan Son Nhut in Captain Fry's Mohawk. Griffin wondered if he had caught the clap yet. The door gunner, in large polished boots, one-piece flight suit, thick gloves, head surrounded by a huge bulbous helmet, face masked behind a sun visor, sat on the floor, feet dangling above the skid outside. He looked like a robot or the man from the fumigation company.

The door gunner sat as still as an artist's model, studying the squares of flooded paddy below with the concentrated intensity of a chess master. He made Griffin nervous. What did he see? What was he expecting to see? What was he waiting for? Griffin looked down. It all seemed pretty routine to him, farms, roads, trees, hootches, the same routine in fact that was forever erupting into violent surprise. Idyllic valley one moment, howling badlands the next. The door gunner's job obviously was to watch, to detect quickly the signs of impending metamorphosis, his care a matter of SOP, not an omen. Reasoning so, Griffin coaxed himself into an alert relaxation, allowed his body to settle into the webbing of his seat. He was only a passenger anyway, there was nothing he could do. His fate in other hands, he was soon asleep again, eased into unconsciousness by the magic fingers of Bell Helicopter.

When he woke Pimplechin was staring at him with an annoyingly clinical expression. The same dreary landscape was moving endlessly past the door. He might have been out for a minute or an hour. How far from Chu Lai? The door gunner, now semierect, leaned easily in the doorway as if he were a bus rider awaiting his stop. Griffin tapped him on the leg. The door gunner bent over to listen, then seemed to lose his balance on the slippery vibrating floor. Griffin reached up to steady him but just as his hands touched the door gunner's arm and chest the man fell clumsily across Griffin's lap. "Whoops," said Griffin, smiling, and saw in the dark sun visor of the door gunner's helmet a modest white-rimmed hole radiating silver cracks across the unrecognizable reflection of Griffin's horrified face pushing the door gunner off his knees onto the floor. Quickly unbuckling his seat strap, he stood, looking about the small interior of the helicopter in frantic confusion as if he had lost something personal or forgotten something important. Across from him Pimplechin continued to sit quietly in his seat looking up at Griffin with an air of serene amusement. This person is insane, Griffin thought. The helicopter rocked hard to one side. Griffin held on to a handful of exposed wires overhead. The pilot, a chubby burr-headed warrant officer, was turned halfway around in his seat, waving his arm, and yelling something Griffin could not understand. The helicopter rocked again. Griffin's body swayed back and forth. Pieces of paint and dust shook down into his eyes. Pimplechin, his unamused face now a marble gray, pointed to Griffin's hand. Blood from somewhere was dripping off the tips of the fingers. There it is, he thought, it's coming out and I can't stop it. A sudden roll slammed his body painfully against the wall. The door gunner did not move. Pimplechin was trying to unbuckle himself, but his hands couldn't seem to manipulate the lock. What the hell was the pilot shouting? Repel all boarders, it sounded like. Blood was pumping out of a white plastic hole. A thin rivulet was winding its deliberate way among the corrugations stamped into the metal floor. Griffin was still trying to remember. The helicopter shook and shook like a wet dog. In a moment the gears and all the bolts would come loose, trickle out the bottom in a runny metallic shit. If he could remember all of this would stop. The engine sounded like gravel in a blender. Griffin heard a voice in his ear, "Waste those motherfuckers, oh goddamn goddamn," and his hands were shaking the machine gun and his arms were shaking too and Pimplechin shaking up and down beside him was helping to feed the belt into the gun that shook to the trees, the paddies, the huts, the bugs on the ground, the bugs everywhere, shaking and shaking, his own parts coming loose, sliding around like yolks in a pan, shaking the bolt out of the center of the world so a trillion agitated pieces come falling down like Christmas snow in a plastic ball in synchronized vibration until all the bugs were gone because the pilot had swung the damaged machine away to sputter along off the bone white coast above the unarmed sea. Griffin hunched over, heaving, unable to get enough air, his tongue turned to sand. He felt a hand on his shoulder. "Hey, you're okay," said Pimplechin. The pilot, again twisted around in his seat, held up a thumb. The floor was awash in red fluid as if a hydraulic line had burst. The wind screamed through the open doorway. Molded to the machine gun in front of him were a pair of ugly sculptures in wax, his hands. The crotch of his pants was wet. "You ever do that before?" asked Pimplechin. "No," replied Griffin, wondering where he could find a clean pair before anyone else noticed. "I think you must have got at least two of them," said Pimplechin. "Two what?" asked Griffin. Pimplechin punched him playfully on the shoulder. The red fluid flowed around Griffin's feet and out the corner of the door, whipped to a spray by the wind. Pimplechin was squatting over the door gunner, feeling through his pockets. Then there was a wallet between his fingers and a wad of bills he slipped inside his boot. He looked up at Griffin and shrugged. Behind him a wall of green ocean water blocked the door. Griffin's hands, bouncing up and down, remained locked about the gun all the way in to Chu Lai. Now and then he glanced with cold curiosity at the door gunner beneath him who lay in the most awkward position imaginable but so still and relaxed he might have been stretched out on the softest mattress in the world.

The Huey settled with a bump onto a huge red cross. A team of businesslike specialists removed the door gunner from the floor. The pilot came around to shake Griffin's hand. "Fine work," he said. "You ever want a job with us, let me know. We got plenty of openings."

A medic led Griffin to an unoccupied bed and a pair of clean fatigue pants that actually fit. He collapsed into dreamless nothingness until the following noon when a doctor with smudged glasses taped to his nose and what looked like a butcher's smock tied around his waist woke him up shouting, "Everyone to surgery ASAP." Griffin stumbled outside and hours later located a Marine Chinook bound for Saigon with half a dozen Marine officers in starched khakis, a squad of armed teenagers representing the army of the Republic of South Vietnam, and a couple families of refugees with a seven- or eight-year-old boy carrying a bamboo cage containing a white duck that, obviously frightened and air sick, quacked and dribbled gray shit all over the floor throughout the flight. One of the Marines said the duck was probably the boy's sister.

Griffin could never have been completely prepared for Saigon. It had been too long, months in public time, busy eons by the private clock, since he had seen a building taller than one story, a music store, a glass window, the name of a restaurant in neon script, private cars in all shades of paint, and sidewalks crowded with civilians untied and uncaged. In his present state his eyes, unable to process the color and clamor, simply transformed the city scenery into undemanding pasteboard. He was still so tired. He had hitched a ride into town with an efficient looking PFC who said he worked as a courier at MACV. He drove the jeep like a blind man. Traffic was a chaotic jumble of army vehicles, taxis, civilian automobiles, motor scooters, and bicycles weaving among each other with aggressive abandon. The street hovered perpetually on the edge of accident. A flinching Griffin kept himself braced stiff-armed against the dash. Even on paved road the jeep continued moving in and out of mysterious clouds of white dust that left a metallic taste in the mouth. The air streaming in over the dirty windshield reeked of burning rubber that worsened the further on they drove as if the center of the city must contain a large lot piled high with old smoldering tires.

"I hate this fucking place," said the PFC suddenly, his first words since leaving Tan Son Nhut. For emphasis he leaned on the horn. A gaggle of bicycles dispersed before their hood, but one bike, unable to move quickly enough because of the crush of traffic to its side, was caught by the jeep's bumper and bike and rider went down. There was a thump and a crunch. The jeep rolled on.

"Hey, wait a minute," said Griffin, turning around to look, "aren't you going to stop and see if he's hurt?"

The PFC glanced in the mirror. "He's okay," he said.

Behind them an adolescent boy limped to the curb dragging a wreckage of pedals and spokes.

"You could be a little more careful," said Griffin.

"I don't think so," said the PFC. "That's the third accident this month for me. And I'm the best driver in the shop."

They passed a theater on Griffin's side, the line already a block long. A giant billboard showed men in thick mustaches and bandoliers atop galloping horses and bronzed women.

"What is it," asked Griffin, "a kind of office contest? Wall chart, little stars pasted next to your names, winner gets a case of beer at the end of the month, something like that?"

"Hey," said the PFC. "I didn't have to give you a ride."

"Want me to get out?"

Silent, the PFC drove on with furious energy, working the gearshift like he was banging a stick around a box.

Suddenly the jeep swerved to the right, skidded to a halt outside a tall gray building with bars on the windows. Faded crimson letters above the door spelled PARADISE HOTEL.

"Thanks for the ride," said Griffin, rubbing his knee. The jeep screeched back into traffic, scattering bicycles and pedestrians right and left.

On the sidewalk in front of the hotel lay a beggar wearing only a pair of khaki shorts. He dragged himself over to Griffin with his right arm, his one remaining limb. On his head was a steel helmet riddled with holes which he took off and held up like a bowl. He appeared to be about twenty years old. Griffin gave him five dollars in MPC, a violation of currency restrictions. Monetary transactions with nationals were supposed to be conducted in piasters. Now this beggar could scuttle around the corner into the alley beside the hotel, hand the bill over to the waiting VC agent who would use it to purchase arms or inflate the already blimplike economy. "Hey," said Griffin, calling the man back, "here's another five." The man raised his one arm, tossed Griffin a salute.

"Okay," said Griffin, "okay, okay."

The lobby of the Paradise looked like a fancy washroom, bushy green plants in large ceramic vases, a mirrored wall, a pair of beaming Vietnamese attendants in black tie and white shirts. To the right was the entrance to the dining room where Griffin glimpsed customers reading leather-bound menus and eating off porcelain plates with shiny silver utensils. The snowy white tablecloths seemed as exotic to him as shoes to an aborigine.

"Monsieur?" ventured a voice. "May I help you?"

Behind the polished wood desk a bald Vietnamese with no eyebrows offered him the register and a fountain pen.

"Yes, could you tell me please which room Chief Warrant Officer Ernest Winkly is in?"

"Oh," exclaimed the clerk, recognition and mirth lighting his black eyes. "Monsieur Boom-Boom." He called over to the black ties. "Monsieur Boom-Boom." Everyone laughed heartily.

"Excuse me, please. You are Monsieur Grief-on?"

"Yes."

The clerk reached under the counter, handed Griffin a folded piece of paper. "For you," he said.

It was a message from Captain Patch: Winkly here. Return at once.

After the horse has broken its leg, the canteen run dry, the sandstorm obliterated the trail, there comes a moment when, watching the rattlesnake that has just punctured your leg slither off under a rock, you lay yourself down on the pebbly ground, thinking Thank God, now I can get some rest. Griffin refolded the note, returned it to the clerk, nodded politely, and walked back out of the Paradise. The beggar was gone. Off spending his newly acquired wealth on shiny needles and uncut dope no doubt.

Griffin took a cab back to Tan Son Nhut. The driver, suspiciously enthusiastic, grinned repeatedly at Griffin in the rearview mirror, exposing one brown tooth, and shouting, "Hokay, hokay." Three blocks from the hotel he produced a joint apparently rolled in tarpaper, which he proceeded to savor with one hand while the other maneuvered the cab recklessly through the city. Still, despite distractions, he was a better driver than the PFC, missing by several feet a procession of school girls and a street vendor whose overturned cart displayed delicacies resembling fried fetuses. The closest accident occurred when the cab was sideswiped by a blue busload of Air Force personnel jeering from behind screened windows. Griffin, convinced his driver was either a lunatic who understood no English and would keep driving until they ran out of gas or a cunning thief on a mission to deliver one hapless American GI to a garage full of thugs with tire irons on the outskirts of the city, searched the streets for familiar landmarks from his ride in. He recognized nothing. The driver looked at him in the mirror. "Hokay," he said, laughing. "Hokay." Griffin saw himself stripped and bruised, picking his teeth out of a puddle of oil. He was just about to order the driver to stop the cab when they rounded a corner and there, spread miraculously before them, was the fenced expanse of Tan Son Nhut. Griffin was so relived he overtipped generously. "Hokay, hokay." He hadn't been in Saigon more than an hour and a half but at least there were two residents who would remember his visit.

Thirty minutes later, astonished at his unexpected change of fortune, he found himself on a plane north all the way to Nha Trang. A temporary tilt in the heavens. He was stuck in Nha Trang, home of the famous Green Berets, for thirty-two hours, sleeping on the floor between indigestible meals of warm Kool-Aid and cold hamburgers that tasted like the plastic lining inside old refrigerators. Up the rest of the coast he hopped like a frog: an overnight stay in Tuy Hoa (steak dinner, fresh sheeted bed compliments the U.S. Air Force), twelve hours in Qui Nhon (shave, shower, interminable movie about Gregory Peck searching for gold in bleak Southwest), and finally five hours in friendly Da Nang entertained by the same group of singing Australians he had encountered there hours or days or weeks ago. At one in the morning Griffin rode home on a C-130 crammed between huge loading palettes of powdered milk and green beans.

"Where the hell have you been?" demanded Captain Patch.

"Get your wick dipped?" asked Chief Winkly.

"Excuse me," said Griffin, "I don't think I feel too well."

Bad ice, he thought, between the chills and the cramps of the next two days, too many cups of flavored water from every Vietnamese snack vendor in every air terminal in South Vietnam. Now here he was poisoned. The chief, it turned out, had been arrested in the Bronco Bill Bar and Grill by club-wielding MPs the night Griffin left. Apparently he punched a prostitute in the face following a sexual remark forever lost in the ensuing melee. The chief proudly exhibited the deep nail scratches across his cheeks as battle wounds worthy of a Purple Heart. Griffin, dragging his ragged intestines from bunk to latrine, wished the girl had had a knife. Seated on one stool and leaning over to take advantage of the adjoining one, he looked up from his misery to see Wendell crouched in the doorway, camera purring. "I'll glue your lens cap on for this," croaked Griffin. "Great," exclaimed Wendell. "Simply great. The War In Vietnam: America On The Pot." Back in his room Griffin lay on his side, sweating, hands tucked between his legs, the nausea rolling through him like heavy seas. Between spasms he would dream about winter again and a helicopter would wobble out of the whiteness and it wouldn't be like dreaming anymore but like someone shaking him awake. His insides bubbled and squirted. There was a fever like a machine gun. Countryside zipped past like film on fast forward. His blanket was the texture of a flight suit. There was a big helmet on his head he couldn't get off. He was suffocating and the visor was so darkly tinted no one could see his face, no one knew who he was. Some bugs dashed out from under cover and tried to bite him. He squashed them with the sole of his boot. None of this ever really happened.

Meditation in Green: 12

The sun is white, the sky starched.

The gravel plain, flat as an anvil, projects its speckled black surface into the mirage of a horizon.

In the opposite direction is piled the sand, the high yellow dunes that record the shape of the wind. There is only silence and the abstract beauty of light and shadow, lines curving up, lines curving down, the razor edges of definition drawn against a monotonous intensity. The wind remains constant, hot and dry, lifting a white spray off the curl of a dune. The sand is moving, grain by grain, slipping patiently on, a landscape in motion. Between the dunes a hard corridor leads to a black finger of rock pointing upward.

At noon the color bleaches out. Shadows disappear. Dunes climb on top of one another and the world turns two-dimensional. Rock and gravel and sand burn with a fire that seems to have been ignited from within. In a moment, though, the sun moves on and perspective returns.

A cloud drifts in from nowhere, then incredibly, is joined by another. The clouds approach, merge, rain begins to fall. It evaporates before touching the ground.

Shadows lengthen. The sky glows yellow. The sun sinks. Night pours swiftly in.

A cockroach emerges from a small hole and proceeds to make its way from one point to another.

In the light of the moon the dunes look like mounds of snow.

"My brother's in the hospital with infected heart valves," announced Huey. She stood in the kitchen, toasting a marshmallow on a fork over the gas burner of the stove. "He's tried to escape twice now so they have him tied to the bed with medieval leather straps. Are you listening to me?"

These most common of all rocks are made of debris. Color is extremely varied. Hardness is generally low. "Yes," I said. "A junkie's disease."

"He won't let me visit."

"Send flowers."

"I did. He threw them out the window. The vase broke a light on an ambulance roof. That's when he ran for the elevator and they buckled him down."

"Hasn't the gang been around to cheer him up?"

"I don't care. I'm finished. I'm through worrying about him. These marshmallows suck." A ball of fire drooped off the end of the fork and into the sink, hissing. She reached into a grimy canvas bag on the floor beside the refrigerator and pulled out a bare stub of black crayon. "Remember Mrs. Armstrong?" she asked, coming into the room where I sat examining glossy photographs with a magnifying glass. "No show today. First time she's ever missed an appointment. Something's wrong. Those scheduled hysterics are what get her through the month."

"Maybe the gas has been turned off for nonpayment and she's rigid there in her rocker, arthritic fingers clenched about her knitting, hard glaze coating each frozen eyeball, ice sculpture. The Golden Years."

"I think we'll send someone over there tomorrow morning." Turning her back, she stepped to an open space on the wall, raised her arm above her head, and quickly began to draw.

"Mukluks. Packed sleds. Dog teams. Get the medicine through to the Eskimos."

Brief furious strokes. Energy revealed itself as clearly as filings under a magnet. A field was created that drew its surroundings down into it. Then the rhythm altered and motion unwound into a complex of curves and swirls, a patterned density somewhat Islamic in appearance, almost frightening in its simultaneous connotations of speed and textured order, intensity and a disdainful calm.

"That's no Chinese ideogram."

"Don't watch me."

The composition of this clastic rock is primarily grains of quartz cemented together by lime, silica, or other material. Crossbedding and ripple marks are fairly common. This rock is used principally for construction.

The sound of crayon rubbing on plaster stopped. I could feel her staring at me.

"Okay," I said.

"You know how it is when boundaries start rising into view like lost continents and your own body assumes a definite cookie cutter shape and space becomes a culture for renegade form."

"I may have to tack a curtain over that one."

She crossed to the window and paused, contemplating exteriors. For a moment she was simply a missing piece from a jigsaw puzzle of a gray sky. When she turned briefly to glance back at the drawing on the wall, the angles of her face had a polished cast, softened surfaces. The laving of the light. "What's the book?"

I held up the cover.

"*A Field Guide to Rocks and Minerals*? Did I miss something?"

"Thinking about starting my own counseling service. Pebble Peace."

"Why aren't you meditating? You're never in the john anymore." She bent toward the window, her breath flowing in opaque clouds across the cold pane. With the side of her curled hand and the tips of her fingers for toes she made miniature footprints marching up the lowering sky.

"A new motto: If you can't trans-cend, you might as well descend. I'm scoping out the bottom here. Acquainting myself with our amazing mineral friends. Look at these specimens, for instance. Mass. Density. Permanence. Finality. Termination. Rock. Even the word conveys heft, a certain assurance. No loss of focus here."

"But what happened to all this plant jive?"

"I don't know. It's not working out. Maybe plants are too creepy, swaying between worlds, mind/no-mind, like what's going on there. It's scary. Now a rock is something that has weathered the crisis. A rock is a survivor. Look at this stuff. No growth, no decay, no streaming fluids. The substance of walls, of fortification. Like to see a deuce and a half breach two solid feet of that."

"Words, words, words."

"I should, of course, experience the various species in their native habitat. Down in the damp bowels. I need to crisscross the globe from one mammoth cave to the next with my miner's hat, my reinforced climber's rope, my geologist's hammer. We could go together, a spelunker's holiday, visit all the world's great holes."

"Listen, why don't you get yourself a nice window box, a package of seeds, and try growing something real for a change? Brighten up the room, test how green your thumb really is."

"Exactly what Arden suggested."

Arms braced against the sill, she leaned delicately forward, touched her puckered lips to the glass. In the middle of the frost, when she drew back her head, was one clear, precise, perfectly rounded O.

Deposition. Compaction. Stratification. Consolidation. Sediment.

Night. The moonlight was unusually strong. The long row of officers' hootches sat silent and dark. For the space of several breaths nothing moved. The door to the first hootch—the CO's—opened and Major Holly descended the steps, turned to his right, and began walking down the road toward the O club. Suddenly from the shadows between two hootches a figure leaped out at the major, knocking him to the ground. The attacker's left hand stuffed a wad of cloth into the major's mouth, the right hand rose and fell in mechanical strokes inserting and then withdrawing a large knife, perhaps a bayonet, into the hunched curl of the major's back. Blood splashed freely all around. The attacker's face was marked by a monstrous grin, visible even in the moonlight, an expression unchanged even as he ceased his stabbing, climbed off the major, and directed his attention and the violent movement of his hands to the major's groin. The figure straightened up, looked around, and after wiping the blade on the major's shirt, tucked it in his belt, and disappeared back into the shadow. The major's right forearm outstretched on the ground before him twitched for a moment, fingers quivering like a spider's legs, then stopped. The ground around the body darkened. The moonlight was unusually strong.

"Freaky," said Griffin.

"The blood's green paint," Wendell explained. "He had rubbers filled with it taped under his shirt."

"I hardly recognized Vegetable. Amazing the resemblance between him and the major. I never really noticed it before."

"The filter helps."

"And Simon. Who would have believed he was capable of such ferocity."

"The camera's an X-ray machine."

They were locked inside Wendell's hot cramped room for a special sneak preview of the rough cut.

"What'd you use for the knife? Looked like a real blade going in and out."

"Sssssh. Attention to the film, please. Questions later."

The film ran over four and a half hours. Griffin didn't know whether it was this body-bruising length or the generous amount of refreshment he consumed during the showing, but when the wall finally went blank he wasn't sure what he had seen.

"Well?" asked the director.

"Wendell, uh, this movie . . ."

"Yes?"

"I don't believe it."

"Yeah."

"It's a mess."

"Huh?"

"I don't know, maybe it's me, but I couldn't make any sense out of it at all. I mean, there's no beginning, no middle, no end. There's no coherence. It just kind of settles over you. Like a musty tent."

"You know nothing about cinema."

"Okay, but was I hallucinating or was there really about five minutes in there tracking a cockroach across a floor?"

"It wasn't just a cockroach."

"And what was that egglike thing cracking open with the pus thing inside?"

"What do you think it was?"

"Sunset over the South China Sea?"

"Cute."

"Hey, I liked the murder part and the scenes I was in."

"They can be cut."

"Wendell, I'm sorry."

"The War in Vietnam: Philistines At Large."

Dear Folks,

Not much time now. Just a note to let you know what's happening. They've been sending me out on patrol the last couple weeks because of a shortage of infantry in our area. Seems the casualty rates have been climbing pretty high lately. Won't bore you with the details of those excursions. Now they've put the entire base on 100% alert, which means we aren't getting much sleep. A lot of activity at night, flares, some shooting every now and then, but nothing major so don't worry. The CO says this sort of stuff happens occasionally and usually nothing comes of it. Just thought I'd write so if you saw anything in the paper about a big battle shaping up or something you wouldn't worry. VC have only broken into this base once in its history. We know how to beat them now. Semper Fi. See you all in 87.

Love,
Me

At 0218 one humid morning a high explosive artillery shell scheduled to leave a steel tube at Fire Base Ringgold for coordinates 619238 detonated instead in the air above 238619. Directly below, Vegetable, the night's gate guard at the 1069th, was awakened by a clap of God's hands and the hot spittle of his breath. Across the street the line of hootches known as Officer's Row emptied in an instant; men in their underwear milled about in the darkness asking each other what had happened. Speed Graphic came out of the photo lab carrying a film canister that had been on a shelf no more than six inches from his elbow. There was a warm hole punched through the top and an exit hole in the bottom. "I've been hit," cried Chief Winkly, pointing to the specks of blood on his shorts, and everyone laughed, more lurid details for his sex stories. Captain Marovicci had a circular bite taken out of the fleshy part of his forearm. "This means another Purple Heart," he said, "for the collection." Lieutenant Tremble had to be waked up and told that he had just missed getting killed in his sleep. Everyone kept going over to Vegetable, who simply stood there silent and sheepish, not a scratch on him, and these officers kept rubbing his head and patting his butt. "Drunks and potheads," exclaimed Sergeant Mars in wonder, "Drunks and potheads." "Who's missing?" asked somebody. "No one," came an answer. "Aren't we all here?" said someone else.

Then they discovered Lieutenant Mueller.

Peering over the round blue lenses of his sunglasses, Griffin examined the corroded thermometer hanging from a bent nail on the wall outside his hootch door. The painted scale of graduated lines and numerals, once glossy and distinct, had become pale and flecked with rust, the enamel blistered and peeling. Even in the bright surgical glare of high noon the temperature, if anyone cared enough to try, was difficult to read; beneath a clouded moon it was impossible.

Griffin reached into his pocket and pulled out a battered cigarette lighter engraved on one side with the initials F.T.A. and, on the other, a cartoon drawing of a dog lying blissfully supine along the peak of a doghouse. Below the picture was the caption: SCREW IT. Mueller's lighter. Holding it aloft like Liberty's torch, Griffin satisfied himself that the temperature still stood above the ninety-degree mark. "Wonderful," he muttered. He paused a moment, then placed the flame directly under the bulb at the thermometer's base and waited until the column of tinted alcohol climbed to the top of the glass stem and the narrow cylinder exploded. "Wonderful."

He walked between the darkened hootches, Thai and his doggie friends romping in the sand about his feet. A figure lurched out of the shadows. "Do you believe money is the root of all evil?" demanded a raspy voice. It was Wendell. "No," replied Griffin, "I don't believe that." "Good. Have you ever read a book called *Man Schluggled*?" Griffin thought for a moment. "Do you mean *Atlas Shrugged*?" "Yeah, you ever read that?" "You've asked me this a hundred times." "Wait till you get to page seven-oh-four." Wendell stumbled back into darkness. "Wonderful." Griffin continued on past Officer's Row, the latrines, the squat sandbagged O club where even over the labored whine of the air conditioners he could hear whoops and shouts from within. A door banged open, emitting light, laughter, and a pair of running men, one in pursuit of the other. A crowd of officers spilled out onto the dirt gravel road, drinks in hand, looking off into the night where the two men had disappeared. "Rip his pants off, Brad," someone shouted. "Tear his goddamn pants."

Griffin slipped around the club, cut through the bright deserted hangar. Opposite the wide floodlit doors the planes, thick and snout-nosed, each centered and momentarily dormant within the shadowy safety of its own revetment, resembled obscene insects, pregnant dragonflies heavy with the unborn larvae of some metallic monstrosity. He entered a revetment, patted a cold fuselage, and clambered up a wall of corrugated steel already coated with greasy beads of moisture though the sun had set only a few hours before. He settled himself on top, legs dangling childishly over the side, and lit a joint. How often had he come out here to this perch overlooking the airfield, particularly in the early weeks of his war, alone, innocent, anxious about the future. He had reasoned then that if repetition could dull the meaning of a word, imaginative rehearsal could abstract the fear from the reality. So he sat above the planes and meditated on the worst. But these mental drills seemed to be directed by a strong separate will more perverse than his own. Once admitted to consciousness each scenario surged effortlessly out of control up into the wide terrors of terminal escalation. They all began in the dark with the sound of billowing sirens and rifle fire crackling far away and mounted furiously to a towering cadenza of fiery wind and mechanical thunder that neatly erased one entire grid square from the surface of the world map. In between, of course, there were running feet and taut faces the color of solidified dough and torn cries that went on and on and wouldn't stop and then pinging silence. Over the globe, in America where the sun was still shining on yesterday's business, people went to work and came back home, the sky was still blue, and the clocks ticked steadily into tomorrow, but today Griffin was zippered in plastic and lifted to eternity on a mud-green UH-1 flying machine. Peace. And each time he had always felt the same wet dread sliding loosely through his insides.

He flicked the joint off into the darkness and gazed out beyond the smoking arc lamps and barbed wire coils of the perimeter, out there where the night began. Three red lights flashed rhythmically back at him. They were attached to the tall antennae of a communications relay station that nested on the summit of a mountain he never knew existed until one morning when the monsoon rain abruptly dissolved and a massive verdant peak thrust itself through the shifting clouds like a jagged green thorn. The lights blinked slowly on and then off, on and then off as though glued to the palms of a triple-armed Oriental goddess who opened and closed her hands in alternating gestures of greeting and scorn. On a clear night her message was visible for miles: Hello. Fuck you. Hello. Fuck you. Hello. Fuck you.

Behind him in the revetment sat Mueller's plane. Already there was someone he didn't know—a muscular warrant officer with an FBI agent's face—flying it. Strangers were beginning to fly all the planes as one by one the pilots Griffin knew either died or went home. Prompt replacement of parts mechanical and human had become a priority mission since the cancerous onset of The General's obsession with that Fifth NVA regiment. "They're out there somewhere," he had been heard to declare recently, "plotting our military embarrassment." The latest attempt at locating this legendary band, a final unrestrained effort of panoramic reconnaissance was supervised by The General and had been personally christened by him Operation Shooting Gallery, a designation Mueller would have enjoyed immensely. "Clawhammer?" Griffin could hear him screeching incredulously. "Clawhammer? The Secretary of the Army drops in for a twenty-minute visit and it's Operation Clawhammer. What happens if the President comes calling, Operation Bootinyournuts? Who've they got thinking these gags up, chief cartoonist of GI Joe comics? Reminds me, you ever hear about Masher, Operation Masher for Christ's sake, big First Air Cav sweep, even Johnson couldn't stomach that, had to change the name to White Wing, same operation but now it's White Wing. Holy God. What we need around here is an Operation Creamcheese, a Project Lords A-leaping, a Mission Negotiable. All these Greek and Roman and Nordic appellations for everything from a moon rocket to a general's fart. How about Operation Sow's Ear or Mickey Mouse fragmentation devices or the Saint Francis of Assisi surface-to-air missile?" And in spite of Griffin's preparations it had been Mueller who was finally zipped in a bag and shipped out like a stale sandwich. Operation Sweet Chariot. Fire Base Ringgold apologized. A freak accident, they explained. The careless gun crew had been reprimanded, the lieutenant in charge reassigned to a desk job. Operation Milk of Magnesia. And it was here atop the revetment wall that Mueller had spoken so often about "the secret structure" of the war: the huge oil deposits off the coast American corporations were already preparing to steal, the numbers of RVN government officials on the CIA payroll, the manipulation of the weak economy by New York banks with branch offices in major cities, the obvious imperialistic need for more and more markets, the less obvious but more frightening demand for blood to oil the rickety gears of capitalism. Griffin didn't know whether any of these theories were true or not—he didn't really care—but he certainly would miss hearing them. Out of conspiratorial odds and ends Mueller had been able to construct a habitable shack inside the wasteland of his experience here until the experience blew him up of course. It was anticipation of such an event that had kept Griffin from developing any coherent war view of his own. Catastrophe lacked coherence. Every separate day was built anew and then dismantled at night, the successive constructions becoming less and less elaborate, lonely props thrown up against hope by a weariness so deep his bones felt tired with sand in their eyes. The day before his frustration had brought him out here at the height of the terrible afternoon heat to sit baking in a masochistic stupor as the same dull planes roared in and out of a blank sky. In the dense miragelike air even the Phantoms seemed to move more slowly, their black needle noses opening flight paths with ponderous difficulty. The weight of the enormous sun softened the tarmac, its spinning stone sharpened the metal edges of hangar roofs and wing fins, polished glass into blinding mirrors that reflected almost casually the fire blazing hidden beneath each surface, the fire of space, the fire of time, bleaching out color, melting distinctions, until all matter seemed to have been immersed in white phosphorus, the eternal combustion burning and flowing and fusing the world into one scalding lump of molten light.

Two weeks later a helicopter carrying Major Quimby and Kraft broke radio contact somewhere in the central highlands and Griffin promptly volunteered for the search team. The previous morning, bent in a jeweler's hunch over one particular frame of defoliated earth, lens magnification multiplying intensely upon one unnaturally smooth-curved shadow—the projection of a truck hood? a random heap of stripped timber?—20×, 30× . . . the surface of the film itself came abruptly apart plunging him down among the crystals, a pure landscape of geometrically perfect black-and-white pyramids, the tombs where all the images were stored like ancient kings. Then triangles ballooned into concentric circles, his field of vision filled again with white phosphorus, and he slid off the stool, his unresponsive hands reaching out too late for the firmness of the counter that was no longer there. Normality returned in a clean gray vista of linoleum floor tiles shining away toward a distant gray wall. His friends stood there laughing, that Griffin and his dumb jokes, gonna fuck himself up real good one of these days. Griffin was frightened; he didn't know what had happened. That night he dreamed of tundra again, ice-caked gloves tearing at his wet snow-blind eyes.

Twenty-four hours after the news arrived of Quimby and Kraft, the crash site was located on reconnaissance film, a small somewhat circular wound opened in the rough green skin of a rock bone mountain. A medevac, promptly dispatched to the scene, hovered forlornly above the ragged hole in the foliage. No signs of life. No rhythmic beeps on the emergency channels. Dipping downward for a closer peek, the medevac drew fire, several punctures carefully centered on the large red cross painted on its hull. It was automatically assumed that the enemy had Quimby's briefcase, the detailed maps, the classified memoranda, the complete set of current code books, an assumption confirmed later that same day when an anonymous attempt was made to call in artillery fire directly upon a besieged ARVN company using the codes, which had of course been immediately changed hours before. It was also assumed that passengers and crew were either captured or dead, probably the latter, but that the bodies still needed to be recovered, the wreckage searched. Word of Quimby's disappearance sent one long chilly shiver down the I Corps intelligence spine. The man knew virtually everything; he had to be found, dead or alive. Conrad and the agency people offered their services. Major Holly, however, instinctively sensitive to the ever-shifting boundaries of bureaucratic responsibility and power, wisely decided to keep this operation in the family. He would employ a contingent of 1069th volunteers in addition to an armed element of experienced Marines who would ride shotgun on the mission. A quick study of the terrain determined that the nearest point for a safe insertion was a grassy field about three kilometers from the crash site. The search team was presented then with a difficult uphill trek through unbroken jungle, across a couple streams of unknown speed and depth, and up or around several walls of slippery overgrown rock. A violent encounter with those who had brought the helicopter down should not be ruled out.

Griffin outfitted himself in full battle gear for the first time since Basic and, self-conscious as a bride, headed for the waiting choppers. Simon wished him luck. "You're a braver man than I am."

"Gunga Din," replied Griffin and waved good-bye in the jaunty manner of the movie heroes of his not so distant youth.

Griffin hadn't set foot in a helicopter since his Chief Winkly-arranged "vacation" to Saigon in another life. As he climbed aboard he noticed that neither of the two (two this time!) door gunners was wearing a sun visor. He settled himself into a seat, concentrating for a moment on his breaths, long and deep now, long and deep. As his chest loosened up, he opened his eyes and looked around. He was surrounded by Marines. This was the wrong helicopter. He started to get up. Squatting in the doorway, a Marine captain who might have been an Olympic decathlon champion in civilian life glanced at the monstrous watch on his wrist and signaled with his hand. Outside the ramp dropped away, the door swung into blue sky, Griffin smiled at his traveling companions. Across from him was a row of high school yearbook pictures in helmets and he couldn't help wondering, okay, who isn't coming back? as the wind numbed his face and gave his skin the tight feel of a plastic mask. The clouds, spectacular heaps of fluffy white cream, flowed by like time-motion studies of an advancing cold front. All the strength in his body seemed to be draining down his legs, through his soles, into the trembling floor of the helicopter. He gripped with both hands the rifle barrel between his thighs. When the moment came, would he be able to stand, to get through that door? He felt as stoned as if he had just consumed an entire lid by himself. None of the Marines appeared the least bit jumpy; all their nerves had been replaced by brass tubing on Parris Island. The ground was a shrieking green blur. Up ahead the long jade vertebrae of the highlands rose and dipped as though some dreaming creature had begun to turn, to awaken from sleep. Bright squares of flooded paddy flashed past like windows on a train. The Marine corporal beside Griffin began tapping on his leg with tan stubby fingers a soundless arhythmic tune. The *Marines* were *nervous*! Now Griffin was really scared. He had the claustrophobic sensation of being moved in a crowd down some concrete tunnel, dim screened-in bulbs overhead lighting the shadowy way to a huge vaultlike door. Under each armpit, dark deltas spread slowly southward. Suddenly he realized with perfect clarity why he had volunteered for this ride. He wanted to experience some portion of this madness as his own, not as accident or bad luck or whim of his superiors but as choice, freely made, the consequences freely accepted; he wanted a purge, a flushing out of the corners, primitive sacrament if necessary, so that when he returned the office would be simply an office again, neutral objects arranged between four neutral walls, and the film would remain solid as pond ice in January, no cracks, no holes please and maybe a simple unsophisticated unprogrammed muscle of his soul wanted simply to exercise itself and do those things in the flesh that one was doing anyway abstractly and on paper because one guy went crazy and some nights the prisoners cried until dawn and half your superiors were fools and you kept dreaming of blizzards in the tropics and your friend got killed and what else was there to do anyway?

The mountains loomed closer, a sharp file of green teeth sawing back and forth. The Marine captain, smiling, pointed out the door. A pair of Cobra gunships streaked past, trails of smoke pouring from their rocket canisters. "Here we go!" someone shouted and Griffin's stomach tilted like the bubble in a carpenter's level. He could see a field of yellow grass rising toward him on balloons of brown smoke left behind by the Cobras' strafing run. Griffin searched the grass for crouching figures, flashes of light. Under his fingers the rifle barrel was cold and hard. A towering mass of mountain slipped ominously into view. The helicopter began to vibrate more vigorously, its prop wash deflecting off the ground. "Go go go go go!" screamed a bouncing door gunner, the ejected cartridges from his M-60 seeming to erupt out of his open mouth as he directed a stream of fire into the dark solid wall of jungle surrounding the landing zone. Marines, their rifles at port arms, started leaping out the door. "C'mon!" ordered a Marine sergeant. He had a gap between his front teeth. "Let's move, troop." He grabbed Griffin's arm above the elbow. Griffin stumbled toward the door. In the long blades of flattened grass rippling outward from the downdraft a bobbing line of heads and shoulders was drifting slowly away, survivors of a sinking ship, backpacks for life preservers. Griffin paused for a moment, hands clutching the metal edges of the doorway. A boot kicked into his butt and out he went. The grass was much taller than he had guessed and, misjudging his fall, he came down hard, his right leg twisted painfully beneath his body. Flat on his back he looked up through a tunnel of swirling grass and watched the empty helicopter lift dramatically away. He felt like a tiny spider dangling on a thread. The helicopter vanished, the thread snapped, the rustle of the grass ceased. The drone of an engine faded into silence. Silence. No rifle fire. No one was shooting at him. Griffin struggled to his feet. The leg was sore but apparently neither broken nor sprained. He followed the nearest head through the whispering grass toward a tree line so dense and flat it might have been painted on rock. In the shade Captain Raleigh, the mission CO, was conferring with the Marine captain; they looked at a compass, then at a map, then into the bush, visibility no greater than the length of an arm.

"We all here?" asked Captain Raleigh. Sergeant Lacrosse was counting heads.

"Okay," said Raleigh. "Let's do it."

One by one the patrol began picking its way through the foliage. Griffin was fascinated. He had never before seen a limb or a leaf this close or without the interdiction of a lens. He felt like a spy in the camp of the enemy, a judge locked into a prison of those he had condemned. As he moved in deeper and deeper, he had the eerie sense of vegetation thrusting itself at him for inspection and comment. Green tongues lapped at his calves, elastic branches tugged at his arms. And there was no end to it. You pressed through one layer to arrive at another just like it and then one beyond that and another and another like passing through doors in an estate of measureless dimensions. The hallways opened into other halls, the tall ornate stairs led to identical stairs even higher —jungle as architecture—pillar after pillar, arches framing arches, rooms connected one to the other in receding series, drapes and rope and tiered balconies, Gothic ornamental expanding geometrically in every direction, and below, who could be certain what was bubbling and fizzing down in that crypt? The bush was a stifling enclosure—the air as thick and stale as an overinflated tire—of gigantic proportions in no need of tenants or staff. Collapse and regeneration occurred at the same moment. Buckling walls and decaying furniture were repaired automatically here in this home of the future where matter itself was perpetually pregnant. The effort to bring down this house, of which Griffin was a part, seemed at this close distance to be both frightening and ludicrous. On the ground, crawling like a bug through the bed of those deceptive film images, he sensed a force the camera could never record, a chemical hardly subdue. Getting out alive was the major priority now. Already his uniform was as wet and uncomfortable as if he had showered in it. Following the others up the mountain, one leg lifting mechanically after the other, sliding on the slope, tumbling into a blind tangle of roots and branches, lungs working useless clouds of must and pollen in and out, heart thumping in his ears, he realized that were he to die in here among these botanical springs and gears, a Green Machine larger and more efficient than any human bureaucracy or mechanical invention would promptly initiate the indifferent processes of converting flesh and dreams into plant food. He felt weak, out of shape. Even the rocks in here appeared green, fossilized droppings. Physical discomfort and fear combined to produce a painful sense of isolation even though he could see and hear the others all around him. Drops of sweat lined up on his nose to take turns leaping off the tip. He popped salt tablets to no effect. He thought of Claypool. A stream provided momentary relief, wading waist deep across a yellow flow of foul silt. Then it was up the opposite bank, the climb continuing, the incline turning steadily steeper and rockier. They came to a place where all the vegetation seemed to be growing sideways; they crawled for yards, bumping their heads, scraping knees on hard tough horizontal stems. "What is this shit?" Griffin heard someone whisper. "Bamboo?" He hadn't the vaguest notion. He couldn't see where he was going, he thought he might actually faint, he felt as though he were locked in a stuffy closet packed with broomsticks and rubber raincoats. He was experiencing a vegetable overdose, a chlorophyll freakout. Then Griffin got mad, indignant, why was he being forced to endure this unnecessary agony? The whole stinking forest should have been sprayed long ago, hosed down, drenched in Orange, leaves blackened, branches denuded, undergrowth dried into brittle paper. The mountain was surely overrun with VC and their camouflaged crops, secret manioc fields, banana groves, rice paddies, water wells. Who permitted these outrages, where was the technology when you needed it? No wonder we were losing the damn war. In spite of the sweat in his eyes, the raw sore rubbing open on his left heel, he discovered he was smiling. Yes, you too, you fucking American.

Then they came to a collection of boulders, narrow passages you could slip through sideways, high walls you climbed hand over hand up the vines clinging to their sides. "What is this?" asked someone on top, pointing out clumps of green excrement. "Monkey shit?" No one knew. No one had heard or seen an animal of any kind. Beyond the boulders there was a second stream, swifter and deeper than the first. Two men slipped under and were carried downcurrent into a rock dam. One man lost his rifle. Griffin kept a careful grip on the rope and safe on the opposite bank watched his pants deflate as the water poured out onto the ground. The rest of the day his feet seemed encased in warm sponges. He was beginning to feel hungry. Suddenly they were on a foot trail or an animal run or a convenient convoluted length of natural erosion. The Marines put their clear-eyed booby trap expert on point. The pace picked up. Griffin, of course, was convinced the ground had been smoothed by hundreds of rubber-sandaled feet. They were close to finding the wreckage. Past the crisis, Griffin's earlier emotional and physical distress had calmed. Accustomed now to the muscular aches, the tightening of the nerves, the suffocating air, the claustrophobic botany, the sweat slick as slime on his face, he realized at first with a shock, then with a curious mix of pride and embarrassment, that he could actually take this torture, that despite his intentions he truly was a soldier, a fact he had never before been able to imagine. For a moment he saw himself through other eyes, the thin fatigued body in a wet wrinkled uniform, scarred rifle clutched in grimy hand, flushed baby face staring dully beneath battered helmet. Yes, all the details were correct. He had become a photograph, a new image to interpret.

Up ahead a shaft of direct sunlight penetrated the green shadows as if somewhere above there was a skylight built into the foliage roof. Griffin followed the others into a clearing and with freshly-discovered soldier's eyes saw this: the helicopter, suffering a compound fracture, lay in an uneven heap along a ridge of broken rock, the rocks and surrounding grass littered with hundreds, thousands of variously shaped and sized pieces of bright metal, one window on the pilot's side having survived the plunge completely intact, reflected a square of blinding sun back up into the sky—a fragment of unexplainable wonder so often left behind by the universe of catastrophe as a sort of perverse signature. His soldier's eyes tried to avoid the centerpiece of this arrangement, but the soldier's muscles in his neck kept rotating his head back and back again as if his skull was one huge metal ball uncontrollably drawn by the force of an irresistible magnet. The crew and passengers of the downed helicopter were hanging at spaced intervals from the rotor blades, strung up by the necks with twisted lengths of bicycle chain. Bicycle chain? Their unbuttoned unzipped pants drooped in folds about their ankles. Groins and thighs were black with stale blood, alive with insect movement. Protruding between the lips of each mouth was a small gray mushroom, the severed remains of each man's penis. Swollen faces had begun to turn colors. Body fluids dripped off boot soles like leaking motor oil, staining the grass and providing puddles of nourishment for thirsty ants and centipedes. In the stillness the sun buzzed like a fluorescent lamp. One of Major Quimby's boots was missing and revealed, dangling in midair, a long bony foot whose green sock, heavy with blood, had begun slipping off. Griffin thought of how embarrassed the major would have been to be seen like this.

Someone gagged.

"Let's go," muttered Captain Raleigh, "get them down from there."

Men put down their weapons and moved toward the wreckage.

"Sometimes, you know, I get to feeling kinda shitty about what I've had to do in this stinking war," said the Marine captain. "Not anymore."

The men as they worked traded simple obscenities: "Hell," "Christ," "Goddamnit."

"These people ain't even human."

"Fuck this fucking shithole of a country into a fucking parking lot."

Counterintelligence specialists searched the helicopter. Major Quimby's briefcase was gone, of course. There was no sign of Kraft anywhere.

Those with the highest security clearances attended to Major Quimby. Griffin and Seeley, one of Raleigh's new interrogators, each took hold of the bare leg of one of the crew, lifted, and began walking the chain off the end of the rotor blade.

"Make a wish," said Seeley, smiling grimly around a thigh.

Griffin wished he had tied a handkerchief around his nose like many of the Marines had done. He tried breathing through his mouth. This was a novel experience. He had never touched a body before. It was extremely heavy, it was like pushing a side of beef through a warehouse. Iridescent flies and black hairy gnats swirled about his face. They were pulling the chain off the last couple inches when the man's groin wound, jarred by the movement, split open spilling out a fermented mixture of blood and juice and insect eggs and shiny larval things. Griffin let go, Seeley lost his balance, and the former helicopter crewman fell to the ground with the sound of a dropped watermelon.

"'Hey!" shouted Captain Raleigh, "watch what you're doing there."

"Sorry, sir," said Griffin to both the living and the dead.

"He weighs a ton," said Seeley.

"Abbott and Costello," muttered Raleigh to the Marine captain.

A Marine sergeant passed out body bags. Neither Griffin nor

Seeley had ever zipped a man up before. Griffin held his breath and the muscles in his throat; he was close to vomiting. The man wouldn't fit inside, the bag was too small, did they come in various sizes?

"Excuse me, girls," said a Marine, pushing them aside.

Apparently unconcerned that the corpse might simply come apart at any moment, he spread the bag on the ground, rolled the body into it, zipped briskly. Obviously someone with prior experience. Despite his daintiness Griffin had gotten his hands smeared with blood. He wiped them on a green army issue handkerchief which he tossed away into the tall grass. Then one of those banana helicopters came and hovered over the hole in the jungle. A winch was lowered and up went the bags one by one. Everyone took a smoke break. Griffin wished he had a joint. He rinsed out his mouth with canteen water and spat on the ground.

The wreckage was rigged with explosives and detonated. That single frame of unbroken glass erupted into a giant mushroom of black-and-brown smoke. They slipped back into the bush and searched for signs of Kraft. A second trail was located and further on a bulletin board plastered with paper notices in Vietnamese.

"What's this?" asked the Marine captain. "Nature hike info?"

"Morale boosters," said Captain Raleigh, leafing through the wrinkled sheets. " 'Long live the glorious revolution, the glorious soldiers, the glorious et ceteras,' et cetera."

"Stand clear," cautioned a Marine sergeant. He raised his rifle, squeezed the trigger, shredded the wooden board. "Chopsticks."

"Stupid," replied Captain Raleigh.

The trail wound on, up and down, a twist and a turn, a path through a maze. Griffin's body lumbered forward on auto pilot, brushing stupid leaves out of his dumb face with idiotic hands. He had seen enough plant life. A current crackled and leaped from one man to the next. Griffin was attempting to remain insulated. He tried not to think. He listened to his breath, he counted his steps. His finger was cocked around his trigger but he really didn't want to kill anybody. The man behind kept popping his chewing gum. Griffin turned, telling him to fucking stop, and saw Major Quimby's face blowing a bubble.

Then when no one was looking a Marine corporal screamed, spun about, and fell to the ground, tensed fingers clawing at the stubby shaft protruding from his chest.

"What the fuck?" someone exclaimed.

The corporal squirmed around for a few moments like a bug on a pin and died before the medic had time to open his shirt. They found the crossbow under a bush, the trip wire rigged across the trail. Two men had passed safely over the trap. "Three on a match," commented one of the Marine officers.

The body was bagged, the patrol moved on.

There was a sense that that arrow had been set some millennia ago and had waited patiently through the centuries for its victim.

They swept the mountain, moved down into a valley on the other side and back again. Beside one of the streams they found the imprint of a bare foot, either a child's or an extremely small VC. They found an old abandoned village and a tunnel system to explore. They burned the huts, collapsed the tunnels. The group voltage began to drop.

There was no sign or scent of Kraft anywhere. He had apparently vanished. "Well," said Captain Raleigh to his Marine colleague during a break, "he was one of them spooks."

Seeley wanted to talk to Griffin. He pestered him at every opportunity. He told about his life, about breaking a finger in Basic, about Coach Pappas and the can of deodorant, about his one-eyed dog Tony, his father's fits of temper, his girlfriend's ring he wore around his neck and his ring she wore about hers.

Griffin pictured himself back in the office, shading this area in on a herbicide map. He never wanted to leave his stool again.

In the late afternoon they made their way down into the morning's field for what Griffin heard Captain Raleigh refer to as their "extraction." Griffin felt totally dull, dirty, and dazed. The photograph again. He remembered now. Survivors of Guadalcanal. The helicopters returned. They made their way through the green sea of heaving grass and clambered aboard. Griffin tripped over his rifle, his knee slammed into the hard edge of the doorway. He limped to a seat, collapsed in a rattle of metallic sounds. He took off his helmet, wiped his forehead with his arm. The helicopter lifted into a soft orange sky. "You're bleeding," said the Marine next to him. He looked down at his leg. A dark blotch in the shape of Africa had taken form on the green material of his fatigues. "Wonderful," he said.

Whenever The General came up on one of his periodic briefing visits Major Holly liked to show him around the compound, impress him with the order, the cleanliness, the growing beauty of the 1069th's physical appearance under his command.

This trip, hoping to elicit a more elaborate compliment than the usual "Well done," Holly was escorting The General to the flower beds he had had planted around the orderly room complete with little white fencing and tulip bulbs flown in courtesy of an old Air Force connection when The General stopped, sniffing the air.

"What in God's name is that?"

They looked down at his boots.

"I'm sorry, sir," Holly apologized. "I'll have them cleaned up right away, sir."

The General's polished boots were caked with fresh dog shit.

That afternoon the clerks could hear the CO through the closed door giving holy hell to the First Sergeant.

The First Sergeant sent for Sergeant Anstin. "The dogs," he said. "Take care of them."

The next morning Sergeant Anstin and his handpicked crew came through the compound with gloves and ropes.

The dogs were delighted. No one played with them often enough and here was a whole pack of men and a new game. They ran barking up and down the sand. They leaped out from under the flying lariats, they dodged the hands, they tugged on the rope ends. Then the men got serious. The animals were herded against the barbed wire around the motor pool and one by one were roped and dragged to a waiting ambulance, the only vehicle with a closed space. The ambulance was driven out to the dunes between the end of the runway and the base perimeter. The back door was opened and, as sporting gentlemen, the people with the rifles gave the animals a running start, shooting them as they swarmed out of the ambulance, M-16 impact knocking the dogs backward to the ground. The ones wounded in the spine or back legs tried crawling for cover, their retreat blocked by exact shots to the head. The howling sounded eerily like a nursery of unhappy babies. A black and brown German shepherd, sensing too late what was happening, charged one of the men, growling, teeth bared. A burst of automatic fire removed the furry top of his skull. Afterward, the men dragged the blood-damp carcasses into a field, drenched them in JP-4, and ignited the pile. The stench, drifting back to the compound, ruined lunch in both the officers' and enlisted men's mess halls.

Trips didn't know what happened until he returned from work —his daily nap in the operations office—and whistled and then whistled again and looked around in bewilderment for the excited animal who had been there to greet him without fail for almost a year. "Where's Thai?" he asked. No one could tell him. Griffin tried, but hadn't even gotten to the main event, said the words, when Trips stepped cursing to his locker, rummaged around inside, and strode out the door with the attitude of someone embarking on a mission so critical he didn't care if he ever came back. Half an hour later he returned, tossed the unbloodied knife onto his bed, muttering about witnesses and close quarters and what he really needed was a bomb to take out the entire NCO club and all the cowards in it. He left again, everyone assuming of course he was out hunting up an adequate explosive device or building it himself because he was gone all night, only Griffin to know finally he had spent the hours sitting beside a mound of freshly bulldozed sand where for the first time in fifteen years he cried with tears and blubbering. Then he dug up one of his Maxwell House cans and locked the door to his room and got into bed and stayed for three days and even after he was up and walking about it was still more than a week before he talked to anyone. No one was to mention Thai's name again. It had taken this much to get over it and he didn't want to repeat the process, but sometimes of course a person forgot or pretended to forget and the dog's name hung in the air like a stale odor that won't go away and anyone could tell by the pure cold light that came into his eyes he hadn't gotten over anything.

Meditation in Green: 13

1. Before sowing treat seed with a fungicide, for example, a .25% solution of formaline. Wash seeds and allow to dry.
2. Mix seed with sand at a ratio of 1:2 and sow in a light, friable, but rich soil at a depth not to exceed ¼ inch.
3. Soil can be kept moist but take care not to overwater.
4. Germination usually lasts from two to three weeks. Three to four weeks after germination the first four leaves of the plant are formed.
5. After the leaves have appeared the plants should be thinned out so that they are spaced about 3–4″ apart.
6. In warm temperatures the plant reaches full development in 40 to 60 days.
7. Flowering occurs during the day. Each flower remains open 30 to 40 hours after which it begins to wither.

Huey stopped dead in the doorway. "Okay, what's this now," she asked, "boarding a family of vampires?" She entered the room cautiously between the narrow boxes of black dirt. "But where did these come from? How did you get them up here? What on earth are you doing?"

"Best soil money can buy."

She wandered the aisles, astonished. She bent down, squeezed clumps of dirt with her fingers. "There are tiny green things here," she declared, "shooting up out of this mud. It's a garden, you've turned your apartment into a garden."

I showed her the closet stocked with bags of fertilizer, the green hose winding its way in from the kitchen tap.

"What have you planted?"

"Let's wait until it blooms and be surprised."

"You could grow your own food in here, organic fruits and vegetables."

"We'd never get cancer."

"Flowers, though, would be spectacular, a roomful of fresh flowers in the center of the city."

"We could hold a beautiful wake."

"Think of all the oxygen the leaves are going to make. We'll be able to breathe again." She turned around in surprise. "But where's your couch and the chairs? Your desk?"

"Them's city conveniences, ma'am, don't need none of that trash out here in God's Country."

"Good Lord, the bed's gone, what have you done with your bed? Where do you sleep?"

"Among the furrows."

"Now what are you doing?"
"Taking off my clothes."
"If you think I'm getting down on that dirty floor."
"Not on the floor, on the dirty dirt."
"O no." She began to laugh. "What are you doing? O no."
"Ancient farm ritual. To ensure the success of the harvest."
"O, this is kinky."
"Well, try to calm yourself, all this laughing is frightening the bees."
"O, o o o o o."
Stamens and pistils.

IIIIIIIIIIIIIIIIIIIIIIIIIIIIIIIIIIIIIIIIIIIIIIIIIIIIIIIIIIIIIIIIIIIIIIIIIIIIIIIIIIIIIIIIIIIIIIIIIIII

One morning Franklin settled himself into his chair with his usual exaggerated care, studied the occupants of the room, stuck a joint in his mouth, lit it, and began smoking.

The clerks looked at one another.

"Fraaaaaaaaaank-lin!" bellowed the First Sergeant, "I don't believe I'm actually seeing this."

Franklin grinned behind purple glasses.

"Put it out, Private!"

Franklin shook his head. "I can't, Top. A man's got to do what a man's got to do."

"Well, here's what I do." The First Sergeant came out from behind his desk, strode over to Franklin, and yanked the burning joint from his mouth.

Suddenly, with the quick fluid motion of a working magician, Franklin caused a long glittering knife to appear in his hand.

"I thought I confiscated that."

"A white devil don't know how to think."

"Give it up now and this unfortunate incident doesn't have to leave the room."

"No, but I do."

"And where you gonna go?" The First Sergeant smiled pleasantly. "This ain't downtown Chicago."

The clerks were frozen in their chairs.

The telephone on top of the First Sergeant's desk began ringing.

"Get that, Simon," said the First Sergeant without taking his eyes off Franklin.

"Ten sixty-ninth M.I.G., Specialist Simon speaking, sir."

Franklin's chest had started to heave.

"No, sir . . . yes, sir, but I don't believe . . . yes, sir, I'll tell him, sir." Simon replaced the receiver.

"Major Coggins out on the perimeter says we owe him another man this month."

"Fine, Simon, sit down."

The knife was quivering in Franklin's hand.

"Now, Franklin, if anyone knows how patient a man I can be it's certainly you. I've sat here day after day listening to your gripes, your complaints, your bad mouth, your drivel, and I think I've been fairly decent about it. So I can be decent about this, too, if you'll just give it over right now. Wait much longer and I don't know what will happen."

The First Sergeant extended his arm. The knife flashed. There was a bright streak of red from elbow to wrist. The First Sergeant looked at his arm in disbelief, looked at Franklin, looked at his arm again. "Why you goddamn cocksucking nigger I'll kill you for this!" he shouted, lunging toward the figure already halfway to the door.

The First Sergeant lost him more than a mile down the road somewhere in the warren of tumbledown shacks and huts that served as housing for the 131st FAC. Major Holly was secretly pleased. At last the CID had cause to enter the case, but a month later Franklin was still missing and there were no leads. Captain Rossiter of the CID figured that by now the fugitive was probably down in Saigon shacked up with some prostitute on Tudo Street. Don't worry, we'll find him. Months passed. Griffin wondered if maybe he wasn't living in a rabbit hole under the Voodoo Hootch but none of the brothers were talking. Or maybe he had really done it, gone all the way over, gone *out there*, beyond the safety of barbed wire and bunker, to roam about those dark wilds, to wait and to watch with lighted eyes.

Each day was a tube you curled yourself into a ball and rolled through. Zip. Dark tube connected to dark tube, a tunnel to tumble down. Zip.

Zip, zip, zip.

Griffin sat cross-legged on the bed, a firm erection glowing in his lap, as he poured with a chemist's methodical care a clear plastic vial of white powder into the emptied tip of a Kool cigarette. He twisted off the end, lit it, inhaled deeply. His lungs were golden honeycombs, his veins the root system supporting Eden.

Zip went the day.

Once the days had gone squeeeak, now they went zip.

He glided over time in swift hydraulic comfort. Faces were like cities, the night was a smoky black mirror, the sound of a single word filled the chamber of the universe. He heard the bells in the great Himalayan temples, he rode on cockroaches to the end of color, he watched the machines dissolve into gray fluid that bubbled away into the ground. The future was here, ladies and gentlemen, now.

Once he had been so backward as to think thoughts such as these: if mind was an engine requiring maintenance and tune-ups for dependable performance down reality road, what happened when you mislaid the tools and your feeler gauge came apart, blades of metal falling into the big oil drum, lost. This, following a ninety-minute monologue on demolition derby from Hagen, a hungover and homesick mechanic. Simmering in the boredom of Sunday morning. Sleep, when it came at all anymore, appeared in snatches, periods of minutes. Marijuana had lost its magic. Trips dropped in with news of a deuce and a half leaving for the beach. Griffin pulled a dirty towel off the floor and wandered out to the truck.

Entertainment on the ride was provided by Trips's jukebox favorites, today's tune: how I dropped acid on the rifle range and shot off my drill instructor's Smoky The Bear hat, mistaking him for a plastic target silhouette. Griffin stared out the back at the road pulling away between parallel clouds of yellow dust. Behind the concertina and the garbage on each side were relocation centers, human kennels constructed from discarded ammunition crates and flattened Coke cans. Packs of stray children ran after the truck, shouting adult obscenities and hurling imaginary hand grenades.

The beach was clean, white, and empty.

Stripped to his shorts, Griffin sat in the soft sand at the water's edge, warm waves foaming over his legs, and searched the horizon. He wanted to see merchant vessels bound for Hong Kong, cream-colored ocean liners crammed to the rails with happy tourists, Russian fishing trawlers, leaping dolphins. He lay on his back and listened to the sea, a constant echoing roar like something huge hurtling through a pipe. Behind him the thousand windows of a luxury hotel. He heard a woman laughing.

His eyes opened. A helicopter was descending. The approaching blades whipped sand in his face and he turned away, spitting. The helicopter settled onto the dunes, disgorging a mob of officers in swimming trunks and bermuda shorts, their hands filled with metal food canisters, tubs of iced beer, assorted balls and a net. Griffin rolled over onto his stomach.

"Lookee what I got." Trips was standing beside him, holding a transparent walnut between thumb and forefinger.

"Cocaine," said Griffin.

"How'd you know?"

"Brother at the PX long time ago offered me some."

"And you turned him down?"

"There's no coke in Asia."

"Who says?"

"Take it from your resident botanist. No coca trees in rice land."

"So what is it then?"

"Crushed aspirin. Corroded battery acid."

"Let's do some up and see."

"Why not?"

Down the beach was an empty shack that served as a bar and refreshment stand during unit parties. Crouched inside, Trips arranged the powder into four identical lines on his military ID card. The shack smelled of fungus and stale urine. "Okay," said Trips, "who's been pissing in the brew?" They giggled nervously and took turns snorting through a rolled-up twenty dollar MPC note. Suddenly it became urgent that Griffin stand up. Struggling to his feet, he lost consciousness and fell, the side of his head banging against the wall. When he awoke Trips was shaking him roughly by the shoulders. "Hey, you okay, huh?" "Yeah," answered Griffin, frightened by his uncharacteristic concern, "sure," on his hands and knees, breakfast eggs splattering over the wooden floor. "You okay?" "Yeah, yeah, I'm okay, what'd I just say." He wiped his mouth on a green army towel. "Let's go outside and goof," said Trips.

Griffin staggered into the light. He seemed to be traversing some immense outdoor trampoline, the flutters in his stomach gathering momentum for the next eruption. He stood still for a minute, hoping the dinghy-in-a-high-sea motion would subside. Then, delicately lifting his head, he forced his awareness into as objective a survey of the surroundings as his reduced concentration could achieve. His eyes and the world shattered simultaneously. It was like staring into a cracked kaleidoscope at bright pieces of color that no longer resolved themselves into any unified pattern. One splinter reflected the intense blue of a sky higher and deeper than any he had ever known, another the hypnotic heaving of a mass of sewage that must have been the sea, another the blob of putty that was Trips's face; scattered shards: the lighted beacon of a beer can, a smiling ball sailing through crystal air, the half-buried treasure of a shod foot (his own), seasick palm trees, amazing movable fingers, the miracle of a knee; there were visibly shoddy seams where things refused to fit properly together, each object stood apart from the others, a sovereign form; a desert of salt undulated upward into heaven, every grain shadowless and distinct, embodied geometry. "C'mon, what the fuck's wrong with you now?" The cottonwood seed floating impossibly past his nose became a city-sized cloud miles away. The lion in his ears, a remnant of reason informed him, was the ocean breaking against the shore. "I'm okay, okay?" He followed Trips up the fluorescent slope to a slumped shoulder of sticky licorice road. Trucks with white stars on their shells clattered past like giant crustaceans. "How you feeling, good buddy?" "About a hundred and two." Across the road in the storage lot of a supply depot long rows of new tanks faced each other like elephants preparing to charge. The letters RESTRICTED AREA hung in the air six inches in front of the sign. The barbed wire glowed. The traffic howled and Griffin teetered in the wind, a pit opened and closed, opened and closed. From out of nowhere a scrawny yellow dog ran barking beneath the chortling wheels of a U.S. Army garbage truck. The soft asphalt sprouted a patch of wet fur, the echo of a yelp dangled in the gray monoxide air. Turning simultaneously, Griffin and Trips presented identical expressions to one another. Wow. They looked back to the dog, looked again at each other. Griffin—dog—Trips—Griffin. The moment welded into a triangle. A mystic crown. Griffin, scratching his skin, felt spiders skittering along under his epidermis. An eye burst into flames. Then one said a word to the other—which one who could say?—or one only thought the word to himself and the other instantly knew or no one thought or said and the word was simply there between them, a revelatory sound arcing two minds.

"Meat!"

Mother Nature's secret ingredient.

"Meat!"

The barbecue on eternity's grill.

"Meat!"

Make love, squeeze a trigger, pave a road.

They rolled in the tar-speckled gravel, enormous wheels whirring inches from their hilarious heads. Griffin's side began to ache and he had difficulty getting enough breath. None of that mattered though, he had penetrated a mystery and seen there at the secret center of things a rubbery pair of laughing lips. And it wasn't until he was back in his hootch, prone on his own bed, that he realized he was back in his bed and that one whole interminable day was actually over, had, in fact, gone zip.

You never spoke the proper name. (Slang kept the demon contained.) In a leather pouch tied to your dog tag chain you carried two capsules of Dexedrine given to you by Doc. (In case of an emergency.) You were careful only to smoke. (Smoking prevented addiction. Everyone knew that.)

He forgot about his workday headaches, the weather turned cool, what was insomnia? The particulars of his environment no longer oppressed him since particulars were irrelevant. Bunk, mess hall, roof top, office stool. Distinctions merged. Time was a landscape of delights. A quiet uncomplaining Griffin spent hours at the office, patiently sharpening pencils and with stoned devotion shading in his wall map with tinted squares and rectangles of orange and blue and white. The colors of the banner under which he marched. The irritatingly random clusters of black dots on Cross's radar maps and the epidemic of measles on McFarland's infrared maps couldn't compare with the clean line and bold composition of Griffin's bright wastelands. The film was another matter. It was all special effects out there. Crops aged overnight, roots shrivelled, stalks collapsed where they stood into the common unmarked grave of poisoned earth. Trees turned in their uniforms, their weapons, and were mustered out, skeletal limbs too weak to assume the position of attention. The topsoils melted away, the sun baked the crust into bricks of laterite, nature's parking lot. Like an impotent king locked in a tower, Griffin sat on his stool and watched the land die around him. Crater eyes stared mournfully into his own. With a grease pencil he drew in comical glasses, moustaches on the mountains, black rainbows, silver lining inside the clouds. He dreamed of chemical showers, of winged nozzles sweeping the provinces from end to end, of 100 percent coverage. Before he left for home he wanted to color in all the remaining blanks on the map, complete the picture.

At night he smoked classified trash. Hours flicked past like minutes. Captain Patch often discovered him in the morning hunched over a cluttered desk. For no obvious reason Patch liked him, spoke of Griffin as "a model troop," "one of my best people," so when complaints started coming in—Air Force grumbling about defaced negatives, communications about indecipherable handwriting, the pilots about mismarked targets on their flight maps—the captain simply transferred Griffin to the day shift where he could keep a fatherly eye on his favorite boy.

Griffin hadn't spent a night in his bed since his second week in-country. He adjusted quickly to the new schedule. Early to bed each evening, he'd set his alarm for a 0300 smoke, he liked his engine to be already running by the time he got up for work four hours later.

He worked now in an office of strangers. Of the original crew only Cross remained and he and Griffin had discontinued communication months ago. There were unfamiliar presences everywhere, the compound was being infiltrated. One day an alien face who called itself Lieutenant Shramm introduced him to another alien face, rosy and freckled. "Want you to take good care of Ingersoll here," droned the lieutenant. "He's your replacement."

"Wonderful," replied Griffin.

Speed Graphic, the photo lab's amateur artist, drew him a short timer's calendar in the shape of a mango leaf. The drawing was divided into numbered squares Griffin was supposed to cross out, one by one, to mark the passage of each day. When the leaf was black, he could go home. Eighty-six, eighty-five, eighty-four . . . In a week he had begun to forget, one day passed, then another, unnoticed by the calendar. After several such lapses the mathematics involved in relocating his place wasn't worth the information it provided. He was zipping too fast to be plotted and charted. The unfinished calendar hung on the wall above his head, a half-finished leaf.

Zip.

"I would have gotten sick," said Chief Winkly, "falling down puking sick. Don't believe I could have tolerated a sight like that."

His collection of photography had broadened from tits and ass to blood and guts. Every day he asked Griffin for more details of the Quimby patrol.

"Yeah," said Griffin.

"Too bad you didn't pack a camera."

"Yeah."

"Guess you can barely keep your hands off the prisoners these days. I know I'd be waiting to split a few faces by now, snap some fingers. You want a turn in interrogation, let me know, I'll see what I can do."

"Yeah," said Griffin, releasing a cloud of smoke into the chief's ripe leer.

Look ma, no telltale odor, what's he got in that cigarette?

One day Griffin passed out at work. Chief Winkly, picking his ear with a paper clip in the other room, smelled something burning and pulled him off the light table. Several frames of film had melted against his face. He didn't feel a thing. In the mirror the shiny red scar produced images no one else could see, a mountain stream, a dirt road, a forest of trees branded into his skin.

Captain Patch often found him staring at the wall, a mess of unfinished paperwork clutched in his hands.

Griffin realized it didn't matter whether he was on this airfield or back on the block, RVN or USA, here, there, space was so insignificant once you had truly learned how to occupy an interval of time.

Then he might have volunteered or perhaps he was ordered to spend a couple weeks as the II section's representative on the perimeter.

"I'll sleep better each night," said Trips, "knowing it's you out there on the watchtowers."

"Eternal freedom is the price of vigilance," said Griffin.

So he went to the perimeter and listened to a sergeant who walked like a rooster describe the order of weapons to be employed in the event of a ground attack, a barrage of bombs and bullets culminating in the detonation by storage battery of something called foo gas, drums of explosives and jellied gasoline buried on both sides of each bunker that either blunted the enemy penetration or permitted your ghosts to cheer jets from Da Nang obliterating the runway from commie hands, thank you gentleman, off-duty hours may be occupied filling sandbags and stringing wire.

During the day Griffin couldn't keep his finger off the trigger of the M-60 machine gun mounted on a wooden table inside the bunker. That cool metallic curve. Framed in the window slot before him was a continuous showing of the full-color travelogue Welcome To Beautiful Vietnam. Those women in their black silk pants, green rice fields and conical hats, the brown children with sticks perched atop the water buffalo, lumbering flanks, dark massive horns, solid as tanks, how much metal to bring one down? How many seconds—his finger stroked thoughtfully—from *National Geographic* to Gray's *Anatomy*? His stubbled chin rested against the plastic butt of the gun. Muzzle velocities, trajectories, impact patterns. All this physics concentrated in the soft tip of his finger. "They had weapons under their blouses, Sarge, they wouldn't stop." His tongue slid out, touched metal. Yes, death might very likely taste like that. The buffalo he'd pay for, of course, in monthly deductions from his salary. At the sound of an approaching motorboat he swiveled the gun to the left and sighted on a small red Honda bouncing through the field toward the perimeter, its rider, a Vietnamese teenager, outfitted in black pointed-toe boots, crimson velvet pants, blue satin shirt, and white ten-gallon hat. A cassette recorder strapped to the handle bars blasted out Blind Faith, almost completely obscuring the boy's familiar cries of "Acid, speed, grass, and scag; acid, speed, grass, and scag." The milkman. His daily rounds.

At night Griffin sat naked and alone on top of the bunker, listening to the rats and centipedes who lived in the wire. In the nearby village a light glided back and forth, appeared, disappeared, a ghost in a castle, and then abruptly went out. Darkness swirled around him like black dust. It made no difference if his eyes were open or closed. He couldn't see the skyline, the sandbags, his own hand. He could feel the jungle, huge and silent, move right up to the wire and lean its warm dark presence against his skin. A spider's web broke delicately across his face. The night flowed in and out of his body. He wanted to walk out into it, float away through the black and green tide. Something scurried in the weeds. He masturbated on a sandbag.

Zip.

Back at the office, he was informed by Captain Patch that the herbicide missions were being phased out. "Big stink in the press, shit storm in Congress, goddamn," he shouted, furiously pacing over the intelligence emblem on the floor. "Only war in history lost because of bad PR. What the fuck do they think we are, a goddamn Broadway show?"

Griffin ripped his map from the wall, tore it into confetti he tossed in a burn bag as Ingersoll looked on, pretending to be shocked.

He quit going to work. No one seemed to care. He sat on the roof, under sun and moon, playing "Remember."

"Remember the old Old Man? Funny little dude, wasn't even American was he?"

"Wonder who booby-trapped his plane?"

"Me too."

"Remember when Lieutenant Tremble ran his three-quarter into the side of the orderly room?"

"And the CO made him do fifty push-ups in the mud."

"Remember the night Noll chugged that bottle of Obesitol and scooted around the compound for three days like a choo-choo train?"

"Remember when Sergeant Anstin caught Alexander screwing Missy Lee out behind the revetments?"

"Did you see his last letter? Wishes he were back here with us. Says the American people are all pigs."

"Guess he's given up on his political career."

"Remember that runty new guy Trips kept on acid for a week? What was his name?"

"Remember when Wurlitzer used to talk?"

"He was smart once, wasn't he?"

"He still ain't so dumb. You realize you can answer any statement with 'Check it out,' 'What can I say?' or 'How do you figure, man?' "

"Can you see him stepping off the plane in Springfield, pink shades, thirty-six strings of beads, mother hugging and kissing him, 'Gosh, son, it's so wonderful to have you home again.' 'Aaaaah, how do you figure, man?' "

"Remember the shithouse fire?"

"The soda wars?"

"The roach stampede?"

"Remember when Sergeant Ramirez started hemorrhaging, and he stood there throwing up blood all over the hot grill?"

"Remember the night Vegetable tried to hang himself?"

"He couldn't even tie a decent knot."

"Remember those grunts who rode in to the Spook House with the stiffs propped up in the jeep like they was out for a Sunday drive?"

"They had funny party hats on 'em for Christ's sake."

"What a freak show."

"Somebody shoulda done something. Like their skin was coming off, man."

"Remember Mueller?"

"Remember Thai?"

"Civilians?"

"Women?"

"Remember temporals?"

"Huh?"

"Brain tubes, man, something to do with memory or something. Simon thinks we've lost them, gonna leave 'em behind when we go."

"Hell yes, shit yeah, I'm leaving my corporals and my generals, too."

Up on the roof his skin darkened to Oriental shades. He looked like a California lifeguard.

Griffin's war was over, processed and distributed. A looped reel wound through his head. A sequence of images projected onto a cold screen. The computers awaiting final interpretation.

He thought that in a helicopter once he might have killed some people.

"So now you're a man, my son," Trips replied.

The night spread away from them. The roof swayed and swelled and in the advancing fog the back of a beast lifted into view, the Delta where in bygone time Trips had humped for Uncle, a gin-youwine grunt who knew John Wayne was a dickhead but believed he was smarter. Recon. Search and destroy. Malaria, heat stroke, paddy foot. The screams of the wounded in the dark were the worst. Shrapnel tore off his helmet and he died once and heaven looked like a Doors concert on acid. In the strobe lights Mad Louie and an NVA regular rolled grunting across the dirt. Trips stuck the barrel of his rifle into the man's ear. He pulled the trigger. A light dew settled back on his hands and face like the spray on opening a can of warm beer. Mad Louie stood up. Dangling down his cheek was a fisherman's bob, a miniature piñata that swung like a pendulum when he moved. There was no eyeball in Mad Louie's left socket. He turned and ran into the darkness. One night. Down in the Delta.

The lights of the base expanded and contracted. The stars revolved. Along the rim of the jungle, a suggestion of light appeared, a dim widening line, the lid of an eye coming open.

"I don't know," said Griffin, the sigh of his breath momentarily visible in the morning air. "It's like we're all these weird spacemen or something and everyone's got marooned on his own chunk of rock and we just whizz past each other like asteroids speeding along at different rates, burning up at different temperatures, know what I mean?"

A gob of spit sailed out over the roof into the blue sand below. Trips said he wanted to fight somebody. Would Griffin do him the honor of serving as his second? A minute later he was flat against the roof, snoring.

Griffin awoke tangled in gray sheets, a moth's cocoon in his mouth. He sat up in bed and peeked between the slats of his screened window. Outside it was snowing. He put on sunglasses and walked out into a blizzard of light; he trudged through dunes and mounds, down slippery roads, across unshoveled walks, nodding to animated snowmen in their magical hats. At dusk the air turned colder and he zipped up his field jacket.

"You look like MacArthur in Korea," said Trips.

"I have returned," said Griffin.

"Wrong war."

"Wrong place."

Silver needles tumbled through cold space, the glitter of tooled precision. Wanna ride? He could never pick his way through a scab with straight pin and eyedropper. For style and elegance the instrument of choice would have to be an old-fashioned doctor's model with glass tube and steel finger grips. Proper works heightened the erotic element. Shooting up was nothing more or less than fucking yourself, in a single act combining penetration and penetrated, roles united into one entity, the circle of desire completed, the mandala of technology.

He lay on his back, blowing smoke rings, blue neon quoits breaking over his groin.

The war encapsuled him in peace. Events arranged themselves into machines of quiet harmony. Objects tended to rest in the serenity of an ancient comprehension. All things simply slowed slowly slowing except the days, of course, and the days, they went zip.

The First Sergeant received an emergency call from representatives of the Red Cross. What was going on up there? The parents were frantic. Their boy's life was threatened daily. Couldn't something be done? What about a transfer to a less dangerous area? The mother was already under the care of a physician.

"Specialist Simon," said the First Sergeant, "you want to tell me now about all these letters you've been writing home?"

One night a tear gas grenade went off in the O club's air conditioner, sending the assembled leadership hacking, crying, stumbling for the doors.

A deed so popular, the First Sergeant informed Major Holly, that more than five people immediately claimed credit for its success.

One night, the XO claimed, some unknown person or persons took a couple shots at him as he strolled down the officers' walk near the CO's hootch.

Had they mistaken him for me? thought Major Holly.

One morning the First Sergeant, while cutting flowers for the orderly room's daily bouquet, discovered a head in Major Holly's tulip beds. Oriental, male, late teens–early twenties, identity unknown. "Maybe it just growed," suggested the Flight Surgeon. "Get it out of here," ordered Major Holly.

Was that a message for me? he wondered.

One morning, as most of the unit stood in insolent attitudes of at ease listening to the First Sergeant's monthly medical lecture on the horrors of the Black Syph, Uncle Sam, the unit's Vietnamese carpenter, a hammer dangling from his web belt, castoff combat boots curled up at the toes like a genie's slippers, and his tool-box-toting crew crossed the dirt road before the tracking eyes of the entire formation and entered the orderly room. In a few minutes the morning calm was shattered by the sudden comical sounds of outrageous banging and sawing. The First Sergeant visualized the venereal enemy for them as a thousand-legged, hairy-bodied, sewer-colored bug with honed pincers and razor teeth that loved nothing better than dining out on nerve ends and soft tasty brain matter.

After a while the noise stopped, an empty truck pulled up, and Uncle Sam and his crew began carting out of the orderly room basket after basket of fresh dirt. The First Sergeant advised everyone to check their underwear regularly and if it ever looked like someone had blown their nose in there it was time to visit the dispensary.

By noon the whole 1069th knew.

"It's a tunnel," reported Simon, "from the orderly room to his hootch, from his hootch to the command bunker. We'll probably never see him again."

And outside of the occasional office glimpse no one ever did. Their commanding officer had gone underground.

At Fire Base Hula everyone was a mole. The gun crews slept in stinking dirt caves and ate their cold C-ration meals squatting in the trenches. The last man to take a peek over the top had developed a third eye and seen paradise. At night there was the Orient Express roaring in, during the day random but incessant sniper fire. The surrounding hills and jungle were scoured constantly by foot patrols, battered by artillery, bombed by shrieking jets. Occasionally a deserted tunnel was found. There was a standing offer of a three day R&R in Da Nang for anyone who shot a sniper so binoculars and rifle scopes and protective vantage points to look through them from were at a premium. When the sun was at a certain angle the base twinkled with lens reflections. Everyone was tired of nights without sleep and monotonous days broken by cans of food that despite the label claims contained the same inedible gunk and of themselves and each other and the dirt and the smell and the unflagging tense expectation. Often there were outbreaks of crazy fire when a charging bush would be "wasted," a moving shadow "waxed," so no one was surprised one warm dawn when the weapons started chattering up and down the perimeter and the familiar frantic cry, "I see him, I've got one, I've got a gook over here!" and all the glasses turned until someone said, "My God, I think he's white!" not even astonished yet because by now the legend of the American who lived in the bush and ran with the Cong was part of the general folklore of the war and if you could get three days in grubby Da Nang for zapping a gook what must be the reward for bagging an out-and-out traitor?

Everyone with a rifle started blasting away at the tree line.

"Wait a minute, wait a fucking minute! Hold your fire down there! I think I hear something."

They lifted their fingers from the triggers and listened. What was that? It didn't sound like gookese, it sounded like . . .

"Timothy Leary!" in a faint cry, "Eldridge Cleaver! Jimi Hendrix!"

They went out and brought the man in. He had obviously been out there for some time, fatigues filthy and torn, eyes bloodshot and ringed, right arm broken. He seemed to be okay mentally, he told them his name, rank, unit, the details of how he had come to be where they found him, but what he wanted to talk about most was the jungle, its aloofness, its beauty, its breathing life, and certain nonverbal secrets it had imparted to him through the intimacy of its soft green touch.

"Sure," they said, "you'll be fine now, a helicopter's on its way."

Above the clouds every day was merely the game light played with space, breaking, falling, the passage of purity across an inviolable expanse. Above the clouds the quick crisp air stung like antiseptic. Heights of pleasure in the sheer blue. Above the clouds the superior leader enjoyed a transient security.

Through the window a shaft of blazing sun struck The General in the chest, igniting a forest of purple-green palms on his yellowish-orange Hawaiian shirt, and rendering almost transparent his white white hand. The hand held a small plastic-wrapped package.

"Ham and cheese?"

Major Holly shifted in his seat and took the sandwich without comment.

"You're disappointed."

"No, no, not at all."

"You were expecting cracked crab at the club with linen and Filipino waiters."

"This is fine."

The bread was cold and damp.

"I know I'd be damn well disappointed. I hate these picnic lunches." The General poked around in the open cooler. "No Swiss."

"Here, take the ham out of one of these."

"No, it's just as well. Had a couple bouts with air sickness last week that took me by surprise I can assure you."

"That bad ear acting up again?"

"Feels like one of those damn Asian bugs that hunkers down and hangs on for weeks."

"The Cochin crud."

"Couple of congressmen at the Ambassador's last night drank me under the table. Pitiful thing when you can't even keep up with the goddamn civilians."

"You always claimed politicans had no insides."

"But they require such special handling."

"Thick gloves and snake boots."

"Complexities of strategic thought are not readily obtainable to the mind engaged in the rush for public office. Something to be said about The Opponent's advantage in that area—no elections."

"Is this plane bugged?"

The General smiled. "We sweep it daily. But as I was attempting to explain to the representatives around the pool this morning our program is winding down to a satisfactory close. Vietnamization is proceeding right on schedule, at least as well as could be expected within the parameters of our given circumstances. The ARVN have demonstrated conclusively they've got the stuff to do the job.

The governments of our neighboring client states are firming up rather nicely, pointing out another lesson we might well ponder. Do you see The Opponent bogged down in the mire halfway around the world? Hell, no, he has his proxies do the bloody work for him. Hope to God we've managed to learn a few things from this affair."

"What lessons do you think the congressmen took home with them?"

"Count your martinis and punt."

The General laughed and the plane banked on a long slow curve to the left and then began descending through the clouds. "Here we are," said The General. "This might be interesting." He leaned toward the window. The clouds broke apart and Major Holly found himself once again confronting the long lean inescapable geography of South Vietnam. The mountains looked like a raggedy green tarp dropped over a body. The rice fields appeared flooded in mud.

"I was still in Vientiane when the call came this morning," said The General. "Rushed out without changing my clothes. Spooked the congressmen. I think they thought we were invading North Vietnam."

"Or vice versa."

"I miss you at our briefings, Marty. No one has the gumption to speak to me that way. It's become pretty boring."

"Who says this outfit is the Fifth?"

"Nobody *says* anything. It's a strong suspicion. Prisoner picked up in the vicinity yesterday morning claimed affiliation."

"If his words were translated properly, if he wasn't too scared to agree to everything, if he wasn't a plant."

"You've disappointed me on this one, Marty, you know that."

"There is no Fifth NVA Regiment."

"Well, the First of the Twenty-second has got somebody in the squeeze out there."

Together they looked out the window. There was nothing to see but the bumps and pits, shadows and variations of triple canopy tropical forest. The door to the cockpit opened on the sunburnt face of a chubby major. "Excuse me, sir, Colonel Findley would like to speak with you."

"Keep your eye out," said The General, unbuckling his seat belt.

The plane circled in a holding pattern over a spot that to Major Holly seemed indistinguishable from any other spot. He scanned the ground for movement, the flash of weapons until his eyes started to burn with the effort. The country was distressingly opaque.

"Remember Barney Findley?" asked The General, returning to his seat. "One hell of a soldier." He motioned toward the window. "There's a terrific battle going on down there."

"Is it the Fifth?"

"They're not sure, probably VC."

Holly studied his reflection in the glass. The horizon was a bluish-gray blur. Why was there always haze in the sky? Did the land naturally emit its own organic pollution?

"Don't get smug," said The General. "Wait till we flush those rascals out and you'll have to look me in the eye with your hat in your hand."

"I was just thinking that if we put a dome over it, dehumidified and air-conditioned the atmosphere, Rome plowed the earth, and treated the water we might have a fairly decent prison farm. And yes, you put the Fifth on a platter and I'll eat it."

The General pulled out his black briar, his bag of Egyptian blend. "How's it going, Marty," he asked quietly as he filled the bowl. "I mean back at the group. This underground business, you can imagine what we thought."

"Beards, beads, hair."

"An amusing image for about half a day."

"The men like to pretend I've gone over to the other side."

"Of course there's no denying the danger, one of the hazards of command. Unfortunately we have lost some good people in a few of these cowardly incidents. Reprehensible behavior. But tunnels now, are they really the proper solution?"

"I'm not hiding out. I'm in my hootch at night, in the office every day. I come and go as I please. So I've made a couple holes in the ground. I'm simply being prudent. The tunnels also serve a useful security function by connecting the command bunker to the orderly room and my quarters. I fail to see what's improper about such preparedness."

"Well, I've spoken to Captain Rossiter. He seems to feel that with this Franklin individual out of the picture the potential threat is reduced markedly."

"There have been several incidents since Private Franklin disappeared."

"I never heard about this."

"Do you think I'm going to bother you every time a weapon is discharged in the company area."

"Was it close?"

"Near enough."

The General sat still for a moment, sucking in silence, the familiar odor of smoldering mummy wrappings slowly engulfing the cramped cabin. The General leaned forward and rapped on the cockpit wall. The plane completed one final circle, lifted its nose and its passengers toward that realm above the clouds where the days were always golden, the nights dark silver.

"How's that Annie of yours?" asked The General, pipe wiggling between his teeth.

"You mean Anh?"

"You know who I mean."

"She's pregnant."

The General's expression went from startled to concerned to bemused. "Is there anything we need to do about that?"

Major Holly shrugged. "She says it's not mine."

"Who else's could it be?"

"I didn't ask."

"Look," exclaimed The General, pointing off into the clear bright sky, "Arclight," and as if at the direction of his extended finger scores of tiny black cylinders began dropping from the long bellies of a formation of big green B-52s, the sticks of heavy explosive wobbling downward in neat perpendicular order and vanishing into the soft endless cloudscape below.

"That ought to shake up the nest," declared The General.

"Sometimes, on very quiet mornings, I've been able to feel the vibrations from strikes in the Ashau."

"Hard lessons," remarked The General. He poked about in the bowl of his pipe with the tip of a penknife blade. "Have you given any consideration to your future in the coming peace?"

"Lately it's been difficult to imagine me having one."

"Oh, there will definitely be a peace all right, the question is how long will it last. The smart boys are all learning Spanish."

"I would have guessed Arabic."

"I hear Bolivia."

"Up in the mountains, isn't it, cool and clean."

"Colonel Tuttle informs me you've worked wonders on that compound."

"You'll have to drop in for a tour."

"Fine, maybe next week after the tournament. You're planning on attending the tournament, aren't you?"

"A couple hours on a golf course at this point would be like two weeks R&R in Honolulu."

"We've put together quite a lineup this year. Stone from the First Cav, Kingsley from the Twenty-fifth, Concannon from the Eighty-second, and Charlton Heston has promised to try to get in for the day."

"My calendar's already cleared."

"Here, have some of the orange juice in this thermos or my steward's going to be miffed."

A towering wall of thick shifting cloud appeared before them. The plane plunged in.

"By the way," asked Major Holly, "what happened back there anyway?"

The plane seemed to be surrounded by suds, immersed in a multiplying mound of soapy sparkling bubbles.

"Back where?"

White foam streamed past the windows.

"On the ground."

"What do you think?" replied The General, puffing busily. "We won. We always win."

Meditation in Green: 14

1. Two weeks after the petals have fallen off watch for these signs:
   a) darkening of the upper green stalk
   b) yellowing of the lower leaves
   c) hardening of the capsules accompanied by a color change from light green to a darker green with a brownish tinge or light green to a dull metallic blue sheen
   d) most important, the time clock of the plant, the ring at the base of the capsule where the petals were joined darkens in a single day to dark brown or black
2. On a clear, sunny, calm morning, taking special care with your Amasya knife to cut neither too deep nor too shallow, make several circumferential incisions about the ripe capsule.

So I turned full time to gardening, brown fingers puttering between the greening rows, that rich crotchlike odor, the silent company of vegetable life. At dusk I sat in the window, agreeably fatigued, surveying the yield as the red sun fell at my back, stretching a shadow across leaves and stems. It was a bumper crop. Nodding heads wall to wall.

I rarely left the room anymore. The plants required attention, I required attending. I weeded, I watered, I whispered encouragement. I dragged the boxes one by one into the bright window light and out again. The seeds burst, and the soil broke and I used to lean against a box, eye to the ground, and monitor a miracle as tiny separate shoots, tender as a baby's fingers, poked curiously through a wall of earth. The strength in such softness. The simple mystery. I could watch and watch. Later, I read dozens of botany books but diagrams and nomenclature couldn't satisfactorily explain the direct wonder of one growing plant. You had to feel your way into understanding. I could see myself stripped to the skin, lying in a box of my own, swollen root burrowing into the ground. Blossoming all over.

I quit my sessions with Arden. I was hopeless. I was a bad seed. He hardly had time for me anyway. The business was branching out, new outlets in half a dozen locations, everybody wanted to be a tree. I occasionally watched him on television Sunday morning, cushioned on a big satin pillow, flanked by rubber plants, holding a cabbage, and chatting with a New Jersey sprout king. He looked great.

Huey's brother recovered from his heart valve infection but died later somewhere out on the street, electrocuted by one of those charged drug terminals no one knows enough about to approach safely. Huey left her job at the welfare office. She was tired of feeling like the witch in the candy house. We spent a lot of time going to old movies.

I was counting the days to harvest time.

One late afternoon the telephone, which had been quiet for weeks, rattled to life. I picked up the receiver to hear a click followed by a dial tone. I hung up, it rang again. Click. Hum. And a third time. Guess who?

I finished my chores, washed the fertilizer from my hands, pulled on a jacket, and went out. Eugene was in the corridor, pacing, alone. He stopped, glared at me through swollen eyes. Someone had left the front door to the building ajar and while Eugene loaded a washer in the basement Chandu slipped out for a closer look at a world he had experienced only from a fourth-floor window. The world greeted him in the form of a hit-and-run Coke truck. We were all responsible. "Fuck the Eskimos!" Eugene shouted at me.

"Fine," I said, descending the stairs. "That's fine."

Outside I automatically checked the sky, an old man's reflexes already settling in, weather? I can remember weather. A low gray lid was being closed over the city. The wind, gusting hard and raw, pressed into me, tearing my eyes. Up ahead the skyline appeared etched in metal, all the buildings sharply filed, a clawful of arrows.

It was a long chilly walk, too long complained the leg.

I found Trips, saltshaker in one hand, half-eaten apple in the other, making faces through the glazed window at the sullen diners packed inside Cleo's Chuckwagon.

"C'mon," he said, grabbing my arm. "Let's move." He had on his Delta look.

"Where we going?"

"To the zoo."

"Slow it down, huh. You know I can't handle this pace."

"To look at the fucking animals."

We went ten quick blocks in breathless silence, cutting down alleys dripping with black water, zigzagging across the barren park, the drained pond. The night came on, cold and early. The first snowflakes stung my face like tossed sand. The leg was giving me a twinge now on every step. I hoped this adventure would be stupid and dangerous enough to be worth the trouble.

The streets got quieter, the lights farther apart.

Suddenly Trips pulled me through a prickly hedge.

"Jesus Christ!" I grumbled. "I think my cheek's bleeding. So's my hand."

"Shut up."

We squatted down on a rectangle of hard dirt, the token front yard of the immense apartment house behind us. "Look," Trips whispered. I peered between the thorns. Across the street beyond a row of parked cars and bare stunted trees stood another smaller building. It was one we had spied on once through binoculars from the rooftop at our backs. Sergeant Anstin's residence. All the windows were dark.

"Now what?"

"Wait."

"It smells like dog piss in here."

"Breathe through your mouth."

"I need something to sit on."

"Here." He pulled a rolled-up newspaper from his back pocket.

"What is it?"

"*Wall Street Journal.*"

"Wonderful."

The snow started pouring down like confetti. I took half the paper and made a tent of stock quotations to cover my head. The inevitable joint was produced and shared quietly, an occasional pedestrian passing us on the other side of the hedge not more than an arm's length away. Under me the ground turned damp and soft. Trips sat hunched forward, chin on his knees, and stared intently out into the empty street, tendrils of smoke curling between tensed lips. Slowly all the scenery was going to white. Up in the stormy sky a red antenna high atop an insurance tower blinked steadily on and off.

"I'm freezing," I said. "What are we waiting for?"

Trips nudged my arm. "Hi-de-ho," he whispered.

A man with a dog on a leash rounded the corner. Trips parted the bush for a clearer look. The man climbed the steps, fished a key from his pocket, and led the dog through the door.

"Fucking cocksuck."

A light went on in a second story window.

"Shit-eating lifer slime."

I remembered a night in the bunker at the end of the runway overlooking the POL dump, four in the morning, drifting off on tropical currents of spilled jet fuel and jungle decay when someone suddenly stood up beside me on the other side of the bunker wall. I tumbled screaming off the sandbags, rifle clattering to the ground. I scurried about on all fours like a frantic bug, trying to find the rifle in the dark. A hand seized the collar of my shirt and hauled me to my feet. "I just slit your white throat, specialist," growled Sergeant Anstin's voice. My legs were shaking. "I just jammed a frag grenade up your nose." He tugged on the hair above my ear. "Get a haircut."

The light in the window went out.

"Yeah, that's right, Jack," muttered Trips. "Try to hide."

"He's gone to bed."

"We'll see."

The cold ground had been seeping steadily into the leg. I began massaging my thigh. "It's tightening up," I said. "I can't sit out here much longer."

"We ain't going to." He pulled up a pant leg and from inside his boot produced a handful of oddly bent, pencil-length pieces of metal. "Lock-picking tools," he explained. "Official issue."

"What do you have in mind for tonight, anyway?"

"Nothing special, my man, a casual meeting, an exchange of pleasantries, a reunion of the guys."

"I'm not breaking into that apartment."

"Now come on, Grif, how you gonna be?"

"We're not about to do the colonel's plane again, are we?"

Trips laughed. "You thought I had something to do with that?"

"Who else?"

"Noll, you fool, The Mutant Man. What do I know about planes and hydraulic lines? I wanted to set up a Claymore under his bed."

"Noll?" I couldn't even remember his face.

"Yeah, Noll. Look."

Across the street the door opened. A man, dogless, exited, tested the door handle, descended the steps, and turned quickly right, moving uptown. From the rear he did exhibit that characteristic E-7 strut.

"Hit it," said Trips.

We came through the hedge right on top of a couple out for a leisurely evening stroll. The woman screamed. The man's hands began to go up. "Boo," whispered Trips, shouldering past.

The cone of a street lamp halfway down the block illuminated a fury of flakes and the top of our sergeant's balding skull.

We cut across the street, squeezing between illegally parked cars, leaving handprints in the snow on trunks and hoods. By the time we reached the corner, Sarge had disappeared into lights and laughter, a forest of people. Fun Night in Fat City.

"There." Trips pointed.

A bald head bobbed across a distant intersection. Visibility was diminishing by the minute.

Trips ran interference through the crowd. I hobbled along behind, cursing my leg, cursing the Sarge. We soon lost him again. Half the town was on the streets frolicking in a winter wonderland. Before the floodlit entrance to a mausoleum of a hotel milled a dense mob of plastic-hatted, name-tagged conventioneers. Trips cleared a path. "Hey, what the . . ." "Do you mind?" HI I'M ROGER "This is my wife, buddy." "Fuck you in the ear." "Did you see that?" Above us flags whipped in the wind like rotor blades.

We emerged from the Eastern Sales Division of Motorola to glimpse the Sarge crossing at the next light and ducking into a corner drugstore. We set up an observation post in the recessed doorway of a closed shoestore across the street. I flopped down on the icy pavement, bent over my outstretched leg, trying to work out the ache. Trips lit a joint. "Bad?" he asked, crouching beside me.

"I don't know. It's like a used car, you never know when it's going to go out on you. It needs exercise every day. I've been inside too long with my plants."

"Your what?"

"My plants. You've got to come visit."

Some kids danced past, swordfighting with broken car antennas. Two drunks were trying to hit each other with clumsy snowballs.

"Plants." Trips stood up, studying the figures in black silhouette crossing to and fro the lighted windows of the drugstore. "What the hell is he doing in there?"

"Listen," I said, my fingers clenching around the stubborn meat of a thigh that no longer seemed mine. "The cables are all twisted up. When he comes out go on without me or you'll lose him."

The hard prominences of Trips's skull glowed orange as he sucked on the joint. "No," he said finally, smoke exploding about his head. "Never left nobody behind, ain't gonna start here."

A patrol car slid silently by, cop faces like dolls behind shatterproof glass.

"You could always leave me with an extra bullet."

"Don't try telling me you don't want a piece of this. I heard you back there huffing and puffing, 'I'll kill that motherfucker, goddamnit, goddamnit.' Don't try telling me."

"How do you know who I was talking about?"

"Shit." The saltshaker was in his hand again, long restless fingers unscrewing the shiny cap.

"What I need is one of those wooden platforms with the little metal wheels to drag myself around town on."

Trips licked his thumb, eyed me sideways like a crazy dog. "It is him, you know."

"Yeah. Yeah, I guess it is."

A man exited the drugstore, slipped around the corner.

"C'mon, there he goes." Trips yanked me to my feet. I tested the leg. Pins and needles. "Let's go," Trips shouted, dashing out into honking traffic, flash and metal, sphincter aflutter. When I reached the opposite curb the leg was in flames. "Go," I said, leaning against the winking DON'T WALK light. "You go on. Knock him down and I'll come along to get in a few good kicks."

"I'll carry you," said Trips.

I tried a couple quick steps. It wanted to collapse. "God damn this thing!" I cried. I was turning in circles, beating a fist against it, the wires crackling up and down. "God damn!"

"Put your arms around me."

"I'm fucking sick of this!" I kicked the light pole as hard as I could. A shower of hot white sparks flamed across my eyes. It had been a long time so when it came up it moved suddenly with the enormous lift of a black wave spinning up storms of sand, tattered ropes of brown weed, broken shells, barnacled sections of unrecoverable wrecks, bloated sea horses with eaten-out eyes, and always breaking and always about to break, frozen in that charged moment between as in woodcuts or watercolors or ebony sculpture of an Oriental style. I turned away, my cheeks wet.

"Are you all right?"

"Yes, yes, I'm all right, I'm always all right, now will you go on, he's getting away."

"I'm not leaving you."

"Okay, watch, I'm moving, see this, I'm right behind you, see, I'll scuttle along like a crab. Look ma, no crutch."

A block of concrete darkness opened into a hollow of vibrating light. We covered the distance as best as I could, slipping and sliding in the slush, Trips glancing back repeatedly, me shouting, "Yes, I'm still here." Then there was Sergeant Anstin's head bathed in flashing color. DANCE DANCE DISCO DANCE shrieked the neon. A crowd of people moved in and out of a silver door. "Sarge!" Trips called in a huge friendly voice. "Sarge, hey, wait up!" There was something in Trips's hand. I could barely see ten feet in front of me. The storm was approaching total whiteout. It was like being trapped in static. The silver door rippled with blurry bars of light. Faces flowed toward me out of the fuzz on currents of laughter and perfume. "Hi Sarge, remember me?" There was something in Trips's hand. Sarge turned, his profile clear in a corona of neon emerald. "Trips!" I cried. The hand was coming up. I grabbed a city trash can and lunged forward, feet slipping out from under me, and swung as hard as I could into Trips's back. I saw a flash as we went down and heard someone scream, gun and can skittering away on a sheet of iced cement that opened my pant leg and the skin over my knee. Trips was squirming around under me. I hugged him tightly about the waist. He beat on my head and shoulders with his fists. "Stop it!" I screamed. "Stop! It's not him, you hear me, it's not even him!" He looked up at me, eyes like milky ice cubes. "Understand? That's not Sergeant Anstin." He stopped moving for a moment, then nodded his head. "You fucking fool," I said, lifting myself off him. "I think I busted my knee. The good knee." And even though I really saw nothing, my body reacted instinctively to the click, jerking backward, so when I did feel something solid moving through jacket and shirt it didn't get in deep enough to matter. I howled like an animal and leaped for the knife. It flicked at me quick as a snake, drawing blood across both hands. "You goddamn motherfucker!" I drove my other knee with all the force I had right into his groin. He gasped as the wind left his lungs and I seized the wrist of his knife hand with both of mine. Yes, I wanted the knife, I wanted the cutting to stop, but at that moment even simple tempered steel seemed too inadequate, too technological, for the lusts that were on me, I wanted to feel flesh—skin, muscle, the airhose of his throat—swimming between my bloody fingers, I wanted to feel it recoil, I wanted to feel it crack, desire never so fierce, and all the time the blade, in the grip of our combined touch, was weaving between us with a sovereign will like a planchette anxious to spell a message from the other side and then abruptly the spirits were fled and I was sitting up examining the mess of my knee, my mangled hands, the amazing pearl handle projecting from Trips's field jacket like a switch you could turn on or off. He was folded up on his side, the falling snow already busy building a pretty white layer down one motionless arm, along the length of one bent leg. I pulled out the knife and opened up his jacket. His LIVE TO RIDE, RIDE TO LIVE T-shirt was soaked through. I wadded up a glove, pressed it in against the wound. "You stupid shit," I murmured. Beside me stood a pair of quaking legs. "Who is this guy?" asked "Sergeant Anstin." "I never saw him before in my life."

"Sorry," I said.

There were veins and arteries, places to be squeezed, pressure points, I couldn't remember all that stuff, half a day of training inside a stifling garage somewhere in the middle of Fort Campbell, Kentucky. That familiar helplessness. Why hadn't I been sent to medics school, brought back something useful from those lost years? My hand was getting wet. A red amoeba swelled slowly across the pavement, coloring the snow pink. My heart was pounding in sync with the beat of the music spilling from the open silver door where a crowd stood, quietly watching. I looked around. I was at the center of an arena of shocked eyes. The stained knife occupied its own clear space on the sidewalk like something fallen miraculous and glowing out of the night sky. I didn't know where the gun had gone. Trips's pulse was weak and irregular. The chills started then, it was so cold and unprotected out here on the concrete, brushing the snow off Trips, trying to keep it from covering him completely, the fine crystals falling like salt all around us. The black wave began rising, pushing out of unglimpsed vaults, higher and higher, there was no stopping it this time, so it rose and it peaked and it broke and I didn't care, all control gone, slumped on the sidewalk, warm blood washing over my hand, and under the flashing lights, the gaze of the crowd, I cried and I couldn't stop. The snow tumbled out of the darkness, draping a mantle over angles and edges, shrouding the world at last in softness and silence.

Finally the ambulance arrived, its domed lights swinging in counterpoint to the neon DANCE DANCE DANCE. A pair of burly bearded guys who appeared to have just driven in from a beer commercial in Colorado jumped out and attended to Trips. The police talked to me.

"You the hero?"

"I hope not."

"Okay, what's the story here?"

"I don't know," I said. "Somebody killed his dog."

I rode to the hospital, rocking beneath a siren, in the back of the ambulance, staring at a white hand dangling off a stretcher. Someone said there was no major penetration, they thought he'd probably make it. Ice built up under the wipers, the tires occasionally skidded sideways. Someone offered me a whiff of oxygen. Someone took a history, nodding approvingly. Everyone got hurt these days, accident, disease, organs breaking down, and no one had proper coverage. Living was expensive enough but dying now was a luxury. A veteran, though, he's got his own hospitals, his staff, his lab tests, his food, his paid care, his security, yes a veteran, why he was home free.

At 0218 Looking Glass 24, a nightly infrared mission, vanished from the radar screens at I Corps air control in Da Nang. Radio contact was broken. The following morning search planes located the wreckage of a Mohawk reconnaissance aircraft approximately three hundred meters from the peak of a rock mountain. There wasn't a section of wreckage exceeding six inches in length. A medical team arrived by helicopter. "I couldn't find enough pieces to fill an envelope," commented Flight Surgeon Beams, speaking of the mortal remains of the crew, Captain Alvin P. Fry and Specialist 5th Class Monroe Wurlitzer.

Kraft wouldn't come out of his room anymore. He ignored orders directing him to the Spook House, he declined an invitation for a drive to the 92nd Evac. He wouldn't move, he rarely spoke. He sat on the floor, head slightly cocked, the muscles of his face fixed in an expression of intense bafflement as though attending to a sound or an interior process distant and subtle. No one knew what was wrong with him. Sometimes when questioned, his hands would lift in gestures of helpless amazement, and he'd look away saying softly, "The plants . . . they're so . . . the trees . . . I . . . I don't know." Finally they left him there like that because he was obviously useless and he only had forty days to go and no one cared anyway.

At last the landscaping, the interior decorating, the washing, the painting were done. Major Holly's vision had become a reality. The hootches were spotlessly white, the polished roofs shone. There were rocks lined up neatly along the road, the sidewalk was swept daily, there were newly planted palm trees beside the mess hall and the O club, flowers were blooming around the orderly room. Everyone always wore a hat and all boots gleamed. The compound looked so neat it reminded Griffin of a Monopoly game. The hootches were the little houses lined up on Boardwalk and he was a metal shoe stuck on Chance.

There was no hope of escape now. The burning pickup bounced across the field, trailing gasoline and fire it couldn't possibly outrun. The truck exploded. Through the open cab window you could see the bodies twisting in the flames. Out in the darkness restless shapes gathered now at the edges of the light. As the fire subsided, they crowded about the warm doors. Reaching in, they pulled at the meat with bare fingers. In the scuffle a handful of intestines spilled shiny and loose onto the ground. A man chewed on a heart, a woman crouched behind a tree gnawing at the charred flesh of an arm.

Someone said, "Wow!"

There were astonished whispers, hysterical giggles, shrieks of delight.

"Save me a breast!" shouted someone else.

The chapel echoed with electric laughter.

One of the men had been locked out of the farmhouse. He banged on the door with his fists. Deformed faces turned toward the sound of his cries.

"Uh-oh."

"Poke 'em in the eyes with the torch!"

"Kick 'em in the nuts!"

A woman screamed. Arms were plunging through the walls.

Simon leaned over. "Is it legal to be showing us this picture?"

They sat on a bench against the back wall. Trips was staring open-mouthed at the images flowing across the white sheet tacked above the altar.

"Look," said Griffin, dressed in field jacket and sunglasses, "I think this kid is gonna eat her mother."

The audience began bouncing up and down in the pews.

Someone stood bowlegged in the open doorway. There came a noise of splashing water.

"Jesus Christmas, Mutant Man, ain't you got no couth at all?"

The film rattled through the antique projector, its sound track scratchy and distorted. A polluted tide of blue smoke drifted along the cone of movie light.

Someone lying on the floor shifted position, empty beer cans went clattering over concrete.

The ghouls milled around in the night, searching for a way in. On the farmhouse porch dead feet tramped steadily across the boards.

"The one with the black eyes and rotten teeth looks just like the CO."

"How about Sergeant Anstin's twin there in the bib jeans?"

"Ma!"

The shadow of someone's upraised hand formed a bat silhouette against the screen.

"This is the grossest movie I've ever seen," murmured Simon.

"I like it," said Griffin.

Armed gangs of potbellied men roamed the daylight countryside hunting for the ghouls.

"Burn 'em or beat 'em," the sheriff advised.

When the sirens began everyone laughed. Then they jumped up, heading for the exits.

"Every time we get a good flick," someone moaned.

"Makes you wonder if they've got a copy of our film schedule or something."

Okay, thought Griffin. Okay. He crawled under the bench and covered his head with his arms.

In R&A a tray of Scrabble tiles was knocked to the floor. "Well, gentlemen," drawled Sergeant Maloney, "looks like the Fifth NVA has found us first." Huddled in his plywood box Lieutenant Tremble wondered if he'd survive the night. He had wanted so badly to make captain.

Around the Spook House the fence was electrified. A unit of Green Berets manned the bunkers.

In the NCO club Sergeant Sherbert put on his flak vest and poured himself a glass of Jack Daniels Black.

The First Sergeant, rolling out of bed, heard the Chinese bugles of the winter of 'fifty-one.

The first mortar round detonated in the empty field between the EM club and the laundry, the huge crunching sound of its impact resembling a monster chewing on bone. The second redistributed the garbage dump behind the mess hall. The third hit the gas tanks in the motor pool.

On top of the mess hall the sirens shrieked, a piercing mournful cry.

Griffin peered out from his hiding place. The chapel was empty, the projector ran on unattended. The warm wind coming through the door smelled of urine.

"There's one," shouted the sheriff. A shotgun fired. The ghoul went down like a rotten tree.

The incoming was making two sounds now. A mortar scored a hole in the basketball court, a rocket removed the kitchen from the rear of the mess hall.

The Officer of the Day and the Sergeant of the Guard ran through the compound, trying to round up the men assigned to this night's Reaction Force.

Scrambling for cover, Chief Winkly banged his head against the bunker opening. He lay down inside between everyone's feet, a moldy towel pressed to his bleeding nose.

Sergeant Anstin ordered two privates to take down by flashlight and note pad the names of those without helmet and flak jacket.

The sound of impacting rounds moved gradually away. The giant stomped off toward the runway. Griffin waited a moment, then crawled out from under the bench. Framed in the chapel doorway down a dark corridor of sand between the hootches the hangar was in flames and miniature black figures scurried back and forth in front of the light. Shouts and screams were muffled, sounds from beneath a heavy blanket. Incredible corollas of orange and white bloomed at random across his eyes. Then the sirens changed pitch and rhythm, began making noises Griffin had never heard before. The signal for ground attack? He stood transfixed in the doorway. Every sudden explosion of sound and color ignited a dazzling rush through his body. His insides sparkled. The air burned, the floor vibrated. He felt close to orgasm. Something flew out of the sky, thumped against the chapel wall. He bent down and saw a combat boot that had miraculously landed upright. He peeked inside. It still contained a foot. The top of the stump bubbled and heaved like a volcano about to erupt. So. He supposed he would need a weapon. Fear was in him somewhere but dimly heard, a screaming voice trapped behind double panes of glass. He waited for a lull in the downpour, then lowered his head and sprinted out umbrellaless into the storm. Behind him in the abandoned chapel a voice patiently explained, "Kill the brain and you kill the ghoul."

Captain Fry's replacement, a twenty-two-year-old lieutenant from Honolulu, raced to the revetments, buckled himself in, and was taxiing down the flight ramp when a mortar round fell into his right wing. The cockpit exploded and melted around him. In an amazing display of accuracy the mortars leapfrogged down the flight line, leaving behind in each sandbag and steel revetment a crackling pyre of aeronautical rubbish.

Wendell stood in the tunnel outside the command bunker, beating on the door with his fist. No one was answering. This infuriating plank of reinforced wood was barring him from the dramatic climax to a great motion picture. The missing footage, the bunker documentation. Tense counsels, questioning eyes, bare bulbs burning above huddled heads, dust shaking down onto the map tables, the chirr of field phones, the cackle of the radio, furrowed faces watered with sweat, assessments, decisions, arguments, the tracing of stress patterns, the deterioration of poses, panic, delirium, death. He was missing it all! Furious, he began kicking at the door with a booted foot. "Hey!" he shouted, "c'mon, open up, I know you're in there." But no one answered. No one seemed to be at home.

The sand was blue, the hootches were huge and black as boulders. Griffin slipped and staggered on. His sunglasses fell off. The plummeting shriek of a whistle made him pause and look up. The darkness opened on a blast of light that tossed him against a wall. He lay on the ground, arms crossed over his head, chuckling quietly as hot metal clattered down onto nearby rooftops. He patted his body. The shoulder was sore but he had sprung no leaks. Of course, he had on his magic field jacket. Tonight nothing could harm him. A small dark shape crept out from beneath the nearest hootch. It was a dog, one of several unnamed mongrels who had appeared in the compound since the famous "canine incident." The animal crawled slowly toward him, whimpering softly. Its skinny body trembled under Griffin's hand. "Hey," he whispered, stroking the bony chest, "it's okay." From a radio left on in someone's room a female country singer was whining nasally about bourbon, Bob, and bouncing beds. Another whistle forced him to cover his head. Lightning cracked behind his eyes. He heard someone screaming in a nearby bunker. The dog looked at him. He scratched its neck. He tried to hug the animal closer to him and muttered in disgust. The dog had peed on him. He felt around the animal's flank. Without warning his fingers slid through fur and skin, were plunged knuckle-deep into wet warm darkness. No wonder the dog had seemed to calm under his comforting. Globs of sticky jellylike things squeezed forward, surrounding his hand. He lifted the gilded hand into the light, then wiped his fingers across both his cheeks. The dog looked at him. Good-bye dog, he said silently. He got up and stumbled across the road. An officer's hootch had received a direct hit. There were splintered chunks of wood and twisted roof tin scattered about a smoking crater. It was like an explosion in a barbecue. Portions of the product were everywhere. He almost stepped on a pale unattached hand. He saw a hairless blackened head lying on the ground like an abandoned bowling ball. He didn't want to examine too closely, he was afraid he might recognize the owner. Up on the hill a crowd had gathered around the window of the arms room. "Number!" demanded the squeaky voice of Potter, the clerk, "No number, no weapon." "I'll show you a number," yelled someone and the cluster of men surged forward to mangled cries and the sound of objects hitting wood. Rifles and loaded magazines began flying out the window. The crowd toppled to the ground, fighting for weapons. "Goddamn that Holly, goddamn him!" Griffin waited until the tangle of limbs and barrels had unknotted. He found an M-16 in the weeds. Flares were popping now in the black sky over the perimeter where ground fire could be heard like gravel rattling down a chute. Was everyone deploying his weapons in the proper sequence? He clutched the rifle in his hands and looked about in bewilderment. He was supposed to have been assigned a defensive position in the event of a night like this but Sergeant Sherbert, his group leader, never showed up for their only drill months ago. Griffin stood there watching the shadows start to come alive.

Trips had broken into Wendell's room easily enough by knocking the door off its hinges and once inside had opened the footlocker with a firm precise blow from his entrenching tool, but he couldn't get into the metal clothes locker, the hasp was too strong, the bolts too tight, proof that this was where Wendell kept his jewels, the gems he had been bringing in from Thailand to finance his first civilian picture. He pushed the locker onto its side and began jumping up and down on it. The door started to bulge. All he needed was a space big enough for his arm.

Lieutenant Tremble ushered his terrified band of Remington rangers out to the cover of a guard bunker on the road between the orderly room and the motor pool. Of course, the bunker was abandoned. "The coward who deserted this post," vowed Lieutenant Tremble, "will find himself tomorrow in a world of hurt." An overloaded jeep ground up the hill from the burning garage, seats piled high with silent, bareheaded soldiers, several men flung spreadeagled across the hood, and sideswiped the bunker and gunned away, its lights off, its horn stuck in a relentless howl of inanimate pain. Some live rounds banged into the metal roof above Lieutenant Tremble's head. He checked his pulse. His own men were huddled there shoulder to shoulder behind an untrustworthy wall of moldering sandbags, their rifles clattering awkwardly together, "watch where you're pointing, shithead," helmets either too big or too small, magazines jammed in backward, their round eyes peering out at the pluming flames and an impossibly hostile confusion and Lieutenant Tremble had a vision: if the commies ever do hit the beaches of California, here is a preview of what to expect—clumsy panic in a defensive position around the parking lot of fast-food Burgerama. "Hey," whispered Sergeant Maloney, touching his sleeve. Apelike shapes were slinking down the dark road. Then, for one amazing moment, there were no thoughts, there were no fears. Lieutenant Tremble simply propped a rifle against his cheek, aimed, and fired. The nearest shape slumped to earth like a puppet with severed strings. He aimed, he fired again. Score two. My God, he was good at this. He was really good.

Ingersoll rounded the corner of the chain-link fence enclosing the II Section. "It's stuck," he shouted hysterically, "I can't get it out!" He ran toward Griffin, tugging on the pin of a hand grenade. "It's stuck or corroded or . . ." The pin snapped, Ingersoll stumbled, the grenade tumbled gaily along the ground. "Get down!" shouted Griffin, dropping onto his chest. Arms outstretched before him, Ingersoll ran mindlessly on, hoping apparently to find his lost toy and heave it away before anyone got hurt. The underside of Griffin's eyelids glowed red for an instant, a hot iron pressed the wrinkles out of the back of his field jacket. When he dared to raise his head, he saw a log in the center of a bonfire. "My God," exclaimed a voice, "was that a gook?" A helicopter stuttered overhead, its bright searchlight swinging wildly back and forth. "They're coming in!" someone screamed in the escalating decibels of a cinema heroine. "They're coming in!"

Sergeant Mars dismissed the security guards and assumed responsibility for the situation in the interrogation building. The detainees began wailing the moment he stepped through the door. He used a sixteen on automatic and it only took two magazines to complete one row. It was easier than mowing grass. He was reloading to do the other side when Lieutenant Phan rushed in, armed and breathless. "Sergeant!" he cried. "What you do?" Mars shot him in the face. Most of the remaining detainees were blubbering by now, crying, begging with hands thrust between the bars, some huddled in back against the far wall trying to put as much space as they could between their helpless bodies and the iron mouth of his white man's gun, some stood in place, their backs turned. Old Uncle Fish, who hadn't uttered a sound through the water and the bamboo and the long distance calls, sat stoically on crossed legs in the center of his cage. Mars began with him. A wave of teletypelike thunder broke down the length of the long room, crashing over the screams, and sweeping away into a sea of silence. Then Mars rolled a fragmentation grenade down the center aisle and bolted for cover. The prisoners' interrogation was now officially concluded.

Wendell zoomed in on the fire, slowly circling backward around the remains of Ingersoll. In the viewfinder flesh fell away from the dripping bone. Denied high psychological drama, all that was left was cheap close-ups.

In the II office Griffin found a trio of confused and frightened strangers. One was squatting under Captain Patch's desk, one was shredding documents by hand, one was fiddling with the dials of a safe. "These won't open," he complained in a hoarse plaintive whisper. He looked at Griffin's face. "My God, you're wounded." Griffin shoved him aside and quickly moved down the row of steel filing cabinets, unlocking one drawer after another. He watched his hands opening and closing, attending to their tasks as though they were the bulky gloves of a spacesuit. He picked up a dusty thermite grenade from the cardboard box on top of the safe. "Where'd Ingersoll get that phosphorus?" His voice too seemed to be transistorized, crackling over headphones. Nobody knew. "If we had been properly trained . . ." muttered one. "Go on out to the bunkers," said Griffin. "I'll handle this." He was inside his helmet, protected from the alien atmosphere. He began with the drawers containing the herbicide reports. He placed a grenade in each one, then slammed the drawers shut. In a few minutes there'd be no record of the work he'd done in this war, he'd be ready to die. The outer door opened, Griffin swung his rifle around. Captain Patch dashed into the room, waving a pistol, shouting incoherently, wide eyes rolling around like those of a horse trapped in a barn fire. The left side of his face was slashed open, his shirt was bloody to the waist. "Fresh weight," he seemed to be crying, "fresh weight." "It's okay, sir," said Griffin, "I took care of it." His finger tightened around the trigger. If this man didn't get out of here in about one minute . . . Patch grabbed a manila folder on his desk and ran from the room. Griffin stood in the center of the office, home for almost a year, atop the intelligence insignia on the floor, and waited for the secrets to melt. The safes were glowing like furnaces. Then he remembered. Copies had been telexed to MACV, CINCPAC, JCS; evidence was strewn like a highway crash all over the globe. He'd never be free of this mess, even in death. A bullet tore through the wall, hit the back of Captain Patch's chair and sent it spinning around and around. Griffin ran out the red door.

On the opposite side of the runway all the hangars of the 101st Airborne were burning merrily, a row of lighted hearths collapsing into ash. A flaming plane drifted across the flight ramp into a line of parked helicopters. Huge metal blades spun like windmills through the billowing explosions.

Brief domes of white-and-orange light swelled upward from the perimeter as drums of foo gas were detonated. Now there were wide holes in the wire big enough for the whole night to slip through.

The Reaction Force had finally been assembled into trucks and under the leadership of Sergeant Sherbert driven out to plug the dike. The ambush caught them completely by surprise. Dead reinforcements sprawled bleeding among the sand dunes.

Shadows sped swiftly inward.

Anstin's privates recorded the names of those breaking down in their group.

Hidden under a musty piece of canvas, Vegetable lay on the floor of the guard tower, head exposed to the nose over the edge of the platform, peering from this choice balcony seat into the spectacle below. Somewhere between his last guard shift and the attack he had mislaid his rifle so all he could do now anyway was watch. He seemed to be so high the action down there was unreal, kitchen match fires, plastic toy soldiers. When the photo lab blew up, he saw a little man pop into the sky and separate into little pieces that fell flaming back to the ground. That was the best so far. He had seen the motor pool inferno, the mess hall eruption, the hangar collapse, the planes bursting like overdone potatoes, and soon it all looked the same, fire and smoke and noise everywhere he turned. What a time they were going to have smoking and joking and talking about this night. Privileged with such a good view, he was trying hard to collect interesting impressions. Now he noticed something. There were naked men creeping in between the hootches. A naked man carrying an AWOL bag sneaked up to a bunker and tossed the bag inside. There was a flash, a muffled boom, sandbags bouncing and falling. There were naked men everywhere. Two were crawling right below the tower toward that bunker. Trips's bunker, Wendell's bunker, his bunker. On the ground the NVA sapper team heard a savage cry and looked up in astonishment at the man plunging toward them, arms outstretched, a length of canvas fluttering up behind him like a cape. One short burst of automatic weapons fire was more than adequate to blow off Batman's head.

Staff sergeants Anstin and Perkle were pinned down in a gulley behind the officers' latrine.

"Can you see him?" asked Perkle.

Anstin lifted his head. Bullets spattered sand into his face. "Motherfucking Christ," he hissed. "You hear that, cocksucker's shooting at us with one of our own weapons."

"How many you think there are?"

"I'll bet you a bottle of Regal that's Joe the barber. Remember that pacing all the time, goddamn gook was measuring targets. Now he's come in for final shaves on his favorites. Fucking prick. Never did trust him, razor and fish breath."

"Think you can reach him with the grenade?"

"Damn well try." Anstin moved up into a crouch, cocked his arm, and heaved. The grenade fell short.

"What's that?" asked Perkle.

"He's laughing, shiteating gook is laughing at us. Now I know it's that gook fairy. Gimme the fucking rifle."

Anstin positioned his feet firmly, then suddenly stood erect, the M-16 swiveling from his hip in a wide cutting arc, rounds singing into the darkness, tapdancing on the dunes. When the magazine was emptied, he dropped to the ground. There was no return fire.

"What happened?"

"Think I got him."

"Fancy shooting, Millard."

Anstin peered out from his cover. "Yep," he declared, "believe I got me one dandy kill."

After exposing himself several more times with no response, Sergeant Anstin crawled out to the gook's position. There was no body, no blood. Feeling around in the sand with his fingers, he found some expended cartridges, a couple empty magazines, and fragments of what appeared to be a dog tag chain and one article of jewelry, a gold beetle.

The sky was filled with moving helicopters. A banana-shaped Chinook hovered in place above the runway, its miniguns spewing metallic fire. A defensive line composed of 101st Airborne troops and a company of Green Berets had been set in place perpendicular to the air terminal. The Opponent would proceed no further. So The General had informed by phone the base commander.

This is my third Purple Heart, thought Chief Winkly, the blood still dribbling down the back of his throat. Lying there in the dark he couldn't see how much he had lost, but the handful of towel pressed to the nostrils of what was certainly a broken nose seemed disturbingly damp. A natural healer he had seen on television once claimed that relaxation promoted the clotting process. Think about women. A crew of naked women with lighted hats and picks and shovels crawled through a grimy mine shaft, prying chunks of coal from the dank walls. Their sleek muscular bodies gleamed with sweat and black dust. The air rumbled. "What was that?" asked one of the officers. "Awful close," answered another. Teams of naked women in helmets and shoulder pads hustled out onto the Astroturf. The ball was snapped. Jiggle, jiggle, bounce, bounce. Then somebody tossed a long bomb into the bunker and a giant hairy clam closed its lips over Winkly's head and the chief was gone.

Wendell couldn't believe his luck: Captain Raleigh and a genuine VC in black shorts locked in a lover's clench on the gravel outside the O club and stabbing one another at intervals with long knives. Wendell circled them carefully, tracking the angry movement of arms and blades. He squatted in the shadows, attempting to backlight his protagonists against the bonfire consuming Chief Winkly's hootch. Beautiful. Through the viewfinder Cain and Abel grappled in some bizarre biblical epic. The next instant Wendell was slammed to the ground, nose and mouth stuffed with grit. He tried to get up again but the only part of his body he could move was his left hand.

"Where's my camera?" he screamed, spitting out dirt. "Where's my damn camera?"

He didn't know what had happened to him or to his actors.

"Help! Someone help me find my camera!"

It was Griffin exploring the landscape of this foreign planet who heard his cries.

"Who's that?"

"Where's my camera?"

"Oh Wendell."

"Don't touch me!"

"You need a tourniquet on these."

"I need my camera. Over there somewhere."

"I can't see anything in this. Who are those two?"

"Extras. Please God, don't let it be broken."

"Something tore hell out of here, the ground's still warm."

"Need to be dragged, Grif . . . drag me into the light, please."

"I found it."

"Thank you."

"Okay, here I'm putting the camera into your hands, okay, got it? Okay, hold on, and I'll get some help."

"No! Too late . . . here, you've got to do it for me."

"Do what?"

"Shoot, you mangy cocksucker, shoot me, shoot them, shoot the whole fucking compound. The War In Vietnam: The Final Hours, huh?"

"Wendell, you need help."

"Yeah, finish the picture. I know you don't like it, Grif, but here's your chance. There's no time for anything else, anyway. Here, socko ending."

"Oh Wendell, I don't know . . . I'm . . . I don't know . . . I'm so fucked up."

"Let's not argue anymore."

"Like this? Is this the trigger here? I look through this?"

"Honorary cinematographer."

"Now what?"

"Focus on my head and begin, slow pan down my body, slow as you can go without shaking the lens, good, now move off the boots onto the road, down the road, let the rise of the ground lift the camera level, good, ease up onto the orderly room, now pan, pan, 7 DAYS WITHOUT AN ACCIDENT, get it all now, the big flames, the busting wood, the jeep, get the overturned jeep, keep it coming now nice and easy, Winkly's barbecue, okay, the flattened latrine, real good, the untouched O club and now back onto me, my head and out. Great. Welcome to the union. You just completed an astonishing 360 that will have 'em moaning in their seats. Okay, give me the camera. Now you can go for help."

"Hold on, Wendell, I'll be back in a second."

"I'm never going to know how it comes out."

"How what?"

Wendell's hand was pawing at the side pocket of his fatigue pants. "My book."

Griffin reached over and pulled out the dog-eared paper brick of *Atlas Shrugged*. "It's okay," he said. "Money saves the world."

"Grif."

"Yes, Wendell."

"Thanks."

Griffin put his hand into Wendell's remaining good one and squeezed and got a squeeze in return. He was trying hard to manage the first emotion he'd felt in months when he realized he didn't have to. He didn't have to go for help either. Wendell's hand still curled about his own, he stretched out beside him and looked into those huge open eyes, eyes now blank and motionless as camera lenses. The irises, he noticed, were green. Why had he never seen that before? Now he wanted to miss nothing. He leaned in closer. Yes, those were still Wendell's eyes, that was Wendell's face, but Wendell was gone. Something else occupied his spacesuit. In the cold surface of his eyes, flat and hard as those of a fish, all he could see were the frantic lights and shapes of the mad world around him and the dim reflection of himself peering into what he would be when he and this whole screaming planet had been sucked down into the bottomless pupils of those eyes and turned into stone forever. What had Wendell seen at that instant? What was he seeing now?

Shortly after the ground attack sirens had begun, Simon left his bunker and crawled into the cramped space under his hootch, a move that had saved his life. Now, huddled in the dark sand, he felt something against his leg, something alive, something sliding up his body. He didn't even have to look or feel with his hand. Sergeant Mars's interrogation aids had broken out of their cages. The pythons were loose in the compound.

The First Sergeant was having a lively night. Game plans, conference calls, brain storms, fire fights. Utilizing the major's ridiculous tunnels, he shuttled between his office and the command bunker, rallying, mobilizing, dispatching, with the formalized nonchalance of a traffic cop at the apocalypse. Reports were good. The enemy was taking a beating on this one. After hand-holding sessions with the officers he went outside and renewed his combat infantryman's badge. Aided by the CQ and five good men, he had managed to keep the orderly room from harm. No goddamn gook was going to ransack *his* files, squat on *his* desk, rifle *his* drawers. A rocket dropped in, killing instantly the man beside him and seriously wounding two others. He shook his head. He brushed the debris off his shoulders. First sergeants never die.

Griffin sat on top of the roof, rifle cradled in his lap. Up in the sky those three red antenna lights were still winking calmly back at him. Further down lines of tracer fire squiggled comically toward one another. Legend had it that whoever controlled the mountain controlled the base below. A flurry of blips and blurs indicated the questioning of control. Flares were suspended over the perimeter like lights above a used car lot. One of the helicopters patrolling the sky suddenly erupted in flames and plummeted to earth, a giant meteorite. There was intense weapons fire around the EM club, in back of the mess hall, in front of the orderly room. Griffin had seen a pair of big boots curled at the toes protruding from a collapsed wall of the Officer's Mess. Yesterday Uncle Sam had been laying down duckboard for The General's visit. Tonight he had picked the wrong place to hide. There were still occasional explosions along the road to the 131st FAC. A jeep careened past Officer's Row and crashed into the guard shack at the gate. A grenade went off inside the mechanics hootch. A signal shop trailer blew up, scattering wires and circuit boards. Griffin pulled out Mueller's old lighter and had a last smoke. In the darkness between the supply building and the II section he could see parts of Ingersoll still glowing a fungus green as though contaminated with radioactivity. He hardly recognized the compound anymore. Half the structures were gone, there were craters everywhere, the people had vanished. The battle for the airfield moved on to the runway where weapons barked and flashed. More helicopters arrived to hover anxiously overhead with lights and loud ordnance. The sky rained fire. Scores of flares descended in stately procession like a fleet of UFOs. Inside a monstrous transparent egg of flame the last hangar, its shape reduced to a spiderlike frame, appeared to take one tiny step forward and collapse on brittle broken legs. Everywhere light was punching holes through the darkness, revealing at last the tarpaper flimsiness of protection from the awful brightness beyond. The crystal of his mind trembled in its clarity. An enormous fan opened then on a landscape of rock and crevice he had never known, and then another, and another, quickly, like a tearing of skin, arrangements of form and texture disturbing in their alienated familiarity, and these wedges drove into him with splitting force, and he lifted on a peak of vertigo, and then the last fan unfolded, and he looked upon a weaving of lines as distinct as the tracer fire on the mountain, and the tension in those lines was connected to the revelation that his body was certainly a machine, deafening in the roar of its parts, and he saw into the hidden work of a moment, the innumerable strands wiggling in the wind of possibility, and the other lines, those threaded few that were being drawn through him by every separate movement of muscle (thought had never mattered much), and winding out into that spiral of rope dropping away into the infinite past. He saw how the gestures of each instant since his induction and probably from further back than he wished to know had conspired to lead him gently as a domesticated animal to the violence of this moment, binding him to this roof, atop this horror. And it was frightening and it was right and it was beautiful because it was right. He began to swoon into the sensation that must occur when one is at last in the possession of meaning. Then the fan snapped shut and the side of the mountain started to burn. Somebody was using big bombs now. He sucked steadily on the OJ. By the time this world and its visions came tumbling down he expected to be entering another. Particle by particle, the smoke of a plant grown in this violated land would rearrange his elements, render him finally invisible, ready for reconstitution in a more permanent spacetime. The others drew near him now, Claypool, Mueller, Major Quimby, Wurlitzer, Wendell, and all those like the helicopter door gunner whose names he never knew. They sat beside him along the peak of the roof, shared this final smoke. He could hear Mueller's voice, insistent and excitable as ever, We missed it all, you know, too late for WW II, pulling in rhythm under occasionally inspired coaching against a team in unvariegated black toward an indisputable goal and the sweetness of that victory and the crusader's conviction in the cause before war got bureaucratized by uniformed business majors who ruined the fun for everyone. And Vietnam? Well, boys and girls, the dope had been incredibly fine. Someone ran by, shouting up at him. He couldn't tell if the words were English or Vietnamese. Suddenly, as furious as he had ever been, he seized his rifle and fired away at the shadow. The weapon jammed in mid-burst and he tossed it as hard as he could out into the dark. Maybe he had gotten him, maybe he hadn't. Now he seemed to remember a curious scene. Something had happened between Wendell and the roof. He had tried to return to his room, to see if it was still standing, to retrieve what? Letters from home. The money under the bunk. His personal stash. Something important. Rounding a corner. The half-naked man. The gook. Hands slipping on the greased body, jungle sweat in his nostrils. The bayonet in his fist plunging, driving out the life before it. Fingers filling with doggie goo. Once, twice, three times. The details were out of focus. In fact, he couldn't be sure whether this incident was an actual occurrence or simply hallucinated desire. The mind apparently was not so clear as he had imagined. Over to the left there was still a radiance visible inside the chapel and he wondered how the movie had come out, unaware the spectatorless film had concluded long ago, the ghouls shot in their heads, the bodies dragged to crematory fires on glistening meathooks, and now the reel spun round and round, the last foot of celluloid slapping repeatedly against the projector. The screen was blank, a rectangle of burning light. There were bugs crawling up his legs, cockroaches heading for higher ground. He jumped up, brushing frantically at his pants. Then he left the roof and he flew, it was amazingly easy, on and on through the night, carrying medicine to the Eskimos. He hit the ground like a dropped sandbag. The sky exploded, the earth screamed. A hot wind whipped over him. Darkness fell in sharp pieces across his back. He closed his eyes. He waited. He had been ready for this for a long time. He opened his eyes. On the flat platter of dirt in front of his nose a small stone jiggled up and down like a kernel of popcorn in hot oil. He didn't know it yet, but he was outside of sound, existing in a moment of pure silence that rushed out from him in long widening concentric circles. Then the sky knifed down and up through his legs and hearing returned and he was sick, face bathed instantaneously in greasy sweat, body burning, falling away from him in long trickles. He heard a wolf howling. Nothing hurt. He knew he was dead. The ground rumbled beneath him, heaved several times in quick succession as though trying to toss this aggravation off its back. The command bunker. They were blowing up the command bunker. Who was in charge tonight? Not Major Holly. He had left yesterday morning for The General's Annual Vung Tau Invitational, golf clubs strapped to the helicopter skids. The ground shuddered. Griffin dug into the dirt and held on. The stone rolled against his hand. His fingers closed over the hard rough surface, squeezed. His legs, wax sticks set too near the fire, melted, sent roots into the sandy soil. Lifting onto his elbows, he looked back at himself. His legs stretched to the dark horizon where they burst into foliage, leafy tree toes. His body's increasing familiarity with the ground was beginning to terrify him. Consciousness, like seeds on the white head of a dandelion, seemed ready to scatter at the slightest breath. He refused to pass out. He clutched the stone tightly. Through the pads of his fingers he concentrated himself onto it, explored contour and texture until the stone was as large as the moon, all craters and mountains and swift smooth seas of sand to glide across in a pleasant rush toward the final room of lights and eyes and giant masked figures bending ominously near, metallic hands flashing like polished claws.

Once he recognized a face, the Flight Surgeon's, Major Beams, demented butcher of doomed youth in a movie someone he once knew had made.

There was a bed he came to periodically, a rectangle of starched white inserted between great blocks of shiny darkness where you were suspended in timelessness like an insect in plastic, a paperweight. This darkness, illuminated by its own private light, was certainly preferable to the white world of tubes and bottles, draped bodies, moans, cries, a piercing brilliance at whose unavoidable center rested what remained of his legs encased in sleeves of stiff white armor. Even his hand was empty, the stone stolen by these cardboard people who could never comprehend the customs and values of the land beneath the bandages. He slipped back into the blocks. Then came a major disturbance, clumsy alien hands lifting him onto wobbly wheels and rough passage in a green ambulance to a glossy aluminum plane and the high whine of a vacuum cleaner sucking him up and away and, struggling sideways, straining against the straps toward the tiny oval window recessed behind his head and one last unrepeatable look back at the surprise of monsoon waters flooding the fields almost to the end of the slick black runway and the shadow of the plane streaking over the paddies, a dark fleet shape diminishing in size as it gained in speed until a speck in the corner of the eye it rose up lost in silver clouds and Griffin's body began to quiver in a fever of sweat and cold anxiety that was either a side effect of medical treatment or a delayed emotional response to his wounds or merely the onset of an unpleasant bout of withdrawal symptoms.

Meditation in Green: 15

1. Remove the latex from the capsules with a flat blunt metallic blade, taking care not to scrape the epicarp.
2. Place coagulated gum in bowl, cover with rice paper.
3. Set bowl in sun for period of two weeks.
4. Roll into balls.
5. Insert ball into pipe.
6. Ignite.
7. Who has a question for Mr. Memory?

My first glimpse of home: the big, brilliant, clean, inconceivable mountains of Washington, cones of powdery white sparkling in the cold winter sun—a vision of space and light, then narrow dim months of pastel walls and dusty television screens. I was a slow healer.

Once I sent a piece of my leg to the President of the United States. I had an amber vial then (50 DIAZEPAM Take As Required) in which I kept my fragments, my therapy. Some played card games, some collected coins, I gathered lost cinders of shrapnel that rose surfacing in the milky pool of my thigh like broken bits of sea coral. I fished them out on the tip of a knife.

The disinfected light, the beds teeming with cripples.

Problem of the age: how to occupy the diminishing intervals between fire and wind and flags.

There's the room and there's the street. Where do you want to hide?

Here I am somewhere behind this forest of leaves. A hardy annual with demonstrable versatility, our plant can be baked into cookies for a friend in the hospital, arranged in bouquets for the woman who comes and goes, dried into rattles for the neighborhood children.

I think my thumb has always been green.

In the spring I'll wander national highways, leather breeches around my legs, pot on my head, sowing seeds from the burlap bag across my shoulder, resting in the afternoon shade of a laurel tree.

At night I carve peace pipes from old cypress branches.

Everywhere the green fuses are burning and look now, snipping rapidly ahead of your leaping eye, the forged blades cutting through the page, the transformation of this printed sheet twisted about a metal stem for your lapel your hat your antenna, a paper emblem of the widow's hope, the doctor's apothecary, the veteran's friend: a modest flower.

STEPHEN WRIGHT was drafted into the U.S. Army in 1969, attended the U.S. Army Intelligence School, and served in Vietnam through 1970. After the war he attended the Writer's Workshop at the University of Iowa, earned an M.F.A., and later taught there. This is his first novel.